John L. Lincoln, Henry S. Burrage

Brown University in the Civil War

A Memorial

John L. Lincoln, Henry S. Burrage

Brown University in the Civil War
A Memorial

ISBN/EAN: 9783337222772

Printed in Europe, USA, Canada, Australia, Japan

Cover: Foto ©Andreas Hilbeck / pixelio.de

More available books at **www.hansebooks.com**

BROWN UNIVERSITY

IN

THE CIVIL WAR.

A Memorial.

PROVIDENCE.
1868.

PROVIDENCE PRESS COMPANY, PRINTERS.
16 Weybosset St., Providence, R. I.

‘Ηγεῖτο γὰρ αὐτῶν ἕκαστος οὐχὶ τῷ πατρὶ καὶ τῇ μητρὶ μόνον γεγενῆσ-
θαι, ἀλλὰ καὶ τῇ πατρίδι.

For each of them considered that not for his father and mother only was he born,
but also for his fatherland.

Demosthenes De Corona.

———

Lord of the ages, thanks
　For every pure career
Of champions, in a hundred ranks,
　Who girt their armor here;
Then bore the day's long toil,
　Or laid a young life down,
For duty, tho dear natal soil,
　And the celestial crown.

Bishop George Burgess, Class of 1826.

PREFACE.

During the late civil war no class of our citizens exhibited a purer patriotism or a truer heroism than the graduates and non-graduates of our colleges. At the commencement of the struggle they hurried to the defence of the Capitol with all the ardor of youth; and thenceforward, in defeat and in victory, till the rebellion was overthrown, they shared the toils, dangers and privations of a soldier's life. Their services have not been forgotten. Indeed, no one will doubt that at the present time, because of the deeds of these men, the colleges which they represented have a stronger hold upon the affections of our people than they had before the rebellion, when, by too many, it was supposed that studies are unfavorable to the development of a character equally fitted for the duties of peace and of war.

Our own University is of the number of these; for throughout the struggle her sons stood side by side with those of her sister colleges, who, at Bull Run, at Antietam, at Murfreesboro', at Port Hudson, at Atlanta, at Fort Fisher, at Petersburg fought *pro libertate et pro reipublicae integritate.* Moreover, on these widely separated battle-fields, she offered with them her costliest sacrifices.

With her sister colleges, therefore, Brown University has a patriotic record. This volume, which presents that record, has been prepared under the pressure of other duties, and with little assistance from class secretaries. Indeed, in most of our classes, the office of secretary seems to be merely a nominal one. All other available sources of information have been exhausted.

My thanks are especially due to those who have contributed biographies. In the preparation of the Roll, I have been aided by President JAMES B. ANGELL and JOHN G. LORING, Esq., class of 1849; Captain E. L. CORTHELL, class of 1867; and Lieutenant G. B. PECK, JR., class of 1864. The Roll of Students who entered the University after leaving the army was prepared by Sergeant JAMES McWHINNIE, JR., class of 1867. The account, in the Introduction, of the reception at the College of the tidings of the fall of Richmond and of the surrender of General Lee, was furnished by Captain W. H. SPENCER, class of 1866. For much valuable assistance, my thanks are also due to Professor JOHN L. LINCOLN, class of 1836; REUBEN A. GUILD, Esq., class of 1847; and the Honorable ELISHA DYER, class of 1829; and especially to Professor WILLIAM GAMMELL, class of 1831, who has kindly aided me in reading the proof sheets of the entire work.

There is yet one other name which should be recorded here. Professor ROBINSON P. DUNN, class of 1843, whose sudden removal from his place among us we all so deeply deplore, cheerfully gave to me, even to the last week of his life, not only words of encouragement, but also whatever assistance I desired. The portion of the work which he himself prepared — the biography of Commander THOMAS P. IVES — was completed only a short time before his death. Surely it was fitting that he whom the Alma Mater had long and lovingly cherished should lay his last offering upon her altar. Had he lived, the entire work would have passed under his eye; but alas! the silver cord is loosed and the golden bowl is broken. We look for our instructor and friend, but he is gone. "All who were about him bemoan him; and all who knew his name say, How is the strong staff broken, and the beautiful rod!"

HENRY SWEETSER BURRAGE.

NEWTON CENTRE, MASSACHUSETTS, January, 1868.

TABLE OF CONTENTS.

THE BIOGRAPHIES.

1840. Henry Stearns Newcomb. - - - - - -
HENRY SWEETSER BURRAGE, B. U., 1861.

1847. Joshua James Ellis. - - - - - - -
REUBEN ALDRIDGE GUILD, B. U., 1847.

1847. Walter Herbert Judson. - - - - - -
REUBEN ALDRIDGE GUILD, B. U., 1847.

1848. Fayette Clapp. - - - - - - -
DAVID RICE.

1852. Sullivan Ballou. - - - - - - -
HORATIO ROGERS, Jr., B. U., 1855.

1852. Miles Johnson Fletcher. - - - - - -
JAMES COOLEY FLETCHER, B. U., 1846.

1852. Charles Bertrand Randall. - - - - -
JEREMIAH LEWIS DIMAN, B. U., 1851.

1854. Thomas Poynton Ives. - - - - - -
ROBINSON POTTER DUNN, B. U., 1843.

1855. Louis Bell. - - - - - - -
JOHN BELL BOUTON, D. C., 1849.

1857. Josiah Gordon Woodbury. - - - - -
SAMUEL WARREN ABBOTT, B. U., 1858.

1857. ROBERT HALE IVES. - - - - - - -
WILLIAM GAMMELL, B. U., 1831.

1858. CHARLES LAMBERT KNEASS. - - - - - -
WILLIAM LEETE STONE, B. U., 1858.

1860. ALBERT GARDINER WASHBURN. - - - - -
DAVID VINCENT GERALD, U. C., 1860.

1861. JAMES CLARK WILLIAMS. - - - - - -
JAMES ANDREWS DeWOLF, B. U., 1861.

1862. WILLIAM IDE BROWN. - - - - - - -
HENRY SWEETSER BURRAGE, B. U., 1861.

1863. HERVEY FITZ JACOBS. - - - - - - -
SETH JONES AXTELL, B. U., 1864.

1864. CHARLES LOUIS HARRINGTON. - - - - -
MISS LUCY LARCOM.

1864. MATTHEW McARTHUR MEGGETT. - - - - -
JAMES WINSOR COLWELL, B. U., 1864.

1864. EUGENE SANGER. - - - - - - -
SAMUEL COFFIN EASTMAN, B. U., 1857.

1865. LEVI CAREY WALKER. - - - - - -
JAMES McWHINNIE, JR., B. U., 1867.

1867. JAMES PECK BROWN. - - - - - -
EDWARD PAYSON BROWN, B. U., 1863.

INTRODUCTION.

THE UNIVERSITY IN RELATION TO THE REBELLION.

THE UNIVERSITY

RELATION TO THE REBELLION.

IT is the design of this volume to perpetuate the record of the graduates and non-graduates of Brown University, who entered the military or naval service of the United States during the late Rebellion. And yet, it cannot but be regarded as both fitting and desirable to preface this record with an introductory chapter, giving a general view of the University with reference to the same period,—a view illustrative of the spirit of loyalty which pervaded its halls throughout the momentous struggle in which our government then was engaged. Such a view will establish the fact, that during this conflict, treason found no entrance within those venerable walls which sheltered the patriots of '76. It will confirm, also, what is otherwise manifest, that the work of education in our Alma Mater has been entrusted to men who, with Milton, call "a complete and generous education, that which fits man to perform justly, skillfully, and magnanimously, all the offices, both private and public, of peace and war." At the same time, such a retrospective view will show that the dwellers in Hope College and University Hall did not live "recluse

from human converse," bewailing the troublous times on which
the country had fallen; but with one heart they followed the
course of our armies, and with one prayer implored their success;—nay more, many of them, not content to remain at a
distance from the fields on which their brothers were toiling,
bleeding, dying, laid aside their books, and forsaking "the still
air of delightful studies," went forth to the conflict, willing to
stand where the need was sorest and the danger thickest.

At the outbreak of the Rebellion the University was in a
prosperous condition. This fact will appear if we compare the
number of its students in 1860–1 with that of preceding years.
The following tabular statement will be sufficient for our purpose:

	Resident Graduates.	Seniors.	Juniors.	Sophomores.	Freshmen.	Partial Course.	Total.
1857–8,	5	29	42	58	65	6	205
1858–9,	0	30	39	60	57	3	189
1859–60,	7	27	51	57	70	0	212
1860–1,	5	38	45	70	74	0	232

This increased prosperity of the University was due, undoubtedly,
to the changes in the plan of collegiate instruction introduced by
Doctor Sears, who was elected to the Presidency in 1855. "Under
his administration," says Professor Dunn, in an article in the
University Quarterly for July, 1860, "the system introduced by
his predecessor has been considerably modified. The increased
opportunities for practical education are still offered. The course
of study for academic degrees has returned to its former order
and limit. The Bachelor's Degree in Arts is given at the end of
four years of prescribed study; the Master's Degree is conferred
in course; the Baccalaureate in Philosophy is retained as originally prescribed. In the order and the course of study, Brown
University does not now differ essentially from her sister colleges
of the United States. . . . . . Retaining all that the times called

for, and all that she found worthy in her 'New System,' she proceeds as of old, on the well-tried basis of a sound and thorough Christian, classical and scientific culture, and offers and gives to her pupils an education in keeping with the spirit in which she was founded, and with the intention of those who have enriched her with their munificence, and cherished her with their love." In thus returning to the course of study pursued in the best of our American colleges, the University entered upon a new and more prosperous era. Men no longer were repelled from its walls by the confusion which the "New System" had introduced; while, as a still further result of these changes, there was manifested at once among the several classes in the University that *esprit du corps* which under the "New System" had not existed.

This was the state of affairs in the University at the opening of the year 1861. Dear, however, as the interests of the University were to all within its walls, higher interests now claimed the chief attention. The hour was full of peril to the nation. As with men throughout the land, so with the students of Hope College and University Hall, the condition of the country was the all-absorbing topic of discussion in public and in private. In the South, with the opening of the spring, the mustering of soldiers for a conflict of arms had already commenced; and yet how did the first gun which was fired at Fort Sumter startle the whole North! The announcement of the attack reached the University late in the evening of April 12. It might almost be said that "no man slept in Athens that night." Certainly the most intense excitement was at once manifested. The despatch, announcing the attack, was meagre indeed; it stated merely, that the bombardment, so long threatened by the rebels, commenced at four o'clock that morning, and continued through the day without any decisive result. Did this mean war, civil war? was the question on the lips of all. Anxiously the morrow was awaited.   When at length it came, it brought a confirmation of the tidings received the night before, and at the same time it afforded the first glimpses of the uprising of a united North. At the recitation of the Senior Class in History, that morning, Professor Gammell alluded to the attack on Fort Sumter. He said: "It looks as if our flag there must go down; but, gentlemen, if it does go down," he added, "it must go up again, and that, too, at whatever cost." The day slowly passed, and when the night came, there came with it the realization of our fears. Fort Sumter had surrendered, our flag had been lowered, and the rebel ensign was then waving over the ruins of the Fort.

On Monday, April 15, after the morning recitation, the Senior Class held a meeting, and appointed a committee to wait on President Sears, for the purpose of obtaining permission to raise over University Hall, the flag that on Saturday had been hauled down in Charleston harbor. University Hall was to be honored thus, above the other buildings of the College, because of the Revolutionary associations which are connected with its history. To these associations President Sears alludes, in the Centennial Address delivered at Brown in 1864, when, after speaking of the Commencement held in 1776, he says: "In just three months from that time, the British fleet entered Newport harbor, and the Royal army landed on the island. 'This brought the camp in plain view from the College with the naked eye.' 'The King's army,' says the President, 'is in sight of my house.' Upon this, 'the country flew to arms, and marched for Providence; there, unprovided with barracks, they marched into the College and dispersed the students, about forty in number. The President gave notice to the students, 'that their attendance on College orders is dispensed with until the end of the next spring vacation.' He should have said, till the end of the war; for the interruption, instead of being limited to six months, continued for six years."

President Sears cheerfully granted the request of the class, and arrangements at once were made for the erection of a flag-staff, and the purchase of a flag.

On Saturday, April 13, the day of the surrender at Fort Sumter, Governor Sprague tendered to the Government his own services, a regiment of infantry, and a battery of artillery, whenever and wherever desired. On Monday following, the offer was accepted, and the work of raising and equipping the troops was at once commenced. On that day, A. E. Burnside, then treasurer of the Illinois Central Railroad, while engaged in the business of his office in the city of New York, received the following despatch: "A regiment of Rhode Island troops will go to Washington this week. How soon can you come on and take command? William Sprague, Governor of Rhode Island." Both the answer and the answerer were ready,—"at once," was the reply. The next morning Burnside was in Providence, organizing the first regiment, Rhode Island detached militia. Four of the Senior Class, —DeWolf, Hoppin, Jenckes, and Sackett,—with several from each of the other classes, enlisted in this regiment as private soldiers. Throughout the University, studies languished. The patriotism of the Freshman Class would brook no restraint. True to the American instinct, the members of that class held a mass meeting, and passed a series of resolutions, (which appeared in the Evening Press of April 16,) sustaining the administration, and expressing their appreciation of the worth of their classmates who had entered the military service.

Wednesday, April 17, was a day long to be remembered by those who were in the University in 1861. At five o'clock, in the afternoon of that day, in the presence of the Faculty and of the undergraduates of the College, and also of a large throng of the citizens of Providence, the Senior Class raised the stars and stripes over University Hall. After the flag had been unfurled, and the band had played "The Star Spangled Banner," President Sears, standing on the steps of Manning Hall, delivered a brief address. He said he deprecated civil war. He regretted the necessity which it imposed upon us as a people. But, he continued, the time for deliberation is past. Every man is now called upon to show himself worthy of the country of his birth. It is fitting, then, that to-day the young men who have come to this University to learn — to learn to be patriots he would hope — and who have everything at stake in this crisis, should show that they appreciate the inestimable blessings which they have inherited from a brave and noble ancestry. In closing his address, President Sears introduced to the assembly the Right Reverend Bishop Clark.

Bishop Clark said that eighty-eight years ago the old Revolutionary flag waved over University Hall. It meant that our fathers were striving to establish the sacred institutions of a free government. The flag, we raise to-day, means that we intend to preserve those institutions. We deprecate war, he continued, especially civil war. All our interests, all our feelings are against it. But enemies have arisen among us. They have commenced the most wicked contest ever waged. We do not hate them, yet we cannot sit tamely by while they are endeavoring to destroy the very foundations of our political fabric.

Bishop Clark was followed by the Reverend Doctor Hall, who said it was not a time when any one should be silent who loves his country and his God. We are men of peace, he added, but here is a thing inevitable. It is government, or no government. The South does not wish to go peaceably. If we have erred at all, we have erred on the side of forbearance. But the past is gone. Let us show by our action that we continue to love our whole country. The hymn, "My Country 'tis of thee," was then then sung by the students.

The Reverend Doctor Caldwell was the next speaker. He said that on the previous Sabbath he could not but feel it was a time for praying, rather than for preaching. The time for words was now past, the time for deeds had come. Be assured, he added, that what we see going on around us is going on everywhere, from Mason's and Dixon's line to the lakes. A conflict is impending, but we go into it not in passion; we simply seek to vindicate the honor of our country in restoring its rightful authority.

Ex-Governor Dyer delivered the last address. He commenced by saying that in the whole course of his experience he had never been subject to such conflicting emotions as were passing through his heart at that moment. Yonder is our country's flag, and the chimes of our city are ringing out our national anthems; but is it possible, he asked, that that flag, and that music, are needed to remind us, that we are citizens of one of the noblest nations of the earth? We are called to contend with traitors, the victims of delusion, all party distinctions, therefore, should be laid aside, and each man should be ready to make whatever, sacrifices the honor of the country may demand.

Such is a brief outline of the addresses which were delivered on this interesting occasion. In the form in which they were spoken they have no existence. They did not float away, however, on the soft winds, then laden with the freshness of returning spring. There were those grouped about the Chapel steps, who then, as never before, were "stirred with high hopes of living to be brave men and worthy patriots"; and to whom the words at that time spoken were an inspiration for good, as in the years which followed, when weary from long marching, watching, fighting, they recurred to them for added strength in entering upon fresh trials of endurance.

The Marine Artillery left Providence for Easton, Pennsylvania, the next day. On Saturday morning, Professor Gammell omitted

the recitation of the Senior Class, in order that the men might
have the day with their classmates and friends, who, on that 20th
of April, were to leave for Washington with the first detachment
of the first Rhode Island volunteers.   The detachment was formed
in Exchange Place at one o'clock, P. M.   In a few earnest words
of farewell, Bishop Clark addressed the troops, and at the close
of his remarks commended them to the God of battles.   Then
wheeling into column the detachment, with Burnside at its head,
marched to Fox Point, where a transport was in waiting.   The
troops were soon embarked, and then, amid the waving of handkerchiefs, and followed by the good-by of friends and the cheers
of the crowd, the steamer swung off from her moorings, and
started down the bay.   The second detachment of the regiment
left Providence on Wednesday, April 24.   Before leaving, the
troops were addressed by Doctor Wayland.

The spring vacation commenced on the following Saturday.
At the close of the vacation, when the students again came
together, it was apparent that there was sufficient military spirit
among them to warrant an attempt at an organization of a College company.   Accordingly on Saturday, May 11, at a meeting
of the several classes, a committee was appointed to make the
necessary arrangements for the organization of such a company.
In a few days these arrangements were completed.   The company was know as the University Cadets, and at its organization
consisted of seventy-eight men, rank and file.   Its first officers
were as follows :—

Captain, Charles F. Mason.	1st Sergt., George T. Woodward.	
1st Lieut., William D. Martin.	2d "	William W. Bliss.
2d " Charles H. Chapman.	3d "	Oscar Lapham.
3d " George M. Newton.	4th "	Henry B. Miner.
4th " William W. Douglas.	5th "	Benjamin F. Clarke.

1st Corp., Simeon Gallup.   3d Corp., Henry G. Gay.
2d   "   Charles E. Willard.   4th   "   Harrison Cole.
Clerk and Treasurer, Benjamin F. Clarke.

It is a fact worthy of notice, that, during the Rebellion, eight of these fourteen officers served with distinction in the Union armies.

By an arrangement with the National Cadets, the armory of the latter became the head-quarters of the University Cadets. Their muskets also were used for instruction in the manual of arms. For a while the company met for drill every night; but after the school of the soldier, and the rudiments of the school of the company, had been mastered, three drills a week were deemed sufficient. The Campus in rear of the University afforded a suitable drill ground; and such was the proficiency to which the company soon attained, that the tri-weekly drills of the Cadets attracted, in a short time, not a little attention.

Class Day occurred on Thursday, June 13. In the absence of the Class President, Mr. William W. Hoppin, then serving with the First Rhode Island Volunteers, the Class Secretary, Mr. William W. Douglas, presided at the literary exercises in the Chapel. In a brief and appropriate address, he alluded to the absent members of the Class, who, at the call of the government, had entered the military service, and would celebrate the day under other skies, and amid far different scenes. He then introduced the Class Orator, Mr. Sumner U. Shearman, of Providence, Rhode Island. Mr. Shearman announced as his theme, The Claims of the English Language upon our Earnest and Faithful Study. In closing the oration, he thus gracefully referred to the conflict just commencing: "Going forth into the world with such determinations, listening to the claims of our mother tongue upon us, and obeying them with all our heart, let us cultivate it, and cherish it, and keep it from corruption. It is true that for

2

such purposes, we enter upon the stage of active life at a most unhappy juncture. With this country launched upon the surging billows of a fratricidal contest, the citizen can find but little leisure for study, or science, or art. Amid the uncertainties and convulsions of civil strife, scarcely a solitary loiterer lingers in the deserted walks of literature, and the temple of science, like some mouldering ruin of the olden time, finds hardly a single friendly hand to prop its tottering columns. But let us not despair. Let us hope that such unspeakable disasters are far away, and that the storm, which the mustering of hosts and the tramp of armies warns us is about to burst upon our beloved country, may soon disappear, and the clear noon-day sun of prosperity once more shine forth in unclouded brilliancy. Let us believe that our country has not yet fulfilled her destiny, that she is not yet to be engulfed in the tumultuous flood of anarchy, that the dismal scenes of the feudal ages are not again to be enacted in this nineteenth century, so full of centralizing tendencies, that social order and good government are to be ultimately triumphant, and that the banner of the Union, doubly dear to every loyal American in this hour of his country's peril, will yet float in triumph over every portion of this broad Republic, South as well as North, West as well as East, and will still hold its place among the flags of the nations, the beautiful symbol of a proud and glorious nationality." It may not be regarded as unworthy of remark in this connection, that the President of the Day, the Class Orator, and the Class Poet, afterwards entered the military service, and were mustered out with the same rank.

In the afternoon of Class Day, the University Cadets had their first public parade. The line was formed on the Campus at three o'clock. Then, preceded by Gilmore's (Pawtucket) full band, the company marched through the principal streets of the city, eliciting the praises of all for the soldierly bearing of the men, and their proficiency in drill. Late in the afternoon, the Cadets visited the camp of the second Rhode Island volunteers, where, in the presence of Colonel Slocum, (who was killed at the battle of Bull Run in July following,) and of the officers of his regiment, they went through the form for dress parade. After receiving the congratulations of Colonel Slocum and of his officers, among whom were two sons of President Sears, the company marched down Westminster street "in four ranks open order," and returned to the College. Still later in the day, the Cadets escorted the Senior Class to the Aldrich House, where the Class Supper was served.

Until the close of the term, the Cadets had regular company drills. Their evening dress parades, on the Campus in rear of the University, attracted thither not only the friends of the College, but the lovers of the military art. A short drill preceded the parade, and it may truly be said that in their company drills, the Cadets equalled, if they did not excel, the other military organizations of the city.

The appointment of an orator and poet for the annual reünion of the Literary Societies at Brown, in 1861, fell to the Philermenian Society. By a vote of the Society, the poem was assigned to Fitz James O'Brien, a young man of fine poetical talent, then engaged in literary pursuits in the city of New York. The invitation was forwarded about the middle of April. Weeks came and passed, but brought no reply. Accordingly, another appointment at length was made. After some time had passed, the committee of the Society received from Mr. O'Brien the following letter, which, it need hardly be said, was deemed a sufficient excuse for his long delay in the matter. The letter is without date, but must have been written sometime in June:—

100 NASSAU STREET, NEW YORK.

MY DEAR SIR:

Excuse my long silence. The suddenness with which my regiment (the Seventh New York National Guard) was ordered to Washington disrupted all my business arrangements, and when I returned, I became so actively engaged in preparations to return to the war, that all other affairs went by the board. I must, I am sorry to say, decline your kind invitation. This is no time for either writing or reading poems. A regiment of rifles, which I am now engaged in raising, demands all my time. If you can put me on the track of one hundred good men, you will please me better than if you crowned me with bays. If there is a spare population up your way, I would take a recruiting trip thither, and present my regrets in person.

Yours fraternally,

FITZ JAMES O'BRIEN.

We give this letter a place here, not only because of the noble and patriotic spirit which it breathes throughout, but from a desire to embalm with the names of our own dead, that of one, who, of like devotion, laid down with them a young life on the altar of a common country. How well he succeeded in recruiting for the regiment of rifles of which he speaks, the writer cannot say. He only knows that O'Brien went back to the field, and then, or afterwards, was appointed *aide de camp* on the staff of Brigadier General F. W. Lander. February 14, 1862, General Lander, in an official report of the fight at Blooming Gap, West Virginia, makes special mention to General McClellan of the services of his aid, Fitz James O'Brien, and adds: "While out scouting, O'Brien was shot through the breast by a rebel." The Baltimore American, of April 7, 1862, contains the following brief announcement: "Died, at Cumberland, Maryland, from the effects of a wound received in the fight at Blooming Gap, Virginia, Lieutenant Fitz James O'Brien, of General Lander's staff."

The exercises of Commencement week, in 1861, brought together the sons of our Alma Mater under circumstances new and peculiar. The country was in a state of war—civil war. The roar of a great battle had just died away—other conflicts yet more severe were to follow. It was manifest, however, throughout the exercises of the week, that but one spirit breathed in the breasts of all. The Reverend J. Lewis Diman, of Brookline, Massachusetts, now Professor Diman, delivered the oration before the Literary Societies on Tuesday afternoon, September 3. The discourse was a vindication of the "Spiritual Forces in History." "The moral of this discussion," said the orator, in conclusion, "need not be a long one. I have asserted to no purpose these spiritual laws that shape the destiny of states, if you have failed to see how pregnant they are with application to our present needs. Vainly have we climbed this Mount of Vision, if we do not worship that overshadowing Destiny which makes

> ' The path of life we walk to-day
> As strange as that the Hebrews trod.'

No modern state embodies in its growth, as we have done, these ideal elements which are the light of modern ages. It is not a narrow national conceit which bids us recognize in our history the operative, and pervading presence, of that new Life which draws such indelible lines between the liberties of pagan and the liberties of Christian states. 'America is the place, of all others,' says De Tocqueville, 'where the Christian religion has preserved the most power over souls.' The great impulse given to the human race by the revelation of man's import as a spiritual and immortal being,—this is the masking Power that hides itself beneath our distinctive forms. Rightly has the South blazoned the old serpent on her flag, for she seeks to show that a nation may do violence to the law of all its growth, give the lie to the deepest lessons of its life, mock the holiest convictions of the human heart, and not surely die.   For us, with the traditions and instincts that we inherit, but one course is open. 'The greater,' says Bunsen, 'the Christian vocation of a nation, the higher the problem it will have to solve, or perish.' The promise of our future rests in our recognition of this principle. We cannot re-write our heroic history; we cannot put off the work that is given us to do. To this end were we born, and for this cause came we into the world.

"Give us statesmen, then, baptized into this confession; statesmen who shall drink at these 'primal springs of empire'; statesmen who shall clóthe with act these august convictions; who, comprehending the vast moment of the nation's growth, and drawing inspiration from the increasing purpose that runs through its continuous years, shall make it a perpetual excellency, a joy of many generations."

The Reverend S. F. Smith, D. D., of Newton Centre, Massachusetts, delivered the poem.   The following were the opening lines:

> " But who would not sing for the true and the brave,
> A song for the free and a shout for the slave ?
> When liberty summons from valley and hill,
> From the farm and the city, the forge and the mill,
> From pulpit and fireside, college and chair,
> The active to do and the valiant to dare !
>
> All nature sings wildly the song of the free—
> The red, white and blue float o'er land and o'er sea ;
> The white, in each billow that breaks on the shore,
> The blue, in the arching that canopies o'er
> The land of our birth, in its glories outspread,
> And sunset dyes mingle the stripes of the red.
> Day fades into night, and the red stripe retires,

But the stars in the blue light their sentinel fires ;
And tho' night be gloomy, with clouds overspread,
Every star keeps its place in the arch overhead ;
When the clouds are dispelled, and the tempest is through,
We shall count every star in the field of the blue.

I see the brave legions—their banners are spread ;
The timid take heart at the sound of their tread.
They come like the mist from the breath of the sea—
Like snow wreaths that gather o'er mountain and lea.
They come, as they came in the days of our sires,
With torches fresh lighted at liberty's fires ;
The troops of the freemen—they come sweeping down,
From county and state, from village and town,
From ocean and land, from college and farm,
To tell that the Union is rescued from harm ;
And little Rhode Island, tho' least, not the last,
With her gallant commander, nails to the mast
The flag of our freedom, and—'Live we or die,
We've fastened it there, and there let it fly,
Till, rent by convulsions of nature, shall flee
The red, white and blue from the sky and the sea.' ''

The next day occurred the ninety-third annual Commencement of the University. To the order of exercises at the church the following note was appended : "At the time of the final examinations, and the assignment of parts, the following members of the class were absent from College, serving as volunteers in the army of the United States; they were therefore not appointed to speak :—

James Andrews DeWolf, Providence.
William Warner Hoppin, Jr., Providence.
Leland Delos Jenckes,* Woonsocket.
John Williams Rogers, Mansfield, Massachusetts.
Frederic Mosely Sackett, Providence.

* Wounded and taken prisoner at Manassas (Bull Run).

Of these DeWolf, Hoppin, and Sackett, having returned to Providence at the expiration of their term of service, were present at the Commencement exercises. Lieutenant Rogers was in Virginia with his regiment, the Seventh Massachusetts Volunteers. Jenckes remained a prisoner in the hands of the enemy till May 23, 1862, when he was exchanged. The following words from an editorial in the Providence Journal of September 4 — Commencement day — fitly expressed the lesson of the hour: "At this literary festival we would not if we could, shut out from our minds thoughts of the great struggle in which the nation is engaged. Nor could we if we would. For by the Commencement programme itself we are reminded that four of the graduating class deserve their portion of the laurels which the Rhode Island regiments won on the plains of Manassas, and that one of them, wounded, now lies a prisoner at Richmond. Another of them is with his regiment to-day on the banks of the Potomac, perhaps facing death in the din of the terrible contest, while we are so quietly listening to his comrades. Two of the undergraduates are also prisoners at Richmond, and others are already enrolled in the army of the Union. And all along the line, from the ocean to the Rocky Mountains, the graduates of Brown are found, standing up bravely in defence of those institutions without which science, and letters, and arts, and industry, and wealth, are all of no avail. It is fitting, then, as well as inevitable, that the feeling which burns in every heart, should give tone even to the joys of the literary festivities of this day. Let the children of the Alma Mater, who opened her halls as a hospital for soldiers in the Revolution, and sent her sons out cheerfully to the perils of the battle, find that their patriotism has gained new strength, and that their impulses to self-sacrificing devotion to their country have quickened by their meeting at this time."

At the dinner, which followed the exercises in the church, President Sears addressed the Alumni as follows:—

" We meet to-day, for the first time in the memory of any of us, under circumstances of great national calamity. We are engaged in a great civil war. Some of our brethren are not with us, but are arrayed in arms against us. Several of our graduating class have been on the field of battle even before receiving their diplomas, while of former graduates, a large number flew to arms at the call of their country, and not a few will never return.

" But, friends, would we not have it so? May our Alma Mater always have brave sons, ready to meet all the demands of patriotism. '*Præsidium et dulce decus!*' In paying our filial respect to her who has nourished us, let us love and venerate her as the mother of a whole race of patriots and heroes.

" We hold a close relation to that free and liberal State that gave us our liberal charter. Hand in hand with each other, have the State and the University ever maintained, and eloquently advocated, the principles of civil and religious freedom. They have been the firm friends and supporters of constitutional authority, and civil order. In common with other States, but not behind any of them in energy, liberality, and devotion to the interests of the country, she has, since we last met here, won new laurels, and achieved a name of which we may well be proud, and which history will not let die. He who has so well represented her in the field, is with us to-day. Neither he, nor his followers, refused to go to Washington by way of Baltimore, nor were they undistinguished in the most fearful battle ever waged on this continent. All honor to the brave man, and the brave men, who, in that hour of peril, thought of nothing but their duty, and the nation's safety. *We* celebrate heroic deeds; *they* performed them. If I were a poet, and were to write an Æneid, I would begin as Virgil did, even if I could say but the first three

3

words, or, pointing to the hero, I would simply say, '*Arma virum-que.*'   I give you, the brave young Governor of Rhode Island."

Governor Sprague, in responding, declared his belief, that the Union could not be dissolved, that the interests of both sections of the country favored this idea, and that, when peace was restored, the country would hold a more honorable and commanding position than it held when it was distracted and full of bickerings.

President Sears then introduced to the Alumni and friends of the University, ex-President Wayland, who, in the course of a spirited address, thus alluded to the state of the country: " Passing events call to mind a remark made by Burke, at a critical period in English history, 'It is a time for a man to act.' Never, in our country, since the Declaration of Independence, has there been a time for a man to act, like this 4th day of September, 1861.   The College has sent its first fruits, and I do believe that the principles imbibed here, the culture bestowed, and the prayers offered up, are a sufficient guarantee that those who go from this College to the war, are noble, honorable, patriotic, self-denying citizens.   If these strong hands can sustain the stars and stripes, if these breasts can form a rampart to put far away the wickedness of slavery, (slavery! slavery! what man was born to be a slave?) let us form an impregnable barrier against the waves of rebellion, of sedition, of the most infamous conspiracy ever known, and let us say, 'thus far shalt thou go, and no further.'" Few who listened to the venerable ex-President, that day, can ever forget the scene, as, raising those "strong hands," and crossing his arms upon his breast, he poured forth these burning words.

Among the guests at the table, was President Felton, of Harvard University.   That no man was more welcome there than he, was manifest from the reception which he received, when he rose to respond to a sentiment offered by President Sears.   "It gives me great pleasure," said President Felton, "to attend this literary anniversary, and especially the present year,—a year so unique, so unexampled, in the history of our country. There are duties of peace as well as of war. Indeed, without the just and magnanimous performance of all the duties of peace, the country would be in no condition to meet the perils and trials of war, for the one is a preparation for the other.

"But one of the misfortunes which have sometimes attended a condition of war, is, that progress in literature and science ceases; school houses are closed; the halls of universities are deserted; and liberal studies, that before occupied so large a portion of the best and most ingenuous minds, lose their interest in the midst of the clang of arms. But, Mr. President, you will remember, and the scholars who are before me will remember, that in the most illustrious state of antiquity, and in the midst of the most desperate war which that state ever encountered, literature, science, and the arts, were still kept at their very height; and that, in Athens, while the armies of the foe were in sight of the Acropolis, the tragedies of Æschylus and Sophocles were listened to by large assemblies of Athenian citizens, as the sun rose above the craggy heights of Hymettus and Pentelicus.

"Perhaps I speak with a little professional feeling; but it has been to me a matter of pride, in visiting schools and academies, high-schools and colleges, to find that, while this great subject of civil liberty and national existence fills our minds, and stirs up every heart, the great interests of literature, science, and education, have not ceased to have their hold upon the New England mind. I know it is different in other parts. I know that the fruits and desperate results of this barbarous rebellion, have been the closing of schools and universities in those rebel States; and I regret the result, because it makes the prospect of bringing them back to their real interests, and to loyalty to our common country, a more difficult task; inasmuch as it is more difficult to enlighten ignorance than to convince intelligence."

The above extract derives a melancholy interest from the fact, that it forms a part of the last Commencement address, which fell from the classic lips of the eminent scholar and educator, then at the head of our oldest University. President Felton died February 26, 1862.

At the conclusion of President Felton's address, the Reverend Doctor Smith, in response to a call from President Sears, read the following poem:—

> "Fling out the banner on the breeze,
>   Shake out each starry fold;
>   Summon the stalwart soldiers forth,
>   The mighty and the bold;
>   The bell of freedom from its tower
>   Its solemn call has tolled.
>
> The sound sweeps wildly o'er the land,
>   Sweeps o'er the bounding sea;
>   It echoes from each mountain top
>   The anthem of the free;
>   It snaps the chain which sin has forged,
>   It rings for liberty.
>
> Marshal the legions for the fight,
>   The youthful and the brave;
>   Stand for the noble and the right,
>   The glorious Union save;
>   Stand for the cause for which their blood
>   Our patriot fathers gave.
>
> Dread not the angry focman's rage,
>   Dread not the tempest's crash;
>   Dread not the billows, tho' the cliffs
>   Along the shore they lash;
>   Dread not the awful thunder's roar,
>   Nor lightning's piercing flash.

Above the clouds the brilliant sky
   Shines in immortal blue;
And light, like Heaven's approving smile,
   Streams in its glory thro';
Be patient till the strife is o'er,
   Have faith to dare and do.

With willing heart Heaven's high behest
   Fulfil without alarm;
The foe has planted for our hand,
   And nursed the conqueror's palm;
And he who bade the sea 'Be still,'
   The stormy waves will calm.

Then fling the banner to the wind,
   The emblem of the free,
Strike the sweet harp-notes that proclaim
   The reign of liberty;
And bid the melody rebound
   From every trembling key.

And count each star that studs the blue,
   Whate'er the past has been,
A wayward wanderer welcomed back
   To fill its place again;
A loving band of sister lights
   Just like the old thirteen.

Strike not one jewel from the crest
   The loving mother wore;
Re-set the gem upon her breast,
   Each where it stood before;
Clasp in the glorious cynosure,
   The entire dear thirty-four."

Such were the public expressions of patriotic sentiment at the literary exercises of Commencement week, 1861. Yet not less devotion to the Union cause did they breathe, who, renewing the associations of earlier years, while wandering with classmates through the halls of the University and under the elms around, could not forget the perils which threatened the nation. One heart beat in the hearts of all, and the children of the Alma Mater went back to their various fields of duty, bearing with them not only her benediction as of old, but also added strength and purpose.

At the opening of the collegiate year, which immediately followed these Commencement exercises, it was apparent that the military ardor of the students was still strong. The University Cadets, with ranks augmented by additions from the new Freshman Class, now entered upon a yet more prosperous career. The following were the officers of the company:—

Captain—William D. Martin.

Lieutenants—1st, George T. Woodward; 2d, George M. Newton; 3d, Edward P. Brown; 4th, Oscar Lapham.

Sergeants—Frank D. Douglas, John D. Edgell, Fenelon A. Peirce, John Tetlow, Jr., Benjamin F. Clarke.

Corporals—Henry G. Gay, William P. Davis, Job R. Smith, George L. Herrick.

Early in the fall, the company drilled on the Campus, in rear of the University; but, on the approach of winter, the men repaired to the armory of the Providence Light Infantry, which was kindly thrown open for their use.

Late in the month of May, 1862, almost as stirring scenes as those of April, 1861, were witnessed in Providence. Let us go back to May 25, when, at midnight, a despatch from the Secretary of War was received by the Governor of Rhode Island, announcing the defeat of General Banks, and calling for troops. At one o'clock, A. M., May 26, an order was issued for the organization of the National Guards for active service. At seven o'clock, P. M., of the same day, the several companies referred to in the order, reported six hundred and thirteen men as ready for duty. The next day the regiment, henceforth known as the Tenth Rhode Island Volunteers, left Providence for Washington, under the command of Colonel Z. R. Bliss.   Company B, commanded by ex-Governor Elisha Dyer, was recruited almost entirely from the ranks of the several classes in the University.   Governor Dyer says: "The students of Brown University could brook no restraint, and, almost *en masse*, came to our recruiting rendezvous for enrollment. It was a source of the deepest solicitude on the part of President Sears, to know how far he was justified in resisting these resolute expressions on the part of the young men who had been placed under his protection and instruction.   The offering would not have been too large, had he consulted his own feelings alone. But it was the widow's son, and the orphan's brother, who desired release.   He came to me in the conflict of duty and enthusiastic patriotism, and, telling me of his embarrassment, said : 'If you yourself will take these young men to the field, I can no longer refuse them.'   I gave the pledge.   The young men came, were enrolled, and, without leaving the armory, entered upon the duties of a soldier.   They proved themselves worthy of their Alma Mater, and the sacred cause for which they enlisted.   Always prompt, obedient, and efficient, they won for themselves an honorable record.   For no delinquency, or misdemeanor, did any name of theirs ever find a place on the morning report.   On the muster out of the regiment, September 1, 1862, many of these young men immediately reëntered the service, and, as commissioned officers, extended a record of which the University may well be proud."

In our admiration for President Sears, and the young men of the University to whom reference is made in the words just quoted, let us not forget that other son of the University, whose pure, self-sacrificing patriotism, appears in his tribute to the worth of others,—who, having received the highest honors in the gift of the people of Rhode Island, and when of an age which might claim exemption from military duty, cheerfully abandoned the quiet delights of home at the call of his country, and took upon himself the labors and responsibilities of a captain of infantry. His was the shining example which is reflected in the record of the men of Company B, Tenth Rhode Island Volunteers.

Class Day at Brown occurred June 12, 1862. Mr. Joshua M. Addeman, the Class Orator, was, at the time, a private soldier in the company and regiment to which we have just referred; but, obtaining a short furlough, he returned to Providence, and delivered his oration on the appointed day. He introduced his theme as follows: "On this day, around which cluster memories and associations of the past, and fond hopes and anxious forebodings of the future, one thought transcends all others in importance. As if embodied in some fair form, beseeching us for aid, our country rises before us, and excludes all minor and selfish considerations. No theme seems more appropriate to the day, and of more vital importance in its bearing upon the future, than The Alliance of Scholarship and Patriotism." The orator, accordingly, proceeded to discuss the duties of the scholar with reference to the State; and then closed his address with the following earnest words: "This is an age when events follow each other more rapidly than in the prophet's inspired visions; when years are heaping up more for history, than centuries of the past; an age which converts a nation devoted to peace into a vast army, bristling with bayonets, and marching with serried ranks to the field of battle; which summons men of science and of letters from their experiments and their books, the lawyer from his brief, the instructor from his pupils, the preacher from his desk, and bids them gird on the sword, and hasten to the defence of the best, the freest, the happiest country on which the sun ever shone. Obedient to its call, classmates have hastened on before us, to discharge the patriot's duty. In thunder tones their example speaks to us of courage, of manliness, of devotion to country. It forbids our retiring, like the monkish recluse, from the active scenes of life, and the performance of the important duties they impose. . . . . . By the increased responsibility conferred by education, by the sacred rights and liberties entrusted to our keeping, by the examples transmitted for our emulation from all preceding ages, by the heroic devotion of our countrymen, and by the noble spirit of sacrifice displayed by our classmates, we are called upon never to falter in our country's cause. Let us strive for the attainment of that perfection of mind and of heart, that will render us equal to the most trying occasions. Let us see to it, that we faithfully discharge our duties as

' Ever in our great taskmaster's eye.'

The benedictions of a grateful country will then rest upon our labors, and, above all, the satisfaction of an approving conscience will be our 'exceeding great reward.'"

The Class Poet, Mr. Henry F. Colby, sung of the power that a nation possesses in the remembrance of a glorious past:—

> " Go ! trace in thought the eddying course sublime,
> Of History's current down the hills of Time.
> Where'er it sweeps the rocks of human woe,
> And gains a clearer voice, a statelier glow,—
> Where'er the murmuring tones of trampled life
> Swell to the grander song of patriot-strife,—
> Beneath its waves the naiad memory dwells,
> And tunes its music to her sounding shells.
> When Greece, the land of heroes and of song,
> Had felt the keenness of the captive's wrong,
> And the foul ravens of foreboding fate
> Perched on the ruins of her fallen state,
> Came Byron's song across the western wave,

4

And roused the spirit of her sleeping brave.
The ancient fire that burned in Grecian veins
Was not all buried on her battle plains;
For recollection, like the brier that blooms
In freshening glory round the falling tombs,
With blissful fragrance cheered the heart forlorn,
But roused the spirit with its lurking thorn.
The storied past alarmed them by its calls,
When victory gleamed on Tripolitza's walls.
Bozzaris heard them on the field renowned,
And Navarino thundered back the sound.
The cheerful light that once had brightly shone,
Again revived at thought of Marathon,
And weeping, trembling, suppliant Greece was free,
At the *remembrance* of Thermopylæ.
 * * * * *
But let us not 'mid foreign splendors roam,
Forgetful of the nobler scenes of home.
Our native sunsets wear as brilliant dyes
As fringe the azure of Italian skies.
No fairy tale of eastern clime has told
Of wealth unequalled by our mines of gold;
And memory here may find a lustrous gem
To deck the circlet of her diadem.
In other lands she's led the hosts of war
Against the bulwarks of established law.
Here Justice leads her, and no plighted word
Prevents the dealings of her righteous sword.
In times of peace we love to turn and gaze
Upon the struggles of those fearful days,
When men were Freedom's martyrs, and each heart
Throbbed with ambition for the hero's part.
We learn to sympathize in all their fears,
In all their ardent hopes, and prayerful tears,
And pass the story of each honored name
Along the whispering galleries of fame.
But these fond memories in the present hour
Became the instruments of wondrous power.
The guns of Sumter sent a startling thrill

> Through hearts still mindful of Bunker Hill;
> And April's tears wept o'er a war begun,
> As in the trying days of Lexington.
> An unseen spirit caught the flaming brand,
> And swept on lightning wings the startled land :
> ' Come from your homes, ye free !' its trumpet cried,
> ' Preserve the country of your father's pride.'
> And from the North, where sighing forests rise
> In state primeval to the bending skies,
> From granite hills, and battle fields whose sod
> The feet of patriot heroes once have trod.
> From the bright shores of Narragansett's bay,
> Along the silvery Mohawk's wending way,
> Soft as the rippling tide on Erie's shore,
> Loud as the tumult of Niagara's roar,
> From lakes majestic, from the Western plains,
> Rich in the billows of their ripening grains,—
> From every city's street and rural home,
> Came up that single answer : ' Yes, we come.'
> And they *did* come.   Potomac's wooded banks
> Gleamed with the bristling steel of serried ranks :
> The sentinel's strange voice was echoed there,
> And blazing camp-fires lit the evening air.
> From the foul dragon's-teeth of civil strife
> A numerous army sprung to active life.''

The exercises of Commencement week, 1862, opened on Tuesday forenoon, September 2, with an address before the Rhode Island Alpha of the Phi Beta Kappa, by the Reverend Thatcher Thayer, D. D., of Newport, Rhode Island.   The oration was a profound and eloquent discussion of the controlling theme of the hour—The State.

In the afternoon, the Reverend James O. Murray, of Cambridgeport, Massachusetts, delivered the oration before the Literary Societies.   The subject presented in the oration was, "Nationality and Literature in their Mutual Relations."   Mr. Murray closed an address of rare interest and power, with a brief allusion to the probable results of the Rebellion in their effect upon the future of American literature.

On the following day, Wednesday, September 3, occurred the exercises of the graduating class. The valedictorian, Mr. James H. Remington, having just entered the military service for three years or the war, delivered his oration in the uniform of a Captain of Infantry. Others of the class, who had received appointments for the day, were already at the front, awaiting, with our army around the Capitol, the movements of the enemy, then just disclosing his plan of a campaign in Maryland. Still others, who had but recently returned from the "sacred soil," were happy in finding themselves in season to bid their classmates once more "hail and farewell." Back to the College also came some, who, though no longer claiming a residence within its walls, still sought the counsel of the loving mother who bore them. That counsel did not in the least repress the martial enthusiasm which our cause had awakened. Indeed the Alma Mater had no kinder words than when she spoke of the patriotic devotion of her sons in the field, and no more earnest prayer than when she offered in their behalf the petition, that in the service of the country they might become "dear to God and famous to all ages."

An editorial in the Providence Journal, of that morning, called attention to the prosperous condition of our colleges in New England, notwithstanding the draft which had been made upon them by the war. "It is an interesting fact," says the writer, "that the prosperity of our chief New England colleges is not much affected by the war. We believe that the prospect is, that we shall have about as large Freshman classes this year as usual. And this is not because the colleges are not deeply interested in the war, and thoroughly patriotic, but because professors and students are enthusiastic and efficient in sustaining the government. The people are seeing, as they have never seen before, that the colleges are the very nurseries of patriotism, that they furnish the mental, and what we may call, not using the word in a religious sense, the spiritual training which fits young men to do, and dare, and suffer and die for their country. Never was the sympathy between colleges and people so close. Never did the public so feel that the stuff of which heroes are made is admirably moulded and sharpened in the highest schools of study. Some of the most efficient officers in the service are men whose names we used to read on the roll of college Faculties. And many of the most heroic young men, who have sealed their devotion to their country with their blood, were fresh from the halls of learning, their academic laurels having scarcely faded on their brows. By their patience, their endurance, their docility, their superior intelligence, their aptness to learn and to teach, and by their heroic courage, they have vindicated the cause of American colleges, and showed to the nation that good soldiers, citizens, patriots, are the fruits of academic training."

At the dinner which followed the exercises of the graduating class, President Sears, having welcomed the Alumni to their annual festival, introduced ex-President Wayland, who said: "I spoke a few words to you at the last Commencement, and ventured the promise that the sons of Rhode Island would always be true to their country, and ready to bare their bosoms in her defence. They have nobly fulfilled that prophecy. To the Rhode Island battery we owe the taking of Pulaski, and this College may inscribe Pulaski on its banners, as one of its graduates commanded the battery that riddled the fortress. Thus has it been everywhere. Though our State is small, her doings have not been small. Everywhere, where danger calls, her sons have been prominent in the tented field. With an uncomplaining energy and courage, that has never been surpassed, they have met the enemy of our country. They will do the same always, and now, in the hour of our greatest need, now, while all we hold dear is trembling in the balance, we know that Rhode Island men are always to be relied on, and that they will do their duty in the presence of God and man.

"But I must go still further. While the balance is thus trembling, we know that it is held by an omnipotent hand, which is guided by justice, by mercy, and by equity. There is not a man of you, who would not, for the cause of our country, peril property and life. But I would have every one of you look up to that throne that judges in equity. I believe God is chastening us for our neglect of him. I call upon you, ministers of the gospel, to state these things before your people, passing by secondary matters. Relying on his promises, though the day be dark, and the news not cheering, I believe that God, in his infinite mercy and power, is for us. God is just, and the trial will be for the greatest good of the country, and we shall yet come out of it the first nation on the face of the earth."

Among the guests at the table, that day, were the governors of four of the New England States,—Governor Washburn, of Maine; Governor Berry, of New Hampshire; Governor Andrew, of Massachusetts; and Governor Sprague, of Rhode Island. Their words were spirited and invigorating, and evinced the patriotic devotion, and unyielding determination, of the people of the States which they represented. It was evident that no reverses, like those which had recently overtaken our army in Virginia, could shake, in the least, their unwavering belief in the ultimate triumph of our cause.

Early in the summer of 1863, the University Cadets became connected with the military organizations of the State, and the company thenceforward was known as Company 1, First Regiment, Second Brigade, Rhode Island Militia. At the time of its reörganization under the laws of the State, the following officers were elected :—

Captain—John Tetlow, Jr.

Lieutenants—John R. Dorrance, William C. Ives.

Sergeants—Charles E. Willard, Edward Judson, Benjamin C. Dean, John B. Mustin, William C. Angell.

Corporals—Charles T. Lazell, George F. Jelley, Minor R. Deming, Joseph E. Spink, Edson C. Chick, Martin S. Smith, Francis M. Tyler, George W. Shaw, John H. Appleton (color corporal).

Not long after this reörganization of the Cadets, the State of Rhode Island and Providence Plantations was suddenly filled with alarm, by a report that the pirate Taconey was on the coast, with her prow turned towards the peaceful waters of the Narragansett. To avoid the havoc and desolation thus threatened, the Governor of the State determined to make good the defences at the entrance of the bay. Accordingly, the needed force and material were at once hurried to the front. To defend the West Passage, a company of infantry was deemed sufficient. What company in the State was so available as the University Cadets— what company was so adequate to the responsibilities of the position? Company I, First Regiment, Second Brigade, Rhode Island Militia, was therefore ordered to prepare for instant service in the field. The following account of this campaign of the Cadets, was prepared by Mr. F. T. Hazlewood, of the Class of 1864 :—

Among the noteworthy examples of patriotism, which the historian of the late war shall embalm for posterity, none is more refreshing, than the memorable campaign of the students on the shores of the Narragansett, in the summer of 1863. Even at this late day, the roll of the drum, calling Brunonia's faithful to the defence of the West Passage, has not ceased to reverberate within the College walls; while the valor of these Spartan heroes is still the theme of Sophomore declamation, and Junior poesy.

It was a fortunate day, indeed, for the impoverished ranks of Captain Tetlow's company, when the Governor of the State so generously guaranteed exemption from the impending examinations to all who would take up arms against the Taconey, then supposed to be on the coast. Ah me! how the deserters returned to their ranks, how the new recruits strove to prove that their names had always been upon the roster. Then it was that an added charm appeared in the words, so often read in the class-room, "*Dulce et decorum est pro patria mori.*"

Of the tearful embraces, of the long farewells, of the gentle waving of handkerchiefs, as the pilot boat steamed down the bay, I cannot speak. Such pictures are worthy of a diviner pen than mine. But of the long exile of *two* weeks, broken by only an *occasional* furlough,—of the tedious night watches, spent in sound sleep within the folds of warm blankets,—of the blistered hands, won in preparing clambakes,—of the heavy marches, in quest of berries and milk,—of the midnight attacks, on poultry yards and sheep folds,—of the daily exposure, to the hot sun on the beach, —of the mysterious disappearance of the guard so soon after being posted, and of the fear which it inspired,—of the courage with which the veterans, leaving the ordinary duties of camp life to confirm the claims of the new recruits to have served their country, entered the houses of the enemy, to feast on "sweet white bread," and "milk drawn by David Larkin's willing fingers," or found their way to the school-house, to inspire by their presence a due respect for the blue coat and brass buttons,—it is fitting that I should speak. For these are the records of a patriotism, which could willingly sacrifice the examinations of the University for the recreations of the Bonnet, and the mush and milk, and bread puddings, and pork stews, of the commons, for fresh fish, and sweet berries, and baked apples swimming in cream.

But let it not be supposed that through all the hard service spoken of above, there were no hours of recreation. Hither

were brought the bases of the University Nine, and in the cool
of the morning, and in the shade of the evening, many were the
happy hits, and the home runs, which won the *encore* of a
delighted audience. Hither, too, came the players on instruments, the violin, the guitar, the flute, the cornet, the triangle
and the bones; and in that hour when

> "Still as a slave before his lord,
>   The ocean hath no blast,
> His great bright eye most silently
>   Up to the moon is cast,"

there went up on the evening air sweet melodies, that sometimes
awakened "thoughts from hiding places ten years deep." Hither
came to us in our isolation, the North Star, laden with packages
for the brave men, who were far away from home, fighting for
their country. How we blessed the little hands that shaped the
crullers and made the pies, and the kind hearts of fair maidens,
in whom an appreciation of the heroic is never wanting. Nor
were these patriots forgetful of the pious trainers of their youth.
Often, in the relief from fatigue duty, they would recount their
virtues and drink their health with merry song.

Thus passed those two long weeks away, when the company,
after having distinguished itself for the terror which it had
inspired throughout the surrounding country, was ordered home.
With sadness they packed up their fiddles and music books, their
fishing rods and herbariums, and returned to the bosoms of the
families from which they had been so long separated.

To the future historian, whose duty it shall be to analyze the
motives which led to such self-sacrifice, nothing but the most
unselfish devotion to the interests of the country will be apparent. What else could induce men absorbed in literary pursuits
to forego, in the heat of summer, the subtilties of logic, the intricacies of mathematics, the familiar talks of Thucydides and

5

Demosthenes and Socrates and Plato, for clambakes, and surf-
bathing, and fishing, in a locality more beautiful than the Utopia
of More and of Southey. Posterity alone will do them justice.
For, true it is, that not one of these veterans of a bloodless campaign escaped the rigid examinations from which he so gloriously
fled; while the story of unrequited patriotism may be read in
the diminished rank of many a diligent student, as it stands on
the records of the Register.

About this time, a full length portrait of Major General Burnside, painted by Emanuel Leutze, of New York, was presented to
the University by some of the citizens of Providence. Honorable J. R. Bartlett, Secretary of State, was mainly instrumental
in securing this gift to the college. It represents the General in
the act of directing the famous charge of his troops at the Stone
Bridge, at Antietam. This portrait, with others of the fine collection in possession of the University, now adorns the walls of
Rhode Island Hall.

The ninety-ninth annual Commencement of the University,
which occurred September 7, 1863, brought together its Alumni
and undergraduates under circumstances most gratifying. The
victories, which, since the last annual festival, our armies had
achieved at Antietam, at Vicksburg and at Gettysburg, had lifted
the darkness that then hung over us, and had flooded the hearts
of all with the light of a new and brighter day.

George William Curtis, of New York, opened the literary
exercises of the week, with an oration before the Philermenian
and United Brothers Societies, on Tuesday afternoon, September
6. He announced as his theme, The Way of Peace.

Peace of a certain kind, he said, is always possible. The
American colonies had only to submit to taxation without repre-
sentation, and there would have been no war. If an assassin
enters your house at night, to murder your wife and children,

you have only to lie quietly in bed, and there will be no trouble. Where the system of government does not tend to freedom and equality, there can be no peace. Our fathers went to Bunker Hill to keep the peace. Had their faith failed them, the Bell of Lexington would not have rung through all history like the morning hymn of liberty; and if the fathers' faith failed now in the hearts of their children, every victory they won we would lose, and great as was their glory, our shame would be greater.

The way of permanent peace could be found only in three ways: either by compromise, disunion, or by the war pushed to its natural results.

Was compromise peace? No, merely defeat and surrender. The speaker showed that the day of compromise had passed; that the questions at issue touched the fundamental principles of government; that compromise was impracticable, because the rebellious chiefs understand that this is a contest for a vital principle, and because they are unwilling to reünite themselves to a people whose character and habits would presently compel them to reconstruct a reconstruction. They would say to us, "You propose to relinquish rights, traditions, etc. It is impossible; we tried under the old Union and failed. You are not able to do what you think you are."

The orator next argued that disunion could not bring peace. He alluded to the difficulty of securing national boundaries, the immense amount of territory we should be called upon to relinquish, the great interior boundary line to be maintained and defended, the impossibility of yielding the mouth of the Mississippi to a foreign power, and the inevitable difficulties which would arise in the case of slaves seeking freedom over our border. For these, and many other reasons, aptly illustrated and eloquently urged, disunion could not secure peace.

The third course was to push the war to its natural results, as the only method of securing a permanent peace. The safety of the country demands a prompt and vigorous support of the administration, and especially in its emancipation policy, which alone will prevent the rebels from retiring from the unequal conflict, only to resume it when their strength is renewed. By every principle of patriotism, and by every obligation of our holy religion, said the speaker, in conclusion, the lover of freedom, and of humanity, is called to persevere in this glorious work.

Among the speakers at the dinner, which followed the addresses of the graduating class, on Wednesday, was Brigadier General, afterwards Major General, John M. Thayer, of the class of 1841. General Thayer had served under General Grant from the commencement of the war, and was fresh from the scenes of the recent victories of his chief. The worth of General Grant had been recognized long before in the valley of the Mississippi—it was now the confession of a loyal people, and General Thayer met the wishes of his college friends, when he placed before them the leading traits in the character of the man, who was destined to lead the armies of the country to ultimate victory.

Speaking of General Grant, he said: No better commander, or soldier, ever took the field. He is as modest as he is determined, as honest as he is brave. He has the unlimited confidence of his officers and men, and let me say that his army, (and I claim nothing for that army above the other armies of the Union), is imbued with but one spirit, and one determination, viz.: to crush this infamous rebellion. And I say to you, and I think it no idle boast, that whatever that army with General Grant undertakes, it will accomplish. General Grant is a man of most inflexible determination, of unconquerable energy, and, better than all in a commander, of good practical common sense.

The celebrated campaign of the University Cadets at the West Passage, near the close of the previous term, by no means exhausted the military ardor of the students. The opening of a new collegiate year found the company in a flourishing condition. Its ranks, diminished by the withdrawal of the members of the late graduating class, were swelled by recruits from the entering class. Lapham, its new commander, moreover, was an accomplished officer, having served in the field as Lieutenant, Adjutant, and Captain. Under his instruction, the company made rapid improvement, both in drill and in general discipline. At the October training of the militia, the Cadets presented so creditable an appearance, that they were detailed to serve as camp guard. This was the last public appearance of the company. The State Militia was disbanded not long after, and Company I, on delivering up its arms and equipments, closed a brief but memorable career.

The class of 1864 held their Class-Day Festival June 9. General Grant, having just fought the battles of the Wilderness, Spottsylvania, and Cold Harbor, was then resting his army, preparatory to a movement to the south side of the James River. The Class Orator, Mr. Charles T. Lazell, chose for his theme, "The Power of History in Life." In the last sentence of the quotation that follows, Mr. Lazell breathed a thought then fondly cherished in many a northern home, but realized only when another year had given us the victories of Petersburg and Appomattox Court House. "It was not possible," said the orator, speaking of the inspiration that may be derived from the contemplation of human agency in history, "that men from the old Bay State, marching on the 19th of April to the defence of that city which bears the name of him who led our fathers through the Revolution, should not feel the inspiration of that first battle of the Revolution, fought on their own soil eighty-six years before. How much of the spirit of '76 must have been in the hearts of those who, on the return of that day which marks the year '76, followed their victorious leader into the fortifications which had so long resisted their strength at Vicksburg.   And is there not something of that same spirit now in our soldiers, who, under the leadership of that same General, are hastening their work, that we may have a triple cause to celebrate our coming Independence Day ?"

The Class Poet, Mr. J. F. Ober, though singing of Music, found a place for an allusion to the conflict then waging under the eye of Lieutenant General Grant:—

> " Tho' Treason, Avarice, drink the country's blood,
> And Evil *seems* to triumph over good,
> Be not dismayed.   For these eventful years,
> Which flood the nation's heart with streams of tears,
> At length will all their wrathful vials pour,—
> And peace will follow when the storm is o'er.
> This fearful woe and mutual hate will cease,
> Bright o'er the land will bend the bow of Peace ;
> Hope, Truth, begin anew their golden reign,
> And Music's lyre, re-strung, a happier strain
> Around the ransomed, joyous land shall fling,
> E'en as of old the morning stars did sing.
> In coming years the epic muse will tell,
> How righteously a modern Illium fell.
> Ah yes ! some deathless lyric yet shall chant
> The simple glory of our hero—Grant."

On Tuesday, September 6, 1864, occurred the first Centennial Celebration of the University.   But all the memories of the century gone, could not shut out from the minds of the sons of the College, thoughts of the conflict still impending.   At the dinner, which followed the Centennial address of President Sears, Honorable John H. Clifford presided, and welcomed to the University, one to whom, as he said " we, as a country, were much indebted for a timely and kindly word, at a time when such words were most needed by America in her great struggle,—uttered, too, when they were worth something, and cost something,—Professor Goldwin Smith, of the University of Oxford, England."   In the course of his address, Professor Smith said : " I thank you for acknowledging in my person, the fellowship of learning and science on both sides of the Atlantic ; and I earnestly pray, that when this evil hour is past, Englishmen and Americans may be bound together, not by the fellowship of learning and science, alone.

" When the Prince of Wales, the representative of George III., paid a visit to this country, he was received, not only with courtesy and hospitality, but with enthusiastic affection ; and we might have hoped that the friendship of the two nations was strongly established. Now, however, a feeling of hostility seems again to have arisen between us, though I trust it will not continue forever.

" You must not suppose that the want of sympathy, or,—as I fear I may say,—the antipathy of which you have had to complain, on our part, during this struggle, extends to the whole English nation. It were idle for me to deny that the privileged classes of my countrymen—the aristocracy, and the clergy of the established church,—are, in a certain sense, your enemies. To these classes, you are a standing menace, not in a military, but in a moral and political point of view. They know that the success of your institutions must ultimately involve the doom of those under which they hold their power.

" Therefore they are glad that the model Republic should, as they imagine, end in failure, and they sympathize with those who are laboring for its overthrow. It is not right that they should have this feeling, but it is natural, when they perceive, so keenly as they do, the tendency of your institutions indirectly to subvert their own. The feeling is not one of malignity towards the American people, but of political fear, and of opposition,—which, in the case of a class circumstanced as they are, is inevitable,—to your principles of society and government.

" The upper middle class, to a certain extent, follow the lead of the aristocracy. It is very wealthy, and perhaps its wealth has had its usual effect to make it a little regardless of questions of principle, by which, at a former period of your history, it would have been deeply moved. I fear it is not above being influenced by a feeling that the side of those who are opposed to you, is the more genteel. But the sentiments of this class are less hostile to you than those of the aristocracy and the bishops. The great middle class paper, the Telegraph, has a circulation double, I believe I may almost say treble, as great as that of the Times. And this journal, though strongly opposed to the war, has not been, like the Times, hostile to the American people. A great number of my countrymen, let me say, are sincerely opposed to the war, without being hostile to America. They sincerely believe that the war is leading you to ruin. My friend, Mr. Bright,—than whom the American people has no better or more powerful friend,—wrote in a letter to me the other day, with a feeling of sorrow amounting to anguish, of the affliction which has fallen upon your nation. Others, seeing the greatness of this affliction, may mistake its cause and speak of it in less friendly terms; and yet they may not be your enemies, they may even be your friends.

" Of what we call the lower middle class, the greater part, I believe, are friendly to America; especially the nonconformists, who are the natural allies of your free churches.

" If we go still further down, we find the agricultural laborers indifferent to this, as they are to all political questions. They are, in fact, in political intelligence, as in political rights, scarcely above the level of mediæval serfs. But the intelligent operatives of our towns, especially in our manufacturing districts, have, in spite of the suffering brought upon them by the war, been, almost to a man, ardently in favor of your cause. They have followed your fortunes with the warmest sympathy, from the moment when the great issue between freedom and slavery was fairly presented to them,—and I must remind you, in justice to my countrymen, that this issue was not presented from the first.

"The party in England favorable to your cause, has alone been able, with success, to hold great public meetings. Our adversaries have attempted to hold great public meetings, but with little success.

"I wished to correct, as far as I could, the impression, which I find prevalent here, that England, as a nation, is animated by hostile and malignant feelings towards the American people. I would not think of touching on any political question which can divide American opinion. We are met here to-day, in honor of one of those institutions which are not, like the divisions of this evil hour, transitory, but permanent; and which will remain well-springs of intellectual life to the nation, when the civil war is a thing of the past, and its fierce passions have ceased to glow."

At the conclusion of Goldwin Smith's address, the President introduced to the Alumni and friends of the University, Honorable S. P. Chase, late Secretary of the Treasury, and now Chief Justice of the United States. We give his address only in part; that part which expresses the public sentiment of the North with reference to the course of England during the Rebellion.

"It was my misfortune," last fall, he said, "to be a good deal quoted in England, as the author of some sayings not altogether friendly to that country. I said, that in my judgment, England had not been altogether just in her dealings with us; something less than magnanimous; a good deal less than generous and kind; and that sometimes I could not help feeling like taking our old mother by the hair, and giving her a good shaking. The phrase was not very elegant. It was an off-hand utterance, to one of our great assemblies in the West, and got into print; and as it expressed, though in homely language, a genuine feeling, I thought best to let it go.

"How could any American feel otherwise, when the Alabama—

> 'That fatal and perfidious bark,
> Built in the eclipse, and rigged with curses dark,'—

went forth upon the ocean, from a British shipyard, equipped with British stores, armed with British cannon, manned by British sailors, to prey upon defenceless American commerce? 'Built in the eclipse'; yes, in the eclipse of national faith and honor! 'Rigged with curses dark'; yes, with the curses of broken amity, and kindled strife! May God, in his goodness, avert the evil omens!

"Allusion has been made to the reception of the Prince of Wales in the United States. It is never best to disguise our real sentiments. We did welcome the Prince of Wales right cordially. We received him with a warm gush of genuine American feeling. Our hearts went forth to him as the representative of the great branch of the Anglo-Saxon family beyond the water. We wished to draw yet closer the bonds of common lineage, common literature, common religion.

"But when this Rebellion broke out,—when men, in the madness of their devotion to slavery, sought to pull down the pillars of the Republic, and establish a slave-empire on its ruins,—and when, in return for the love and generous sympathy with which we greeted the representative of England, we received cold and averted looks; unkind and ungenerous words; taunts and jeers, in the hour of our calamity; and last, and worst, saw piracy sheltered, provided, equipped, and armed, for the conflagration of our merchant ships, and the plunder of our commerce,—and all this done by Englishmen,—how could we feel otherwise than hostile to England? We did feel so, and we feel so still.

" But we hope for better days. We look for the time when England will see that she consults neither her true interest, nor her true honor, when she indulges unfraternal sentiments towards America. And we rejoice to know that there are illustrious men on the other side of the Atlantic, who dare to rebuke such sentiments, whenever uttered.

"Among those who have thus spoken,—among those upon whom we must rely for the return of amity, and fraternal sentiments, and Christian good-will,—is the honored gentleman who has just addressed you. In your name, in the name of my fellow citizens of the great State beyond the Alleghanies, in the name of all the loyal men and women of America, I thank him."

Near Governor Chase, in the uniform of a Major General, and wearing on his breast the badge of the Ninth Army Corps—his old command—sat General Burnside. No one, on that day, received from the Alumni of the University, a warmer welcome than he, as he rose to respond to the sentiment, " Our Honorary and Regular Graduates in the Army—*Decus et Præsidium.*" The General referred to the services of the sons of the University in the army, and closed his address with an expression of thanks for the honor in which their names were held.

George William Curtis, of New York, responded to a sentiment in honor of the adopted sons of the University. Nobly did he assert the duties of the scholar, with reference to the government under which he lives.

" Our bond of union is scholarship. But to what end is scholarship ? Let him answer,—Sir Philip Sidney, the English scholar of three hundred years ago:—'To what purpose should our thoughts be directed to various kinds of knowledge, unless room be afforded for putting it into practice, so that public advantage may be the result?' But while this truth is in your minds, and on my tongue, while you seek among these, for whom I speak, and to whom you have granted scholastic honors, those who have given all their knowledge, all their skill, to the public service, I see you glance around this table, and ask, as you seek the shining example, what McDowell, looking for the tried soldier, asked, when he saw, at the first Bull Run, that there was to be sharp fighting. He rose in his saddle; his eyes swept the field; the words leaped from his lips—'Where is Burnside?'

"One more, sir. Another of your children, by adoption, is not here. No man, of all our statesmen, more scholarly than he. When all shook, he was steadfast. When all was dark, his eye flashed victory. You have invited him to-day, but he cannot come, for he is putting his various kinds of knowledge into practice. Yet, he sends a message. He spoke in the appalling tumult of the opening war. It was the clear bugle-call of heroic loyalty, that rang triumphant through that fierce yell of rebellion, and brought the bewildered nation to its feet: 'If any man hauls down the American flag, shoot him on the spot.'

"Yes, sir, we meet as scholars, but with no forced, or timorous avoidance of the solemn thought of the hour. It is an insult to literature and to man, to whisper, during a fierce contest for civil order, that politics are unfavorable to literary leisure. Is the scholar a sheep, that he should bleat peace when the wolves are abroad? Literary leisure! To what, in the name of justice, *is* literary leisure favorable, bought at such cost of manhood as that? There is no fairer passage in the life of our University, than the brief record, in our brother Arnold's history, that when the enemy landed at Newport, in 1776, 'The College exercises were suspended, and the building was occupied as barracks, and afterwards, as a military hospital.' I do not doubt that the College would respond now as it responded then; and, meanwhile, that the enemy is further away, I am glad to believe, that Hope College, and University Hall, are each barracks four stories high, crowded with sons of liberty, and that Manning and Rhode Island Halls are not only schools of learning, but hospitals, for the thorough cure of lame loyalty and paralytic patriotism.

"It has too long been the reproach of scholars that they were parasitic,—content to be the ornaments, not the springs of political power, nourishing a false, and, therefore, fatal, conservatism. But the artist, Michael Angelo, is never a nobler figure than when strengthening the walls of Florence against her foes; and Archimedes never manlier than when he puts various kinds of knowledge into practice, that public advantage may be the result, by burning the hostile Roman fleet with mirrors. *Se non e vero, e ben trovato.* If the story be not true, it shows the instinct of the heart, the popular instinct, that, in every time of emergency, the men who go ahead should be the educated, and the intelligent.

"Let who will, therefore, plead, with Montaigne, that politics are not favorable to literary leisure, and so withdraw to their chateaux, and literary leisures. · Not so did John Milton, greatest of English scholars, in the civil wars of England. His was no cloistered virtue, unexercised and unbreathed. Forever reverend in the history of scholars—all the glory of genius, all the spoils of learning, he laid upon the altar of patriotism, giving the power of the poet, and the accomplishment of the scholar, to the duty of the patriot. And, sir, no more splendid vision did the sightless bard behold, than that which the patriot Milton saw, and which, at this very moment, while the land shakes with the glad exultation of national victory, we may seize from his lips as a prophecy:—

"'Methinks I see in my mind, a noble and puissant nation, rousing herself like a strong man after sleep, and shaking her invincible locks: methinks I see her as an eagle mewing her mighty youth, and kindling her undazzled eyes at the full mid-day beam; purging and unscaling her long abused sight at the fountain itself of heavenly radiance; while the whole noise of timorous and flocking birds, with those also that love the twilight, flutter about, amazed at what she means, and in their envious gabble would prognosticate a year of sects and schisms.'

"Such be our satisfaction, sir, and brothers; such be the vision that we behold to-day, on this academic mount. And as we go hence, to-morrow, let it be our Alma Mater's joyful pride, that she sees us truer to God, truer to man, truer to our country, because we are scholars, and because her hand of benediction has been laid upon our heads."

Brighter days for the country came with the spring of 1865. Early in the year, Sherman entered the Carolinas in triumph, and late in March, Grant led forth the Army of the Potomac to the victory for which it had so long labored and waited.

While now the Rebellion was tottering to its very foundations, it was impossible for the students to bring their minds to a consideration of the calmer subjects of thought which the text-books of the course afforded. Lessons were very hastily learned, or not learned at all. Everything pertaining to the studies of the place seemed insignificant in the light of the great events that were making that early spring such a memorable one in our national history. Every ear was attent to catch the reports of new victories; and fresh bulletins were eagerly scanned for the latest tidings from Grant and Sherman.

When, at length, the fall of Richmond was announced at the College, the students generally felt that they ought in some way to signalize the event. They waited, however, for tidings yet more glorious. Those tidings soon came. A little before midnight, April 9th, a telegram was received, announcing the fact that Lee had surrendered, with his whole army. The bells throughout the city at once repeated the announcement; and speedily, above their joyful clamor, a section of artillery thundered the tidings into the ears of the drowsy citizens. Men rushed from their houses into the streets, and then into Market Square. The College buildings were suddenly deserted. At first, the students joined the crowd in the square, where the citizens were making bonfires of the recruiting houses, in the belief that the usefulness of these establishments had passed away. But one feeling animated the ever-increasing crowd, and that was one of unmingled joy. The thought that the war at last was ended, filled every heart with praises, and leaped forth in all manner of jubilant expressions. The words of Old Hundred, The Star Spangled Banner, and America, found a new meaning then and there, as they rose heavenward from grateful hearts. Men cheered, they shouted, they grasped the hands of friends in fervent congratulations. But, however expressed,—in songs, or cheers, or tears,—all their feelings bespoke the unfeigned joy of loyal hearts.

The natural desire of the students for an independent jubilation, soon drew them back to the hill, in eager quest of materials for a bonfire at the College. There was no rowdyism in this. Nothing was done except by consent of the President, or rather in accordance with his hearty desire. Empty barrels found ready purchasers, and nimbly did they leap from dusky hiding places, and merrily roll toward the blazing pile in the centre of the Campus. Never before did crackling flames have such a significance to the excited crowd of students there assembled. To some they spoke of hard service on the battle-fields of Virginia, and of crippling wounds which had cut them down while marching "on to Richmond," and which had sent them back to the books they had dropped for the musket and the sword. To others they spoke of the blood of classmates and of kindred, shed for a holy cause, now gloriously triumphant. To some, they spoke of instantaneous relief from a constant dread of the draft. To all, they spoke of the coming reign of peace; for in the jubilant noises of that memorable night, in the clangor of bells, in the thunder of cannon, in the singing and shouting of excited men, this was the source of exultation so lofty and wild, "The war is over!"

Not satisfied with this impromptu demonstration, the members of the several classes in the University made arrangements for a more fitting celebration of the victories which our armies had recently won. The evening of April 13th was selected for this celebration. Various colored lanterns were suspended from the windows of the several buildings, and from the elms on the Campus. The front of Manning Hall was decorated with flags and streamers, and a stand was erected near, for the use of the American Brass Band, and the University Glee Club, who furnished music for the occasion.

The illumination commenced at eight o'clock. Not long after, Mr. J. G. Dougherty, Chairman of the Committee of Arrangements, introduced President Sears to the throng of students and friends of the College, who had assembled in front of the Chapel. President Sears spoke of the deep interest which the College, as a body, and by its individual members, had taken in the progress of the Rebellion and in the efforts of the nation to suppress it. Three young men were then present, each of whom had sacrificed a limb upon the altar of his country. Now that the chief army of the Confederacy was destroyed, now that the serpent's head was under our feet, and we cared not for the contortions of the powerless body, the College was ready, with triumphant exultation, to celebrate the dawning of peace. The country was saved. Rebellion was crushed, and the powers of Europe must henceforth respect a nation powerful, united, irresistible.

Addresses were then made by ex-Governor Hoppin, Mayor Doyle, Reverend Doctor Caswell, Honorable Abraham Payne,

Reverend Doctor Caldwell, Reverend Mr. Woodbury, and Honorable William M. Rodman.   At the close of the addresses, a large bonfire was kindled on the Campus, in rear of the College, around which the students gathered, and continued the festivities of the evening with songs, national and collegiate.

Before the week closed, all this rejoicing was turned into sorrow, by the tidings of the assassination of President Lincoln. Silently the emblems of victory in the Chapel, gave place to the emblems of mourning.   The exercises of the College were for a time suspended.   All within its walls joined in the general grief. The citizens of Providence, in their affliction, at once repaired to the residence of Doctor Wayland, desiring to learn from his lips, the lessons of the hour.   Thither followed many a young heart from the University over which that venerable man had so long presided.   Professor Chace, in his eulogy on the virtues and services of President Wayland, has sketched the scene with a master's hand : "The country had in an instant been plunged from the height of joy into the deepest mourning.   Its honored and beloved chief magistrate, at the moment when he was most honored and most beloved, had fallen by a parricidal hand.   The greatness of the loss, the enormity of the crime, and the terrible suddenness of the blow, bewildered thought and paralyzed speech. It seemed as if Providence, which had just vouchsafed so great blessings, was, from some inscrutable cause, withdrawing its protective care.   In this hour of darkness, to whom should the citizens go, but to him who had so often instructed and guided them? As evening draws on, they gather from all quarters, and with one common impulse turn their steps eastward.   Beneath a weeping sky, the long, dark column winds its way over the hill, and into the valley.   As it moves onward, the wailings of the dirge and the measured tread, are the only sounds which fall upon the still air.   Having reached the residence of President Wayland, it

7

forms itself in a dense throng around a slightly raised platform in front of it. Presently he appears to address, for the last time, as it proves, his assembled fellow citizens. It is the same noble presence which many there had, in years long gone by, gazed upon with such pride and admiration from seats in the old Chapel. It is the same voice whose eloquence there so inflamed them, and stirred their young bosoms to such a tumult of passion. The speaker is the same ; the audience is the same. But how changed both ! and how altered the circumstances ! That hair playing in the breeze has been whitened by the snows of seventy winters. That venerable form is pressed by their accumulated weight. The glorious intellectual power which sat upon those features is veiled beneath the softer lines of moral grace and beauty. It is not now the Athenian orator, but one of the old prophets, from whose touched lips flow forth the teachings of inspired wisdom. The dead first claims his thought. He recounts most appreciatively his great services, and dwells with loving eulogy upon his unswerving patriotism, and his high civic virtues. Next, the duties of the living and the lessons of the hour, occupy attention. Then come words of devout thanksgiving, of holy trust, of sublime faith, uttered as he only ever uttered them. They fall upon that waiting assembly, like a blessed benefaction, assuaging grief, dispelling gloom and kindling worship in every bosom. God is no longer at a distance, but all around and within them. They go away strengthened and comforted."

April 17th, at a meeting of the Faculty and Students, in the Chapel of the University, President Sears being in the Chair, the following resolutions, reported by a committee previously appointed, were unanimously adopted :—

Whereas, It hath pleased Almighty God to permit Abraham Lincoln, the President of the United States, to be slain by the dastardly hand of an assassin, Therefore

RESOLVED, That we bow with submission to an inscrutable Providence, which, in the very hour of our national triumph, has removed our Chief Magistrate, to whose integrity and wisdom that triumph was so largely due.

RESOLVED, That we revere his memory as that of one whose purity of motive, honesty of purpose, political sagacity and unsullied patriotism,—publicly recognized by his reëlection to the highest office in the gift of the nation—entitle him to a place beside that of "the Father of his Country."

RESOLVED, That we hereby declare our profound abhorrence of the crime of the assassin, that we regard it as the legitimate fruit of " the barbarism of slavery," that we pledge ourselves anew to the cause to which our beloved President has fallen a martyr, and that we pray God to overrule this crowning act of national rebellion to the best interests of our country and of humanity, and to his own eternal glory.

RESOLVED, That we hereby express our tender sympathy with those most nearly bereaved by this mournful event, and our common share in the overwhelming national sorrow ; and that in testimony of this, the Chapel be hung with black, and that we wear a badge of mourning for thirty days.

Professor R. P. DUNN,

JOSEPH WARD,	C. C. DAVIS,
LABAN E. WARREN,	WILLIAM H. LYON,

Committee.

The surrender of Lee was followed by the speedy dissolution of the rebel armies, which still remained in the field. Then, once more, throughout the land,

" War's red eyes were charmed to sleep,"—

Rebellion was at an end—

" And bells rang home the boys returning."

When next the sons of the Alma Mater came together, to celebrate her annual festival, the loving mother gathered around her those, who, during the Rebellion, had served in the Union army or navy, and, in the address of Professor Angell, (now President of the University of Vermont,) which follows, gave them a formal greeting :

" Gentlemen who have served in the Army or the Navy :

"I had expected, until within a few hours, that an older graduate, whose eloquence is worthy of this impressive occasion, would have discharged the pleasant duty which is now devolved upon me. Summoned at the eleventh hour to fill his place, I could not but recall the words of one whom we are proud to rank among our honorary Alumni, that gallant and noble leader, whom so many of you have been proud to follow into the thickest of the fight—General Burnside. When asked by telegraph, at the opening of the war, how much warning he wanted to take command of the First Rhode Island Regiment, he answered instantly: '*Just one minute !*'   And when invited to speak a word of welcome to you, my heroic friends, how could I ask for more than one minute to prepare to utter that word, which is now trembling on every lip, and is ready to leap from every tongue in this vast assembly, Welcome ! thrice welcome ! welcome evermore back to this, your home. We come here with no formal utterances. We need here no studied words. But, with overflowing hearts we grasp you by the hand, and thank God that you are with us again. These beaming eyes, these radiant faces, these familiar scenes, all welcome you with a fervor and an eloquence, which no poor words of mine can rival. The very winds that linger in this academic grove, seem to whisper lovingly your dear names, and to welcome you back to their friendly shades ; and, though there were no other tongue but theirs to tell of your noble deeds, they would with their heavenly music recite them to all coming generations. The Venerable Mother, who, with aching but patriotic heart, has sent you out from her halls to stand on the perilous edge of death, now, with inexpressible joy, gathers you fondly at her feet, to lay her hand upon your heads, and pronounce her benedictions upon you, 'well done! well done! good and faithful servants.'

"In the weary hospital, on the bloody battle field, in the fetid prison-pen, where you underwent the sufferings of a living death, at every post of duty and of danger, you have been teaching that great lesson of patriotism, which it is one of the chief aims of this University to impart. You have taught it with such impressiveness that your most refractory pupils understand, as they never did before, the unity and individuality of this Republic. It was this lesson that you pounded into them at Gettysburg and at Vicksburg, and they learned. Under Farragut, with his old sea dogs, you thundered it into their ears at Mobile and New Orleans, and they learned. Under Porter at Fort Fisher you belched it from the guns of your hundred ships; and under Terry you flashed it from your sabres and bayonets, and they learned. Under Sherman you wrote it in blazing letters of fire over a thousand miles of the South, and they learned. Under Grant you swept them from their forty miles of forts, like the leaves in these autumn winds, and they learned. And now, in every ruined village and town, in every smouldering house and cabin, in every acre stripped, trodden, desolated and peeled, they read that this nation is now, and shall be, by God's blessing, one and inseparable to the end of time. That is the lesson you have been teaching.

"It would rejoice us to-day to dwell upon the services of each of these brave sons of Brown, however familiar the story may be to all. We should be glad to tell each other how Major General Wheaton, fighting with distinguished bravery and skill, through the four years of terrible campaigns in Virginia, has added even fresh lustre to the name, which the world-wide reputation of his learned kinsman, Henry Wheaton, had already covered with such an effulgence of glory, that it seemed well nigh impossible to wreathe it with new honors.

"We would gladly follow the career of my classmate and room-mate, Major General Underwood, from the time that he entered the service in the Second Massachusetts Regiment, in 1861—that regiment with which—His Excellency (Governor Andrew) will permit me to say it—we in Rhode Island esteem it a glory itself for a man to have been connected,—until he at last fell, mortally wounded, it was at first supposed, while leading a midnight attack up a precipitous height at the bloody battle of Wauhatchie, below Chattanooga. His unconquerable courage and cheerfulness, by the mercy of Providence, have borne him through all these painful months of sufferings, and though seriously disabled and crippled for life, he comes back to his old home here to-day, with the fresh laurels, which President Johnson has just laid upon his brow, to share in our festivities and to cheer us with his presence.

"It were pleasant to tell of the services of Ewing, him of the masculine intellect and noble heart, who left the chair of Chief Justice of Kansas to risk his life in the field, and won the highest commendations for his generalship in Missouri.

"As my eye runs over the roll of heroes, how many names and forms of these brave men throng my memory; for I am proud to say that nearly all of them were either my fellow students or my pupils.

"It were delightful to hear again, if there were time, how Metcalf and Brayton and Ames and Mitchel and Douglas have nobly represented us in the Carolinas; and General Thayer, whom we are glad to welcome here to-day, from his distant home in the

West, and the brave Tourtellotte, who stood by Corse in the renowned defence of Allatoona; how Rogers, on the bloody fields of Salem Heights, snatched the colors from the standard bearer and led the wavering ranks into the thickest of the fight, and how, at an earlier day, he sent his Rhode Island cannon balls through and through Fort Pulaski, and by those shots also pierced every granite fort in Europe; how Colonel Browne and Tobey and Remington and Lapham faced the terrible fire at Fredericksburg; how Pell and Goddard were found wherever there was danger; how Colonel Frederic Brown and Monroe and Weeden and Waterman and Bucklyn and Jastram and Mason and Sackett and Dwight and Corthell and Sears—you remember I am used to calling the roll—and Cushing and Whittier made their artillery everywhere a terror to the foe; how Spooner and E. P. Brown served with high honor through the memorable campaigns of the gallant Fourth Rhode Island; how, on a hundred fields, Major James Brown and Duncan and Rogers and Adams and Barker and Draper and Blanchard and Fales and Axtell and Babbitt and Edgell and Woodward have sustained the honor of Massachusetts; and Corbin and Gay and McWhinnie and Smith and Jacobs that of Connecticut; and Bliss and Cunningham that of New York; and Sanborn and Quimby that of Maine, and Sanger that of New Hampshire; how Addeman and Zephaniah Brown and Cragin and Southwick and Smith have shown us to what discipline colored troops may be brought under such officers as they; how Sayles and Parkhurst and Whipple have led our cavalry; how Ely and Shearman and Jenckes and Smith and Bowen and Chapman and Burrage, after displaying splendid valor in the field, endured the horrors of rebel prisons; how Lieutenant Commander Ives and Avery and Thurston and Diman and Caswell and Seagraves and Bradford and Nelson served upon the sea; how Dorrance and Peck, the last representatives dispatched to the field, were struck down wounded by the Parthian shots of the fleeing and perishing rebellion ; how Dennison and Wayland and Burrows and Lane and others ministered as chaplains, and Carpenter and Brownell and Carr and Millar and Abbott and Perry and Hosmer and Porter and Trull and Judson and Keene —where shall I stop ?—and others, as surgeons to the sick and dying ; how on every field of strife, in every part of the land, these and other sons of Brown, whom I have not named, have won unfading laurels for themselves and for their Alma Mater.

"Would that they were all with us to-day ! Some, alas ! will never sit at these festive boards again.

" The first sacrifice our College offered, was BALLOU, who fell on the day when the first of the red harvests of blood, which waved on the fields of Virginia, was reaped at Bull Run ; BALLOU, the memory of whose frank and manly face and generous heart dwells with us as an inspiration even to this day. On that same field of Bull Run, his classmate, RANDALL, first fleshed his maiden sword, never to be sheathed till death struck it from his hand in front of Atlanta. How many of you remember with affection the genial KNEASS, who fell with his face to the foe as the cheers of victory were ringing in his ears ? There was IVES, the centre of how many and how fond hopes, who, scorning the exemption which many in his circumstances would have claimed from the hard service of the field, went forth on such a fair September day as this to meet at once his baptism of battle and of death. Well sang his loving friend, of the gain of the College even in the death of these two young heroes :—

> ' She gained her crown a gem of flame,
>   When KNEASS fell dead in victory gory ;
>   New splendor blazed upon her name,
>   When IVES' young life went out in glory.'

"That brave son of New Hampshire, General BELL, who fell while leading his troops through the terrific fire of shot and shells into that well nigh invulnerable work, Fort Fisher, was also a son of Brown, though not a graduate.

"And yet one more we mourn. Just as we were hoping that death had completed his roll of victims from our ranks, as the rebellion was tottering to its final downfall, the fatal bullet sped to its mark, and Major BROWN, of the Eighteenth New Hampshire Regiment, was gone forever. In every battle and every skirmish he had been at his post, and at his post he fell, as complete victory was about to restore him to us and to all he loved. Would you know his sweet and noble spirit? Hear what he said with tearful eye and swelling heart, as he was about to set out for the field with a new regiment, to which he had been assigned: 'I am not afraid to face death; I am not afraid to meet it, if need be. But what if my regiment should disgrace itself?' True-hearted soldier and Christian! A regiment with such officers as thou wast, never disgraces itself.

"These are the precious sacrifices which our Alma Mater has offered to the country. Let the monumental marble, either in yonder sacred chapel, or in these academic groves, preserve their names, and perpetuate their memory, as the choicest treasure of the University.

"Comrades of the fallen brave! as the University beholds your proud record and theirs, she is inspired with new hope and new courage. You have vindicated the claim, which the friends of academic training have made for it, that it prepares men for every honorable calling in life. Your learning has not degenerated into weak dilettantism or timid and palsied conservatism; but your training in these halls has made your whole life more manly, more high-toned, more brave in the presence of death, more heroic in every hour of trial.

8

"In fighting the battles of liberty, of order, of good government, you have also fought the battle and won the victory for the cause of sound learning, of academic discipline, and especially of your own beloved Alma Mater.   Happy the college that produces sons of such heroic mould, of such true manliness of soul.

> ' Felix prole virum,
> Laeta Deum partu, centum complexa nepotes,
> Omnes coelicolas, omnes supera alta tenentes.' "

Major General Underwood, Major General Thayer, General Rogers, and Major Burrage, briefly responded in behalf of their comrades.

Already in these pages, attention has been called to the fact of the general prosperity of the University during the Rebellion. This fact is worthy of additional notice.   We present, therefore, the following tabular statement of the number of students in the several classes of the University for the collegiate years 1861-2 -3-4 and 5.   A glance at this table will show that, amid the stirring events of the present, the friends of liberal studies, and of sound learning, did not forget the demands of the future :—

	Resident Graduates.	Seniors.	Juniors.	Sophomores.	Freshmen.	Total.
1861-2,	5	31	55	72	51	214
1862-3,	6	34	48	53	58	199
1863-4,	0	40	50	56	56	202
1864-5,	1	37	48	47	52	185

With this statement, we close the patriotic history of our University during the Rebellion.   It is a history of which every graduate and non-graduate of the College may well be proud. Nay, more : we cannot but believe that those whom the Alma Mater shall gather around her in all the future which is before her—and "she is a comely matron yet, and will bear more children, we trust, to bless the world, than can be counted upon a thousand such rolls as she exhibits now"—will love her the more for what she was during the troublous times through which the nation has just passed.

BIOGRAPHIES

OF

STUDENTS WHO DIED IN THE SERVICE,

OR FROM

DISEASE CONTRACTED IN THE SERVICE.

HENRY STEARNS NEWCOMB.

ENRY Stearns Newcomb, a son of Henry Stearns and Rhoda (Mardenborough) Newcomb, was born at Newport, Rhode Island, August 31, 1821. He was the sixth in descent from Francis Newcomb, the founder of the family in this country, who came to New England soon after its settlement. At Roll's Court, Westminster Hall, in the record of the list of passengers, who sailed for America on board the ship Planter, April 6, 1635, is the following: "Francis Newcom, 30, Rachel Newcom, 20, husbandman, wife, and two children." Francis Newcomb is said to have landed at Plymouth, and to have settled at Braintree, on a spot still designated on the map as Newcomb's Landing.

The family, as the surname attests, is of Saxon origin, and is one of the oldest in England. A descendant of Francis Newcomb, who was taken prisoner during the Revolutionary War, was thus addressed by one of the King's judges, to whom he had given his name: "We know the Newcombs. They live in Oxfordshire. They are brave men, and in their veins flows the purest Saxon blood in England." Mr. Newcomb was also related to some of the principal founders of New England. His grandmother was descended from Isaac Stearns, (or Sterne,) of Watertown, Massachusetts, who came to America in 1630, and whose admission to the rank of freeman, is the earliest in date of any on the record. Mr. Newcomb's grandfather, Judge Newcomb, of Keene, New Hampshire, was highly esteemed by all who knew him; and the history of the town is replete with references to his usefulness and public spirit. Daniel Webster, when introduced to his daughter, on a certain occasion, remarked as he took her hand: "As the daughter of Judge Newcomb, of Keene, you must be good indeed not to offend the shade of your father."

The father of the subject of this sketch was Lieutenant Henry S. Newcomb, United States Navy, a man alike remembered as a gentleman and an officer. In the war of 1812 he played a prominent part. By his gallantry on different occasions, he aided not a little in extending the list of those brilliant achievements which made the fame of our young navy illustrious. As a token of their appreciation of his services in the defence of Fort McHenry against the British fleet, the citizens of Baltimore presented him with a gold-mounted sword. His reputation as a gallant officer was such, that the citizens of Boston, having fitted out a privateer for the protection of their commerce against British cruisers, placed the vessel under his command. He did not live, however, to enjoy long the honors he had so worthily won; for, some years after, when in the Mediterranean, he took passage for America in a merchantman, of which nothing was heard after the vessel left port.

The second son of Lieutenant Newcomb,—Henry Stearns Newcomb,—is the subject of this sketch. A mother, whose uprightness, simplicity and kindness, won all hearts, watched his early development, and nourished in him those generous impulses and affections, which distinguished her son through life. He received his early education in the schools at Providence, Rhode Island. Afterwards, in the academies at Plainfield, Connecticut, and at Andover, Massachusetts, he studied the classics, preparatory to a college course. He had inherited, however, his father's fondness for the sea, and desired to enter the naval service; but having completed his preparatory studies, he yielded his preference in accordance with the wishes of his mother, and in September, 1836, at the age of fifteen, entered the freshman class of Brown University. But he was not interested in the studies of the place. He longed for a more active life. The profession in which his father had won distinction was alone attractive to him. Accordingly, the next year,—the year in which his brother, Charles K. Newcomb, was graduated,—he withdrew from the College. Not long after, his mother, deeming it unreasonable to attempt longer to check his desires, visited Washington, and secured for him an appointment as midshipman. The boy's dreams were now to be realized. He entered the service of the United States, July 21, 1838, and made his first cruise in the Ohio. He was soon promoted to the rank of passed midshipman. While in this rank, by leaping into the sea, and rescuing a seaman of his vessel who had fallen overboard, he evinced that generous manliness which, in public and in private, characterized him throughout his career. For this humane act he received the thanks of the Secretary of the Navy. June 28, 1853, he was promoted to the rank of Lieutenant. Subsequently, while on duty in the African squadron, he was detached from his vessel to bring home the Panther, a captured slaver,—a service which he performed at great peril, in consequence of the unseaworthy condition of the ship. In the war with Mexico he was present at the bombardment of Vera Cruz.

It was not till the outbreak of the Rebellion, however, that he found full scope for his powers. He was a Lieutenant at this time, but was soon promoted to the rank of Lieutenant Commander, and then, in September, 1862, to that of Commander.

In the action at Port Royal, he commanded the steamer R. B. Forbes. The flag-staff at Fort Walker was cut down by a shot from his vessel. Afterwards, he was in command of the brig Bainbridge. He was next transferred to the steamer Magnolia. In September, 1863, he was appointed to the command of the gun-boat Tioga,—an appointment which he received with great pleasure. This vessel was then with the East Gulf Blockading Squadron. He joined the Tioga at Key West, early in October. On Sunday, October 24, he was suddenly taken ill. The best medical skill was of no avail; and in a few hours life was extinct.

Long and well, Commander Newcomb had served his country. His sea-service amounted to seventeen years and ten months; shore and other duty, to four years and three months. He was unemployed three years. In all, he was in the service twenty-five years and two months. One who knew him as an officer, speaks of him as "a most unassuming man, very gentlemanly in his manners, and kind to all officers and seamen under his command." Faithful in all his relations—a loving son and brother, a kind and considerate officer, an affectionate husband and father— he has left the record of a useful and honorable life. Such a life is a precious legacy.

The following account of the burial of Commander Newcomb, is from the pen of an eye witness: "The funeral took place on Monday morning, from the government wharf, at Key West, and was attended by a large number of officers of the navy, and by a few citizens. On each side of the hearse were half a dozen seamen, after whom came a guard of marines, with arms reversed. The seamen of the Tioga, two abreast, followed. Then came the officers of the Tioga, also two and two. Several carriages, containing other officers of the Navy, and citizens, brought up the rear. Admiral Bailey and General Woodbury occupied the same carriage. In this order the *cortege* moved off to the cemetery, where the remains of the gallant officer were committed to the grave. The funeral rites were celebrated by Mr. Bowman, the Admiral's Secretary. The usual volley was then fired by the marine guard, and the grave closed over the dead."

Captain Newcomb's remains were afterwards removed to Providence, and now rest in the old North Burial Ground.

JOSHUA JAMES ELLIS.

Class of 1847.

————●————

I CANNOT better commence this sketch of my departed class-mate and friend, than by introducing, in substantially the language of the original, the following letter, written at the time of his graduation. It gives, in words more fitting and impressive than any that I could frame, the history of the writer's childhood and youth :—

"BROWN UNIVERSITY, PROVIDENCE, R. I., 1847.

"Cowley speaks truly, when he says, 'it is a hard and nice subject for a man to write of himself; it grates his own heart to say anything of disparagement, and the reader's ear, to hear anything of praise from him.' As you have requested me, however, in connection with our much esteemed classmates, to commit somewhat of my personal history to writing, that you may with greater vividness, in some future hour of quiet reflection, recall the happy scenes of 'long ago,' I do most cheerfully attempt (notwithstanding the discouraging opinion of the great master of the seventeenth century) to record the more striking incidents of my past life, and to express, though not without many misgivings, the hopes which, on the eve of our college course, I dare to cherish.

"I was born in Boston, Massachusetts, September 13th, 1826. My father, with whose name I was christened, resided in Garden Court street, at the North end, having in early life left the home of his parents at Southwick, 'to seek his fortune,' as was common for poor young men of his time. He was a man of extraordinary perseverance, and business energy,—one of that class of whom we hear it often said, 'everything prospers with them.' From . the vocation of a shoemaker, by means of frugality, he became in a very short time a thriving merchant. He succeeded in amassing considerable wealth, although what would certainly be deemed rather paradoxical in a man in our time seeking gain, he possessed a warm and benevolent heart. I should naturally allude to the house of my father. It was built as a rival to the mansion of Governor Hutchinson, though it was far superior to it in size and structure. The original owner was Sir Harry Frankland; and it was from his heirs, who had become somewhat embarrassed in their affairs, that my father made his purchase. Many were the visitors which its quaint English architecture, and curious workmanship attracted thither. Though long since removed to make room for more modern dwellings, it has been made a subject of history, and any one may find it faithfully described in a romance, (by Cooper,) styled LIONEL LINCOLN, with only a slight change of locality, Beacon street having become in the time of the author, a more consistent location for such a mansion as he was describing, than one of the outlets from North Square.

"It was in this venerable house, that I, the youngest of a family of five daughters, and quite as many sons, was born,— the first and only issue of my father's second marriage.

"Not long after I was born, my father died. Our family then was broken up, and my mother and I removed to Scituate, Massachusetts, her native town. My residence at this place may be said to form the second period of my life. Here upon the banks of the beautiful North river, on an estate made classic from having been improved by one of the earliest families of Plymouth Colony, we lived the solace of each other. The mother was the wise counsellor and faithful guardian of her only son, and he, of course, was the object on which was centered many a fond hope. My mother was a noble woman, and though, from the very circumstances of the case, inclined to indulgence, early taught me to be obedient to her authority. I was often made the subject of her correction, and while I loved her, I was constrained somewhat by fear. For four years I spent my time at the schools and in sports, as most children do at this age. At the expiration of this time a new affliction was in reserve for me, in the decease of my mother. I was eight years old when this event occurred ; but, young as I was, I keenly felt her loss, and, with all who knew her, shall ever remember her as one of the truest of women.

"Thus I might seem to have been left completely alone ; but immediately upon my mother's death, I found a friend in Daniel Phillips, the husband of her daughter Louisa, who had been selected by my mother before her death, as the most suitable person for my guardian. To his home, in Marshfield, Massachusetts, I immediately repaired, where from that time till now has been my home ; and thus a third period of my life was commenced. Mr. Phillips has discharged his duties, *in loco parentis*, faithfully and well. To his wise supervision, and interested regard, all that I am or hope to be, I owe. He has guarded with cautious eye the little legacy which was bequeathed me by my father, and, as a good illustration of the practical sense generally found in an intelligent New England farmer, has ever acted in regard to me from the belief, that a small patrimony can be secured to a youth with larger interest, by a systematic intellectual cultivation therewith, than by a training which would expose it to the risks of a mercantile life, or to the doubtful issues of the trades.   He early placed me at reputably good schools, taught for the most part, till 1 was fourteen, by damsels, and those anomalies of humanity, unmarried women.   From their teachings, I think, I did not derive much serviceable knowledge.   I used to shirk much of the time, since I had them somewhat in my power; and yet, as one may suppose, after subjection to such gentle influences, early I became very tractable and lamb-like.   At fourteen 1 undertook the study of the Latin, after much entreaty and many tears.   Having pursued it one year with a gentleman in Hanover, Massachusetts, I concluded that I would now prepare for a college course.   Accordingly I repaired to the school of one Paul Wing, of Sandwich.   The isolation to which I now subjected myself, afforded abundant opportunities of preparation for the life which my friends had designed me to lead in one of the Universities.   Two years of hard study, and poor instruction, the most monotonous of my whole life, dragged slowly away, when I was considered a worthy candidate for admission. to college. Brown was the spot to which controlling influences inclined me, and from this time-honored seat of learning, if the Fates are propitious, I shall graduate this year.

"Hitherto my life had been far from being an eventful one. Its tenor had been even, nor have these college days with me been mixed with much romance.   To me they have been working days.   On entering College I was forced to toil from necessity; but no sooner had I in a measure atoned for the deficiencies arising from a scanty preparation than, I think, my exertion might seem to have been governed somewhat by ambition.   I have been ambitious.   Such is my nature, that upon being subjected to such influences as we have here, I could not well help being so.   But while I confess this, it is but just to say that my aspirations have not reached much higher than to rub along.   My intense application, for which I have gained a college reputation, has been a need and not a virtue. Thus the whole history of the past four years, with me, can be expressed in one single, brief word, 'study;' which, as I recall it, seems to me like a remembered, but an unrecorded warfare, impossible to turn to much fruition. Those bright spots which stand out so prominent before many, and which so many can hail as glad mementos of college life, alas, are not mine to recall. This path, the end of which we must so soon reach, in my case has lain along but few 'green dales and bright meandering streams.' My social relations have been restricted and confined, and I have been conscious of unpopularity among my fellows. I have attached to myself some particular friends, among whom I take pleasure in recognizing all who have been my chums. I am sure that but for these, I should have quitted these classic halls long ago. As I have lived at Brown, so I expect to live, when I have left its halls, toiling, and toiling, with no hope of bringing anything to pass. My health has been somewhat impaired while here, but if it continues to be good 'to struggle in the world's rough race,' I shall in all probability become a second-rate doctor, or a second-rate pedagogue over some village school; and these are at present my highest aspirations.

"But, chum, there is one event which before all others stands conspicuous in my college life, and to which I cannot help alluding before I close this already protracted sketch ;—an event which, if it be not the means of modifying my hopes in respect to the future in this life, will, I trust, be ever hailed as the foundation of that hope which is as an anchor to the soul, sure and steadfast, and which entereth into that within the veil. The event to which I allude is the consecration of my heart to God. For many years I had been convinced of the importance of an experimental acquaintance with the Saviour, and more than once had the Holy Spirit striven with me, to convict me of sin, and to lead me to the Lamb in whom I could find pardon. While at

10

Sandwich, my teacher, a man of most ardent piety, labored faithfully by prayer and entreaty to lead me to become a true child of grace. Nor did his counsel seem at the time to be ineffectual or unblest, for I did then have some evidence—from sorrow for sin, delight in prayer, and in the reading of the Scriptures,—that I had been born of the Spirit. But the hope which I was then inclined to cherish, could not have been based upon the everlasting rock. By slow degrees I yielded to temptation till I had no more abhorrence of sin than before. Prayer was neglected, or offered at wide intervals, and my Bible was read only to still the monitions of conscience. On my admission at Brown, I had relapsed into a state of alarming passivity. Ambitious views now supplanted every holy aspiration, and had God seen fit to cut me off at this time, where Jesus is I could not possibly have gone. For a long period my religious sentiments, if I had any, were imperfect and corrupt. I paid an outward respect to religion, indeed, in that I attended church upon the Sabbath, and the Friday meeting of our class, and abstained from gross sins; but as for the religion of the cross, in *me* it was wanting. I tried to arm myself against this. I favored a doctrine that it belongs to humanity to save the soul. I scouted at my former experience, as an infatuation and a lie. In such a state of hardness, I remained till the summer of 1846, when God saw fit to awaken me again to a sense of my duty, by a sermon which I heard from R. H. Neale, of Boston. Yet I resisted all invitations of the Spirit, till it called upon me to repent a third time even. During the second term of our senior year, the entreaty of Christian friends, and especially my studies, caused me to see that my condition without Christ was hopeless. The Spirit seemed to tell me that if there was a God, I must not only know that He existed, but love Him, and obey Him;—that if this life, of doubtful duration, was but probationary to another, which

I knew to be eternal, I must act in such a manner as to obtain
that bliss, and shun that woe, which I had every reason to believe
eternity would reveal;—that if Jesus was the Saviour of the
world, I must not only say, 'Lord, Lord,' but believe on Him, and
put my trust in Him. These impressions, day by day, were deepened, till on the Friday evening succeeding our College Fast, I
could endure it no longer. My whole life, during this evening,
seemed to rise up before me. It appeared one of complete
rebellion against God. I felt grieved that I had sinned so long
against so good a Being. I felt my need of a Saviour; and in
Doctor Wayland's room, while listening to his advice, I gave to
Him my heart; from that time I have rejoiced in knowing that
He is mine. With this short account, then, of what I hope was
the commencement of a new life, I must close this little history,
which I have endeavored faithfully to present. However my
aspirations may be humbled in respect to temporal things, I do
aspire to be a sincere follower of Jesus. If I were sure that I
had sufficient of His spirit, I would preach Him to the world, but
with such a course of life there would be many things to interfere. Hoping that the best of Heaven's blessings may descend
upon you, and that you may be guided in the way of all truth, I
inscribe myself your true friend and chum,

JOSHUA JAMES ELLIS."

Mr. Ellis united with the First Baptist Church, Boston, Reverend Doctor Neale, pastor, in the spring of 1847. As a scholar
he ranked high, being one of the eleven in his class who were
elected members of the Phi Beta Kappa Society. His Commencement oration was a manly production, on the somewhat unusual
theme, "The Eloquence of Silence." A pleasant voice and a
fine personal appearance added much to the effect of its delivery.

Immediately after graduating, he removed to Newport, Rhode Island, where he spent a year in the family of the late Reverend J. O. Choules, D.D., teaching a select number of youth the various branches of knowledge required in an ordinary course of classical and English instruction. To this period in his history he delighted to refer,—and with reason, for here he formed an acquaintance with the amiable and accomplished daughter of Dr. Choules, which resulted in a permanent attachment, and years of happy wedded life.

In the fall of 1849, Mr. Ellis entered the Medical School of Harvard University, where he spent three years in the successful study of his chosen profession. After graduating at this School, he received the appointment of House Physician at the Massachusetts Hospital, where he remained one year. He practiced medicine for a few months in Portsmouth, Rhode Island, and in the year 1854, established himself permanently as a Physician in the town of Bristol. His close attention to business and his professional skill soon acquired for him a handsome practice, and he rapidly rose to distinction among his associates in the healing and surgical art. The following extracts from an address delivered by him before the Rhode Island Medical Society, at an annual meeting held in Newport, July 11, 1860, may serve to illustrate somewhat his character and social position, and his devotion also to a "cherished calling":—

"The older we live to be, and the more variegated our experiences become, the more must we come to be conscious of the fact, that our calling is one which tends to make anchorites of us all; and that the practitioner who lives remote from his fellows and from books, imperatively needs the benefits which must accrue to him from occasional association.

"Every liberal profession of late years seems to have been fortifying itself round the strong rallying point of frequent gatherings, and to have been cementing together their individual members by the double bond of organization and concord.

"Happy for the practitioner, especially the country practitioner, if his duties at the bedside of the sick will allow him to separate himself from them *all*, and once or twice a year come up hither to have his ambition fired to new zeal; and, if for no other motive, to reässure himself that he is associated with a noble body of men, engaged in one of the noblest callings which dignify humanity.

"Gentlemen, we have at last come to appreciate and to appropriate to ourselves the virtues of that unseen, associative force of our co-laborers, the chemists, simple *contact;* and there is that in it, which, while it is a destructive force, can develop as grand results for the professional world, as the world of matter.

"The chemist places his acid and his metal side by side, and he decomposes it; but a new creation, a sparkling crystal it may be, rises upon the ruins. With this frequent interchange of thought, the warm and friendly pressure of the hand, eye meeting eye, and the sympathizing fraternal greeting, this simple contact, while it must break down every discordant element which has been too often attached to us as a body, must inevitably tend to develop us and strengthen us, and raise us in the scale of relative professional importance in the eyes of that public, so constantly our debtors, and to which we have a right to feel ourselves most justly entitled. Under the auspices of as frequent professional intercourse as possible, not only as a State Society, but it should be as district branches of it, I foresee for the Medical Corps of Rhode Island, a reputation already enviable, vastly enhanced, and a glorious future.

"Let the seniors encourage youth by a frequent attendance upon these meetings, and let the juniors 'flock up hither, ever adopting that philosophy as the soundest and safest, which aims to extend the domain of our art, by regarding it as built upon the oldest foundations, while year by year are added for its adornments, the ripened experiences of age.

"To be sure, other systems than those established on long well grounded principles, may germinate, and even attain an apparently vigorous maturity. New dogmas will ever be inculcated; and skepticism, that skepticism, it may be, generated by a life of total indifference to medical concerns, and flashing from sparkling intellects, may threaten the demolishment of this our cherished art; yet the temple of ancient Medicine, in the erection of which we all are artificers, despite every attack upon it, will continue to rise higher and higher, with not a stone in its foundations loosened, and with every pillar perfect, till it towers to the skies."

In July, 1862, Doctor Ellis accepted the appointment of Assistant Surgeon in the Thirty-Seventh Regiment of Massachusetts Volunteers. His whole heart was in the work now before him, and with all the enthusiasm of his nature he devoted his professional energies to the care of the men entrusted to his charge. His letters to his friends during the few months that he was in the service, abound with expressions of sincere patriotism, and contain graphic descriptions of the stirring scenes around him. His natural kindliness of heart, and his Christian sympathies, led him to take a warm personal interest in his men, devoting to them, in not a few instances, far more time and attention than the ordinary duties of a Surgeon required. Lieutenant H. M. Butler, commanding a detachment, First Massachusetts Cavalry, with which Doctor Ellis was for a time connected, thus writes of him: "His conduct as a Surgeon, as a gentleman, and as a man, receives my highest approbation. His care of troops cannot be excelled."

But while thus engaged in the faithful performance of his arduous duties, he was seized with the typhoid malaria, and for twelve weeks was confined in one of the hospitals at Washington. His constitution, never strong, was nearly shattered by this attack, and for a time his recovery seemed doubtful. He was, nevertheless, spared to return to his loved family and friends in Newport, having obtained an honorable discharge from the service. Disease, however, and exposure, had done their work, and·in a few weeks he calmly and quietly breathed his last. On the morning of the day previous to his death, I received a few pencil lines in his familiar hand-writing, urging me to come and see him once more. Immediately I obeyed the summons, and hastened to his bedside. That interview I can never forget. He received me with heart-felt joy, and in the most unreserved manner, reviewed the past years of his life, dwelling especially upon the beginning of his religious career, when in College, and regretting most deeply his departure for a time from his Christian love and faith. His mind seemed filled with devout thankfulness for the goodness and mercy which had so long followed him, and for God's wonderful forbearance and long suffering concerning him. As he entered the swellings of Jordan, his eyes lighted up with holy joy. Death for him had lost its sting. Thus he passed away, in the full possession of his mental faculties to the last, and in the enjoyment of that perfect peace which "casteth out all fear." He died Tuesday afternoon, March 17, 1863, in the thirty-seventh year of his age. His wife and one son survive him. Doctor Ellis, it may be added, was an honored member of the Masonic fraternity, being connected at the time of his death with the St. Alban's Lodge, at Bristol.

WALTER HERBERT JUDSON.

Class of 1847.

WALTER HERBERT JUDSON was born in Boston, Massachusetts, February 14, 1824. In early infancy he lost his mother; hence he was deprived of many of those influences and associations which render childhood happy and home attractive. During his boyhood he attended the public schools in his native city. Restless, however, and fond of adventure, he went to sea, at the age of sixteen, as a sailor before the mast. After spending several years abroad, visiting various ports in Africa and in South America, he returned to Boston. Resolved now to secure a liberal education, he repaired to an academy in Uxbridge, Massachusetts, where he commenced anew his studies, preparatory to a college course. In the Fall of 1843, he entered the Freshman Class in Brown University. Notwithstanding the imperfect manner in which he had reviewed his classics and mathematics, he took a good position as a scholar, graduating the twelfth in rank, in a class of thirty-three members. He was best known among his fellows, however, as a writer. The sprightly lyrics which he contributed to the "Mirror," a semi-monthly periodical, established by the men of his class, gave him a college reputation as a poet of no ordinary genius. His humorous lines, in praise of the Tutor in Mathematics, commencing—

11

> "The Freshmen of New Haven
> Count a hundred boys I hear;
> Let them take our little catalogue,
> And point at it and sneer,"

will long be remembered by those to whom they were more especially addressed. These "Mirror" papers, which it was my privilege to edit, are now before me, and I find a melancholy pleasure in looking them over, and in perusing the memorials which they furnish of a departed friend. It is worthy of mention, that Mr. Judson delivered a poem at Commencement, entitled, "The Victories of War and the Victories of Peace."

The two years immediately succeeding his graduation, he spent in the Dane Law School, at Cambridge, Massachusetts, where he was under the direct instruction of Professor Greenleaf and of Chief Justice Parker. In 1849, he received the degree of LL. B. at the hands of Edward Everett, then President of Harvard University. Having passed a year in the office of Ellis Gray Loring, Esq., of Boston, he was admitted to the Suffolk Bar in October, 1850. He at once opened an office, and entered upon the practice of his profession. The following extract from a letter dated July 25, 1853, and addressed to the writer, in reply to a circular which he had issued as Secretary of his class, finds a fitting place in this sketch, as it tells briefly the story of Judson's life in his own words:—

"I lost my mother when I was but a few weeks old. I have never possessed a *home* in my life. From my childhood I have been a wanderer, either by sea or by land. The years immediately preceding the commencement of my college life, I passed at sea, as a sailor before the mast. In this capacity I visited many of the ports of Africa, and of South America. I entered College with the yellow stains of tar at the roots of my finger nails,—stains which at once attracted the attention of Tutor

Frieze, who conducted my preliminary examination. This examination was sufficiently lame and unsatisfactory to the grave Tutor
and to myself, for my reviews had been very hasty and superficial,
and I was obliged to rely, with only an ordinarily retentive memory, upon knowledge acquired years before. Hence, for a long
time after my admission to College, I labored hard,—indeed far
more severely than any of my classmates suspected,—to maintain even a respectable position among those who had come
to College direct from the drill of the academy.

 * * * * * * * * * * *

"My life has been one of *labor* with my hands as well as with
my head. I have always possessed a taste for practical knowledge
of every sort. I can mow, and reap, and make fences and milk
cows. I can splice a rope, tie a reef joint, steer a ship 'scudding,'
send down a royal yard, and at a pinch make my own clothes.
I have lived long enough to discover that learning without practical knowledge and good sense is powerless, but that with these
it is invincible. I am now a lawyer, with a growing practice,
ambitious, but not impatient, and sure of success if I deserve it."

About this time Mr. Judson became much interested in military matters, and connected himself with the Boston Light
Infantry,—a company more commonly known as the "Tigers."
At the annual festivals of this company, he seems to have been
the popular poet, producing inspiring lyrics similar to those for
which he was distinguished while in College. The following
lines were read by him on one of these occasions:—

> You have often heard of a wonderful knife,
> That was owned by a lady advanced in life,
> Which had nine new handles and six new blades,
> And excited the laugh of the lady's maids;
> But the lady declared with obdurate will,
> That her knife was the same old jack-knife still.

You have often heard of a wonderful ship,
That sunk Johnny's cruisers, and gave him the slip,
Which has had new planking, and ribs, and keel.—
And yet she can dance to the storm-king's reel;
    She has borrowed the oaks from many a hill,
    But the ship is the same "Old Ironsides" still!

You have sometimes heard of a wonderful corps,
Equipped by the fathers in days of yore,
Who first wore helmets, and boots to the knee,
And guarded the roots of the "Liberty Tree;"
    The war smoke lifted from Bunker Hill,
    But the corps was the same old company still!

They borrowed a badge to aid their cause,
A tawny creature with threatening claws,
You may hear his growl at the twilight's fall
In the lonely jungles of far Bengal;
    The yeoman's rifle had ceased to kill,
    But the badge was the same "Old Tiger" still!

The veteran corps of Ninety-eight
Have doffed the helmet and boots of late;
They have donned the skin of the Northern bear,—
And the tidy black has a modern air,—
    But change the skin as much as you will,
    The creature's the same "Old Tiger" still!

There's talk of a movement, new and grand,
That changes the front of the old command,—
That gives to the corps a separate life,
And widens the field of honor's strife;
    But whether the change be for good or ill,
    The badge is the same "Old Tiger" still!

An honest purpose, and heart and hand,
Union, a love for our native land,—
This is the standard our wishes crave,—
The spotless standard the yeoman gave!
    And whether in life, or whether in drill,
    The veteran spirit is with us still!

Let us pledge in silence the men who bled —
The *Day* and the *Name* of the mighty dead!
A growl for the minions of Old King George!
Nine cheers for the heroes of Valley Forge!
    Then up boys, up! nine cheers, with a will!
    The "Tiger" spirit is burning still!

Soon after the breaking out of the rebellion, Mr. Judson, with many of his comrades of the Boston Light Infantry, entered the service of the United States. July 16, 1861, he was commissioned a Second Lieutenant, and assigned to Company C, Thirteenth Regiment Massachusetts Volunteers, Colonel Samuel H. Leonard. The nucleus of this regiment was the Fourth Battalion of Rifles, Massachusetts Volunteer Militia, a favorite corps in Boston at that time. The Battalion was raised to a full regiment in the Summer of 1861, while at Fort Independence, Boston Harbor. The Thirteenth was ordered to Washington July 30, 1861. From the time of its arrival in the field, until the Spring of 1862, the regiment was engaged in patrol and outpost duty. Previous to January 1, 1863, it was in action at the second battle of Bull Run, at Antietam and at Fredericksburg. During the greater part of his period of service, Lieutenant Judson was an invalid. In the Fall of 1862, while attempting to rejoin his regiment at the front, from which he had been absent on account of sickness, he was taken prisoner near Culpepper, Virginia, and carried to Richmond. In consequence of his failure to report, it not being known at head-quarters that he had fallen into the enemy's hands, his name was dropped from the regimental rolls. After an imprisonment of several months he was exchanged, but his health had become so seriously impaired that it was no longer possible for him to resume the active duties of the service. Indeed, it was evident that his life was drawing to a close. Desiring, if possible, to see his home once more, he started for Massachusetts.

On reaching New Haven, Connecticut, he found himself too ill to proceed further, and left the cars. Reason was now almost gone, and his strength rapidly failed him. A classmate, Professor George P. Fisher, D. D., of Yale College, kindly cared for the sufferer so long as life remained. He died on the 10th of March, 1863, leaving a widow, but no children.

FAYETTE CLAPP.

FAYETTE CLAPP, a son of Ebenezer and Lucy (Lee) Clapp, was born in Chesterfield, Hampshire County, Massachusetts, June 5, 1824. His father was a descendant of Roger Clapp, a citizen of Boston, one of its earliest inhabitants, and a man of wide reputation. Fayette was one of a family of thirteen children, eight of whom are now living. His early life was spent in Chesterfield, at his mountain home, where, in the village schools, he obtained the rudiments of a good English education. When about fourteen years of age, he went to Albany, New York. Entering a mercantile house in that city, he soon became a successful salesman. After a clerkship of about three years, he removed to Hartford, Connecticut, where he engaged in business for himself.

It was during his residence in Hartford that he became interested in the Christian religion. He had planned an excursion to New York, but, disappointed by reason of the failure of his plans, he stepped into the Reverend Doctor Hawes' Church, at an evening service, and there listened to a sermon from the words, "And the door was shut." Mr. Clapp's mind was deeply impressed by this discourse. The truth found an entrance into his heart. He saw that he was a sinner in the sight of God; and, with a devotion ever characteristic of the man, he now yielded himself to the service of Christ. In the course of a few days, all his plans in life were changed. New purposes filled his soul. He could not repress the conviction that it was his duty to secure an education, in order that he might devote himself to the work of the Gospel Ministry. Accordingly, after consultation with Doctor Hawes, and with other friends, he abandoned his business, in which he had now become firmly established, and forthwith entered Williston Seminary, at Easthampton, Massachusetts, and commenced a course of study preparatory to a college course. This was in 1843.

Mr. Clapp remained at Easthampton until he was fitted for college. He commenced his collegiate studies at Princeton, New Jersey, where he remained two years. Leaving Princeton, he entered Brown University, then under the Presidency of Doctor Wayland, and was graduated in the class of 1848. He will be remembered by his classmates as a man of fine personal appearance, and of more than ordinary talents. If somewhat extravagant in his expenditures, he was also benevolent,—such was his nature, for he possessed a heart out of which freely flowed the noblest impulses. He had faults,—so have all men,—but he had virtues which strengthened with advancing years, and gained for him valuable friends in every field of labor in which his lot was cast.

On leaving college, he had designed to commence the study of theology, in accordance with the plans he had cherished when he connected himself with the church at Hartford; but, while his religious views remained unchanged, he was so filled with doubts respecting his call to the work of the ministry, that he now relinquished his former determination, and turned his thoughts, respecting his life-work, into other channels.

He soon decided to enter the medical profession, and with this end in view he commenced a course of study in the office of his brother-in-law, Doctor S. Clapp, of Pawtucket, Rhode Island. With Doctor Clapp, and with Doctor David Rice, of Massachusetts, he pursued his studies, attending lectures, also, at the Harvard Medical School, until he had completed nearly the course prescribed for graduation. But, just before his examination should have taken place, Mr. Clapp, fascinated by the reports then afloat on every wind, concerning the newly discovered gold regions on the Pacific coast, attached himself to a company of eager adventurers, and started for California, designing to seek his fortune among the mines. After his arrival in California, however, instead of engaging in mining operations, he commenced the practice of medicine and surgery, in accordance with the wants of those who had been attracted to this new Eldorado. In his practice he was very successful, and he soon rose to the foremost rank in his profession.

After spending two years or more on the Pacific coast, he sailed for the Sandwich Islands. There obtaining the confidence of the King, he was by him specially employed to treat cases of small pox and to vaccinate the islanders.

In 1854 he returned to his native State, though with health somewhat impaired. During this year he received a diploma from the Medical College at Castleton, Vermont, and also from the Massachusetts Medical Society, of which he afterwards became a fellow. He was, also, at a later period, honored with a medical degree, for special surgical merit, from one of the medical colleges of Philadelphia.

After receiving his medical honors he removed to Dixon, Illinois, where he engaged in the practice of his profession, making, however, the practice of surgery a specialty. From Dixon, Doctor Clapp subsequently removed to Columbia, Boone County, Missouri. Here he was permanently located until the Rebellion called him to another, and a more important, field of action.

12

uncle, however, contributed much towards the support of the little orphans. But, though Mrs. Ballou was not possessed of material wealth, she was blessed with maternal qualities, more valuable than silver and gold. She taught her children in their early years, that there was no royal road to success, and that if they hoped to achieve it, they must exert themselves to deserve it. She implanted in their breasts a spirit of self-reliance and a determination to win the reward, which industry always attains. She impressed on their youthful minds the truth that honor and integrity were virtues without which, no success, however rapid or brilliant, could be enduring or even worth obtaining.

Sullivan remained at the public schools in Smithfield until he was fifteen years of age, when he was sent to Rochester, New York, and placed in a dry goods store. This was a sore disappointment to the boy, and his letters home were filled with urgent entreaties that he might be allowed to obtain an education. At length, after dragging out a year and a half in this uncongenial occupation, his request was granted. By the assistance of relatives he was sent to a boarding-school at Dudley, Massachusetts, where he remained six months. Then he was transferred to Pawtucket, Rhode Island, where for a year he studied the classics under the Reverend Mr. Taft. Two years at Phillips Academy in Andover, Massachusetts, completed his preparation for Brown University, which he entered in the fall of 1848.

Sullivan strove to make his obligations to the hand of kindness as light as possible. In his vacations he taught school, and, being an excellent flute player, he gave lessons on that instrument. As he could but ill afford college expenses he boarded at home, every morning walking from his mother's house in Pawtucket to the University, a distance of four miles.

At this time, like most boys, who have a decided bent in one direction, he did not excel in general scholarship. In declamation, however, of which he was very fond, he was distinguished among his fellows, and in it he was *facile princeps*. The court house, the legislative hall, and the lyceum, were to him places of frequent resort. No opportunity was allowed to pass unimproved, that could in any manner conduce to the cultivation of his favorite study. His lectures and orations written while he was in college and a little later, testify that his style at that time was easy but forcible; and, as his delivery was graceful and earnest, his numerous audiences listened to him with pleasure.

At the close of his second collegiate year, an uncle, who had rendered him pecuniary assistance, meeting with business reverses, Sullivan felt obliged to accept an offer to teach elocution at the National Law School, in Ballston, New York. Here he commenced the study of law. Availing himself of every honorable means to replenish his scanty purse, he copied for the professors in addition to his other labors. Letters written by him at this time show how straitened were his circumstances, and how rigidly he was compelled to economize. The following extract refers to the failure of a plan to visit the battle-field of Saratoga, which was only fourteen miles distant; a visit which he had long promised himself:

"The fact was that on Saturday I received a letter from Thomas, and the bad state of the finances at home on all sides, was quite a disappointment to me. I immediately examined my weak and sickly purse, and its long, lank, wasted condition spoke too plainly of the emetics I have given it. Therefore, begrudging the little expenses of the excursion, I thought it the part of duty to stay at home."

He writes to an aunt as follows:

the request, notwithstanding his impaired health. In December, 1862, accordingly, he was appointed Surgeon of the United States steamer Marmora, on which he served, accompanying the Yazoo Pass expedition. IIe was afterwards transferred to the Benton, then again to the Marmora, and was on the latter (or the Louisville) when a portion of our fleet ran the blockade at Vicksburg. IIe continued to act as Surgeon on the vessels of the fleet until June, 1864, when, having contracted chronic diarrhœa while on the Red river, where his labors had been unusually severe, especially during General Banks' Red River Expedition, he was again compelled to return to his home in Missouri. The country around was at that time infested with guerrilla bands. Men who had been engaged in any capacity by the Federal Government were brutally murdered as occasion offered. Dr. Clapp's friends accordingly deemed it unsafe for him to remain in Missouri, and he sought an asylum among his brothers and sisters who resided at Lee Centre, Lee County, Illinois.

By the wayside and in hospitals, on the field and on the vessel's deck, he had given succor to many sick and wounded soldiers and sailors; but so long had he lingered at his post, that his strength was now well-nigh exhausted. Under the watch care of his faithful wife and of the loved ones of his own family, he lingered till September, 1864, when he peacefully breathed his last, happy in the assurance of a rest from all his toils, in a land where there is no war, no loss of friends, and no more death.

He was buried in a cemetery near Lee Centre, where, in memory of his virtues and faithful services, his comrades of the United States steamer Louisville have erected a marble monument. "Greater love hath no man than this, that a man lay down his life for his friends."

SULLIVAN BALLOU.

***

RIOR to the late Rebellion, it was a matter of speculation among us, whether, if opportunity offered, the young men of this generation would emulate the heroism of their patriotic ancestors. In those tranquil times, and to our inexperienced minds, the history of the great struggle for national independence seemed like a romance. Our civil war has at length solved the problem.

SULLIVAN BALLOU, one of the earliest victims of that unnatural war, was among the first to prove that devotion to their country had not withered in the hearts of American youth. He was born in Smithfield, Rhode Island, March 28, 1829, and was the son of Hiram and Emeline (Bowen) Ballou.

He was, in a broad sense, a self-made man. His father died at the early age of thirty-two, leaving a wife and two small children. Sullivan, the youngest, then but four years old, early felt the necessity of depending upon himself for support and advancement.

The slender means of his widowed mother could secure for him no other opportunities for mental improvement, than were afforded by the public schools of his native village. A kind

While residing in Columbia, he formed the acquaintance of an estimable southern lady, whom he married, and by whom he had three children.   IIis practice in this place, as hitherto, was for the most part surgical; indeed, he was esteemed the most eminent surgeon in Columbia, and in all difficult cases his services were in demand.

When the Rebellion came, there came with it a severe trial for Doctor Clapp.   He had formed many warm friendships among his southern friends, the majority of whom were now secession- ists.   They, of course, urged him by every inducement, to espouse the southern cause; but his inbred ideas of loyalty to the old flag were so strong that no reasoning, however specious, could induce him to deviate from what he considered to be the path of duty.   Surrounded, though he was, by so many adverse influ- ences, he remained a staunch and consistent unionist.   Both he and his family, however, suffered much from proscription. They were obliged to bury their household goods, and to endure bitter opposition from their old friends.   In a letter written about this time to his parents, occurs the following: "The attitude of this great nation at this time, is such as to lead us to apprehend most severe trials.   Thoughtless, heartless men, led on by even more heartless demagogues, persevere in their madness, appa- rently bent on the complete destruction of the best form of gov- ernment ever reared by finite minds.   A wicked ambition, or some more grovelling motive, seems to actuate those who have been most implicitly trusted with our dearest rights and privi- leges.   Disunion!   Oh, it has almost made my heart cease to beat, to hear the direful word echoing through this broad land. I never before comprehended the meaning of patriotism.   I never before appreciated the blessings of our glorious government.   I do believe, if it is ever the will of God, that I could cheerfully give my own life to perpetuate and preserve it."   This extract well shows the depth and earnestness of Doctor Clapp's patriotism, while his subsequent sacrifices in the service of his country guarantee his honesty.

Soon after the opening of the Rebellion Doctor Clapp's services were demanded, and cheerfully given, in the Union armies. Some statements follow, compiled from a letter written by his wife. They will form a brief outline of his career as a surgeon in the army and the navy.

The outbreak of the Rebellion found Doctor Clapp a resident at Columbia. Such was his reputation among the Union men of the State of Missouri, that he was entrusted with despatches to General Lyon, while he remained at Booneville. In November, 1861, he entered the United States service as surgeon, on General Fremont's staff. Afterwards, during Fremont's campaign in Missouri, he was detached to act as surgeon of the Fifth Ohio Battery. In December, 1861, he was commissioned by Governor Gamble, with the rank of a Regimental Surgeon, and ordered to Jefferson City, Missouri, and other points, to establish hospitals, and to look after the comfort of the soldiers. In April, 1862, he was ordered to take charge of a ward in the Fourth Street Hospital, in St. Louis, where he remained several months, devoting himself, day and night, to the care of our soldiers, and also of the prisoners wounded at Fort Donaldson, and at Shiloh.

In October, 1862, worn out by hard work in these hospitals, and by exposure while serving in the field, he resigned. In the same month, however, Fleet Surgeon Pinckney sent an appeal to the chief of the Sanitary Commission at St. Louis, urging him to send to the fleet, without delay, a man not only qualified to discharge the duties of a surgeon, but also possessed of such qualities of heart as would secure the kind treatment of the seamen entrusted to his care. Dr. Clapp was summoned from his retirement on this call, and he did not feel at liberty to decline

" Have been waiting a long time, and patiently too, for money from ——, but it does not come, and I can now wait no longer. * * * Tell —— I am ' broke'—' dead broke'—' hawk-struck,' and must have that money. * * * *

" You ask if I am coming home this vacation. It depends, as you see, upon what I can do with ——, as he is my staff after this term. Should I be able to raise thirty dollars out of him, as I hope, why I shall stay and trust to Providence for eighteen or twenty dollars which I shall need next December. When I feel as I do to-day, I want to get home as soon as possible, and do something to earn my bread and butter. I cannot look forward with any degree of patience to next spring even, beyond which time my ambition does not impel me to stay. I know of no means, however, of staying beyond next Christmas, unless the Goddess of Fortune should appear in the sudden emergency, and boost me along, as she always has done. But lest she, who is so fickle with others, may fail me at last, I shall expect to come home 'for good' next Christmas.

" Am getting along as well as could be expected with my studies. Sometimes I miss an exercise; but it cannot be helped. It is utterly impossible to accomplish *all* I have to do, and if I carry it half through, I shall do more than the rest. The first six weeks I stood it nobly. That good constitution, which necessity forced upon me amidst the dust, mud and rain of the Pawtucket Turnpike, has been worth a fortune to me within the present term. It is by no means overtaxed, but in this hot weather one feels a want of energy, a lassitude in driving business."

Ballou returned to Rhode Island after two years absence, and was admitted to the bar of his native State in 1853. He first established himself in the village of Pascoag, in Rhode Island, where he remained but a few months; meeting, however, with gratifying success. That field being too limited for his aspirations, he removed to Woonsocket. There his uprightness, urbanity of manner, industry, and enthusiastic love for his profession, at once secured him a lucrative practice. In a few years this place also became too cramped for him, and he opened an office in the city of Providence. The same qualities which had advanced him in the country, established his success in the capital of the State.

While settled in Woonsocket, he was for three successive years elected Clerk of the Rhode Island House of Representatives. In 1857, he was returned as a member, and was at once unanimously chosen Speaker. His strict impartiality, unfailing courtesy, and eminent fitness for the position, won for him a merited popularity. The next year he declined a re-nomination to the Speakership, as the duties of the chair interfered with his freedom for debate. While on the floor, he was chairman of one of the most important committees. His attention to business, and his effective oratory, made him a leading legislator of the State. At the close of his second year of legislative office, he persistently declined reëlection, having determined to apply himself with undivided attention to the engrossing cares of his profession.

A radical republican in politics, he could not keep aloof from the exciting canvass of 1860, and he exerted himself to the utmost for the elevation of Abraham Lincoln to the presidency. In the spring of 1861, the republicans in grateful recognition of his services, nominated him for the office of Attorney-General of the State. The whole ticket was defeated by what was called the conservative party, and Mr. Ballou remained in private life, anxiously watching the development of the conspiracy which then threatened our national life.

In the summer of 1855, he was married to Miss Sarah Hart Shumway, of Poughkeepsie, New York, and by her he had two

13

children, Edgar and Willie. How many happy homes civil war desolates! Here was a young man, scarcely over the threshold of manhood, just thirty-two years of age, congenially wedded to the woman of his choice, with young children needing his parental care and support. After long years of struggle, he had now won an honorable name and such a measure of success, as bade fair in a few years to place his little ones beyond the reach of those trials, which he himself had encountered. To no one, and to no family, did the world look brighter.

At length came the war of the Rebellion. Sumter fell, the President issued his proclamation for seventy-five thousand men, the troops hurried forward. Then came a call for three hundred thousand more men, this time to serve for three years. Rhode Island promptly responded to the summons, and her Second Regiment was mustered into the United States service June 5, 1861.

A major, however, was still wanting. As the organization had been carefully officered, a man of unquestioned merit was sought. The Governor of Rhode Island, by a sort of intuition, had early learned that the wisest choice of material for officers, where all were unskilled in the art of war, was to select men of ability and education, who would be apt at learning from books, and who would make the most of experience as they obtained it. The *morale* of such, also, inasmuch as their ruin would be great, if they disgraced themselves by misbehavior, would be of a higher standard than that of those, who had but little at stake. Acting on this principle, Governor Sprague offered the vacant Majority to Sullivan Ballou.

The offer was entirely unexpected and unsolicited on the part of Ballou, who at the time was connected with the militia only by the quasi-military position of Judge Advocate-General. In such a crisis, when office sought him, he did not feel that he could decline the appointment. Those of us, who knew him well and watched his arrangements preparatory to his entrance upon military duties, could easily see that the terrible and unerring presentiment that he would never return, haunted him from the very acceptance of his commission. Indeed, the writer of this sketch recalls, as of yesterday, the tender earnestness, with which Major Ballou attempted to dissuade him from entering the army unless his services were imperatively demanded, as if the uniform of the soldier were the pall of death. Major Ballou received his commission on the 11th day of June, 1861. The Second Rhode Island now fully officered and equipped, left Providence on the 19th of the same month and proceeded to Washington.

The regiment went into camp a little out of the city, and near the First Rhode Island. In those pleasant summer days the strictest attention was given to the usual routine of camp duty, for Colonel Slocum, the regimental commander, was a thorough soldier and a severe disciplinarian. Guard-mounting, the daily drills, and the evening dress-parades rapidly advanced the volunteers in military proficiency. Major Ballou, with a conscientious desire to obtain a thorough knowledge of the duties of his position, gave himself assiduously to the study of military science; for, like most officers in the early part of the war taken from civil life, he started with little more knowledge of a soldier's duty, than what is contained in the "School of the Company." A man's letters are his own best portraiture; and in the few which Major Ballou wrote during the single month he was in camp, we find some passages highly characteristic. For instance:—

"It would stimulate your State pride very much, if you were here, and could see the action, and know the reputation of the Rhode Island troops. At the present time our camp is about the only fashionable resort in Washington. The ground is crowded with the *elite* of the city; while we are reviewed almost every night by Mr. Lincoln, some member of the Cabinet, the Speaker of the House, or some other distinguished personage. Some of the enemy also have had the curiosity to look at us—such as Breckenridge, Buckner of Kentucky, and others. The officers of other regiments flock to see us, and the universal exclamation is not one merely of praise, but of astonishment. The men of our Second Regiment have taken to drill wonderfully, and their pride being stimulated by the efficiency of the First Regiment, they are already rivaling the First in public estimation.

"Camp life begins to grow rather dull, and all of us sigh for active service.

"I am not able to write you much about the intentions of our Government. We have as many different stories afloat here as you have, and we soon learn not only to disbelieve them, but to take no interest whatever in them. The patriotism of the troops is by no means abated. * * * *

"If we do not move South this summer, I hope to get a furlough for a week and come home and see you all. I want to see my dear little boys, around whom the tendrils of my heart cling so powerfully. And I assure you, it is a stern conflict between my affection and duty to my country, when I give up my children and take the battle-field in defence of the great principles of American civilization. Do not suspect me, however, of any hesitancy or misgivings;—the world has never yet seen nobler institutions in peril than ours, and men were never yet called upon to die in a nobler cause. I shall do my duty with all my might and mind, and to my latest breath; and if I cannot remain here to care for my children, I shall leave them a name of which they will not be ashamed. But I do not deem it inconsistent with true courage for a soldier, before stepping upon the battle-field, to give some affectionate thoughts to 'the loved ones at home;' and though this is the first time such thoughts have dropped from my pen, yet they fall without reserve to you. I have great confidence, Charlie, in the strength of the foundation on which your character is laid, and know that you will not only honor the institutions which I have pledged my life to sustain, but will have both mind and heart to cherish an obligation for the posterity of those who have fallen in their country's service. Let me ask you, therefore, Charlie, if it is my fate to fall on the field, to be a brother to my little boys. I need not enlarge upon the sacred obligation I thus impose upon you, nor labor to impress it upon your heart."

On Tuesday, July 16th, it having been determined to give battle to the rebels then threatening the Capital, the army was put in motion. The Second Rhode Island was attached to Burnside's Brigade, of Hunter's Division, which formed the middle column of the advance. Crossing Long Bridge, Hunter's command took the road leading to the Little River Turnpike, being the direct route to Fairfax Court House. Nothing to the inexperienced soldier, could exceed the beauty and interest of that march. The first bivouac was at Annandale, and, to the thousands of uniformed men, who, regiment after regiment, filed into the fields to cook their coffee by the camp-fire, and to sleep on hostile soil under the covering arch of heaven, this was the first real experience of campaign-life.

The next day the troops pushed on to Fairfax Court House, passing smouldering fires, trees felled in the road, and abandoned earth-works; for the enemy's pickets retired before our skirmishers, and the rebel advance had, but a few hours before, left the place. On Thursday, the column leisurely proceeded to the neighborhood of Centreville. Here two days of inaction were allowed to pass, on the pretence of concentrating the Union forces. Ample opportunity, therefore, was afforded the rebels to hurry up their reserves from Richmond and Strasburg. Oh, how different from the masterly celerity that marked the later campaigns of the war! Major Ballou, all this time, was with his regiment, patiently awaiting the battle, that was to be his first and his last.

At length, on Sunday, the 21st, at half past two in the morning, the troops were moved out of their camps. Hundreds of these brave men, who started off in that early morning hour, when everything was dank with the dew, were to take their next sleep in the cold embrace of death. Halts and delays ensued. It was late ere Cub Run was passed, and it must have been nine o'clock before Sudley Ford was reached. The Second Rhode Island with skirmishers deployed, formed the advance, and, after passing Sudley Church, felt the enemy on the extreme right. For some reason, difficult to be understood, this leading regiment, entirely unsupported, was ordered to engage the rebels, then in heavy force in its front. This was done, and the regiment held its position until reïnforcements came up.

But, while the Second had thus been mercilessly left, as it were, to its fate, shot, shell and musketry had been mowing down its bravest officers and men. Colonel Slocum, Captains Tower and Smith, and many subordinates had been killed, and " Ballou, the heroic, devoted servant of duty, had fallen mortally wounded." While our forces were pressing the enemy in the thickest of the fight, a round shot striking Major Ballou as he sat on his horse, tore off his leg. He was at once carried to the field-hospital near Sudley Church. When our troops were routed and driven back, he fell into the hands of the enemy, and comparatively little is known of his last moments. His shattered leg was amputated, but his constitution could not bear the shock, and he died on Friday, July 26, 1861, and was buried near the church.

In 1862, when our forces obtained possession of the battle-field, the remains of Major Ballou and the other fallen officers of the Second Rhode Island, were recovered by the aid of exchanged prisoners, who had marked the place of burial. It was then discovered that the bodies of these officers had been most inhumanly violated. But, lest a simple statement of the facts even, might appear to some too incredible to have occurred in a Christian country in the nineteenth century, and we might thus be deemed guilty of exaggeration and injustice to a conquered foe, we insert a few extracts from the report of "The Committee on the Conduct of the War," made to the Senate of the United States, April 30, 1862, and signed by the chairman, Honorable B. F. Wade, Senator from the State of Ohio:—

"The evidence of that distinguished and patriotic citizen, Honorable William Sprague, Governor of the State of Rhode Island, confirms and fortifies some of the most revolting statements of former witnesses. His object in visiting the battle-field was to recover the bodies of Colonel Slocum and Major Ballou, of the Rhode Island regiment. He took out with him several of his own men to identify the graves. On reaching the place, he states that 'we commenced digging for the bodies of Colonel Slocum and Major Ballou at the spot pointed out to us by these men, who had been in the action. While digging, some negro women came up and asked whom we were looking for, and at the same time said that "Colonel Slogun" had been dug up by the rebels, by some men of a Georgia regiment, his head cut off, and his body taken to a ravine thirty or forty yards below, and there burned. We stopped digging, and went to the spot designated, where we found coals and ashes and bones mingled together. A little distance from there we found a shirt (still buttoned at the neck,) and blanket with large quantities of hair upon it, everything indicating the burning of a body. We returned and dug down at the spot indicated as the grave of Major Ballou, but found no body there; but at the place pointed out as the grave where Colonel Slocum was buried we found a box, which, upon being raised and opened, was found to contain the body of Colonel Slocum. The soldiers who had buried the two bodies were satisfied that the body which had been taken out, beheaded and burned, was that of Major Ballou, because it was not in the spot where Colonel Slocum was buried, but rather to the right of it. They at once said that the rebels had made a mistake, and had taken the body of Major Ballou for that of Colonel Slocum. The shirt found near the place where the body was burned, I recognized as one belonging to Major Ballou, as I had been very intimate with him. We gathered up the ashes containing the portion of his remains that were left, and put them in a coffin together with his shirt and the blanket with the hair left upon it. * * *

" The testimony of Governor Sprague, of Rhode Island, is most interesting. It confirms the worst reports of the barbarity of the rebel soldiers, and conclusively proves that the body of one of the bravest officers in the volunteer service was burned. He does not hesitate to add that this fiendish desecration of the honored corpse, was committed because the rebels believed it to be the body of Colonel Slocum, against whom they were infuriated for having displayed so much courage in forcing his regiment fearlessly and bravely upon them."

Should any one desire to read the monstrous details of such barbaric inhumanity, we refer him to this report, to which is appended the testimony of numerous witnesses taken by the Committee.

The remains of Major Ballou, with those of the other Rhode Island officers killed at Bull Run, were brought back to the capital of their native State, and buried with imposing military honors, amid the tolling of bells and the booming of cannon, while all the flags in the city were lowered to half-mast and business was suspended. His remains now repose at Swan Point Cemetery.

Thus lived and died Sullivan Ballou. It is a singular coïncidence, that, like his father before him, he died at the early age of thirty-two, leaving a wife and two small children almost entirely dependent upon their own industry for support.

Major Ballou was a man of unflinching integrity, strict morality, keen sense of honor, with a winning affability of manner, and a quickness of parts and habit of industry, that would have made a long life as brilliantly successful as his short one had been. General Burnside, in his official report of the battle, speaks of him as "deserving of the highest commendation as a brave officer and a true man."

The following letter, which he wrote to his wife the Sunday before the battle, and which was found in his trunk after he was mortally wounded, is his own best eulogy:—

"HEAD-QUARTERS, CAMP CLARK,
WASHINGTON, D. C., July 14, 1861.

"MY VERY DEAR WIFE:

"The indications are very strong that we shall move in a few days, perhaps to-morrow. Lest I should not be able to write you again, I feel impelled to write a few lines, that may fall under your eye when I shall be no more.

"Our movement may be one of a few days duration and full of pleasure—and it may be one of severe conflict and death to me. Not my will, but thine, O God, be done. If it is necessary that I should fall on the battle-field for my country, I am ready.

14

I have no misgivings about, or lack of confidence in, the cause in which I am engaged, and my courage does not halt or falter. I know how strongly American civilization now leans upon the triumph of the government, and how great a debt we owe to those who went before us through the blood and suffering of the Revolution, and I am willing, perfectly willing to lay down all my joys in this life to help maintain this government, and to pay that debt.

" But, my dear wife, when I know, that, with my own joys, I lay down nearly all of yours, and replace them in this life with cares and sorrows,—when, after having eaten for long years the bitter fruit of orphanage myself, I must offer it, as their only sustenance, to my dear little children, is it weak or dishonorable, while the banner of my purpose floats calmly and proudly in the breeze, that my unbounded love for you, my darling wife and children, should struggle in fierce, though useless, contest with my love of country.

"I cannot describe to you my feelings on this calm summer night, when two thousand men are sleeping around me, many of them enjoying the last, perhaps, before that of death,—and I, suspicious that Death is creeping behind me with his fatal dart, am communing with God, my country and thee.

"I have sought most closely and diligently, and often in my breast, for a wrong motive in thus hazarding the happiness of those I loved, and I could not find one. A pure love of my country, and of the principles I have often advocated before the people, and "the name of honor, that I love more than I fear death," have called upon me, and I have obeyed.

"Sarah, my love for you is deathless. It seems to bind me with mighty cables, that nothing but Omnipotence can break; and yet, my love of country comes over me like a strong wind, and bears me irresistibly on with all those chains, to the battle-field. The memories of all the blissful moments I have spent with you, come crowding over me, and I feel most deeply grateful to God and you, that I have enjoyed them so long. And how hard it is for me to give them up, and burn to ashes the hopes of future years, when, God willing, we might still have lived and loved together, and seen our boys grow up to honorable manhood around us.

"I know I have but few claims upon Divine Providence, but something whispers to me, perhaps it is the wafted prayer of my little Edgar, that I shall return to my loved ones unharmed. If I do not, my dear Sarah, never forget how much I love you, nor that, when my last breath escapes me on the battle-field, it will whisper your name.

"Forgive my many faults, and the many pains I have caused you. How thoughtless, how foolish I have oftentimes been! How gladly would I wash out with my tears, every little spot upon your happiness, and struggle with all the misfortune of this world, to shield you and my children from harm. But I cannot. I must watch you from the spirit land and hover near you, while you buffet the storms with your precious little freight, and wait with sad patience till we meet to part no more.

"But, O Sarah, if the dead can come back to this earth, and flit unseen around those they loved, I shall always be near you— in the garish day, and the darkest night—amidst your happiest scenes and gloomiest hours—always, always; and, if the soft breeze fans your cheek, it shall be my breath; or the cool air cools your throbbing temples, it shall be my spirit passing by.

"Sarah, do not mourn me dead; think I am gone, and wait for me, for we shall meet again.

"As for my little boys, they will grow as I have done, and never know a father's love and care. Little Willie is too young to remember me long, and my blue-eyed Edgar will keep my frolics with him among the dimmest memories of his childhood. Sarah, I have unlimited confidence in your maternal care, and your development of their characters. Tell my two mothers, I call God's blessing upon them. O Sarah, I wait for you *there!* Come to me, and lead thither my children.

" SULLIVAN."

MILES JOHNSON FLETCHER.

Class of 1852.

————•————

MILES Johnson Fletcher, was born at Indianapolis, Indiana, June 19, 1828. His father, the late Calvin Fletcher, was the first lawyer who settled in the capital of Indiana, and one of the most eminent members of the legal profession in the west. Mr. Fletcher, senior, was a native of Vermont, and, though he early became a citizen of the then "far west," he so appreciated the educational advantages of New England, that he sent no less than five of his sons to Brown University,*—all of whom, either on the field of battle, or at home, were active in the work of putting down the Rebellion. Miles J. Fletcher was the fourth of the brothers who entered our *Alma Mater*. The first eighteen years of his life were spent in his native State. His father, though burdened beyond his contemporaries with professional duties, was engaged largely in agricultural operations—cultivating several large farms. In cultivating these farms, young Fletcher was his father's most useful coadjutor. He thus performed much labor, and oftentimes shared great responsibilities, until 1846, when he came east to complete his preparation for college. He

---

* Since his death, Albert, the youngest son of Calvin Fletcher, has become a member of Brown University, making the sixth of the family at that institution.

spent a year at Seekonk Academy, and, in 1847, entered the Freshman class in Brown University. During his course he was absent from the college one year, so that he was graduated with the class of 1852.

So far as text books were concerned—with the exception of those connected with rhetoric, history and ethics—he was only an average scholar, as his preparation for the University had not been very thorough. But, as a reader, as a searcher after facts in history, no one of his class surpassed him. He studied history with earnestness and delight. He not only read the works of the best historians, but he studied the philosophy of history. At the same time he did not neglect the study of the present, in his love for the past; and few in the University were more cognizant of what was transpiring in all parts of the world, than Fletcher.

He possessed many noble traits of character, for which he will long be remembered by his comrades. That he was frank, generous and impulsive, is attested by many incidents of his childhood and early manhood. The following is a specimen: When a lad of ten years, he was attending, in Indianapolis, what was then known as the "County Seminary." It was kept by the Reverend James Kemper, a teacher of great reputation in the west at that time. One day, a number of boys (among them Major-General Lew Wallace) in thoughtless sport broke the glass in nearly all the upper windows of the school building. The next morning, Kemper, before allowing the usual exercises to commence, read the statute concerning a trespass of this kind, and stated that the penalty would be fully inflicted, according to the laws of the State. He then read a list of the boys who had been engaged in this transaction. An eye witness says: "I never, in a long experience, saw an audience so deeply impressed as were the boys of that school; many of them then learned for the first time, what is meant when we speak of law, and of its violated sanctity.   They saw in vision, as it were, the court-room, the trial, the jail, and the disgrace which would follow.   As the list was read, the name of one of the Fletchers, who was not within a mile of the building when the mischief was done, was announced as that of one of the guilty party.   Kemper read the names slowly, and, in the intervals, there was the profoundest silence. A boy from one of the back seats was seen to advance to the middle of the room.   There, confronting teacher and scholars, he said in a calm voice: 'There is a mistake, sir.   It was Miles Fletcher, and not Calvin.'   This confession touched the hearts of all in the room, and Kemper could scarcely go on with his list." This little incident beautifully illustrates the open, unshirking nature of Fletcher.   Frequently, while he was in college, there were occasions in which the nobleness of his character was as strikingly manifested.   Indeed, there was no meanness in him.

He was graduated in September, 1852, and, on the same day, he was married to Miss Jane M. Hoar, of Providence, Rhode Island.   Before his graduation he had determined on the career of a teacher.   To him, the cultivation of the mind and the heart, was a high and holy service.   Accordingly, on taking his first degree, he accepted the professorship of English Literature, in the Indiana Asbury University, at Greencastle, and entered at once upon its duties.   To meet the requirements of his department, he labored with characteristic zeal and energy.   In an eminent degree he possessed the faculty of interesting the students in his course.   Moreover, he was a friend to his pupils, not holding them off by any false notions of professional dignity, but wooing them to companionship by the kindness of his manners. He gave them encouragement in their despondency, and employment in their poverty—he visited them in sickness, and closed their eyes in death.

As the teaching of history was connected with the duties of his professorship, Mr. Fletcher commenced afresh the study of English history. We have already alluded to his love for historical studies. One who was with him in college, thus refers to this tendency of his mind :

"Among his classmates Fletcher was distinguished for his general knowledge. He cared but little for mathematics, although he acknowledged their importance; and he was never deep in love with the classics; but in history and in logic, he stood head and shoulders above his fellows. Of passing events and of things gone by, he was a living encyclopedia. At this period, his love for reading amounted almost to a mania. Although the vision of one eye was almost destroyed in childhood by sickness, he injured the other in reading to a late hour by lamp-light."

On taking the chair of English literature in the Asbury University, he imposed upon himself a very thorough course of reading. His favorite authors on topics in which he was most interested, were Sir James McIntosh, and Sir William Hamilton. Indeed, at one time, he was intending to spend a year in Edinburg, under the instruction of the latter.

His work as a professor was intermitted by a year given to the assistance of his father, and by a year — 1856–7 — spent at the Cambridge Law School. Indeed, he was so efficient with his hands, his head, and his heart, that there was a constant temptation on the part of his friends to tax his time and strength.

After two years, he returned to Greencastle. Here he resumed his old professorship with unvarying success, until called in 1860, by the voice of the people, to the responsible position of Superintendent of Public Instruction for his native State. The custom has obtained from the earliest settlement of the west, for prominent candidates to canvass the whole State.   During the canvass, Fletcher was received with favor everywhere.   The excitement was intense in Indiana, for, in addition to the Presidential election, there was a most exciting contest for State officers.   The candidates for the office of Governor and Lieutenant-Governor, were the late Honorable Henry S. Lane, and the Honorable Oliver P. Morton, the present United States Senator from Indiana.   They were exceedingly popular, but, at the election, Fletcher united the largest number of the votes which were cast, running far ahead of his party.   He entered upon his new duties with great zeal.   None except those born at the west and yet educated at the east, can fully realize the great difficulties one must encounter in systematizing the work of education in a State like Indiana, where the larger proportion of the population is from the once border slave States, and not one-tenth from the home of free schools.   It was Fletcher's ambition to raise the schools of Indiana as nearly as possible to the New England standard.   To accomplish this, he divided the State into districts, and visited every one of them, infusing something of his own spirit into the most apathetic. His duties were very laborious, but he brought industry, enthusiasm and perseverance to bear so efficaciously upon the educators of the State, that, at the time of his death, the whole system which he had inaugurated was in fine working order.

In the spring of 1861, when the attack upon Fort Sumter aroused the north, Mr. Fletcher held a commission as *aide-de-camp* to Governor Morton.   At the request of the Governor, he at once repaired to Camp Morton, where he rendered valuable assistance in drilling the men who were there mustered into the United States service.   Soon after, by appointment, he visited the armories of New England, and contracted for the first arms which were purchased for the State of Indiana.   In August, 1861, in search of his brother, Doctor William B. Fletcher, who

15

was captured by the rebels in July, he made a journey to Western Virginia.   Unable at that time to secure his brother's release, he visited Washington during the following winter, and, at length, having ascertained the place of his confinement, he not only succeeded in alleviating his sufferings, but also in obtaining his exchange.

Returning home he reëntered upon the duties of his office, giving himself for the most part to county visitation and to lecturing.   Again, however, he was interrupted in these labors; for as soon as the tidings were received of the battle of Shiloh, he hastened to Pittsburg Landing, carrying relief to our sick and wounded.   Among these he labored with such assiduity as to impair his health, and he was obliged to return home.

On the evening of the 9th of May, at the request of Governor Morton, of whose staff he was still a member, he again turned southward, seeking, as before, the comfort of the wounded at Shiloh. Before the train left Indianapolis, he remarked, in conversation with his father, that he was oppressed with forebodings concerning himself, feeling that he was leaving his home never to return again. With the father's promise that his family should be cared for, he spoke his farewells, and, with Governor Morton, Adjutant-General Noble, and several others, entered the train. ·At Terre Haute the party took the connecting train to Evansville, reaching Sullivan about one o'clock the next morning.   As the train was approach- . ing the station, it ran into a freight car which had been run back from the switch, but remained so close to the main track that the passenger cars jostled against it.   Startled by the noise and jar of the collision, Mr. Fletcher put his head out of the window to ascertain the occasion of the trouble, when something, probably the freight car which the train was passing, struck him on the side of the head, crushing his skull and killing him instantly.

Though Mr. Fletcher did not die on the field of battle, yet as truly was his life sacrificed in the service of the country, as was that of any of the noble army of martyrs whose memory we love to cherish. His remains were brought home by a special train, and, on Tuesday, May 12, they were committed to the grave, in the presence of a large throng of citizens.

At the next meeting of the Legislature of Indiana, Governor Morton, in his message, referred to the character and services of his aide as follows:—

"The death of Miles J. Fletcher was a misfortune to the State. Possessed of fine talents, highly educated, endowed with every accomplishment that can make a man attractive in society, with a heart full of the warmest affections and the most generous impulses, he united with all these an indomitable energy of character that gave no rest, and ever pressed him forward in the path of duty. His industry was a marvel, and the amount of labor he accomplished wonderful. The duties of his office he discharged, not scantily as a task, but with a devotion and pleasure that were satisfied only with a full performance. The cause of education he regarded of the first importance, and the vocation and calling of the ,educator the most honorable and dignified, next to that of the Christian minister. The misfortunes of his country deeply afflicted him, and, notwithstanding the delight he took in the performance of his official duties, and his untiring devotion to the education of youth, he would have resigned his office and gone to the field, had he not been dissuaded by his friends, who urged that he could serve his country better in the position he then held. He devoted much time, labor and money to the care of the sick and wounded soldiers. He visited the hospitals and the field of battle to hunt up and minister to the neglected and the dying, and, in carrying a wounded man upon a steamboat at Pittsburg Landing, shortly after the battle of Shiloh, suffered a bodily injury, from which most likely he could never recover. When he was killed, he had started upon another mission of mercy to the army. I was standing by his side at the moment of his death, and never before did I have brought home to me the full force of the words which declare, 'That in the midst of life we are in death.' Had I been asked a moment before, who, among all the young men of Indiana, bade fairest for a life of great usefulness and fame, I would have answered, Miles J. Fletcher."

While spending a vacation in the village of Uxbridge, Massachusetts, in the spring of 1848, influenced by a letter from a brother, Mr. Fletcher became a sincere and earnest inquirer for the Truth, and He who said, "Seek and ye shall find," soon opened the "wicket gate" to one who sought with his whole soul.

Kindness and generosity were leading traits in his character. The poor and the oppressed ever found in him a true friend. Indeed, no opportunity for benefitting any class of his fellow men was allowed to pass unimproved. In the development of such a character, the influence of Mr. Fletcher's father is to be clearly traced; and especially that of his early guide and instructor, the late President Wayland, whose teachings he cherished and followed to the close of his life.

CHARLES BERTRAND RANDALL.

Class of 1852.

CHARLES BERTRAND RANDALL, son of the Reverend Charles Randall, a Baptist minister, was born at Arlington, Vermont, October 27th, 1831. Losing his mother when little more than three years of age, he was indebted to his surviving parent for the affectionate and judicious training which bore its fruit in his subsequent career. For ten years he was his father's sole domestic care, endearing himself by his ingenuous disposition, and unassuming ways. After fitting for college at the Academy in Brookfield, New York, he entered Brown University in 1848. " Possessed," writes one of his classmates, " of a genial temperament and generous disposition, he drew around him a large circle of personal friends among his fellow students. Vivacious and sportive, he occasionally became involved in the tricks commonly practiced upon the novitiates in college life. But he was entirely free from maliciousness. He would never wantonly or knowingly injure any one. Even his most intimate friends sometimes became the targets for his shafts of wit and ridicule. With all his love of sport, and his almost provoking raillery, he possessed so genial a disposition, and so true a sense of honor, that he was loved and trusted by all his associates." Randall was graduated in the class of 1852, and immediately after, commenced reading law in the office of Senator Harris, of Albany. He also went through the usual course of study at the Law School in that city, at the same time teaching, for support, in a Young Ladies' Seminary. On the completion of his professional studies, he removed to Syracuse, which he made from that time his home. Here, in social life, he showed the same traits which had gained him favor among his college classmates. A love of military exercises led him to join the Citizens' Corps; and his efficient performance of duty, as a member of that organization, enabled him, when the crisis came, to enter at once upon a career which he could not have anticipated, but for which he had been unconsciously preparing. Not in the path which he had first chosen, but in another and more brilliant, he was destined to finish his course.

The breaking out of the war, in the memorable spring of 1861, found Randall in the successful practice of his profession. By diligence and integrity, he had secured the confidence and esteem of his clients, and had already won an honorable position at the bar. Yet, with his growing business, and bright prospects of advancement, he did not hesitate, when the first call for troops was made, to sacrifice every professional advantage, and enroll himself among the defenders of his country. Receiving a commission as lieutenant in the Twelfth New York Volunteers, he shared all its dangers and honors, until it was mustered out at the expiration of its term of service.

When the army of the Potomac started for Manassas, Lieutenant Randall, whose regiment was attached to the division commanded by General Tyler, was placed in charge of the first skirmishing party of the Federal army which entered the woods in front of the enemy's works at Blackburn's Ford. .The following account appeared in a Syracuse paper, at that time: " Lieu-

tenant Randall's skirmishers were acknowledged to be the best in
the battalion, and were complimented by Captain Bretschneider,
commanding battalion, by Colonel Richardson, commanding brigade, by General Tyler, commanding division, and by all who
witnessed their daring advances, within conversational distance
of the enemy's line of battle, and their skillful deploying, rallying and firing.   Lieutenant Randall particularly distinguished
himself for daring courage and imperturbable coolness.   Much
of the time he was far in advance of his line, instead of in his
proper place, twenty paces to the rear.   The boys say that when
within plain sight of the enemy's infantry, and in speaking distance, he coolly filled his meerschaum, lighted a match and took
a quiet smoke."

The following is from Randall's own account of the battle, as
given in a private letter, dated July 25, 1861, to a friend in Syracuse : "I cannot refrain from saying a word or two in praise of
my command on that day.   They numbered forty-six, taken from
companies A and D, of our regiment.   Their names you have
undoubtedly seen in the Standard.   As the commandant of our
brigade said of them after the battle, *they are heroes, every one of
them!*   We have received special mention in the official report.
When deployed we found ourselves at the extreme left of the
line of skirmishers.   We passed across a ravine filled with bushes,
and into an open space of several acres between two strips of
wood, filled with pine bushes from four to twelve feet in height,
and in the intervals between the bushes bough houses had been
built to the number of thousands.   The enemy suffered us to
pass over this ground without molestation, or showing themselves.
We advanced steadily and carefully along into the woods, with
intervals of four or five paces between each two men, until the
left of the line came to a ravine in which was a creek and road
running around the base of a low hill, upon which we were

deployed, and which descended towards the enemy to the left
and front.   One of the boys saw a man in front of him and fired
his piece, which was answered by a solitary rifle-shot, and private
J. W. Walten, of Company D, fell dead by the side of the road,
shot through the breast.   He died like a brave man and a hero,
in the performance of his duty.   The boys kept up the firing as
they could get sight of any one, and steadily advanced from tree
to tree for a few minutes, receiving an occasional shot, when we
received a volley from about fifty pieces, followed in a moment
or two by another of three or four times that number, and immediately we heard the order, 'left and right oblique, aim and fire,'
and we then saw the enemy's line of battle—some thousands of
infantry—along this ravine, within at most from twenty or thirty
feet from us, and fire they did.   The balls flew around, above,
below, and upon all sides, but principally over our heads.   I saw
one of the boys, just before this tremendous volley, fire his
piece and dodge behind a tree, and as the bullets came, more
than a dozen struck the tree, either one of which would have hit
him had he been on the other side.   We then discovered that all
the other detachments had left us, and we made double quick
time in getting out of it ourselves.   We had arrived into the
smooth space among the bushes and bough-houses, when the
bugle sounded forward, and back we went nearly half the distance, when we received the order to rally on the battalion, and
we tumbled out and ran around the edge of a piece of woods, and
were just closing up and getting into something like the shape
of a company again, in the rear of the left flank of the Massachusetts regiment, when along came Colonel Richardson, commander of the brigade, who said, 'Twelfth New York skirmishers, deploy on the left of the Massachusetts regiment, into the
woods, by the flank,' and immediately added very sternly, 'move
forward, sir! move forward, sir!' when 'by the left flank march,'

'double quick, march,' was the command by me, and into it we went, puffing and blowing as we were, over the fence and into the woods, when I gave the order, 'scatter and take care of yourselves.' We advanced up almost hand to hand with the enemy, and, when last seen, poor Cheney was doing his duty like a brave soldier. Several of the boys rallied around one of our pieces of artillery, which was then in the bushes, and beat back the enemy who made a rush upon it, and which was in that way alone, as the gunners say, saved from capture by them. As the artillery left their position we fell back, helped along a little by the rifle cannon balls which came after us by way of parting salutes, whizzing, whistling, thumping and ploughing their way along, but which the boys cared not much for, compared with the little humming birds which they had heard so much about lately. After that we were pretty much scattered, only a few of us in the same part of the field; but it made no difference. Our work was done. We had found the enemy, and his strength. Just then our regiment took its chance in. The boys were all apparently as cool as if on parade, and on our way out they did not neglect to strip every blackberry bush they happened to see. We were first in and last out each time, and at one time were considered as all killed or prisoners."

In the September following the battle of Bull Run, Lieutenant Randall was promoted to a captaincy in his own regiment, a position in which he displayed an executive ability that brought his company into an excellent condition. No officer had the respect and confidence of the men under him in a greater degree. While always a strict disciplinarian, he had the happy faculty of being kind as well as stern, blending the two qualities without any apparent effort.

16

Captain Randall, the next spring, followed General McClellan to the Peninsula, acquitting himself with distinguished bravery in several conflicts. When the battle of Gaines's Mills began, he was lying in his tent, prostrated with fever, but he immediately arose, placed himself at the head of his company, and remained on the field until the action was ended. One of his men remarked, that "he seemed like a ghost moving over the battle-field, so pale and emaciated was he." The effort proved too much for him, and he was compelled for a time to leave the service, and return to Syracuse.

Notwithstanding that most serious apprehensions had been excited, Captain Randall began to regain his strength, and, as soon as he was sufficiently restored, proceeded to his father's home, in Auburn, where he was soon after married to Miss Caroline A. Slade, of Somerset, Massachusetts, to whom he had been long betrothed, and to whose unwearied devotion he owed, under Providence, his rapid convalescence. As soon as his strength allowed, he hastened back to join his regiment.

In the battle of Fredericksburg, December, 1862, Captain Randall gave another striking proof of his characteristic coolness. Lieutenant-Colonel Richardson, commanding the Twelfth Regiment, wished to send an important message to Colonel Stockton, in charge of the brigade. The way lay across an open field, swept by the shells and bullets of the enemy. Volunteers had been vainly called for, when Captain Randall, stepping forward, said, "Hand me the message;" and, wrapping his cloak about him, walked to the place, and returned unhurt. Such an act naturally secured him the profound respect of his subordinates. Soon after this, he received the appointment of Judge-Advocate, in the court-martial ordered for the trial of General Tyler, which, under the circumstances, was regarded as a high compliment to his ability.

In May, 1863, the two years term for which it had enlisted having expired, the Twelfth Regiment returned home, and soon after was mustered out of service. But, in the midst of urgent calls for men, Captain Randall could not resign himself to the quiet of domestic life. He promptly and gladly accepted a commission which was soon tendered him as Major of the One Hundred and Forty-Ninth New York Volunteers. Before, however, the regiment had been mustered into service, he was advanced, in fitting recognition of his merit, to the rank of Lieutenant-Colonel. On the eve of his final departure to join his regiment, he was presented by friends in Syracuse with a purse of two hundred dollars, to be expended in the purchase of a horse.

Lieutenant-Colonel Randall had hardly returned to the army, when his regiment was summoned to share in the bloody conflict at Gettysburg. At the close of the second day's fight, Colonel Barnum, commanding the regiment, was forced by physical disability to retire from the field, and his responsible duties were devolved upon his next in rank. So conspicuous were the skill and courage which Randall displayed, that the regiment paused in the midst of the fight and gave him three hearty cheers. Near the close of the third day, he was struck by a Minié ball which entered his throat, and passed down diagonally through his left lung, and out under the arm. A ball also passed through his left fore-arm. He was borne from the field, as it was feared, to die.

Colonel Barnum, in his official report after the battle, says: "Where so many did so well, it would be invidious to make especial mention of some in the ranks and line who were particularly brave and meritorious. I should disappoint my entire command, however, if I did not call especial attention to the consummate skill and unsurpassed coolness and bravery of Lieutenant-Colonel C. B. Randall, who was dangerously wounded in the left breast and fore-arm, while cheering on the men to their work.

Through illness of myself, he was in command of the regiment after the fight closed on the 2d instant, and during the whole of the fight of the 3d, until he was wounded, which was near the close of the contest."

As soon as he could be safely moved, Lieutenant-Colonel Randall returned to Syracuse. Although he never fully recovered from his wounds, yet he hastened back to join his regiment, which had been transferred to the army of the Cumberland, under Sherman, and shared in all the dangers of the Western campaign, in the latter part of 1863. At Lookout Mountain, Missionary Ridge, Ringgold, Ressaca, Dalton, Mount Hope, and Atlanta, his conduct elicited the repeated and hearty commendation of his superior officers.

Colonel Ireland, commanding a brigade in the battle of Lookout Mountain, wrote: "The conduct of Lieutenant-Colonel Randall, while on the right, was splendid. He, by his example, fearlessly exposing himself during the hottest of the engagement, is worthy of all praise." The following instance of Randall's inventive genius deserves to be recorded: "Our regiment is encamped on the summit of a mountain, almost as high as Lookout Mountain itself, and brigade head-quarters are on a hill nearly as elevated. Between the two lies a deep valley, making communication a very toilsome and difficult operation. This difficulty has been overcome by the ingenuity of Lieutenant-Colonel Randall, who has invented a code of signals, by which messages are telegraphed back and forth, from brigade to regimental head-quarters, with the greatest facility and despatch. Words, letters, and whole sentences, are telegraphed across from mountain to hill-top, by a few waves of a white flag, and thus a toilsome journey is dispensed with. The code, although on a small scale, works admirably and rapidly, and is capable of being enlarged to an almost indefinite extent."

General Geary, after the battle of Mission Ridge, in the presence of his staff, complimented Randall for his conduct, saying: "Colonel Randall, you are one of the bravest of the brave."

At the Soldiers' Festival, on which occasion an elegant medal was presented to Lieutenant-Colonel Randall, by the young men of Syracuse, the following incident of the battle at Ringgold was related by Colonel Barnum: "Our troops had taken position at the right of the line, at the entrance of a gap in Taylor's Ridge, when a fearful fire was concentrated upon them from the right, left and front. They soon broke in great confusion, which General Hooker observing, he turned to General Geary, commanding our division, and asked him if he had men who would stand that fire. General Geary mentioned the Third Brigade, that would do it if any could. The order was given, and that gallant brigade, led by the One Hundred and Forty-Ninth, itself preceded by Lieutenant-Colonel Randall, then in command, advanced at a double-quick across an open field a half mile in extent, swept by the musketry and grape and canister of the enemy, and took position in the gap. The movement was executed with the order of a dress parade, and was pronounced by General Hooker, to have been one of the finest he ever witnessed on the battle-field."

At the battle of Ressaca, Lieutenant-Colonel Randall again attracted the notice of General Hooker, and was thanked on the field for his skill and bravery in capturing a rebel battery of four brass pieces, strongly intrenched, and guarded by a detachment of infantry.

When on his last visit to Syracuse, in a speech in acknowledgement of a beautiful flag and guidons, presented to the One Hundred and Forty-Ninth Regiment by the Salt Springs Company, Lieutenant-Colonel Randall used the following language: "Already the armies of the nation are beginning to move. The columns of General Grant, like highly mettled coursers, are restless and eager for the word of direction from their gallant leader. The One Hundred and Forty-Ninth are attached to the central column at Chattanooga, and may, before I reach them, or even now, be on the march to meet the enemy. We expect to return to you in a few short months, with our work finished, no more to go out from among you. We expect soon to notify you that an inscription has been placed upon this flag,—whether it be Atlanta, Mobile, Charleston or Richmond, we know not, but rest assured it will be returned to you unstained, untarnished—that it will float just as proudly, just as fearlessly, over every field upon which it may be placed, as the former one." These words gave utterance to a conviction which Lieutenant-Colonel Randall was known to entertain, a conviction natural perhaps for one who had escaped so many dangers, that he was not destined to die upon the battle-field. Said one who knew him more intimately than any of his comrades: "I had never thought he could be killed, and he did not expect to be." But at the place where he had promised that his flag should float in victory, with his sword drawn, and cheering on his men, he met the soldier's death. He fell, mortally wounded, before Atlanta, July 20, 1864. The last scene is best described in the following letter from Colonel Barnum, the commander of the regiment: "We had led our corps the day previous in a charge across Peach-Tree Creek, and had driven the enemy about three-quarters of a mile, and held them until the balance of our division formed, and we were then relieved and went to the rear of our column and bivouacked. The next day our lines were advanced about half a mile—the first and second brigades of our division being deployed in front, and our brigade massed in column of regiments, a little distance in rear. Our lines were about being again advanced, when on came the gigantic wave of rebel hosts, and in one moment we were all plunged into one of the fiercest fights I ever saw. Our front lines were soon broken, and our brigade deployed and charged the enemy in the woods which surrounded us all. The ground was cut by deep ravines, and, on climbing the banks of one of these ravines, we found ourselves full in the face of the enemy's line of battle, not twenty feet distant. We were ordered to surrender, and the boys replied with a cheer and a volley. Here the most of our killed and wounded fell. We fought them till the entire line on our right and left had given way, and the enemy had an enfilading fire on both our flanks. Colonel Randall saw this before I did, and withdrew the left of the regiment. The right was forced back also, and I ordered the colors back just in time to save them, as the enemy were closing in behind us. On reaching the crest of the first ridge in our rear, I found Randall engaged in forming a new line, and went up to him, and he said: 'Colonel, I am forming on the left of the One Hundred and Second.' 'Very well,' said I, 'remain here, and put the men in position, and I will go and send those up,' pointing to a squad a few rods further to the left, and started to do so. I sent the men to Randall, and returned. The line was again broken, and Randall was dead! A musket ball had passed through his breast, from the point of the breast-bone to the back-bone, probably breaking the spinal column and cutting the *aorta*. He never spoke after being hit. He was standing with his sabre drawn and encouraging the men, and when struck sank to the ground and was dead in an instant. He probably did not know what struck him."

The body of Lieutenant-Colonel Randall was conveyed to Syracuse, where it lay in state, in the City Hall, the flags floating at half-mast from many of the buildings. Thence, after appropriate religious services, it was removed, under escort of the Citizens' Corps, to Somerset, Massachusetts, and on the 5th of August, with further solemnities, the voice of a classmate, the

Reverend Charles A. Snow, pronouncing the last tribute, was committed to its final resting-place. In a retired and beautiful spot, overlooking Mount Hope Bay, and but a few miles from the scene of his youthful studies, he sleeps the sleep which no morning drum-beat, nor rude alarum, shall ever break.

THOMAS POYNTON IVES.

THOMAS POYNTON IVES, was the only son of Moses Brown and Anne A. (Dorr) Ives. He was born in Providence, Rhode Island, January 17, 1834. He came of a family long conspicuous in the annals of his native State for their enterprise, commercial integrity, and large public spirit, and for years identified with the history and the prosperity of the University, among whose graduates he sacrificed his life in the service of his country. His paternal grandmother was the sister of Nicholas Brown, whose honored name the University bears, and his father was for a long period its faithful Treasurer, managing its pecuniary affairs and promoting its interests with the same skill and devotion that placed him among the first of Providence merchants. All who saw in the growing boy and maturing youth, his unaffected sincerity, his dislike of ostentation, his large-hearted sympathy with his companions and his dependants, his genuine modesty, and his plain, practical common sense, recognized in them hereditary traits of character.

One of his early instructors was Mr. Reuben A. Guild, the present librarian of the University. He was put under his private tuition at the age of twelve. A weakness of the eyes, which for years afterward prevented his long and close application to

17

books, and hindered that devotion to study which he desired, at this time rendered it necessary that he should depend much on hearing books read to him. A large part of his boyish acquirements in learning were made under such difficulties, but made with that earnestness, and resoluteness of purpose, which then as in later years triumphed over the obstacles by which others would have been baffled and disheartened. In an appreciative obituary notice of him published in the Providence Evening Press, Mr. Guild observes :—

"As a pupil he loved his studies; and he especially delighted in having his instructor read to him works of true wit and humor. * * * He also loved to hear the Scriptures read, and seemed never to tire of listening to the 'Sermon on the Mount,' and the illustrations of the 'Golden Rule' there laid down. * * * He always loved what was real and substantial, in preference to an empty show, and cared little for the senseless forms and outward observances of mere fashionable society."

Another of his early teachers was Mr. James B. Angell, afterwards Professor of Modern Languages in Brown University, and now President of the University of Vermont. Describing the impression his pupil then made upon him, President Angell says :—

"Mr. Ives was sixteen years of age when he came under my care. The same qualities both of mind and of heart which he afterwards evinced were then clearly manifest. He had a marked aptitude for physics, chemistry and natural history. The physical sciences were always, I think, his favorite studies. His literary taste was uncommonly pure for a youth of his years. His mental processes, though not very rapid, were singularly accurate. His memory was very retentive. His questions were original and suggestive.   Strength was the distinguishing characteristic of his mind.

"He had a strong love of the sea.   The best tales of sea-life and graphic descriptions of voyages were very attractive to him. I should say that his strongest desire then was to take a long voyage.   There was hardly a day when his conversation did not turn to that subject.   None of us then dreamed how serviceable to the country this love of the sea would render his life.

"No one who associated with him could fail to be struck at once with his modesty and simplicity and sincerity, and with his love of the genuine in everything.   He was silent and retiring in the presence of strangers, and in the presence of friends advanced his opinions with caution and often with diffidence.   Shams and vain display of all kinds he thoroughly despised.   His love for the substantial rather than the showy manifested itself even in the minutest things.   A book, to please him, must be printed with clear type on heavy paper, and must be well bound.   So, in judging of the contents of a book, while he did not overlook graces of style, he did not, like some young men of his age, mistake mere rhetorical ornamentation for ideas.   No prettiness of style could to him compensate for the lack of useful thoughts. His solid, good sense demanded something of the same good sense in companions and in authors.

"I never saw a more scrupulously conscientious person than he was.   I never knew one of his years who was so careful in guarding against all error or exaggeration in statement.   He spoke as if he felt that he was to give an account for every word. While narrating a story or describing an incident, he would often modify the language he had employed in the fervor of narration, even when to most persons it might seem that the subject was not of sufficient importance to render the correction necessary. But he was never satisfied until he had given what he conceived

to be an exactly correct impression to his hearer. Especially
was he cautious in quoting the words of others. This scrupulous
accuracy was one of his distinguishing traits in all his subsequent
life, and was a source of great moral power. Every one felt that
his words could be implicitly believed, that he meant just what
he said, nothing more, nothing less.·

"His perseverance was extraordinary. Without that quality
he could not have overcome the serious obstacles which then lay
in his path. Although the weakness of his eyes prevented him
from reading, he learned more rapidly than many boys who have
the use of their eyes. When he had decided to achieve anything,
he counted no obstacles serious, but with indomitable will and
untiring patience pushed over or through every barrier and
attained his end.

"He was at sixteen mature in character beyond his years.
His subsequent career, with its honorable history of self-sacrifice,
much as it rejoiced me, did not at all surprise me. I had seen
the prophecy of it all. And he was capable of yet greater things
than he did. I felt at the time of his death, and have never ceased
to feel, that only those who knew him intimately, who understood
what reserved forces of good there were in that modest, quiet,
earnest man, who comprehended how capable he was of growing,
and so of filling larger and larger spheres of usefulness, could
fully appreciate the loss which Rhode Island and the country
sustained in the early close of that promising life."

A large part of his seasons of recreation was spent on a farm
which had been for many years in the possession of his family
at Potowomut, about sixteen miles south of Providence, on the
western shore of Narragansett Bay. Here he found his chief
amusement in the management of a sail-boat, or small pleasure
yacht. He thus became familiar with the sea, cultivated a fondness for nautical affairs, and gained such a practical knowledge

and skill in reference to vessels and navigation, as gave a character to his life, and ultimately proved of the greatest advantage to him in that form of service which his patriotism prompted.

He early manifested a taste for physical science; and, being prevented by the weakness of his eyes from entering a full course of academic study, he pursued the studies of only the scientific course in Brown University, and received the degree of Bachelor of Philosophy in September, 1854.

Although he did not look forward to the practice of medicine, his inclinations led him to the study of that science. For this purpose he entered the office of Doctor James W. C. Ely, of the class of 1842, in the city of Providence. Here he was unable to devote himself long and closely to the needful text-books, but, pursuing the method of study which he had been obliged to adopt in earlier years, he had many a page of anatomy read to him by a fellow-student.

In connection with his private course of study in Doctor Ely's office, he attended lectures at the College of Physicians and Surgeons in the city of New York; but, as he did not purpose to practice medicine, and pursued the study of it, only from an interest in science, and a desire to qualify himself for such opportunities of benefitting his fellow men as offer themselves to any public spirited citizen, he did not apply for the degree of M. D.

With similar aims, he in 1857 travelled through the mineral regions of the west, for the purpose of personally observing their resources; and in 1858 he visited Europe in order to make such a study of the public institutions of the old world, as would help him to promote the interests of industry and beneficence in his native State.

On his father's death in August, 1857, he succeeded him in the house of Brown & Ives, and in many of the public trusts long borne by him; of these the most important was that of

Treasurer of the Butler Hospital for the Insane. With ample means, leisure and opportunity both for private culture and public activity, Mr. Ives might well have anticipated a career of usefulness and happiness; but this prospect, like that of so many of the educated and promising young men of our land, was rudely disappointed.

The distant murmurs of the opening of our civil strife were borne to his ear in a sick-room. The first call for volunteers found him just recovering from a severe attack of pneumonia. Contrary to the wishes of his friends and the advice of his physician, who thought that he needed an interval of rest to renew his strength, and restore the tone of his system, he at once began his preparations for active service in such a form as he thought his experience had best fitted him for. It was this too hasty assumption of care and labor, prompted by his ardent patriotism, which planted the seeds of the disease, that so soon cut short his life. Says his uncle, Henry C. Dorr, Esquire, to whose admirable memoir of Mr. Ives, in Bartlett's "Rhode Island Officers," the writer of this notice is indebted throughout: "He offered to the government his own yacht, the Hope, and his personal services without pay, in any department in which they might be available. He determined to continue them to the end of the war, if he should be permitted to see it." The government had at the time in its naval service no need of such vessels as this so generously offered. Mr. Ives however received from the Secretary of the Treasury a commission as Lieutenant in the revenue service. This did not indeed open to him the path in which he would have preferred to serve his country, but with that genuine patriotism which subordinates personal inclination to the desire for public usefulness, he said: "I made application for *service*. I never applied for revenue service, but was ready and willing to take it anywhere." Unattractive as it seemed to him, longing for a more active participation in the work of sustaining the government, and little as its daily routine and unconspicuous hardships and perils filled the public ear, this service at this time proved a most important auxilliary to the blockade of the southern coast.

The waters of the Chesapeake and its affluents offered a ready medium to northern sympathizers with the south, to transmit military and medical supplies, as well as intelligence to their friends beyond the lines.

Mr. Ives' yacht, the Hope, had been duly armed and manned at the United States dock-yard at Williamsburg, New York, and under his command, it was in June, 1861, ordered to Baltimore for service in the Chesapeake. In these waters, during the summer months of that year, did he fulfil the duties thus imposed on him. The climate was unfavorable to one like him but partially recovered from disease. The office of seeking to intercept or prevent all communication with the rebels was one which provoked the bitterest feeling on the part of their baffled and disappointed northern friends. The shores offered convenient ambush for any unscrupulous marksman who might desire to avenge his fancied wrongs by the death of the vigilant officer who had interrupted his supplies. The perils were not less numerous but much less conspicuous than those of a battle-field. But Mr. Ives discharged the duties of his post with a diligence and a faithfulness which greatly impeded the communications across the line, and awakened a proportionate hostility in the secessionists of Baltimore.

Willing as he was to occupy his present position if the authorities so advised, he however longed for other and more stirring service. He even offered to build a vessel at his own cost, if he could be entrusted with the command of it; but before this proposal was accepted, the expedition organizing by his friend, General Burnside, near the close of that year, offered him the opportunity so long desired; and having received from that officer an invitation to take part in the projected enterprise, and a promise of the command of one of the army steamers, he in November, 1861, resigned his commission in the revenue service. "In acceding to this proposition," wrote Mr. Chase, the Secretary of the Treasury, in reply, "I must express to you my thanks for the zeal and alacrity with which your personal service, as well as your vessel, were tendered for the public service under circumstances so creditable to your patriotism." On Mr. Ives' return to Providence he was commissioned by Governor Sprague, Assistant-Adjutant-General of the State of Rhode Island, with the rank of Captain, and was "relieved from duty to take part in General Burnside's Coast Expedition, at the special request of General Burnside."

Captain Ives at once went to Philadelphia, where the Picket, a propeller of three hundred and thirty tons, which had been assigned to his command, was preparing for service. Her light draft and formidable armament admirably fitted her for the kind of work before her. General Burnside selected her as his flag-ship; and on the 22d of December, Captain Ives, with his old crew, who were content with lower wages than in the revenue service because they "wanted to go with him," received on board the Commander of the expedition, at Annapolis. At length, after tedious delays, on the 11th of January, 1862, the fleet started for its destination, Roanoke Island. The Picket, with General Burnside on board, was the first of the army vessels to enter Hatteras Inlet. During the weary days and nights that followed, amidst the perils of a gale upon a treacherous coast, in the face of all difficulties and dangers of a narrow and shallow roadstead crowded with over-loaded transports, many of them incompetently handled, Captain Ives devoted himself to the task of getting the army vessels over the sand-bar which obstructed the inlet, and securing them in the safe anchorage of the Sound. He thus shares with General Burnside, with whom he was closely associated, the praise of contributing by his patience, activity, and nautical skill, to the final success of the expedition. Referring to the feeling of impatience and discouragement at the unexplained delay in the work, which, at this time, was general at the North, he says, in a private letter written January 29th, 1862: "If any one could be made to understand the difficulties we have had to encounter, he would not be impatient at our seemingly long delay. Hatteras is the Cape Horn of the northern coast, and almost as perilous. There is danger of a vessel's grounding, and if she once touches the bottom, the chances are that she never comes off again. We have a large fleet of poor vessels, ill sheltered in a small and crowded harbor. It is capable of holding twelve comfortably, and sixty are here. Vessels that two weeks ago we conceived it impossible to get over the bulk-head, are now safely over and preparing to start."

The attack upon the rebel position on Roanoke Island soon followed. In this the Picket took an active part, first in carrying the orders from the commander of the expedition, and afterwards in leading five of the army gun-boats in their approach to the enemy's gun-boats and batteries. It was one of her shells which fired the quarters of the garrison. Enabled by her lighter draft to approach nearer the shore than some of the other vessels, she followed up the advantages gained, and materially aided in silencing the rebel batteries. When the debarkation of the troops commenced, she was ordered with other vessels to cover the operation. On the day after the battle she was sent on the unsuccessful errand of trying to capture the fugitive General Wise, on the opposite shore of the Sound.

The next important movement of the expedition was towards Newbern. Captain Ives, in the meantime, had been busy in

18

severe weather in getting the remainder of the army transports and gun-boats over the bar into the Sound.   In the advance upon the city his vessel with other vessels, shelled the woods before our columns marching up the river on the shore; and in the attack he bore his part in winning the signal victory which led to the surrender of the post.   As was fitting, the Picket was dispatched by General Burnside to Washington to convey the intelligence of the capitulation.   Captain Ives' further service in North Carolina consisted in covering the landing of the troops under General Parke at Fort Macon; in guarding the Roanoke river; in accompanying General Foster in an armed reconnoissance to Columbia, and in aiding to close effectually the Dismal Swamp Canal.   At the termination of the naval work of the expedition, he asked to be relieved from further service in the North Carolina waters, that he might find elsewhere more active employment.   In reply to his letter of resignation, General Burnside wrote: "I cannot accept your resignation without expressing to you my sincere thanks for your kind coöperation and valuable assistance during your service in this expedition.   I sincerely regret parting with you, and shall always remember with pleasure your gallantry, devotion to duty, and your high social qualities.   All the work for armed vessels in these Sounds having been finished, no one can doubt the wisdom of your course in deciding to change your field of action in the Union cause."

The government was not less ready to appreciate the value of Captain Ives' willing offerings and services.   When, after a brief interval of rest for the renewal of his health, he asked for duty, he was appointed Acting Master in the United States Navy, and given command first of the steamer Stepping Stones, and afterwards of the Yankee.   He was then assigned to the second division of the Potomac flotilla, and stationed at Acquia Creek.

To duties similar to those which he had discharged while in
the revenue service, were now added those of coöperating with
the North Atlantic squadron in enforcing the blockade, and with
the army in Virginia, in keeping the river communications open
with Washington and with the forces in North Carolina.   The
rebels were active in planting batteries on the shore of both the
Potomac and the Rappahannock, and in making reconnoissances
to the water's edge.   The flotilla was constantly busied in checking and hindering their operations.   The service was one of great
peril, and of comparatively little public distinction.   But for this,
Captain Ives, true to his nature, cared little.   Far more than general
notoriety he valued such testimonials as that borne by the department in the Secretary of the Navy's Report, December, 1863 :
" At all times and on all occasions, the flotilla has given active
and willing coöperation to military movements.   While the army
was in the vicinity of Fredericksburg, its services were invaluable.   It opened communication with the military forces, cleared
the river of torpedoes, and drove the rebels from its banks.   It
convoyed transports with troops and supplies going to the army,
and returning from the battle-field with the wounded and the
sick.   The vessels in this service are of light draft, and, as their
construction is necessarily slight, those who serve on board of
them in a hostile country are exposed to more than ordinary peril.
But, whether in clearing the banks of the Rappahannock of sharpshooters, or removing torpedoes from its bed, no less energy and
daring have been exhibited than by others, in vessels of larger
proportions and with greater protection."   Some of the specific
actions in which Captain Ives bore a prominent part in the service
thus generally described and commended, were in an encounter
in December, 1862, between the Yankee and a rebel battery
supported by rifle-pits, in which the latter were silenced and
destroyed, a thorough examination of the Rappahannock at the

request of General Hooker, in February, 1863, and the arrest of a rebel conscription in the middle of February, in the counties lying between the Rappahannock and the Potomac. The high estimate of his experience and skill entertained by his superiors, was attested by his appointment in February, 1863, on a board of examiners of Masters' Mates, for promotion to the grade of Ensign.

With the opening of the spring, his services were called for elsewhere. His gun-boat was ordered to take part in the effort to open the river Nansemond, an important channel of communication between Fortress Munroe and General Foster's imperilled forces in North Carolina. The rebels strained every nerve to obstruct transmission of supplies and reïnforcements; but, after six days of severe fighting, the combined forces of the army and the navy of the United States succeeded in driving them from the peninsula, and thoroughly clearing the banks of the river.

Early in May, he was engaged in coöperating with General Hooker in the Rappahannock, and in the anxious days which followed the reverses of Chancellorsville, maintaining the communications with his shattered army.

In recognition of these and of kindred preceding services, the Secretary of the Navy, under date of May 26, 1863, wrote to him: "Having been officially mentioned for efficient and gallant conduct, you are hereby promoted to the grade of Acting Volunteer Lieutenant in the navy of the United States." The only noteworthy action in which he took part during the remainder of this month, was in the capture of the town of Tappahannock, the seizure of a large amount of rebel military stores gathered there, and the emancipation of a large number of slaves in that region.

On the 30th of May, 1863, Commodore Harwood, commanding the Potomac flotilla, appointed Mr. Ives Fleet Captain, or adjutant, of the flotilla. While still retaining command of his own gun-boat, he was charged with communicating to the several commanders the orders of the Commodore, and exercising a supervision over the eighteen vessels which composed this detachment of the fleet. "The service," says an eminent officer of the navy, "required ability and untiring industry in its performance. Lieutenant Ives brought to bear upon his duty, all the higher qualities of the gentleman and the officer, was always prompt and cheerful in carrying out his instructions, and never, that I recollect, in fault. He had no previous training for the service on which he was engaged but in the management of his yacht, yet I noticed that he always performed his duties with the quiet composure of a man 'bred to the sea.' He always seemed to act upon the principle of doing thoroughly what he had in hand, never looking for applause, or betraying for a moment the consciousness of having done well. These are among the finer qualities of a good officer, and added, if possible, to the respect in which Lieutenant Ives was held by his associates in the regular service."

During the summer, he was occupied with the duties of the flotilla. He aided with his gun-boat in protecting the crossing of the Rappahannock at Urbana by General Kilpatrick, in his famous raid, in blockading the river during his absence, and in covering his return. He, with the other vessels of the flotilla, guarded the upper waters of the Chesapeake during the rebel invasion of Pennsylvania, while the fortunes of the Union were still wavering before the decisive day of Gettysburg.

With the approach of winter he found that the labors and the exposure of the summer had rendered it necessary for him to seek relaxation and rest. It was a painful disappointment to him to be forced to withdraw from duty before the final triumph of the Union arms. Unwilling to forego his services, the department, December 3, 1863, detached him from the Potomac flotilla, and directed him to report in person to the chief of the bureau of ordnance. He was ordered to Providence to superintend the work on guns and shells for the government, at a foundry there.

Having performed this service, he felt the absolute need of rest, and therefore sent to the Secretary of the Navy the following letter :—

"PROVIDENCE, February 26, 1864.

"SIR:—I beg respectfully to resign my appointment as Acting Volunteer Lieutenant in the navy of the United States. I feel the greatest reluctance in taking this step during the continuance of the Rebellion, but the state of my health, the less urgent necessities of the service, and the favorable aspects of the war, seem fully to justify me in so doing. When I was detached from the Yankee, I directed the Acting Assistant Paymaster of that vessel to send my accounts to the Fourth Auditor of the Treasury. I presume that they are now in his office, and that there will appear to be an amount standing to my credit as due me for my services since I entered the navy of the United States. As it is my purpose to draw no pay for any services which I have rendered to my country during the present war, I respectfully request that any sums so appearing on the books of the Auditor may remain in the treasury, and that the accounts may be thus closed.

"I have the honor to be, with great respect,

"Your obedient servant,

"THOMAS POYNTON IVES,

"Acting Volunteer Lieutenant United States Navy.

"The Honorable Gideon Welles, Secretary of the Navy."

The department declined to accept his resignation, deeming his services too valuable to the bureau of ordnance to be dispensed with; and assured him that if he found the duties too burdensome, he was entitled to further relief.

On the 4th of April, Lieutenant Ives was invited by Captain Wise, chief of the ordnance bureau, to act as ordnance officer at Washington. His tastes and his training made this a very inviting proposal, and he at once acceded to it. The faithfulness and the success with which he performed the duties of this office, requiring, as a distinguished officer of the navy remarks, "talents of no ordinary character combined with sound judgment and discretion, * * * could not have been excelled." The government acknowledged the value of his services by promoting him to the grade of Lieutenant-Commander, November 7, 1864. He remained at his post until January 26, 1865, "after which time," says Captain Wise, "his devotion to the country and to the duties of the service had so injured his health, that I felt bound to insist upon his going away."

Commander Ives, therefore, asked to be relieved from duty, on account of his failing health. He received leave of absence for six months, and permission to leave the United States.

On the 5th of April, he sailed for Europe. Change of scene, relief from care and labor, brought with them increase of strength. He looked forward at first with confident hope, to a return to a restored Union and a regenerated country, for which he had been willing to sacrifice his means, his powers, and life itself. But the hope was but brief and fallacious.

On the 19th of October, he was married in Vienna, to Elizabeth Cabot Motley, daughter of the Honorable John Lothrop Motley, Minister of the United States at the Court of Austria. His six months leave of absence had been extended, but with the consciousness of failing vigor he turned his face homeward. That home, so dearly loved, which he had once hoped to enjoy in a peace for which he had bravely fought, he was destined never to see.   On the 17th of November, 1865, he died at Havre, whither he had come to embark for the United States.

With a public spirit akin to that in which he had cheerfully yielded up his life, he, in the disposition of his property, made bequests to several of those public institutions, which, had he lived, he would·have aided with his wise counsel and his unwearied labor.   To the Rhode Island Hospital, whose origin is associated with the name of his honored father, he bequeathed the munificent sum of fifty thousand dollars ; to the Providence Athenæum, in which, like others of his family, he had felt the deepest interest, the sum of ten thousand dollars; and to the Providence Dispensary, five thousand dollars ; thus, as it has been justly said, "leaving to his own and to other times, an example of munificence rarely equalled in a career brought to so early a close."

It is worthy of remark, that during his period of active duty as a volunteer, he served in three different departments of the public service of the United States.   On his first enlistment, he was commissioned as a Lieutenant of the revenue service.   At the call of more active employment, he was attached to the army, and shared in the toils of the opening of its campaign in North Carolina; at the time of his death he was an Acting Lieutenant-Commander in the United States navy.   In whatever capacity he served, he brought to the service a faithfulness and diligence, a courage and a devotion which command high honor and win success.   The greatness of the loss which his death occasioned may be estimated by the noble record of his past and the promise of his future.   Cut off in the prime of his manhood, he has left to the many hearts that mourn his untimely end a memory for evermore associated with the noblest charity and the most unselfish patriotism.

LOUIS BELL.

Class of 1855.

OUIS BELL, the youngest son of the late Governor Samuel Bell, and of his second wife, Lucy, was born at Chester, New Hampshire, March 8, 1837. Among his elder brothers were the late Doctor Luther V. Bell, who resigned the honors and profits of his profession that he might contribute his unrivalled skill to the care of our sick and wounded soldiers, and died from overwork and exposure in the service; the late Senator James Bell, an eminent lawyer and an honest legislator; and ex-Chief Justice Bell, (the oldest of the family, and still living,) whose learned decisions upon questions of the highest legal import, have enriched the jurisprudence of his native State for a period of fourteen years. Surrounded by men of such an antique mould of virtue and probity, and watched over by a loving and pious mother, the boy early imbibed the loftiest sentiments of honor and of religion. To such a youth, reared in such an atmosphere, the love of justice, the fearless assertion and defence of truth, and an uncompromising patriotism, were as much a part of his being as the blood that circulated in his veins.

In him the adage, "the child is father to the man," was aptly illustrated. Those who studied and played with him at the

19

Academies of Derry and Gilford, and who knew him during his precocious career at Brown University, saw in him precisely the same traits of character which, in the flush of his young manhood, won the confidence and love of brigades, and carried the standard of his country to victory whenever victory was possible, or philosophically accepted a reverse whenever that was a part of the Providential chastisement and education.

Louis entered Brown University in September, 1852. Here, where he first came into competition with large numbers of young men, he soon took a high rank in the various branches of study prescribed for a college course. But it was in the natural sciences, and specially in chemistry, that he attained a marked excellence. For original chemical investigations he had a decided talent; and among the stores of mementoes which his relatives and friends now contemplate with fond regret, is a collection of small vials containing the crystallized results of his enthusiastic researches among the mysteries of nature. Nothing but the most complete analysis satisfied his inquiring mind, and he would spend whole days and nights separating and re-combining the elements by the aid of retort and crucible. Had he followed the profession of a chemist, he would undoubtedly have contributed his share to the practical benefits which men everywhere are deriving from the wonderful discoveries of the age. His attainments in chemistry, though not shaping his future career of usefulness, were not wholly lost to the country; for years afterwards, they rained down upon the city of Charleston, in the form of a novel and inextinguishable fire, of which some further account will be given in the proper chronological place. Geology, mineralogy, zoology and botany, also received their share of the young student's attention at the University, and more practically by the explorations of mountains, forests and fields, during his vacations. There were few persons who had so good a general knowledge

of the rocks and the fauna and the flora of New Hampshire, as
Louis Bell before his eighteenth year.

His strong constitution, powerful frame, clear eye, and dexter-
ous hand, made all kinds of athletic sports easy to him. In
riding, swimming, jumping, fencing, and shooting, he excelled.
Things like these, which to some men are difficult, were to him
most easy; and now that we can judge of them by subsequent
results, they are not to be regarded as unworthy of notice as a
portion of that education, though not exactly in the regular
course of study, which was fitting him for the part he was to
play in the salvation of his country.

He had an innate taste for a military life, not because of the
ease which it promised, at a time when the nation was happily
at peace with itself and all the world, but because it offered to
him the future possibility of a sphere for his peculiar combination of talents. Before he went to Brown it was his wish to go
to West Point; and he importuned, though without success, the
aid of several persons influential in government circles. In
December, 1853, he left the University, and entered upon the
study of the law; but his boyish love for the army rose in rebellion, and he applied to President Pierce for a commission in a
new regiment, a part of whose officers, it was understood, would
be taken from civil life. Hoping and expecting to receive a
Lieutenant's commission, he devoted much study to military subjects, and laid away a mass of information of which he afterwards
availed himself in unexpected times and places. But his age—
he was nineteen years old at this time—was considered an objection, and the coveted prize was not obtained,—a disappointment
keenly felt. Louis was accustomed to allude to it regretfully,
when, in after years, he thought he saw how much more skill he
might have brought to the service of his country. Making up
his mind that the army was not to be his sphere of usefulness,

he betook himself to the law with fresh ardor.   In 1857, he opened an office in Farmington, New Hampshire, where he soon began to make his mark as a counsellor and an advocate.   In 1859, he was appointed Justice of the Police Court for that town, and, in 1861, Solicitor for the county of Strafford.   During this time he held the office of Brigade Judge Advocate, with the rank of Major.   His revival of the old action of detinue, which had generally been regarded as obsolete, and its confirmation by the highest court in the State, furnished an illustration of his independent bent of mind.   He was held in high esteem by all his professional brethren.

On the 8th of June, 1859, he was married to Miss Mary Anne P. Bouton, third daughter of the Reverend Doctor Bouton, of Concord, New Hampshire.

President Lincoln's call for seventy-five thousand volunteers, in April, 1861, roused Louis Bell from a dream of domestic happiness.   To him, as to many a chivalric young man, the honor and glory of his country, were more than home, fortune, wife, life itself.   To offer his services in any capacity, he hastened to Governor Goodwin, and was appointed Captain of Company A, First New Hampshire Volunteers.   The regiment, rapidly organized and admirably equipped, left Concord amid the God-speeds of the people, May 25, 1861, arriving at Washington three days after.   Soon after, the First District of Columbia Volunteers, a New York regiment, and the First New Hampshire, were formed into a brigade, and placed under the command of Colonel Charles P. Stone, (afterwards Brigadier-General Stone, United States Volunteers,) for the purpose of picketing the left bank of the Potomac, thus connecting the army of McDowell at Washington, with that of Patterson at Harper's Ferry.   The First New Hampshire occupied the centre of the line, and Company A was stationed most of the time at Conrad's Ferry.   The enemy had a few troops, with two six-pounders, on the Virginia side, and occasionally sent an iron compliment across the river, which was always cordially responded to by a sharp musketry fire. Captain Bell, for the protection of his men, built a small field-work, which was afterwards enlarged, and which, known as Fort Bell, was occupied as late as 1864.

The First New Hampshire returned to Concord August 8th, having been engaged in no important action during its three months service. A new regiment, the Fourth, was at once raised, of which Thomas G. Whipple was made Colonel, and Louis Bell, Lieutenant-Colonel.

This regiment left Manchester September 27, 1861, and late in October embarked with the troops selected for the expedition under General T. W. Sherman and Admiral Dupont, destined to Port Royal, South Carolina. During the winter which followed, the Fourth was stationed at Beaufort. Lieutenant-Colonel Bell's abilities soon won the notice of General Sherman, and he was surprised one morning by a summons from the General, with whom he had no acquaintance, and the announcement of his appointment as Inspector-General and Chief of Sherman's staff.

Upon the resignation of Colonel Whipple, Bell succeeded to the command of the Fourth New Hampshire, and was commissioned as Colonel, March 18, 1862.

In April of that year, the Government sent Colonel Bell and his regiment to occupy the fortified town of St. Augustine, Florida. The expedition was a success, no resistance being offered by the enemy, and the inhabitants apparently acquiescing in the presence of the national troops. Colonel Bell was placed in command of the post. Anticipating an attack upon the principal fort, he at once put it in a thorough state of defence. Among other means employed was a kind of hand-grenade of his own invention, made of a heavy shell, loaded, and arranged so that when thrown from the ramparts it would explode near the ground. The explosion was effected by a string of the proper length, one end of which was attached to the top of the ramparts, and the other to a friction primer, wedged into the fuse-hole of the shell. When the shell was thrown from the rampart, its weight drew the primer, and caused the shell to explode. Colonel Bell not only exercised the garrison in the use of heavy guns, but he also organized and equipped one company of his regiment as cavalry, which patrolled the outskirts of the town as a guard against guerillas. Colonel Bell's administration, firm yet mild, was so satisfactory to the people of St. Augustine that, when he was recalled from the post by order of General Hunter, who succeeded General Sherman, a number of the most respectable and influential citizens of the town united in sending him a letter expressive of their gratification at the manner in which he had performed his arduous duties, and their regret at his unexpected departure.

Colonel Bell was relieved from his command for an alleged violation of one of the Government's numerous orders with reference to slavery. An examination of all the facts in the case—for which space could not be afforded here—shows that the Colonel was entirely innocent of any breach of order, either in letter or spirit; and that General Hunter acted in the matter upon insufficient information, and without that reflection and judgment the exercise of which in this and other weightier affairs, would doubtless have saved him from the humiliation of a recall by the Government in September, 1862. General Brannan, a skillful and judicious officer, succeeded General Hunter, and immediately restored Colonel Bell to his command. On his return to his old regiment he was warmly welcomed.

In October, 1862, the Fourth New Hampshire took part in the expedition against Pocotaligo, near the head of Broad river.

It was the design of this expedition to cut the Savannah and Charleston railroad. The enemy, however, were in great force, and after a short contest our troops were compelled to retire. The Fourth New Hampshire lost about thirty men killed and wounded. On the retreat of our troops to the gun-boats, the regiment formed the rear guard. In this fight Bell received a severe bruise from a splinter struck from a tree by a cannon ball.

In the winter and spring of 1863, Colonel Bell occupied at Beaufort, as his regimental head-quarters, a fine old mansion, last owned by one of the Rhetts. It faced the sea, and was surrounded with trees and flowers. To this bower, deserted by secessionists, he brought his wife and little daughter Marian, and his cousin Miss Eliza Nesmith, of Lowell, Massachusetts, and renewed something of the old graces of home life which had once sanctified the dwelling. The wives of some of his officers also came from their northern homes, and quite a New England air soon pervaded the lazy old village of Beaufort. It was a strange episode of the war—the transplanting of the domesticities and refinements of the north, into the very midst of the southern tempest. But there were true hearts and strong arms ready to shelter and protect those whose presence brought to mind so vividly the loved circles at home. Serenades, excursions, picnics, were among the orders of the day, as long as ladies were permitted to gladden the grim Department of the South. At length, when a course of more active operations was determined upon, an order came that broke up these extemporized households, and sent home the fairer and tenderer portion of them, amid the general regrets of the soldiers, rank and file.

During his brief vacation in New Hampshire, in 1861, the Colonel had made many additions to his little store of military books, so that he took with him to South Carolina a valuable, though compact library. Before him in his new field of labor, were many interesting and unsolved problems in the art of war, which his ambition, no less than his patriotism, impelled him to seek to master. As fast as spare funds accumulated in his hands, he would send to New York for treatises, sometimes the rarest and costliest in that sphere of knowledge; and it was not long before he took a just pride in saying that he had the finest private collection of standard military authors in that Department. A diligent study of these works, combined with his natural aptitude and daily practice in the actual operations of war, fitted him, in the opinion of those who knew him best, for a position of much higher responsibility than fortune had hitherto allotted to him. Most of the volunteer officers confined themselves to the duties of their particular arm of the service; but Bell was familiar with the details of the cavalry and artillery service, and of engineering, as well as with those of infantry. At different times, as occasion demanded, he displayed his proficiency in these widely distinct branches of military attainment.

About this time Colonel Bell was placed in command of a brigade consisting of the Third and Fourth New Hampshire, and Ninth and Eleventh Maine regiments,—superb fighting material. These troops took a conspicuous part in the heavy operations on Folly and Morris Islands, including the siege of Fort Wagner, and the bombardment of Fort Sumter and Charleston. His brigade was almost constantly under fire, and suffered severely. A portion of the time Colonel Bell directed the bombardment of Charleston. There were neither facilities nor ingredients at hand to test the Colonel's skill in the preparation of a substitute for "Greek Fire," which had thus far been a failure. But with such rude apparatus as he could command, and such combustible and explosive substances as he could gather from ordnance and quartermasters' stores, he succeeded in accomplishing his object. The result of his experiments was a solid substance, capable of burning for several minutes with an intense heat, throwing out large tongues of flame, and inextinguishable by water. Small cylinders of wood or brass, open at one end, were filled with this substance, and then, enclosed in bomb-shells, were dropped into the Palmetto city. The explosion of these shells scattered the fire in every direction, and, unless the shell exploded prematurely, or did not burst, never failed to start a lively conflagration. The feasibility of burning the lower part of Charleston, had that been seriously desired, was now demonstrated; but it soon became evident that such was not the wish of the government, and Greek Fire was abandoned. Colonel Bell's mechanical talents, no less than his chemical skill, came into play. While at Beaufort, he experimented many times with a mortar upon a new combination shell-fuse, which was designed to overcome several difficulties, hitherto unsurmounted in shell practice. With coarse fuses made by himself and the regimental blacksmith, he attained a good degree of success. He intended to resume his experiments under more favorable auspices, at some future time, which never came.

Previous to the general movement of the armies in May, 1864, most of the old Tenth Corps originally taken to South Carolina by General T. W. Sherman, including Bell's brigade, was transferred to Fortress Monroe; and, when Grant commenced his grand movement against Richmond, the Tenth Corps and other troops, under the command of General Butler, moved up the James river to Bermuda Hundred. There they soon found plenty of fighting. On the 9th of May, Bell's brigade took part in a battle north of Petersburg; on the 15th, in a severe engagement near Drury's Bluff, on which occasion the Colonel temporarily commanded a division; on the 17th, in the repulse of Beauregard's desperate attack on our entrenched lines; on the 20th and 21st, in repelling similar assaults of the enemy. These

20

onslaughts were made in strong force, with great intrepidity and a perfect recklessness as to losses. The design was to crush Butler before Grant could effect a junction with him; but it failed by reason of the superior endurance of the national troops.

When Grant crossed the Pamunkey river, a part of Butler's command, including Bell's brigade, were transferred by means of transports to the head of the York river. Thence, by McClellan's old route, they marched to join the army of the Potomac. The movement was successful, and, on the 30th of May, these reën-forcements engaged the enemy at Cold Harbor. Bell's brigade formed the left of the line. A few days of desultory skirmishing followed, when, about the middle of June, Grant made another of his flank movements to the left, this time striking Petersburg. The Tenth Army Corps was the first to arrive in front of the Cockade City; and to Bell's brigade was entrusted the task of carrying two forts by assault. This was done in a gallant charge, the Colonel as usual leading his men, and being among the first to enter the rebel earthworks. At the same time, a colored brigade captured a third fort near by. The rebel inmates had surrendered to the negroes, when the latter remembering the Fort Pillow massacre, (which, indeed, had been in their thoughts and on their lips all that day,) were about to retaliate upon their captives, when Bell mercifully interposed, and placed a guard of his own men over the prisoners for their protection.

July 30th, Bell's brigade, forming the second line of attack, was engaged in the unsuccessful "mine" assault at Petersburg. Major E. P. Brown, *Aide-de-camp* on the staff of the First Brigade, Second Division, Ninth Army Corps, met the Colonel in the crater. He speaks of his noble and courageous bearing on that day of dark things, which is also attested by the fact that Colonel Bell was one of the few of the higher commanders in that affair who were not in any way censured by the Board appointed by General Meade to investigate the causes of the failure.

We next find Colonel Bell stationed near the Appomattox, in front of Petersburg, forming with his brigade, an arc in the grand cordon which was gradually to be tightened about that city. Sharpshooting and shell practice were constantly kept up on both sides, and no place in the neighborhood was safe. The daily number of casualties in our army was large.

Butler's troops recrossed the James on the 29th of September. Some ground was gained in the early part of the day, and it was decided to push forward the advantage thus secured. Accordingly Bell's brigade was ordered to charge a heavy and important work known as Fort Gilmer. The space of nearly half a mile in front of the fort was covered with fallen timber. Behind this bristled two lines of abatis. On either side were formidable batteries. From all these difficulties the brigade did not shrink. On pressed the Colonel and his brave men, picking their way over the prostrate trees, their numbers fast thinning out under a galling fire, until they reached the abatis, when it became evident that to proceed further would result in the slaughter of the entire command. Reluctantly the Colonel gave the order to fall back. In this charge his brigade of four regiments was reduced to a skeleton, and actually numbered less than one full regiment.

On the 27th of October, an important demonstration was made against the enemy's right. In this, Bell's brigade participated. The Colonel placed all his old soldiers on the skirmish line, and held his undisciplined troops in reserve. During the afternoon he was ordered to advance his lines. The Colonel, after a careful reconnoissance of the enemy's works, returned word to General Terry, that if he would send him a few old soldiers as a reserve, to be substituted for his raw troops, he would rout the enemy and hold his advance. The veterans were promptly supplied, and the Colonel, in a few minutes of sharp fighting, made good his promise.   After the engagement, Bell was warmly complimented by the commanding General.

Then came the expedition against Wilmington, and the disheartening failure of the first attack on Fort Fisher, the humiliation of which was keenly felt by Colonel Bell.   In vain did he ask permission to assault the fort with his brigade alone, confident that he could carry it.   Information received by the commanding officer of the expedition, after the withdrawal of the troops, proved that Bell was right.   Had his gallant offer been accepted, there is little doubt that the fort could have been taken with a slight loss.

The following extract from a letter written to his wife about this time, exhibits the degree of courage which he would have carried into the fight, and also reveals the exalted sentiments of patriotism which habitually animated him.   He wrote :—

"God knows I will not shrink from any necessary danger.   If I live through the conflict, I will live more for my wife and children than for myself.   If I die, do not forget, my own precious wife, that I die in defence of our country.   Teach our children to die for it if need be, and to regard death with it as far beyond life without it, be that life surrounded with however many blessings. Teach our children, darling Mollie, that liberty and freedom are first freedom for all, and that for it we are bound to lay down our lives.   Should I be killed, do not mourn me, precious wife.   Let me be as one absent, soon to return, and while away gaining a history that will be remembered while history lives.   Let me be buried near my father, and have carved on the northeasterly side of my father's monument a broken sword, and this inscription: (My name and title,) 'killed in battle,' (date and place,) 'aged' (—— years,) 'fighting for the union of his country.'   Let me be buried in uniform, with my sabre resting on my breast. My last thought will be for the future of our children, and for the happiness of my own precious, darling wife, my own loved Mollie.

" Louis."

In a letter relative to the failure, Bell calls it the " Great Wilmington Fizzle," and adds, with trenchant sarcasm :   "My brigade and one other, Curtis', were the only troops landed, and we took a look at Fort Fisher and reëmbarked.   Our whole loss was fourteen men wounded—not one of them mortally."

The army and the people shared in the view of the first Wilmington expedition so curtly expressed in the Colonel's epistle. When the order came for the second expedition, and the same troops were chosen for the redemption of their own and the country's honor, they responded with cheerful alacrity.   Bell was lifted by the order out of the slough of despondency into which he had fallen ; always happy at the prospect of active service, he was peculiarly delighted at this opportunity of wiping out a stigma on a brigade which had never before smarted under disgrace.

It is not the purpose of this brief memoir to give anything like a detailed history of movements and battles, except so far as they serve as a background for the man whose worth these pages record.   Passing over, therefore, the story of the second expedition, from the time of its departure to that of the landing of the troops (Saturday, January 14, 1865,) on the beach, about half a mile north of Fort Fisher, under cover of a heavy bombardment from our gun-boats, we find Colonel Bell cool, cheerful, setting a good example of courage and patience to his men, as he always did.   He knew that he was to be among the foremost, a tall, wide-breasted mark for the rebel sharpshooters, and that the enemy, having now been reënforced, would make a desperate resistance. But this thought did not drive the habitual smile from his lips, or give a gloomy reasoning to his conversation. As he stepped upon the sandy beach, his eye, always on the alert for natural curiosities, espied a beautiful piece of white coral. He picked it up and dropped it into his pocket, saying to his adjutant, Lieutenant Sanford, "This will do for my little daughter."

That night the troops rested on the sand, behind hastily constructed breast-works, forming a line across the narrow peninsula. To veteran soldiers like those, there was nothing terrible in the prospect of the death-grapple which was to take place on the following day. Officers and men talked as eagerly and slept as sweetly as ever. Many of them, not unthoughtful of the possibilities of the morrow, scrawled brief letters to mother, wife, sister,—words that death might render forever precious, because they were their last. Colonel Bell, sitting on the beach that night with no tent to cover him, undistinguishable, except by the eagles upon his shoulders, from the thousands of gallant fellows who reclined upon the sand, smoking their pipes and chatting low and pleasantly, pencilled upon his knee, by the light of the camp-fire, a note to his wife. Such a note, so overflowing with love, so full of the deepest heart-thoughts of the fond husband and father, it would be almost a profanation for others to read. There is no shade of anxiety in it, nor any allusion to the perils that were overhanging him. Love, home, and a happy future, were its only topics.

The assault, which had been preceded by a bombardment of thirty-six hours from the gunboats, was made about 3 P. M., on the 15th. The storming column of marines and sailors, as brave men as ever rushed into the jaws of death, had been beaten back from the sea-front with dreadful losses. With the troops of Ames' Division, of the Tenth Corps, rested the fate of the fortress and the honors of the day. The disposition of the assaulting force

was as follows: Bell's brigade, then consisting of the Fourth
New Hampshire, One Hundred and Fifteenth New York, Thirteenth Indiana, and One Hundred and Sixty-Ninth New York,
marched by the right flank from the beach to the causeway leading from the fort; Pennypacker's brigade were on their right in
advance, in motion; Curtis' brigade on the extreme right, moved
forward at the same time, enjoying the advantages of slight irregu-
larities of ground.   Abbott's Brigade constituted the reserve.

Bell's brigade formed the third line of attack, and was not to
move except upon a signal from General Ames, as agreed upon
at a consultation between Terry, Ames and Bell. The Colonel,
with a ramrod in his hand as a walking-stick, had led his brigade
from their camping-ground, and, after reaching the position
assigned him, awaited the signal.   The advance troops were
heavily engaged.   General Ames had ridden close up to the fort,
and was obscured from view by clouds of smoke.   No signal from
him could be visible, but soon, above the battle-clouds, appeared
the stars and stripes floating from the out-works of the fort.
Seeing this, Bell turned to General Terry, and asked if he should
not move to the attack.   The General assented.

"Forward! double-quick!"

Rapidly the soldiers advanced with close front, bearing aloft
their regimental colors, exposed to a terrible fire from the sharpshooters who lined the parapets of the fort.   Colonel Bell was in
advance of his men.   His eye was watchful along the column to
detect any faltering or flagging.   At one moment, owing to some
inequality of the ground, a small portion of the line, he thought,
had fallen a little behind, and he dispatched an Aide to have it
straightened out.   This done, his face glowed with pride, and he
said to one of his staff officers, " How well the brigade are coming on under so severe a fire."

As the troops, pressing on with resistless valor, approached the fort, and were about to cross the slight bridge which covered the ditch in front of it, the Colonel, who was at that moment on the bridge, received his fatal bullet from a sharpshooter, who lay crouching on the top of the embankment, which rose at a sharp angle fifty feet in height before them. The shot was a plunging one, striking the Colonel in the left breast, and passing out in the lower part of the back. He fell to the ground, saying to his adjutant, who was at his side, "My arm is broken." But that officer, who had heard the bullet as it struck, was confident it had passed through the Colonel's body, and a glance at the prostrate form discovered the rent in his coat. Several officers and privates immediately left the ranks to attend to their fallen commander. The others cast back looks of sympathy and grief for the man whom they so deeply loved, and then rushed on to victory — their commander's eyes, forgetful of himself, following them with hope and pride.

As the men gathered about him to raise him from the ground, he said, with the same courtesy which he always used in addressing others, "Lift me up a little, if you please." He was then borne slowly to the rear, and laid down on the grass until a stretcher could be procured.

Doctor Dearborn, Surgeon of the Fourth New Hampshire, was at the Colonel's side as soon as possible after he fell. The coat, stiff with blood, was tenderly cut away, and the surgeon looked at the ghastly rent which the ball had made. "Is the wound mortal?" calmly asked Bell. "I am fearful it is, Colonel." "Well, I thought as much myself." As through life, so in death — calm, patient, undemonstrative.

Before he was carried from the field the victory of our men was made certain. Half raising himself on the stretcher, when the tidings came to him, he said, "I want to see *my* colors on the parapet." The next moment, as if in obedience to the dying soldier's wish, the flag was planted there. He looked at it, a smile of contentment playing upon his pale lips, and said, "I am satisfied!"

Everything that skill and affection could suggest was done to make him comfortable; and it is a consolation to know that the sacrifice which he that day offered up for his country, did not involve any protracted or acute physical agony. He sunk into his last sleep as peacefully as he might have glided into a grateful slumber after a hard day's work.

All night, until the gray morning hour, when the stars and stripes began to show proudly above the rebel works, the Colonel lay dying in his tent, watched over and cared for by loving friends. From about the time that the surgeon had pronounced his wound mortal, his mind had wandered. The booming of the cannon, the rattle of the musketry, the shouts of the victors, sometimes almost brought him back to consciousness. He would murmur broken phrases about his "brigade," "the sea," "the beach," "the fort," and several times asked, "Is the fort taken?" With these were mingled expressions of love for his mother, wife, and children; and finally, his lips forming their last faltering articulation, pronounced the name of his wife; and, with that thought in his heart and upon his tongue, he died.

The death of the Colonel caused a feeling of profound sorrow throughout the whole division, checking the exultation which followed the victory. The commanding officers of the higher grades mourned the loss of one who had ever been to them an able and trustworthy coadjutor and a beloved friend. But his untimely death was to the officers and men of his immediate command a personal affliction. "His memory," they said, "shall live with us as long as our lives shall last, inspiring us to noble thoughts and heroic acts."

21

Secretary Stanton, General Terry, and General Ames, in their official bulletins and reports of the action, paid just tributes to the memory of the gallant soldier. The Secretary of War, who arrived at the fort the day after its capture, conferred upon Colonel Bell, by direction of the President, the brevet of Brigadier-General, to date from the 15th of January, the day on which he received his fatal wound.

To the peaceful home where his mother and wife were waiting for the return of their loved one, the dreadful tidings came like the crashing of a thunderbolt through the roof. The venerable mother, within a few years, had lost two of the staffs of her declining age — Doctor Charles Bell, of Concord, (Brown University — class of 1853,) and George Bell, Esquire, of Cleveland, Ohio, young men of high promise in their respective professions. Of her two remaining sons, Louis and John — the latter a surgeon in the United States army — one was now taken away, and under circumstances painful in the extreme. The Colonel had been expecting to come home after the failure of the first Wilmington expedition, and wife and mother had prepared everything for his reception. Louis' wishes, his tastes, were all consulted and gratified in anticipation. A note written to his wife on the eve of sailing from Fortress Monroe, had informed her that another expedition was about to set forth. He did not tell its destination, but she was under the belief that it was some important movement which would occupy but a few days, when the troops would return to their old camping-ground north of the James, leaving her husband free to come back to her. This impression was so strong upon her mind, that she was looking for him on the very day that Secretary Stanton's dispatch reached her, announcing the "fall of Fort Fisher," and "Colonel Bell dangerously wounded."

The shock was terrible to both of those waiting hearts. But Louis had a strong constitution, prodigious vital energy; and what might be dangerous to a weaker man, might not to him. His wife, buoyed up by faith and love, which would not admit the possibility of his death, immediately set about preparing to go to him. All night long she sat up, packing her trunk and cheating her fond heart with the thought that she would soon be at his side. How or when she was to get there she had not planned. The next day she would have started for Derry on her long journey, and had her bonnet and cloak on ready to leave, but the door opened and her father stood before her.

One glance at his face divined the sad mission upon which he had come. Her heart had heard the story before it could be told to her ear. She fell into her parent's arms, in a paroxysm of grief and anguish. The mother, entering the room, was the next to receive the terrible news. Upon the scenes that followed— such as were witnessed in many a household during the war— the curtain must be dropped. The broken heart is a sacred thing!

On the 27th of January, 1865, Louis Bell was at home again. The promised visit, so fondly hoped for, was made at last. The son, the husband, the father, had returned to those he loved. He was clad in the full dress uniform which was so becoming to his noble figure. The sword, never unsheathed, save in a righteous cause, rested by his side. Upon his breast was a cross of flowers whose perfume filled the air. His face was pale, and his eyes were closed as if with weariness; but upon his lips was the same smile which he had always brought into that house. His mother, his wife, his children, and many relatives and friends from far and near, were gathered there, not to welcome the hero covered with glory, but to mourn his early death, and bear him to the portals of the Silent Land.

Under the snow, in the frozen ground, was placed all that was mortal of Louis Bell. He was laid in the spot of his own choosing, next to the shaft which marks the grave of his honored father. In the same quiet church-yard are buried others of his kindred. Separated in life, dying in various parts of the country, some in distant lands, they have here come together again, many of them as they sometimes met, when living, around the hospitable hearth. It is a painful story, that of the almost blotting-out of those two families, the ornaments and pride of the little village of Chester. Their children's children will come, sometimes, it is hoped, on pilgrimages to their ancestral homes, and gather lessons of wisdom and of virtue from those graves. Above the resting-place of Louis Bell may they vow in their hearts renewed fidelity to the Union, and to the sacred cause of Human Liberty, for which he cheerfully laid down his life in the fullness of its blossom and fragrance.

In the month of May, when nature was instinct with new life, and the spring flowers were rehearsing the mystery of the Resurrection, almost the same group of mourning friends assembled in the same place to attend another funeral. It seemed harshly out of place amidst all that verdure and music of birds. But death had come a not unwelcome guest to the solitary chamber of the broken-hearted. The weary load of unspoken sorrow which the widow had carried for four months was now laid down forever. Her wounded heart had found its cure in death. She had gone to her other and shining home—the only home in which her spirit seemed to have lived and moved since the joy of her life had been extinguished.

The day before her death she had visited her husband's grave, as she was wont to do every fair day, and had planted a white rose-bush in the green sod, little thinking, and scarcely daring to hope, that soon the emblematic flower would shed its perfume

above them both. The next day, after breakfast, she remarked
to her mother-in-law that she would go out to the fields behind
the house, and pick a few wild flowers for the decoration of
Louis' grave. She had been absent about two hours, when Mrs.
Bell began to be alarmed. The fields were searched for the
missing one, but without success. She was not in her room. It
was then thought that, having picked the flowers, she had gone
directly to the church-yard, nearly half a mile away, without
passing through the house, as was usually her custom. But,
unhappily all conjecture was removed, when little Marian Bell,
who had been up-stairs, came down and said innocently to her
grandmother: "Mamma's hood and cloak are on the bed in the
front-room, but mamma is not there."

Her grandmother hurried up-stairs. On the bed was the
inanimate form of the missing one. The artless remark of the
little child was true. Her tender, loving mamma was not there.
She had joined her husband and her first little Louis. Gone from
our earthly gaze forever, she had left behind the imperishable
memory of her virtues and of her consistent Christian example.

A physician was instantly sent for, and every attempt made
to rekindle the extinct spark of life; but in vain. All the external symptoms, as well as the history of her case, disclosed in
previous attacks, proved that she had died of an affection of the
heart, hastened and brought to its crisis, as that disease always is,
by an agony of grief that could not be allayed. It is supposed
that she was taken with a fainting turn, and threw herself hastily
across the bed, dying without one shock of pain—summoned
away and escorted into the unseen world by we know not what
angelic messengers; passing in a single moment from a state of
sorrow to one of bliss.

The funeral services at the house were beautifully appropriate.
The Reverend Mr. Tomlinson, the pastor of the village church, in

a few well chosen remarks, bore testimony to the Christian life
and many social graces of the deceased, and tenderly applied
such consolation as it was possible to administer to her sorrowing
kindred. Then two voices, from the church choir, fitly attuned,
sang this sweet pæan of victory and trust:—

> " Beyond the smiling and the weeping
>   I shall be soon ;
> Beyond the waking and the sleeping,
> Beyond the sowing and the reaping,
>   I shall be soon.
>   Love, rest, and home —
>   Sweet hope !
> Oh, how sweet it will be there to meet
>   The dear ones all at home !
>
> Beyond the blooming and the fading
>   I shall be soon ;
> Beyond the shining and the shading,
> Beyond the hoping and the dreading,
>   I shall be soon.
>   Love, rest, and home —
>   Sweet hope !
> Oh, how sweet it will be there to meet
>   The dear ones all at home !
>
> Beyond the parting and the meeting
>   I shall be soon ;
> Beyond the farewell and the greeting,
> Heart's fainting now, and now high beating,
>   I shall be soon.
>   Love, rest, and home —
>   Sweet hope !
> Oh, how sweet it will be there to meet
>   The loved ones all at home.

Then the coffin was borne from the house, out upon the piazza
which the living feet of the two dear ones had often pressed,

through the green meadow where they had together tended the flowers and interpreted their meaning, and down the long hill to the church-yard, over the same road which they had travelled many a time in the old days of peace and love.

The procession paused not till it stopped opposite an open grave nestling close to that where Louis Bell was sleeping. There the casket that held so much that was precious was laid away, and upon it were dropped, from faltering hands, wreaths of flowers, typical, to the spiritual eye, of the fadeless beauty of the two lives which death had not long divided.

JOSIAH GORDON WOODBURY.

JOSIAH GORDON WOODBURY was born in Bedford, New Hampshire, July 27, 1833. He was the son of Doctor Peter P. and Eliza (Gordon) Woodbury.

In 1849, he went to Derry, New Hampshire, to prepare for college. There he remained until 1853, with the exception of a few months, which he spent at the Kimball Union Academy, at Meriden, in the same State. In the autumn of 1853, he entered Brown University.

The following extracts, in relation to his character while in college, are from a letter written by an intimate friend of Woodbury's — Charles Blake, Esquire, of Providence, Rhode Island.

"Woodbury was an affectionate, true-hearted, honorable, and pure young man. I weigh well each one of these epithets, and am sure that he merited them. He had an absorbing taste for politics, and spent the largest part of his time in gaining information that might be useful to him in public life. I think no young man at his age, was ever before so well versed in the history of the country, especially in the intricacies of diplomacy, the minutiæ of congressional debates, etc.

22

"His taste for reading was absorbing, and wholly directed towards history, with some digression towards Shakspeare, and more modern dramatists.

"He was very fond of debate.   In this exercise he manifested towards his opponent a courtesy, beyond that of the most polished society. * * * He always heard his antagonist quietly, and without interruption. * * * * *

"Much of his time he spent in his room in quietness, but his mind was ever active; he was always reading, or meditating on his reading.   His veracity was undoubted, and his religious sentiments were deep.

"Best of all was his purity.   Although strong and healthy, he was well disciplined in all his instincts, and never did I hear from him an indelicate allusion, or know of his enduring indecent conversation from others.

"Woodbury was a democrat, having had a thorough democratic nurture in times when democracy was respectable.   I believe he studied law after leaving college, and when the democracy rose against the government, he entered the navy. * * * He was remarkable for his humor.   It was broad without being coarse, and it penetrated his whole nature.   His laughter was hearty, but not boisterous, and his fun was never malicious."

After the completion of two years of study he left college, at his own request, and commenced the study of law, in the office Messrs. Foster and Ayer, of Manchester, New Hampshire. ·

The following extract from a letter written by his sister, gives a brief summary of his life for the ensuing years, until he entered the service of the United States:

"My brother attended the Law School in Cambridge, Massachusetts, and, in September, 1857, was admitted to the bar. Immediately after, he went to Indianapolis, Indiana, and practiced law till December, 1860, when he formed a partnership with C. L. Dunham, Esquire, of New Albany, Indiana.   He soon became much attached to his profession, and to his 'western home.'   The war not long after broke out, and, as he was near the border States, where courts were suspended, he returned to his home in New Hampshire, where, in December, 1862, he received the appointment of Acting Assistant-Paymaster in the United States navy.   In February, 1863, he was ordered to the iron-clad Catskill.   He went with the Catskill to South Carolina, and there remained till his death."

The Catskill mentioned in this letter was one of the nine iron-clads, built in accordance with an act of Congress, which was passed soon after the original Monitor repulsed the Merrimac in Hampton Roads.   She sailed in February, 1863, for the South Atlantic squadron, and, after a stormy passage, arrived at Port Royal about the 1st of March, 1863.

It was on the Catskill, that the writer of this sketch first became acquainted with Woodbury.   We occupied adjoining state-rooms, and sat at the same mess-table during the last few months of his life.

Woodbury had a fine, manly form, a dark, flashing eye, a cheerful face, and was always ready with some interesting story, with which he enlivened many a weary hour of our monotonous stay in Edisto Harbor.   He despised meanness, and his love for the truth, his manliness of character, and his genial disposition, made him a general favorite of the ship's company.   He had a rare literary culture, and had pursued a well-selected course of reading.   Much of his time was spent alone in his state-room in the company of his books.   Carlyle's French Revolution was a favorite with him, and he frequently read aloud, or related from memory for the entertainment of his brother officers many of its stirring passages. He was exceedingly fond of debate, and was at home on all subjects pertaining to national affairs. No event of importance during the war had escaped his observation.

Kind-hearted and obliging to all, he was ever ready to lend a helping hand when assistance was needed. I remember to have seen him during the hot summer days of 1863, (only a few weeks before his death, and while the Catskill was in action with the Morris Island batteries,) cheering on the men who were stationed below, and assisting with his own hands to hoist from the hold the huge shot and shell for the fifteen-inch gun. This was by no means an easy task, with the hatches all shut down, the air below foul with powder-smoke, and the temperature varying but little from one hundred degrees Fahrenheit.

His presence always cheered us, and relieved the monotony of our almost submarine life. His lively conversational powers, his keen appreciation of wit, and his love for all that is social in one's nature, rendered the ward-room a pleasant home for us all.

He was present at the first attack on Charleston, in April, 1863,—an engagement which, though lasting only an hour or two at the most, was one of the most terrific of the war. Nine iron-clads participated, none of which carried guns of less than eleven-inch calibre. On the other side were the rebel batteries, mounting more than three hundred heavy guns. In addition, there were to be encountered obstructions almost numberless, while submarine torpedoes awaited us in every channel. It was deemed advisable to withdraw from so formidable a defence, and the attack was not renewed till mid-summer. During the intervening three months the fleet remained in North Edisto harbor, a few miles south of Charleston.

The time passed away tediously, until the first week in July, when a change of officers in the departments of the South, both military and naval, brought with it a period of unusual activity in both branches of the service. The drifting sand-hills of Morris Island, which had given shelter to the troops of Beauregard, became peopled with the soldiers of the Union.

Early in the morning of August 17, 1863, the fleet of iron-clads steamed up the main ship-channel, to make a combined attack, in connection with General Gillmore's shore batteries, upon forts Wagner and Sumter, which, up to that time, had not been silenced. It was a hot, sultry day, and scarcely a ripple broke the surface of the harbor.

The following account of that day's operations is copied from Admiral Dahlgren's Official Report to the Navy Department:—

"It was now noon. The men had been hard at work since day-break, and needed rest; so I withdrew the vessels, to give them dinner. * * * The officers and men of the vessels have done their duty well, and will continue to do so. All went well with us save one sad exception;—Captain Rodgers was killed, as well as Paymaster Woodbury, who was standing beside him.

"The Weehawken (flag-ship) was then lying about one thousand yards from Fort Wagner, and the Catskill, with my gallant friend, just inside of me, the fire of the fort coming in steadily. Observing the tide to have risen a little, I directed the Weehawken to be carried in closer, and had hardly weighed anchor, when I noticed that the Catskill was also under way. It occurred to me that Captain Rodgers had detected my movement, and was determined to be closer to the enemy, if possible. It was soon reported that the Catskill was going out of action, with flag at half-mast. * * * It is but natural that I should feel deeply the loss thus sustained. The *country cannot afford to lose such men.*"

Mr. Woodbury, the duties of whose office did not require him to remain below, had volunteered to assist Captain Rodgers in this action, by standing at his side in the pilot-house, and recording the times of firing, sizes of shot and shell, and other usual statistics of an engagement.

While standing in this position, a rifled projectile from Wagner struck the top of the pilot-house, in a place where the plating was only two inches in thickness. Portions of this plating were torn off by the force of the shot, causing the instant death of both the Commander and the Paymaster, and also knocking down the pilot and the man at the wheel. Mr. Woodbury was wounded in the back of the head and neck, the sharp iron crushing through the head and spinal column.

Had he remained below where alone duty called him, his life would have been spared; but he chose a far more perilous position, and, as we have seen, fell while cheerfully volunteering his assistance to his Commander.

It was a sad duty for us to bear their lifeless bodies below, and tenderly to care for the remains of those who had so suddenly, in the prime of manhood, been called from earth. The name of Mr. Woodbury will always be cherished by the officers of the Catskill and by her crew, as one who served his country faithfully and heroically. Among the sons of Brown who have fallen in the deadly conflict, or died of disease contracted in the service, we cannot but admire the self-sacrifice of him who, doing even more than his duty, fell almost at the cannon's mouth, in the very face of the foe.

His remains were conveyed to his home in New Hampshire, where they were buried with fitting honors.

ROBERT HALE IVES.

Class of 1857.

ROBERT Hale Ives was the son of Robert Hale and Harriet Bowen (Amory) Ives, and was born in Providence, April 3, 1837. He was descended on his father's side from the Browns, who were so conspicuous in the commercial annals of Providence, and whose ancestor, Chad Brown, was among its earliest planters. On his mother's side from the Bowens, who came from Wales, and were represented in the town for three generations by eminent physicians. His early life was nurtured with the fondest parental care. All the plans and arrangements for his training were designed to combine, as far as possible, the innocent enjoyments that belong to the season of childhood, with the best culture of his mind and character. He was attentive and diligent in his studies, and spending as he did both his school and college days in his native city, he was scarcely ever separated from the genial influences of the happy and cultivated family circle to which he belonged, composed of his parents and his two sisters;—a circle in which he held the place of the only son and the youngest child. He was prepared for college at the University Grammar School, and entered Brown University in 1853, where he graduated, with an honorable rank in his class, in 1857, at the age of twenty years. His life in college was studious and correct. His favorite studies were in the classical and literary portions of the college course, and, though he was never neglectful of the appointed tasks, his general reading was observed to be more varied and extensive than was common among the young men of his time.

But it was not alone, or principally, under the influence of academic studies and teachers that his mind acquired its culture and his character received its development. The family of which he was a member, and the wider circle of kindred with whom he was intimately associated, exerted upon him a moulding influence even more powerful than that of either the companionships or the instructions which he found at school or in college. Here were affectionate relationships and endearing associations. Here too were books and forms of art and elevating social intercourse, cultivated manners, conversation and reading, the visits of the gifted and the good from without, and all that could stimulate the love of knowledge or awaken generous sentiments and manly aspirations. Among the persons with whom he was thus thrown, in his own home and in those of his nearest kindred, in addition to companions of his own age, were both men and women, who illustrated some of the highest virtues and graces of character, and who must have exerted over one in whom they felt so fond an interest, an influence which was destined to be felt in all his subsequent life.

It was undoubtedly amidst scenes and associations like these in which he found his most constant enjoyment, and where he daily met with characters of singular excellence and worth, that the mind of the growing boy received its deepest impressions. It was under influences thus exerted that his modes of thought and feeling were fashioned, and that there were planted in his nature those sentiments of reverence and fidelity, of honor and duty which a true man will always cherish as the most precious

elements of any culture which it is in the power of others to
impart to him. The ideals of character and of life which he
thus acquired always remained in his mind, and probably did
more than all things besides towards giving to his own manhood
"its form and pressure."

Thus passed away his early youth. It was filled with enjoyment and culture, and exposed far less than is common to the
temptations which belong to that forming period of life. He had
been blessed with health and with unbroken happiness, and was
now standing on the verge of a manhood bright with every promise of usefulness and honor which a pure character, a cultivated
mind and an independent position can ever afford. His calling
in life was pointed out and made almost necessary by the traditions and circumstances amidst which he had grown up. His
father and his father's family for three generations had conducted
a mercantile house which still bears their name, and to the same
occupation he was to devote his life. But, before entering on the
position to which he was looking forward, he desired still further
to prolong his period of preparation. Accordingly in September,
1857, immediately after leaving college, he went to Europe, and,
at Paris, in accordance with a previous arrangement, joined his
cousin, Mr. T. P. I. Goddard, who, with his family, was spending
some time abroad. The circumstances were exceedingly favorable to his enjoyment and his improvement, and he was absent
somewhat more than a year, which he devoted to liberal and
careful culture. He travelled with his friends through France,
Italy and Germany, everywhere studying languages and art, and
watching with eager interest the great events which were then
transpiring on the continent, in connection with the emancipation
of Italy from the despotism of Austria. In the summer of the
next year, he was joined by his father and his younger sister, and
with them returned to Paris and made a trip to Switzerland ; and,

23

after spending a few weeks in Great Britain, they came home together in the following autumn.

He now began to take his first lessons in business at the counting-house, and in this occupation he employed the first year after his return from Europe.   But, though he had passed a year abroad, he had not accomplished all that he desired, and, early in the autumn of 1859, he again left home to prosecute still further the travels he had before begun.   In this trip he was much of the time in the company of the same congenial party as before, to which had now been added another of his cousins, of his own age and of tastes kindred to his own.   In this companionship, either wholly or in part, he travelled during most of the autumn and winter in Spain, went again to Rome, and revisited England and Scotland, returning home early in the summer of 1860. Immediately after his return, he became a partner in the business of his cousins, Messrs. Goddard Brothers, in Providence.

The years of his life had thus far passed with but few personal events to mark their history, or to ruffle the quiet stream in which they flowed.   Some of those whom he had always loved and venerated had passed away, and especially his two venerable grandmothers, Mrs. Ives and Mrs. Amory, had gone from the domestic scenes which they had adorned with singular graces both of person and of character, and where they had been objects of special honor and affection.   His elder sister had been married, and little children had now sprung up to call him by a new name, and to become to him objects of new interest and attachment.   His life had been pure, and his tastes were refined and elegant.   His form was manly and erect, his manners affable and well bred and his mind cultivated and informed.   His spirits were lively and genial, and in his heart was a wealth of affection which he lavished with fondness on the chosen few to whom he was attached.   He was no longer to be the light-hearted youth devoted to elegant culture and to social enjoyment, but the regular and methodical man of business, sharing responsible trusts and engaged in important and absorbing duties. Nor was this all of his character, as it now appeared to those who fondly watched its fair unfoldings. Blending with its other qualities, there was also the sentiment of Christian piety, which had already taken root in his heart. He had been nurtured amidst Christian influences, he had been consecrated to God in his infancy by parental vows, and everything in his daily life at home was fitted to remind him of his highest obligations. In addition to this, he had been thrown much in the society of his younger sister, whose Christian influence descended like an inspiration from Heaven upon all with whom she associated. It is to this influence, proceeding from her rare and beautiful character, from her pure and spiritual example and from the frequent expression of the fondest wish of her heart, that we may trace the decision which by the grace of God he had made, that he would henceforth be a soldier and servant of Jesus Christ. The change took place in the recesses of his own moral being, and, as was characteristic of his nature, it was attended with no outward demonstrations. It, however, plainly revealed itself in his habits and tones of thought, in his observance of religious seasons and his interest in all religious things, in the books he read and in the companionships he sought. At Easter, in 1859, he received confirmation from the Bishop of the Diocese and became a communicant at St. Stephen's Church, under the rectorship of the Reverend Doctor Waterman.

As has been mentioned, he returned from his second visit to Europe in the spring of 1860, bearing in his character the fruits of the travel and study he had so liberally pursued abroad. He was soon, however, to experience the only real sorrow which it was his lot to know in the course of his life. Summer succeeded to spring in his happy home, but over that home were now gathering the clouds of a great bereavement. The sister nearest his own age, the companion of his childhood, the watchful guardian of his youth, and, more than any other being, the sharer of his thoughts and sympathies, was now in declining health. The weeks of the summer were spent in watching her fading life, and, ere that summer was ended, she had gone from the world. She was one in whom rare personal charms were blended with the loveliest graces of character, and to her brother she might well be the ideal of all that is lovely and excellent in woman. Her death touched chords in his being deeper and more tender than had been reached by any other event, and her memory rested upon him as a sacred influence through the residue of his life. The bereavement, bitter though it was, evidently came to him with sanctifying power. It deepened his religious feelings and strengthened his faith in the promises of the gospel. It exalted his views of life, prompted him to new usefulness and opened to him more distinctly the vision of immortality.

A friend who had known both the brother and the sister from childhood, thus writes of this great affliction: "Few estimated aright the severe weight of that blow. Her name was seldom on his lips, but her memory was ever fresh in his heart. As her life had been a continued benediction to him, so we believe her death to have been a sanctified affliction. She had not lived unto herself, and she did not die unto herself. His character ripened and mellowed under the influence of her sweet memory; prejudices were softened; judgments of character and action lost edge and sharpness; kindly forbearance was exercised towards those whose habits and opinions made them naturally repulsive to his refined and scrupulous taste. Those who watched the development and growth of his religious life, saw and felt the power of her life and death. In his last illness, she seemed to be with him as a living presence; in his wanderings he called her name as the most familiar utterance of memory; her loving spirit seemed to become his own, as he breathed out good will and affection for all of whom he spake; and, when the last conflict was over, and the released, ransomed spirit soared upward to its Savior and its God, was she not 'first at Heaven's gate' to meet and welcome him?"

The seasons that followed this afflictive event, witnessed the rapid growth of his character and his increasing participation in the active duties pertaining to his station in life. He was earnest and diligent in business, and was fast developing in himself his own ideal of what an educated merchant ought to be. Though instinctively shunning conspicuous responsibilities, he could not but become linked to the institutions of the community in which he lived. In addition to several financial posts which he held, he was chosen a member of the vestry of St. Stephen's church, whose new house of worship was then just begun. He had from the outset taken an active and liberal interest in the undertaking, and he now gave his daily attention to the progress of the work. He also devoted a part of every day to study, and watched with eager solicitude the sullen gathering of the storm of civil strife which was soon to burst in desolating fury upon his native land. His life at this period was singularly independent, and filled to an unusual degree with the opportunities and the means both of the highest improvement and the best enjoyment. He had adorned the apartments which he occupied in his father's house, with the beautiful forms of art, and, for his summer home, he had appended some commodious rooms to the farm house on the ancestral estate at Potowomut, on the shore of Narragansett Bay, in the furnishing of which he had shown the cultivated taste that presided over everything he attempted to do. Here, in the midst of the extended circle of kindred and friends who had their country residences in the neighborhood, he passed while at home, during the last two summers of his life, those hours of every day which were not given to business in town.

In circumstances like these he was passing his quiet though busy days, when the civil war broke upon the country. From how many bright and peaceful homes did the first summons to arms issued by the government, call forth the brave and generous young men of this northern land. The sudden summons was not only a thrilling appeal for patriotic service, but also a searching test of personal character. It sent anxiety and alarm into thousands of households and wrung with agony a multitude of hearts, as it opened up the prospect of separations and partings, of unimagined dangers and sufferings and of bitter bereavements and life-long sorrows. Forebodings and anxieties such as these were in every family and became the common lot of the whole people. From no single class of citizens, however, did the loyal cause at any time receive a more generous support or a more gallant service, than from the educated young men of the country, and especially from those who had been most fully trained by those liberal studies that go to make up what Milton styles a "complete and generous education." It must never be said that such studies are unfriendly to patriotism, to heroic endurance or achievement, or to any of the hardy virtues of daily life. Their natural effect, as well as their true design, is not only to inform the intellect, but to establish principle and invigorate sentiment, to create a high and generous manhood, which is in itself a guarantee both of character and of usefulness. Minds and characters thus formed can not be restricted to a narrow sphere. They expand themselves, of necessity, beyond the social circle in which they move. They send their influence abroad into the general community, they unconsciously become an example and inspiration to others and form a controlling

element in the life of the State and the nation. Never was this
more nobly illustrated than during the recent civil war, when
the young scholars of the country and those who had attained
to the best education, came forth so promptly from every sphere
which they had entered and brought their earnest faith and cultivated intelligence, as well as their gallant services, to the cause
of the Union.

From the moment when the rebellion first lifted its arm in
defiance and outrage, there was in the mind of Mr. Ives the most
perfect appreciation of the duty of all orders of citizens. He was
eager to take his place in the ranks with those who at the very
outset rallied in the defence of the government. But his mother
was then too ill for him to leave her, and, besides this, he saw that
his going would add another pang to the sorrow of recent bereavement which still burdened the hearts of his parents. He used to
say, " it is hard to be kept at home," but, in the circumstances,
none can question the delicacy or the justness of his decision to
sacrifice his patriotic impulses to his sense of filial obligation.
Nearly all his kindred of his own age, and many of his immediate friends, joined the regiments that hastened to Washington,
and the feeling of higher duty which kept him away was undoubtedly a painful one. His most intimate associates saw that he was
uneasy and unhappy, and he would sometimes say, "I am ashamed
to be seen in the streets," as if he feared that his position might
be deemed equivocal, and his example might seem like shrinking
from duty. He, however, became actively enlisted in everything
that would promote the raising of troops and their comfort in
the service, and did all that a patriot citizen could do to uphold
the perilled institutions of his country.

It was in the second summer of the war, so soon as the probability of its continuance was assured, that he determined to take
an immediate part in the service. The great campaign of the

preceding spring had ended in disastrous failure, and the army of
the Potomac had been driven almost from the gates of Richmond,
back to the defences of Washington.   The rebellion was flushed
with temporary triumph, and the hopes of the nation were at the
lowest ebb.   All enthusiasm had subsided, and the dread realities
of war stood before us only in their ghastly outlines.   It was the
gloomiest moment in the annals of the fearful struggle.   Some
of his friends endeavored to persuade him that he could do more
by remaining at home than by joining the service, and also that,
being the only son of his parents, he ought not to leave them.
The manner in which his decision was made and carried into execution, was characteristic alike of his modesty and his independence.   The decision itself was doubtless the result of careful and
religious consideration, and it was formed in the solitude of his
own mind, with single reference to what he thought to be his
duty.   He knew how hard it had been for other parents to
surrender their only son to the dangers of the war, and he was
not unmindful of the circumstances which would make the trial
doubly painful to his own.   In an affectionate nature such as his,
with his deep and delicate filial feeling and the tender memories
that dwelt in his heart, his decision must have been the result of
a severe conflict.   Yet, though it was evident to those who saw
him most that his views of his duty as a citizen were about to
be carried into practical effect, he did not mention the subject to
any of his family or his friends until his determination was
formed.   He then for the first time informed his father that he
thought it his duty, in some way, to engage in the service of the
country.

An accomplished and respected clergyman who at this time
made his acquaintance and won his esteem, has thus recorded
the impressions he received of his character:—

"Lieutenant Ives struck me as a rather undemonstrative man, and therefore not likely to be hasty or impetuous in his judgments or action. I should never have suspected him of being easily borne away by his feelings, and, even in my short intercourse with him, it was plain that what he *did* and what he believed was equally the action and conviction of one who weighed opposite considerations, and came deliberately, but surely, to his conclusions. In saying that he was an undemonstrative man, I do not mean that he was cold or reserved; on the contrary, few things charmed me more in what I saw of him, than the perfect frankness with which he talked out what was in his mind, and gave me pictures of men and things with an utter unreserve of confidence and freedom which was rather unusual. I should have said he was eminently a person of few concealments, not indiscriminately communicative perhaps, but really open and transparent in the very texture of his soul.

"What I have said above of his conversations and descriptions, reminds me of the fine appreciation which he seemed to have of everything that he encountered. This was evident to me in the very inclination of his head; he had a critical eye, his distinctions were nice and accurate, and his perceptions equally precise and penetrative. I should have respected his opinion, no matter how widely I might have differed from it.

"This nice and thorough appreciation of character, made him ready to discern what was false and unreal, and to detest it. I shall not soon forget the honest scorn and real vigor with which he took to pieces the sham pretensions of some foppish and shallow men with whom he had once been thrown. It was very refreshing to me to see how utterly he revolted against all shams; how true and real he was in every fibre of his nature.

"And this came out in his conversation on things pertaining to religion. He did not say a great deal. But his few sentences,

24

dropped now and then, were the utterance of genuine conviction and feeling; tempered but truthful echoes of depths, that in his last hours, as I have been told, were so blessedly revealed to those about him.

"But I think nothing is more fresh in my mind now, than his kindly manners and always considerate temper. If he was not the very *soul* of kindness and genuine courtesy, then I certainly saw the best side of him. An attentive consideration for others, an evident desire to make them happy, a readiness to sacrifice himself—all these, on my first acquaintance, I judged to be the obvious traits in a character which was to me a most winning one. And in this judgment I feel confident that I was not mistaken. For what was his last act, the unselfish heroism and self-consecration with which he gave himself to his country, but the grandest exhibition of a devotion and self-sacrifice, which never would have revealed itself had it not long before been growing and strengthening amid the quieter walks of daily common life."

It was, however, no easy matter to determine in what manner he could best render the service he desired to perform in behalf of his country. He felt called upon to do everything in his power, but he entertained only the most modest estimate of what that might be. He had no thought of seeking any position for which he was not prepared. He had no military aspirations to gratify, no care for merely winning laurels, and no favors to ask of the government. His tastes were all for the pursuits of peace, and he left these pursuits only at the call of what he deemed a religious duty. Educated, however, as he had been, practiced as he was in business, and in all matters of executive promptness and care, and withal an accomplished horseman, it was plain enough that he would be exceedingly useful in any position in which military experience was not specifically required.   Accordingly, so soon as General Rodman, a Rhode Island officer who had lately been made a Brigadier for special gallantry at the capture of Newbern, North Carolina, was assigned to a separate command, he offered himself as a Volunteer Aide on the staff of that officer, preferring to serve entirely at his own charges.   The offer was readily accepted, and Mr. Ives was immediately commissioned as a Lieutenant by the Governor of Rhode Island, and directed to report to General Rodman for service.   His commission was dated August 19, 1862.

On the first day of September, Lieutenant Ives left his home in Providence to join his chief in the army of the Potomac, who had then just been assigned to the command of a division in the Ninth Corps under Major-General Burnside.   It was the gloomiest moment in the progress of the war.   The long campaign in Virginia had just before ended in humiliating failure, the national arms had met with new reverses on the fields of Manassas, and the forces of the rebels, flushed with their recent successes, were hastening to the invasion of Maryland.   The army of the Potomac, now restored to the command of General McClellan, was already beginning to move to meet them, and the very crisis of the republic seemed to be at hand.   The young officer was thus obliged to hasten at once into the most active and arduous service.   Before he had even learned the routine of his new duties, he was fully engaged in discharging them, and that too almost in presence of the enemy.   The Ninth Corps left its bivouac on Seventh street, in Washington, on the 7th of September, and immediately crossed into Maryland.   It encountered the enemy first at Frederick, and drove him from the city without a battle. The march from Frederick to South Mountain was a continued skirmish, and, at South Mountain, a battle was fought at which Lieutenant Ives for the first time was under continuous fire from the enemy.   On the 16th, the army had reached the vicinity of Sharpsburg, and its several corps and divisions were ranged along the left bank of the little river Antietam, which runs into the Potomac a few miles below.   Most of the day was spent in placing the troops in position, and in other preparations.   On the following day came the great battle of Antietam.   It began at an early hour, and, by ten o'clock, the corps of General Burnside was fully engaged; its right being near the stone bridge that spans the stream, and its extreme left, commanded by General Rodman, being opposite a ford three-quarters of a mile below. On the carrying and holding of this bridge, the fortunes of the day were obviously to turn.   The great and critical work was at length accomplished, after several ineffectual attempts and through terrible fighting, at about one o'clock; and, a little later, the division of General Rodman crossed the ford and joined those who had passed over the bridge, on the heights that rise from the right bank of the stream.   The carnage had been frightful all along the line, but the day's work now seemed to be done, and the corps was resting upon its arms.   The enemy, however, still occupied a vantage ground in the neighborhood, and at three P. M., an order reached General Burnside to renew the attack. The position of General Rodman's division was now such as to expose it in the movement directly to the raking fire of certain batteries of the enemy.   A charge was ordered and the guns were carried, but both the General and his Aide fell mortally wounded.   Lieutenant Ives was struck by a cannon shot which tore the flesh from the outer thigh, leaving a ghastly wound, but not breaking the bone.   He was tenderly borne away by some soldiers and placed in the hands of his own faithful servant, a young Englishman, who had come home with him from England, and had been in his service for several years.   Immediately on hearing of his wound, this young man ran forward under the fire of the enemy, at the risk of his life, in search of his master, whom he would scarcely have recognized in the arms of the soldiers, so changed was he by the smoke and grime of the battle. The spot on which he fell was soon again in the possession of the enemy, and the guns were lost, so that if he had not been removed as he was, he might have been borne away in the tide of battle, or trampled under foot by the squadrons that rushed over the ground. He was speedily conveyed to a house adjacent to the field which had been taken for a hospital, and there he was soon attended by his fellow townsmen, Surgeons Rivers and Millar, the former the Surgeon of the division, and the latter of the Fourth Rhode Island Regiment.

Three days later he was visited by his attached cousin, Colonel R. H. I. Goddard, then bearing a Lieutenant's commission, and having just received an appointment on the staff of Major-General Burnside, who thus describes his interview :—

"On the evening of the 19th of September, 1862, I learned from Captain Hills, Commissary to General Rodman, of Robert's wound. He described it as serious, but speaking of it as a flesh wound and giving an encouraging account of his condition when he left head-quarters, I was comparatively free from fears that it would prove mortal. At this time I was at Frederick City, waiting for transportation to the army. I succeeded in procuring a conveyance to take me the next day to the battle-field of Antietam, in the vicinity of which the Ninth Corps was then encamped. Arriving at General Burnside's head-quarters on the afternoon of the 20th, I learned that Robert was in a field hospital, a few miles to the rear, and received permission to go to him and remain with him. It was a warm afternoon and his tent flaps being thrown back to give him all the air possible, he saw me approaching. He seemed much affected and greeted me with the most affectionate cordiality. He had lain there for three days waiting for some one of those he loved to come to him. He knew that his father could not reach him for some days, but, as he was aware that I was on my way to join the army, he was prepared to see me at any time. Though prostrate and helpless, he did not appear to be wanting in strength. His voice was strong, and his desire and ability to converse and talk over the stirring incidents through which he had so lately passed, surprised me, when I was aware of the grave nature of his injury. His thoughts seemed to wander constantly toward his home, and his heart was overflowing with love toward the cherished members of his family circle; and the reserve, which was peculiar to his character, did not appear while talking about and inquiring after each and all of them. He was full of affection and tenderness for every one whom he had loved, and expressed these feelings constantly during the few days I was with him. He was also much interested in relating to me the details of the march from Washington to Antietam, which comprised the skirmish at Frederick and the two battles of South Mountain and Antietam, in both of which General Rodman's division had taken so prominent a part.

"His health had been good, and he had undergone the extraordinary privations and exposures of that memorable fortnight with the facility of a much older soldier. He felt that he had followed the path of duty when he entered the service, and he had no regrets for the course he had taken. I repeated to him some of the expressions which General Burnside and other officers had used, in bearing testimony to the fidelity and zeal with which he had discharged every duty on the march, and particularly in speaking of his behavior on the field of battle. The commendation, thus received, pleased and touched him exceedingly, not that he had any personal vanity to be gratified by such flattering opinions, but because he was conscious that he had striven to per-

form every duty faithfully; and it was a source of peculiar pleasure
to learn from his superior officers, that what he had endeavored
conscientiously to do, he had really accomplished. 'I do not want
to appear vain,' said he to me while sitting by his rough bedside,
'but I would like my father to hear from you what General
Burnside said of me.   I want him to know that I did my duty.'

"His faithful servant, George Griffin, had shared all his privations and dangers, and, after he had received his wound, attended
him with affectionate and tender solicitude.   At Robert's request
I read to him several times from the Bible, which had been his
constant companion.   Before my arrival, George had been in the
habit of reading to him.

"During the day, except when the Surgeon was dressing his
wound, his sufferings were not constant, though sometimes very
intense.   He had intervals of freedom from pain, when he was
cheerful and disposed to converse on many matters of interest.
At night he seemed to have few moments when his sufferings
were not very acute.   If he fell asleep it would be a troubled
sleep, from which he would start after a few moments with the
fancy that the conflict was still raging around him, and that he
was being trodden under foot by the contending armies.   At
other times his mind was perfectly clear and as active as it was
while he was in full health.   He was uniformly cheerful and
hopeful, notwithstanding his great sufferings, and thoughtful of
those who were suffering around him.   In adjacent tents of the
same field hospital where he was lying, were General Rodman,
Colonel Steere and Captain Bowen, all dangerously, and the former fatally wounded.   For these officers Robert was constant
in his inquiries.   I do not think he anticipated at all the result
which was so soon to follow.   He spoke of going home to recover
from his wound, and expressed the opinion confidently that in
three months he would be back again in the army.   The terrible

scenes through which he had passed, the intense sufferings he had experienced could not for a moment subdue his manly spirit, or divert his mind from that line of duty which he sincerely and conscientiously felt himself called upon to follow.

"The profession of arms was one foreign to his tastes and to his habits of life. He entered into it after the most solemn reflection, because, as he expressed to me, he considered the country needed and had a right to expect, the services of every young man who had health and a life to devote to her cause. With such high motives he decided to give his services to the cause he had so near to his heart. Having once entered the army, I am sure, had his life been spared and his health permitted it, he never would have quitted it while the war lasted."

Tidings of his wound had immediately been sent to his father from the nearest telegraph station, but so freighted were all the telegraphic lines with messages of sorrow or of joy to friends at a distance, that the dispatch did not reach Providence till Friday afternoon, eight and forty hours after his fall. It was Sunday evening, the end of the fifth day subsequent to the battle, when his father, accompanied by Doctor L. L. Miller, the most eminent surgeon of Providence, after great difficulty and long delay, at length reached the little cluster of hospital tents in which he and other wounded officers from Rhode Island had been placed. The army had moved from the scene, and these were left behind in charge of the Surgeon and a few attendants. His condition was apparently so comfortable that it was soon determined to remove him from the field to Hagerstown, some sixteen miles distant, and the nearest terminus of any railroad leading homeward. The removal was effected partly on a stretcher and partly in an ambulance, without any special discomfort, and the expectation was still cherished that he might not only reach home, but at length recover from his wound.

It is scarcely possible for those at a distance to conceive the condition of Hagerstown during the days immediately following the battle of Antietam. It had been visited in succession by each of the two contending armies, and it was now crowded with officers and soldiers who had come from the army, and with citizens from distant States who were on their way to look for the living or to bring home the dead. Its supplies of every kind were so completely exhausted, that literally nothing could be purchased for the comfort of the wounded or the sick. Mr. Ives had hoped to proceed without delay with his son on the journey homeward, but the strength of the enfeebled sufferer would not allow it, and he was forced to remain in the crowded and famished town. In these circumstances the condition of the young officer became known to Mrs. Howard Kennedy, a patriotic and Christian lady of Hagerstown, who immediately invited him to her house, and united her own careful ministry with that of his father and his Surgeon in providing for his comfort. Though revived and refreshed by this unlooked-for kindness in a town of strangers, his strength did not return. The fearful wound was too deep for healing, and, on Friday, the day following his removal to Mrs. Kennedy's, his father made known to him the fatal conviction which his own observation, not less than the opinion of Doctor Miller, had forced upon him.

We venture not to draw aside the veil from this parting scene between the stricken father and his only son at the gates of immortality. The brief hours that remained were full of religious consolation and Christian hope. His life was coming to an untimely end in the new career on which he had entered but a few days before, but he had no repinings and no regrets for the course he had taken. He had said to one of his dearest friends as he was leaving home, " Be satisfied that if I should be shot in my first battle, it will be all right"; and now that this had

25

actually come to pass, his spirit remained the same; he was full of cheerful resignation to his Heavenly Father's will.   He received the comforting sacrament of the communion from the hands of a clergyman for whom he had sent, and with words of prayer and trust upon his lips, with tender messages to the loved ones who were away, and with gifts of fond remembrance and of pious charity which he desired to bestow, he passed from the world on the morning of Saturday, September 27, 1862, at the age of twenty-five years and nearly six months.   His remains were brought to Providence, and his funeral took place at St. Stephen's Church on the first day of October, just a month from the day on which he left home to join the army.   A memorial window has been placed in that church opposite the principal entrance, to commemorate the interest which he had manifested in its erection and his heroic death in the service of his country.   Its devices are of chaste and singular beauty.   It contains in one of its divisions, in three separate lines, the inscription, ROBERT HALE IVES, JUN. ANTIETAM. 1862.; and in the other, two well-chosen passages from the Bible.

An intelligent fellow-officer of General Rodman's staff who was almost constantly with him after he entered the service, has furnished the following glowing estimate of the manner in which he performed his duty amidst the novel and trying scenes into which he was so suddenly ushered :—

"The brief military experience of Lieutenant Ives, furnishes perhaps the severest test and brightest illustration of his charac- ter.   Voluntarily exchanging, at one of the darkest hours of our history, a home of luxury for a field of hardship and danger, he gave himself with entire devotion to his new work, and quickly manifested the presence of the highest traits of the soldier and the man.   Capacity, courage, coolness, courtesy and endurance, were called into daily exercise. The readiness with which he acquired a knowledge of his unaccustomed duties and the zeal with which he fulfilled them, quickly secured the respect of officers and men, while his quiet bravery and self-possession commanded their admiration. After a hard day's duty while others were snatching a short repose, he would forego his necessary rest, that he might learn the object of some movement made during the day, whose purpose or execution was not fully understood by him. A striking instance of his perfect self-control occurred at the battle of South Mountain. In obedience to an order from his general, he was bringing a regiment into position, when a huge shell shrieked past and struck just behind him in the head of the column, killing and wounding some twenty men. 'He neither quickened his pace, nor turned his head,' said a spectator; 'I never saw a cooler man.'

"Nor was he less remarked for his uniform and cheerful courtesy to all, whether his superiors or inferiors in rank. It was this same virtue, perhaps, more than anything else, which won the esteem and affection of all with whom he came in contact.

"Of his fortitude and endurance whether in hardship and exposure, or in labor and suffering, there could scarcely have been a sterner trial. For days and nights together on duty without relief, with no rations but crackers and water, almost without sleep, he never flinched or flagged. Already wearied and worn down by this exhausting service, he was called to meet and bear his fearful wound. Most nobly did he sustain himself under this new and sorest burden. Of his unmurmuring patience and Christian submission I will not speak, for they were above praise. No man can say too much of Lieutenant Ives, for his was no vain ambition, but a lofty and unselfish obedience to the call of duty, which answered, 'he felt within him a peace above all earthly dignities — a still and quiet conscience.'"

Thus early closed the career of this young officer in the service of his country. It is one of the briefest recorded in the history of the civil war. As has already been stated, only a month elapsed from the day of his departure from home to the day of his funeral. He fell fatally wounded in the first great battle in which he was engaged, twelve days after he joined the army in Washington. But these days, few as they were, were filled with arduous and trying service, and they signally illustrated the spirit that dwelt in his heart and the qualities that marked his character; his manly sense of religious duty, his modest fidelity to every obligation he had assumed, and his cheerful surrender of the brightest hopes and the fairest prospects to die for the preservation of his country's life. That country's life was mercifully preserved; but it is only when we count the places left vacant in hundreds of thousands of loyal homes, and read the illustrious roll of the brightest and best of our American youth who perished in the strife, that we can form any proper estimate of the amazing cost at which this blessing was finally secured.

CHARLES LOMBAERT KNEASS.

CHARLES Lombaert Kneass was born in Philadelphia, Pennsylvania, December 14, 1837. He was the eldest child of Samuel H. and Anna A. Kneass. During his boyhood he attended the school of Thomas D. James, of Philadelphia. Mr. James' assistant was Charles S. James, a graduate of "Old Brown," and now Professor of Mathematics in the University at Lewisburg, Pennsylvania. In 1852, the state of Kneass' health compelled him to leave his books and embark in some out-door employment. He accordingly obtained a position as rod-man in the engineer corps then at work on the mountain division of the Pennsylvania Central Railroad. At the end of a year's service his health was so much improved that he returned home and continued his preparations for college. After some months of hard study, however, his health again failed him, and he was compelled once more to take the field. He entered the employ of the same company, with whom he remained during the season, making surveys in the northern part of Pennsylvania. He then returned home and resumed his studies, and, having gained experience by the past, he connected with them various athletic exercises, such as boating, ball-playing, etc. In January, 1854, with his brother,

William Harris Kneass, he entered the Scientific Department of Brown University. While in college he was eminently distinguished for his gentlemanly treatment of his fellow students. He was fond of all manly sports, and, while loving a good joke, even a practical one, would never descend to any *meanness* or unkindness to effect it. He was naturally very bright, but had not much application; and, while never falling below the average, was not distinguished in his classes as a student. He was, however, a good scholar in the modern languages. His bearing sometimes appeared to those who were not intimately acquainted with him *brusque*, yet never ungentlemanly, but it was soon seen that it arose from his manner rather than from his heart. Without sycophancy, he was always loyal to his professors, though this was shown rather in a quiet influence among his comrades than in any active demonstrations.

The last year that he was in college he made very great efforts to awaken a martial spirit, believing that it would be an excellent thing for the physique of the students. For the accomplishment of this end he labored for a long while unceasingly, neglecting somewhat, perhaps, his collegiate studies. Finally he, together with Livingston Satterlee, Charles P. Williams, (both of whom now reside in New York,) and the writer, interested a sufficient number of students to authorize the formation of a military company. Kneass was our Captain, and Satterlee our First Lieutenant. A lot of broom-handles, picked up around the grounds and in various rooms, supplied the place of muskets; and thus equipped, Juniors as well as grave and reverend Seniors, for four months, spent their leisure time in the drill, unmindful of the playful sneers of our fellow students.

Had Kneass remained through his entire course, it was his intention to lay before the Faculty the desirableness of the introduction of the study of military tactics as a part of the regular college curriculum. Events, however, have since proved that in this particular he was only in advance of his age.

In April, 1855, leaving a worthy representative of the family in his brother, he dissolved his connection with the college, and entered the counting-room of the Fountain Green Rolling Mill, at Philadelphia, where he remained about eighteen months; finally leaving that situation to go into the iron trade on his own account. He remained in this business until the breaking out of the late civil war, constantly gaining in reputation among his fellow-citizens as an honorable and good business man, and laying the foundation of a handsome competency.

But the reverberations of the first gun fired at Sumter, found their way into the quiet counting-room, and awoke the manly qualities of the youth then busy among his account books. In April, 1861, he "closed" his last account, sold out his interest at considerable sacrifice, and enlisted in the Washington Greys, an old Philadelphia company composed of young men whose only ambition was to feel that they had done something for "the old flag." He went out with this regiment as Corporal; and, "I truly think," writes an intimate friend, "that the stripe on his arm was worn with more pride than if he had commanded a division or worn the epaulette of a Jackson or a Lee." He accompanied his regiment to Washington, and remained with it until his appointment as First Lieutenant in the Eighteenth United States Infantry, on the 14th of May, 1861. He immediately joined his regiment, then stationed at Columbus, Ohio, where he was at once made Post Adjutant. Now his past business experience was of essential value, both to himself and to the service. War was then new to us, and the formation of regiments was a work entirely different from that in which we are occupied in the peaceful pursuits of every day life. His advice and good judgment were therefore of incalculable benefit to his superior officers. In December, he fell on the ice and broke his ankle. The time which he then spent in the family circle while laid up from active service, is among the most tenderly cherished memories of the family. "He came home," writes his brother, William Harris Kneass, "and spent some six weeks with us; and happy recollections we have of that time. His kindness, his great heart overflowing with affection, his patience in suffering, make us all look back to his last visit with peculiar feelings of pleasure and of sadness."

As soon as his ankle was sufficiently healed he rejoined his regiment, and was ordered to Cincinnati on recruiting duty. Here he remained until the fall of 1862, when he was advanced to a Captaincy. He immediately took the field, and was with Rosecrans until his death. He was engaged in several skirmishes, but his first and only "fight" was at Murfreesboro', in which action he fell, while at the head of his company, on the 31st of December, 1862.

"The first news we received of his death," says his brother, in a letter to the writer, "was a telegram from Captain Hull, in these words: 'Charles was instantly killed on the 31st; body not recovered.' Subsequently, we obtained more particulars. The regular brigade was ordered to lie down, as the enemy were making sad havoc with their shot and shell. They remained in this position for some time—their ranks continually growing thinner and thinner—until some of the officers said, 'had we not better shelter ourselves?' Charlie, with the chivalric spirit of a true soldier, at once exclaimed, 'I will take no cover until my men have cover!'—are they not good words? Shortly after the order was given to retreat. Charlie raised himself on his knee in order to gain some knowledge of the situation, when the fatal bullet struck him. He only exclaimed, 'My God, I'm—' when he fell; and throwing his arm over his face died immediately.   The men and officers could not take him away, and he remained on the ground, a dead soldier, a true patriot, a kind son, and a good brother.   We did not obtain the body until about three weeks after, when a board was found marked with red chalk, 'Captain C. L. Kneass, United States Army.'   On exhuming the body of your friend, it was ascertained that the rebels had buried him with his comrades, near where he fell. Even his stockings had been taken to adorn the feet of some chivalric son of the South.   Charles is buried by the side of our father in Woodland Cemetery, Philadelphia, and the little flowers that shed their fragrance over his grave, would, could they speak, tell of a man who with Wolfe would say :—

' 'Tis sweet for one's country to die.' "

26

ALBERT GARDINER WASHBURN.

Class of 1860.

THE sacrifice of a single human life, aside from all moral considerations, and in the cold light of political economy, must ever be regarded as an inroad upon the resources of a nation. But when that life combines present strength with future promise,—the realization of past dreams with a well-grounded hope of a glorious career to come,—the loss is double, —of what was—of what might have been.

ALBERT GARDINER WASHBURN, the youngest of four children, was born at Gloucester, Massachusetts, on the 6th day of February, 1839. His parents were Israel and Elizabeth C. (Allen) Washburn. His father was a Methodist clergyman, and, as the discipline incident to that faith rendered frequent removals of the family necessary, young Washburn labored under that disadvantage which always results to children from a frequent change of location, inasmuch as such changes tend to confuse the mind by bringing it into communion with new teachers, and by introducing new methods of instruction, at a time when regular habits of thought ought especially to be cultivated. No evil, however, exists but has in its composition at least a small measure of good; and it is more than probable that something of the versatility and ready faculty of adapting himself to circumstances, which Washburn afterwards so conspicuously displayed, was derived from the migratory character of his early life.

In September, 1856, after concluding his preliminary studies at Fair Haven, Massachnsetts, Washburn, being then in his eighteenth year, entered the Freshman Class of Brown University. Such was his readiness of perception, that he was enabled to comprehend almost immediately the new position in which he was thus placed, and to it he easily adapted himself. New friendships at once were formed. They were few in number, but those whom he selected as companions and who received him into their confidence, remained firmly attached to him. Even when varying fortunes compelled a separation, these friendships remained unimpaired. Washburn's tastes did not incline him to strive to excel as a linguist. Nevertheless, his standing in the languages was much above the average. It was in mathematics that he seemed most at home, and in that branch of study he took a high rank. The routine of a collegiate course contains little worthy of preservation. Interesting, absorbing at the time, to those whose world is then included within the college walls, it is dull indeed to all except the actors themselves. Washburn was not one of those book-worms,—seekers after academic honor,—who bend all their energies to the accomplishment of an object, which when attained is not worth the labor it has cost, and which leaves the student to find that his ambition has been directed to an aim of little importance, while in the effort years have been trifled away. He was, on the other hand, desirous of securing such a position as would enable him to command the respect not only of his classmates, but also of all within the circle of his acquaintance. He associated freely with the students in the University, kept himself well informed upon the news of the day, and gave considerable time to general reading. In those little contentions which so often arise in institutions of learning, and which are dignified by the name of college politics, he was ever active, and was a tower of strength to the party whose cause he espoused. In the summer of 1858, in connection with several others, he became entangled in a difficulty with the Faculty, which resulted in his asking and receiving an honorable dismission from the University. The same course was taken by most of his friends. Undoubtedly this step gave new shape to his future career.

It was not his intention in leaving Brown University to abandon the acquirement of a liberal education. He therefore at once began to consider where he should complete his course. The merits of several colleges were discussed, but by the advice of his friends he finally determined to go to Union. He entered this institution in September, 1858, and was admitted to the Junior Class. Here he found a line of study which suited his natural taste for mathematics. He at once took a good rank among his classmates, and maintained it throughout his course. In Schenectady he formed many and firm friendships. By all who made his acquaintance he was regarded as one whose society should be sought. Schenectady became in fact his home. The choice of a profession, a matter which sometimes seems difficult, and which often depends upon chance, had been made by Washburn at an early period in his life. The brilliant history of the law had forced his mind to adopt a course of study which promised much distinction in the end, and great intellectual pleasure in the development of such genius as alone could command success in the severest of all professions. Accordingly, after graduating at Union, he entered the Albany Law School, where he enjoyed the privilege of pursuing under favorable circumstances, a study which already possessed for him rare charms. He had thus early, however, made the acquaintance of several journalists, and had written occasionally for the press. In 1861, when he received the degree of LL. B., an opportunity presenting itself, he availed himself of that training which had been undertaken rather as an amusement than with any serious thought of ever making it useful. In June, of that year, he became the editor of the Amsterdam Daily Despatch, a position which he continued to occupy for about six months. About this time, he married Miss Belle Evans, of Schenectady, by whom he had a son, Israel, who is still living. On closing his connection with the press, Washburn commenced the practice of the law, continuing, however, to reside at Amsterdam. Circumstances did not spare his life long enough to allow him to achieve an extended reputation in a profession remarkable for the difficulty and slowness which attend a rise to a position of even moderate prominence, and in which it may well be said there is no fictitious success, no undeserved reputation for either ability or learning.

In July, 1862, the excitement incident to the Rebellion, and the enthusiasm consequent upon a state of civil war, were at their height. Washburn's generous and impulsive nature saw but one course—he must enter the army. He could not afford the time necessary to secure that influence which would obtain for him such a commission as his education and merit entitled him to receive, and accordingly he entered the army as a private soldier. Undoubtedly he was commanded by many officers who were greatly his inferiors both in intellect and in social standing. He was not long, however, allowed to remain in the ranks, but soon received the warrant of a Sergeant and rendered valuable assistance in advancing the discipline and drill of the company to which he was attached. On the 12th of September, 1862, he was commissioned and mustered into the United States service as First Lieutenant, Company I, One Hundred Thirty-Fourth

Regiment, New York Volunteers. On the 24th of November, 1862, he was promoted to a Captaincy in the same regiment, and assigned to the command of Company E. His army life was short, but his duties were faithfully performed. Let the words of a brother officer speak of his conduct as a soldier:—

"Captain Washburn, in July, 1862, enlisted as a private soldier in the One Hundred Thirty-Fourth New York Volunteers. Having a manly and commanding presence, and being at that time moderately well qualified in military tactics, he was soon appointed a Sergeant, and entrusted largely with the discipline and drill of the men of his company. He was a Sergeant, however, but a short time. His gentlemanly deportment and soldierly qualities soon attracted the attention of his Colonel, and he was promoted to the rank of Lieutenant before the regiment left the barracks at Schoharie. He was with the regiment in its marches and experiences in Virginia until what was called the *Mud March*, the time when Burnside's army, then before Fredericksburg, Virginia, moved out to attack the enemy, but was compelled to abandon the attempt on account of impassable roads. Captain Washburn was then sick in his quarters, having been refused permission to go to a hospital. He was now taken to a private house, but so rapid was the progress of the disease that on the return of the regiment to its former position, it was found that he had breathed his last.

"Captain Washburn possessed a grace of refinement and a dignity and impressiveness of deportment which won the esteem and friendship of all with whom he associated. As a man and as a soldier he was greatly beloved, and his loss was profoundly felt in the regiment."

From other sources we learn that Washburn died at Falmouth, Virginia, on the 20th of January, 1863, of typhoid fever, and after a very brief illness. His father, who was at that time Chaplain of the Twelfth Massachusetts Volunteers, learning of his sickness, was able to reach him just before his death, and had the melancholy satisfaction of saving his body from a soldier's burial, and of committing it to the dust of the Vale Cemetery, at Schenectady.

It is a sad thought that during Washburn's sickness, short but terrible in suffering, an intimate friend, an officer in the same army, who had been a room-mate both at Brown and at Union, and whose influence at that time could have commanded those comforts which would have saved his life, or at least would have alleviated his suffering, though within but a short distance, was wholly ignorant of his condition, or even of his presence in that department.

The funeral services were held in the Methodist Episcopal Church at Schenectady, and were conducted by the pastor, assisted by President Hickok, and Professors Jackson and Lewis, of Union College. The flags throughout the city were placed at half-mast, the college exercises were suspended, and the students *en masse* were present at the solemn ceremonies.

In Washburn were combined intellectual strength and fidelity to friends; qualities which united win the devoted love of intimates, and the admiration of all acquaintances. Although fond of society, he nevertheless seemed to feel that courtesy to all ought never to be confounded with a dissipation or dilution of one's affections; and that the substance of friendship ought not to be merged in the show of the gentleman. No better tribute can be paid to his social worth, than those continuing friendships which had their birth at an early period, when the mind was undeveloped and the passions unsettled, and their end only with life. A correct taste must have formed them, and forbearance and constancy alone could have preserved them.

In the life of Captain Washburn, we see the promise of a brilliant career suddenly blighted.   An intellect, capable of extraordinary development and versatile in the highest degree, had been excellently cultivated.   It was ready to repay mankind for those benefits which it had received.   The preparation was complete — the usefulness for which it was intended was enjoined by that Power, with the wisdom of whose decrees we must remain content.   But, in contemplating the dispensation, one is oppressed with the strange and indescribable feeling which always takes possession of the mind when regarding that which is incomplete; and thought is painfully turned to those numberless broken columns which, throughout the cemeteries of the world, mark the graves of disappointed hopes, of promises unfulfilled.

27

JAMES CLARK WILLIAMS.

JAMES Clark Williams was born in Cincinnati, Ohio, April 17th, 1842. He was the son of Clark and Mary (Thompson) Williams, and was the youngest of a family of nine,—four sons and five daughters. His father's residence was situated at the foot of Mount Adams, upon whose summit stood the Astronomical Observatory, presided over by Professor O. M. Mitchel, whose family were on terms of intimate friendship with that of Mr. Williams. In particular, James, the subject of this sketch, and the youngest son of Professor Mitchel, were constant companions and playmates; and this youthful attachment grew into a firm and lasting friendship, terminated only by death.

As a boy he was rather quiet and sedate, and was disposed to shun the boisterous sports of his fellows, and to seek the society of older persons and enter into conversation and argument with them, to a degree unusual in one of his age. He was, nevertheless, popular with his companions, while he gained the esteem and approbation of his teachers by his uniform good conduct.

He was very fond of reading, and generally chose some standard work. When a boy of only eight or ten years of age he employed much of his time in this way; and often one of his companions, on going to his house to spend a leisure afternoon with him, would find him deeply immersed in some book; when, instead of inviting his friend to join in boyish sport or adventure, James would select for him another volume from the library and induce him to amuse himself in the same manner. The writings of Sir Walter Scott had especial attractions for him, and he doubtless often imagined himself one of the heroes so fascinatingly depicted by that master-hand, and burned to emulate their "deeds of high emprise."

The perusal of works of this kind was probably not without its effect upon his character and conduct. At any rate, he possessed, even in his boyhood, a truly chivalrous spirit, which only those who knew him best could appreciate, but to which even casual observers could not be altogether blind; for it evinced itself, in his daily intercourse with others, in a high sense of honor, which rendered him incapable of any of the petty meannesses of which boys are too often guilty. Nothing could induce him to betray a friend, or to reveal a secret of which he had become possessed, to the prejudice of another. If he were abused or ill-treated in any way, he never was known to revenge himself by accusing those who inflicted the injury. He would sometimes suffer the harshest treatment, and scorn to appeal to his parents or others for protection.

It was, perhaps, a result of these tastes and traits of character, that he developed, at an early age, an inclination for a soldier's life; and, after completing the round of elementary instruction in the schools of Cincinnati, he was anxious to enter the United States Military Academy at West Point. His parents, however, who had been educated in the doctrines of the Quakers, and who, moreover, did not care to encourage what they probably considered a mere boyish whim, objected to this project, but finally, as a sort of compromise, they sent him, at the age of thirteen, to the military school of Mr. Russell, at New Haven, Connecticut. Here he remained about two years, when, having decided, in accordance with his father's wishes, to obtain a college education, he left New Haven and entered the preparatory school of Messrs. Lyon and Frieze, at Providence, Rhode Island. In the following year, 1858, he entered Brown University, to pursue a three years course of study.

At college, Williams displayed the same characteristics which were conspicuous in his earlier life. Quiet and retiring, and even diffident in his address, his appearance and demeanor were not calculated, perhaps, to impress a stranger favorably, and few, probably, even of those who were brought into daily contact with him, suspected the spirit which lay concealed behind this external mask of reserve, or the lofty aspirations which were treasured there in secret. But those who passed this barrier, and were admitted into his confidence, found him a warm-hearted, generous friend, true as steel, the very soul of honor, with refined and cultivated tastes, and a mind capable of higher thoughts and purposes than the mere sensual enjoyment of the passing hour.

He had few intimates, but his whole class were his friends, for his amiable and gentlemanly conduct won their esteem, and it may be safely said that he had not an enemy in college.

Although not a hard student, he never habitually neglected his studies, and his standing was always good. The fondness for reading which marked him as a child, did not diminish, but rather increased with his years — indeed, it amounted almost to a passion. A large portion of his leisure time was thus employed, and some hours doubtless, which, in the opinion of his preceptors, at least, should have been spent in study. His favorite amusement in the winter evenings was to meet with two or three " inseparables," at the room of one of the number, and, seated before a good fire, in dressing-gown and slippers, pipe in mouth, to read books of all kinds and upon every subject. Williams, however, appeared to have little relish for "trashy" literature. His reading was generally of a substantial character, and of great variety. Possessing an excellent memory, he acquired in this way much valuable knowledge, and he was exceedingly well informed upon most of the topics of the day.

His old fancy for a "life on the tented field," continued unabated, and, throughout his academic course, he never ceased to cherish the hope that he might yet be enabled to follow out the path towards which his inclination so strongly pointed. When the events which preceded the late conflict began to reach their climax, and war appeared inevitable, it seemed as if fortune were smiling upon him, and opening the door through which he might enter, without hesitation—nay, with patriotic enthusiasm,—upon the career he longed to pursue. At the time of the actual commencement of hostilities, and the first call for volunteers, he was in the last term of his senior year; and, though the first prompting, both of duty and of inclination, was to respond at once, and though he chafed at the thought of delay, especially as some of his classmates and acquaintances were enlisting in the service, yet, in deference to the wishes of his parents, he decided to complete his college course and to bide his time.

It came at last. Having passed his final examinations and graduated with credit, his duty in this respect was now discharged, and, meeting with no further opposition from his parents, whose scruples were outweighed by considerations of patriotism, he felt free to devote himself to his country's service in his chosen profession.

An inviting opportunity presented itself. Professor Mitchel had been appointed a few weeks previously, Brigadier-General of volunteers, and had given his son Frederick—the friend and

companion of James from boyhood,—the appointment of Aide
upon his staff; and the latter, having applied for a similar position, it was readily promised. He soon obtained a commission as
Second Lieutenant in the Forty-Fifth Ohio Volunteers, and was
immediately after—in September, 1861—detailed as *Aide-de-Camp*
to General Mitchel, who was then in command of the Department
of the Ohio, head-quarters at Cincinnati. His regiment, however,
was not mustered into the service, and for several months he acted
in the capacity of Volunteer Aide, being unable to draw any pay,
though for this he cared little, so long as he was now fairly
entered upon a soldier's career. At the end of this year he was
transferred to the Twenty-Fourth Ohio Volunteers, a regiment in
active service; still continuing on the staff of General Mitchel.

His position was far from being a sinecure, even while remaining in Cincinnati. F. A. Mitchel and Williams were as yet the
only members of the personal staff, and, as the General was an
early riser and a hard worker, they were frequently on duty and
busily employed from six, A. M., till ten, P. M.

In the latter part of November, the departments of the Ohio
and the Cumberland having been consolidated, and General Buell
having been placed in command, General Mitchel was ordered
to report to him at Louisville, Kentucky. Here he was placed
in charge of a camp of rendezvous, near the city; but at the
expiration of two or three weeks, he repaired to Elizabethtown,
and assumed command of the Third Division, Army of the Ohio.
In a few days the division moved to Bacon Creek and encamped.
The other members of the General's personal staff were now
(December, 1861,) appointed and assigned to duty.

While at this place, Williams contracted the " camp " or
typhoid fever, which was prevailing amongst the troops, and had
already attacked several others of the staff. About the 1st of
January, 1862, he was sent to Cincinnati on sick leave, where he

was tenderly cared for at the house of his sister, his father no longer residing in the city. Here he remained for weeks, growing weaker and weaker all the while, until at one period, his life seemed to tremble in the balance; but at length the dread crisis was passed, and he began slowly to recover.

In the mean time the men of the Third Division were not allowed to remain long idle. About the middle of February they marched upon Bowling Green, then occupied by rebel forces, who evacuated on their approach. So rapid, however, was General Mitchel's advance, notwithstanding the inclement weather and miry roads, that he arrived at the town in time to hasten their departure by a vigorous shelling, though the burning of the bridge over the Barren river prevented an immediate pursuit. From Bowling Green the division pushed on to Nashville, Tennessee, and thence, after a few days, to Murfreesboro', where they remained during a part of March.

As Williams lay upon his sick bed at Cincinnati, and listened to the accounts of the marches and exploits of his companions-in-arms, he grew restive and impatient of his slow recovery, and anxious to return to the field. His friends restrained him for a while, but finally yielded, long before he was really able to go. "One evening, as I was sitting in my tent at Murfreesboro'," says a brother officer, "I was suddenly surprised to see Williams enter, in a state of nothing more than convalescence,—his face pale, and his whole appearance indicating the near approach he had made to the other world." A kind Providence averted any evil consequences of his rashness, and he ere long regained his health.

From Murfreesboro' the division of General Mitchel started on that short and brilliant, though almost bloodless campaign, which resulted in the occupation of Huntsville, on the 11th of April, and gave northern Alabama into the control of the National forces.

This campaign, although so signally successful, afforded little scope for the exercise of personal courage. It was characterized by long and forced marches, which demanded rather endurance and celerity of movement, for the tactics of the enemy were mainly displayed in securing as rapid retreat as possible. The General and his staff, therefore, were scarcely under fire at all. At Bridgeport, Alabama, however, there was a lively little affair in the capture of a bridge across the Tennessee river, and of Williams' conduct on this occasion an eye-witness says: "His quiet nature began to show signs of an excitement which was generally foreign to him. As the rattle of musketry commenced, he seemed to be perfectly delighted, and utterly regardless of fear. * * * I observed his actions, and from them I judged that he would make a very dashing officer." He always solicited permission to join scouting parties, or any expeditions which offered a prospect of danger or adventure; but they were generally uneventful, for, as a messmate of his remarks, " the enemy, in those days, were always getting away from us without a shot."

General Mitchel remained in command in Alabama, with headquarters at Huntsville, for several months, during which time no operations of special importance were undertaken. Early in July, he was ordered to Washington "to assume an important command," having been previously promoted to the rank of Major-General of volunteers. On reporting at Washington, he found that changes had occurred which materially altered his prospects. Halleck was appointed Commander-in-Chief, who probably preferred to give the "important command" to another. At all events, it was not conferred upon him, but he was, instead, placed off duty, and condemned to a period of inaction which was most irksome.

This was terminated, about the middle of September, by an order directing General Mitchel to proceed to Hilton Head, South

28

Carolina, to take command of the Department of the South. The eagerness with which a return to active duty had been awaited by the General and the officers of his staff, gave place to disappointment when they learned of this assignment. "After our roving campaigns in the West," writes one of them, "you may fancy with what feelings of horror we contemplated being shut up in the swamps of South Carolina." It is a soldier's duty, however, to obey, and General Mitchel was not the man to grumble. But his usual hopeful vigor and alacrity appeared to have deserted him. The depression which was felt by all, when setting out upon this ill-starred voyage, was seen to weigh most heavily upon him, and upon his Aide, Lieutenant Williams. "Nothing," continues the writer quoted above, "appeared to rouse them from a lethargy which had fastened upon them, and which, with their evil forebodings, seemed to indicate the sad fate which awaited them."

Just previous to their departure, the troops serving in the Department of the South were constituted the Tenth Army Corps, and all the staff were promoted, Williams receiving the rank of Captain.

On a rainy, dreary day, (September, 15, 1862,) they sailed from New York, and in a few days reached their destination.

At the time of their arrival, that fearful scourge, the yellow fever, had already disclosed its hideous form at the post, and it was not long in making its appearance at head-quarters.

All the while at Hilton Head, as at the departure from New York, General Mitchel and Captain Williams were very low-spirited, and seemed to have forebodings as to the future, too soon, alas! to be realized. Williams was particularly quiet.

It was about a month after he reached South Carolina, and just as the expedition under General Brannan, against Pocotaligo, for which he would have otherwise volunteered, was about starting out, that the fatal disease laid its insidious hand upon him. The sad events which succeeded are thus described by Captain F. A. Mitchel:—

"There were five of us upon the staff. Williams was the first attacked. The next day another was taken down with symptoms of violent disease; and thus we continued to be stricken, until, of our little military family, all except the senior Aide, Major Burch, and the General, were sick. *They* knew it was the dreaded yellow fever, but kept it from us.

"It was about the 25th of October, that the General, wishing to get us out of the noxious atmosphere in which we were, put us all on board a steamer, and took us to Beaufort. Here we were placed in the Heywood House, which had been reserved for head-quarters. Williams and I were put in the same room, and my brother and the Adjutant-General, Colonel Prentice, in another, across the hall. That night, General Mitchel went down stairs from our room unwell, and we never saw him again.

"For two or three days Williams continued to grow worse, until the black vomit appeared, when he was carried into the next room, and all night I listened to his death struggles. On the 29th of October, the last convulsions came upon him. He knew he was to die; indeed, I heard him say, the day we arrived at Beaufort, that he had rather die than suffer as he had for the past week. He asked his attendant if he was not near his end, and, being answered in the affirmative, said no more, but, closing his eyes, seemed, from the motion of his lips, to be commending his spirit to his Maker."

A few moments more of apparently great suffering, and the struggle was over, and death, as an angel of mercy, came to his relief.

He was buried as a soldier, with the honors befitting his rank, a company of infantry acting as funeral escort, and firing the customary volley over his grave,—a farewell salute on his departure for another world. His body was afterwards removed to Cincinnati, his former home, and deposited in Spring Grove Cemetery.

General Mitchel survived him but a single day. The other sufferers, after severe and protracted illness, were mercifully snatched almost from the jaws of death, and brought to a state of convalescence. But how sad and dark seemed the world to which they had, as it were, come back! There was a fearful gap in their little circle. He who had been the affectionate father of two of their number, and whom they all had learned to love and revere as their kind and paternal chief, and he who had been their friend and companion, and whom long association amid the scenes of camp and field had made doubly dear, were no more ; and they were left to bear their crushing loss as best they might, and, when reviving strength permitted, with heavy hearts to leave the shore which had been to them but a scene of suffering and calamity, and return to their sorrowful homes at the North. "The contrast between our entry" (into the harbor of Port Royal) "and our departure," writes one of them, "was great. On our arrival, the General was received with honors, and, as the vessel passed up the harbor, the ships of the navy and the batteries along shore fired the customary salutes. When we left, the General and Williams were in their coffins, and the rest of us were a cadaverous set of fellows, whose struggles with disease and trouble had made us little like the healthy men we were when we arrived."

The following are extracts from an order announcing the decease of Williams and others, issued by General Brannan, who succeeded to the chief command :—

"HEAD-QUARTERS, DEPARTMENT OF THE SOUTH, }
"HILTON HEAD, PORT ROYAL, S. C., November 5, 1862. }

"GENERAL ORDER, No. 50.

"It is the painful duty of the Commanding General to announce to the Tenth Army Corps, the decease of their late companions in arms, * * * Captain J. C. Williams, A. D. C., (staff of the late Major-General Mitchel,) on the 29th of October.

*   *   *   *   *   *   *   *

"Captain J. C. Williams served as Lieutenant and A. D. C. on the staff of General Mitchel during his entire campaign in the West; and, though quite a young man, had already distinguished himself as a gallant and efficient officer, and was much beloved by his companions for his many good qualities of heart and mind.

*   *   *   *   *   *   *   *

"By order of Brigadier-General J. M. Brannan.

"LOUIS J. LAMBERT,

"*Assistant Adjutant-General.*"

Thus ended a career which, all too brief, and seemingly uneventful, is yet worthy to be placed on record by the side of those which have already found an honored place in the history of the great struggle for national life. Though cut down in the early flush of manhood, he was not twenty-one when he died, Williams lived long enough to display those sterling traits of character which make the true man, and to win golden opinions from all who were brought in contact with him.

Captain Mitchel, his oldest and most intimate friend, says of him:—

"Williams was really one of the most chivalrous fellows I ever knew. Our acquaintance lasted fifteen years, and, during the whole time, he never, to my knowledge, was guilty of a mean thing. As a child and as a man, he always had that high sense of honor which shows itself in one's treatment of all about him, and in a regard for the feelings of others, which always inspires confidence.

"I think he was a natural soldier, and, had he lived, I am confident the country would have heard of him. He was always popular with brother officers and with those subordinate. He had a certain dignity and tact in delivering an order that always won. It was his pride to be a good soldier, and to obey his instructions to the letter. He had no nervous quickness in the discharge of his duties, but he was certain. He never was thrown off his balance, and never forgot anything. If any duty was to be remembered to be done at a certain time, the General was sure to charge Williams with it. 'There is one thing I have learned about Williams,' said he once to me, 'Whenever you order him to do a thing, you may depend upon its being done, and may dismiss it from your mind.'

"As he never was really in action, it is not possible to say much of his personal bravery. But he manifested throughout his life a disregard for death, and, when it came upon him, did not seem to fear it."

Another writes: "His companions and I have heard the General say, that he was intended for a commander; and his manner was such as not only to win the respect of those about him, but also to command the obedience of his subordinates."

Colonel W. P. Prentice, General Mitchel's Adjutant-General, pays the following tribute to his worth :—

" He was one of the most prompt, reliable, gallant and devoted soldiers I knew. I remember well what a dashing staff officer he made as *Aide-de-Camp* to General Mitchel; how highly appreciated he was and how useful. His associates found him a very companionable man, and a gentleman, through and through.

"He seemed to lead a blameless life. He kept it as clear as his sword from bad works, and both he had devoted—without any of the paltry political considerations and prejudices of which we were accustomed to hear so much—to his whole country.

"He had intended to apply for a commission in the artillery as soon as he should be relieved from staff duty, and for such service he was, at the time of his last sickness, making thorough preparation and study.

"Altogether he was a man to be remembered and mourned for, and, in the circle of his personal friends, his place cannot be filled."

Such was he whose life and character we have thus briefly and imperfectly sketched. If, ere his sword could win for him an immortal place in the list of patriot heroes, the hand that grasped it was stiffened in death, his name will yet be an undying one with many. There is one circle, at least,—that of his classmates at Brown,—where his memory will be kept ever green. When, at lengthening intervals, and, alas! with lessening numbers, they gather in the familiar precincts of *Alma Mater*, to renew the old and dear associations, and to call the roll of '61, the mention of "Jimmy Williams," as they love still affectionately to call him, though it can evoke no response from his death-sealed lips, will never fail to touch an answering chord in every heart, awakening feelings of mingled pride and sorrow; and, when they are questioned of the record of the class in the great conflict—of its contributions to the national cause—of its sacrifices in behalf of Union and humanity in the dark days of rebellion and civil war, they can point to his name, inscribed in marble on the college wall, and say, "Behold our costly offering."

WILLIAM IDE BROWN.

———◆———

WILLIAM IDE BROWN, a son of John S. and Deborah (Ide) Brown, was born in Attleborough, Massachusetts, August 27, 1839. Not long after, his father removed to Fisherville, New Hampshire. William remained at home enjoying such educational advantages as the town schools afforded till 1856, when he entered the Academy at New London, New Hampshire, and commenced the study of the classics preparatory to a college course. While at New London, he became interested in the subject of religion, and on the 7th of June, 1857, he made a public profession of his faith, and united with the Baptist Church at Fisherville. The wants of the Christian ministry at once attracted his attention. The question of his own duty with reference to that work, however, was not hastily settled. September 6, 1857, he writes to his father: "In respect to the great question of my calling in life, I feel much the same as when at home, but I think I look forward to the ministry with increasing pleasure. I feel that I need to watch closely the indications of God's Providence, and not trust too much to my own impulses." February 28, 1858, he writes: "I can look forward to nothing else in life with pleasure except the ministry." The decision was now made; and thenceforward, in accordance with the profoundest convictions of duty, he regarded the work of a Christian minister as his life-work.

Early in September, 1858, he entered the Freshman Class at Brown University. Kind and courteous in his manner, he soon won the esteem not only of his classmates, but of the men of other classes. As a scholar he did not take a high rank. In his preparation for college, he had not shared the advantages for a thorough, classical culture which many of his classmates had received. Nor was he ambitious to distinguish himself in his studies. "I do not think," he writes in a letter to his father, " that either my health or my abilities warrant me in aiming for the highest honors." These he would leave to others. Yet, unambitious as he was, his rank was an honorable one, and he received appointments both for Junior Exhibition and for Commencement.

A firm conviction of the necessity of strengthening if possible a constitution by no means rugged, led him to give not a little attention to physical exercises. To no one was the gymnasium in the city a more favorite place of resort. Its advantages, however, were not all that could be desired. With others, he longed to hail the day when the *college* would have a gymnasium — when physical training under the charge of a suitable instructor, would find a place in the college curriculum. Fondly he cherished the belief that that day would come, and no one did more than he to hasten its approach. This fondness for physical exercises led him to engage in boating, which, at the time he entered the University, had just begun to attract the attention of the students. A single six-oared boat then constituted the "Brown Navy." Other boats, however, were soon added, and, for a while — we might say till the outbreak of the Rebellion — no interest in college was more popular with the students than that of boating. Brown joined the crew of the Atlanta — a connection which he

retained throughout his college course.   How true it is that this
physical training which he received in the gymnasium and on
the Seekonk, has a meaning now to us, which at that time it had
not to him.   Little did he imagine that the strength he acquired
then and there, was fitting him to endure the weary marches of
many a lingering campaign.

But his highest aim while in college was to lead an upright,
Christian life.   That life may not have conformed to the ideal
that was ever before him — it probably did not — but it was an
unselfish life — a life without a stain.   He would have every one
know that he was a Christian.   His daily life should attest the
sincerity of his profession.   Moreover, he would array himself
with the Christian men of the college.   Accordingly, on entering
the University, he at once enrolled his name on the books of the
Religious Society.   There are those who have not yet forgotten
the earnest simplicity of his words, when, soon after his matricu-
lation, at one of the meetings of this Society, he spoke of his
previous Christian life, and of his anticipations respecting the
work to which he had consecrated himself.   Throughout his college course he gave to this Society an unwavering support.

At no time while in the University did he lose sight of the
work which he had in view on entering its halls.   He spoke of
it frequently, both in his intercourse with his friends in college,
and in his letters to his friends at home.   Closely he watched
himself, lest unworthy considerations should influence him in
entering on such a work.   "I make this a subject of prayer," he
writes, October 14, 1860.   March 19, 1861, he says: "As I
approach nearer and nearer to active life I am thinking more
and more of the particular part which I am to act.   I think I
am gradually giving up selfish purposes in life for the one holy
purpose which is above all."

During the latter part of his college course his interest in his studies greatly increased. Mathematics and the classics were somewhat distasteful to him. In the natural sciences, in rhetoric and in history—the studies that now claimed his attention—he took much delight. As a writer he at once advanced to a high rank among his classmates. His success, however, was not achieved without labor; but the labor was willingly bestowed. "I have received an appointment for Junior Exhibition," he writes, March, 19, 1861, "and have been casting about for a subject for my oration. Preparation for the occasion will require much extra work. I do not boast myself a genius; therefore my speech will be the result of hard labor. * * * * I do not strike for the first honors of the occasion, for I am aware that my abilities do not warrant me in so doing; but I am confident I can stand much above mediocrity." He was not mistaken. His oration—"The Influence of the Public on the Author"—satisfied the highest expectations of his friends.

During the latter part of his college course—that part to which he had looked forward with so much interest—the political affairs of the nation assumed an aspect which no lover of his country could regard with indifference. The distant mutterings of the approaching storm were heard in Hope College and University Hall. The literary societies in their meetings discussed the questions of the day. These questions also furnished the chief topics in social intercourse. In the spring of 1860, when Abraham Lincoln came to Rhode Island, he found no more attentive listeners to the two addresses that he delivered—one in Providence and one in Woonsocket—than the students of the college who flocked to hear him. Brown writes to his father, March 8th: "Lincoln, of Illinois, speaks this evening at Woonsocket. There is to be an extra train, and —— pays the expenses of eighty or ninety students." The occasion to which these words refer was one which few of the men who were in college at that time have yet forgotten or can forget so long as life shall last. Soon, in the rapid march of events, the western orator became the President of the United States, and Brown saw him next as, in company with McClellan and Burnside, the President passed along the lines in review of the army after the battle of Antietam.

Threatened violence at length appeared armed, and, in April, 1861, the peal of hostile cannon filled the land. But the sound of the first gun which was fired at Fort Sumter did not die away when it reached the walls of the college. It would be impossible to set forth in words the state of feeling which was at once manifested throughout the University. The Senior class procured a flag, and, on the afternoon of April 17, in the presence of the Faculty, the students, and a throng of the friends of the college, it was raised over University Hall. Burnside had arrived in the city the day previous, and was already organizing the "First Rhode Island." Not a few from the several classes in the college entered its ranks. Brown, writing to his father that evening, said: "To-night, as I see the streets thick with uniforms, it begins to seem like war. The excitement here is intense. I hope New Hampshire will furnish her quota of troops in good season." May 8th, he writes, "Junior Exhibition passed off smoothly, although on account of the war-excitement there was less interest manifested than usual. The recitation-rooms bear testimony to the restlessness of the students in these times."

About the middle of May, a military company—the University Cadets—was organized at the college. Brown placed his name on its rolls at the first; and in its ranks he made his first acquaintance with the principles of the school of the soldier.

He had already parted with college friends who had entered the military service. On the 20th of May he went to Boston, to take leave of home-friends, who, on that day, with the Second

New Hampshire, were to pass through the metropolis of New England on their way to the seat of war. Nothing since the outbreak of the Rebellion had stirred his heart so deeply as the scenes which he witnessed then and there. "I felt as if I could give them all a hearty shake of the hand, and a God bless you," he writes. "I was most agreeably disappointed in the appearance and discipline of the men. As the representative of New Hampshire here, I have had to stand not a little of bluster and slurring on account of her slowness in sending out troops. I have not been posted at all in regard to her movements or her soldiers, and accordingly have had to bear it all. But now I can stand up for the Granite State with an intelligent and patriotic feeling."

The year 1861 gradually wore away. Few expected that the Rebellion would long continue, and Brown had his eye still steadily fixed upon the work to which he had devoted his life. February 11, 1862, writing to his father, he said, "I am looking forward with the very pleasantest anticipations to my three years at Newton." But the disasters which in the month of June befel our army before Richmond, dissolved at length the dream he had so long cherished. He was then writing his Commencement oration. Its subject—"The Physical Conditions of Poetical Productiveness"—was little in harmony with the thoughts that crowded his mind. The wants of his country were continually before him. He would not, he could not close his eyes. He would meet the question of duty fairly. He had no love for a military life—he did not thirst for military distinction. "True patriotism," he writes, "is something more than impulse—mere ignorance of the cost—mere indifference—it is the result of a settled conviction that the country needs great sacrifices and is worthy of them. Intelligent and careful thought must precede this conviction; and, when a man has gone through with this process, he cannot help coming out several rounds higher up on the ladder of existence. * * * The patriotism of the country is to be again tested by the call for three hundred thousand more men. Who wont have to go—who can?"

These words reveal the posture of his mind at this time. But it was hard to relinquish long-cherished plans. His eyes were still turned towards Newton. Already he had secured a room in the Theological Institution there. The studies of the place, and the companionship of old friends, attracted him. While weighing the question of duty thus presented he entered upon the vacation that intervened between the close of the term and Commencement day.

As he left Providence—it was early in July—he could not withhold the confession that the attachments of the place were stronger than he had supposed. His affection for his classmates was real. Long before, they had shown their appreciation of his worth in making him their President—a life appointment. He parted from them now, expecting to meet them again when the exercises of Commencement week should bring them together for the final separation. This expectation failed. Some of those classmates he was to meet again only on distant and bloody fields. Some he was never more to meet.

He was soon at home. But there, as in college, he could not forget that three hundred thousand more men were needed to give efficiency to the wasted armies of his country. The question, "Who can go?" could no longer remain in abeyance. His answer was now ready, and he said, "I will go." He at once gave himself to the work of recruiting a company for the Ninth New Hampshire Volunteers. August 10, he was commissioned a Second Lieutenant in that regiment. On the organization of the regiment his company was known as Company K. So urgent was the demand of the government for more men, that the Ninth

New Hampshire was hurried to the front at the earliest moment possible. The regiment left Concord August 25. On reaching Washington it at once crossed the Potomac, and encamped on Arlington Heights. General Pope at that time was in the vicinity of Manassas Junction. General Jackson was between our army and Washington. Jackson retreated on the 28th. On the 29th was fought the second battle of Bull Run. The tide of Rebellion was again sweeping towards the Capitol. "Don't give yourself a moment's anxiety about me," wrote Lieutenant Brown to his father. "Tell mother not to. She would not if she were here. She would wish she had an army of sons to help crush the Rebellion." But the Ninth was not called to participate in any of those sanguinary battles which were fought by the army of Virginia on those last days of August. "The battle autumn," however, was now at hand.

General Lee, after several days, drew off his army, and it was then discovered that he was moving North. All our available forces were at once placed under the command of General McClellan, and a new campaign opened. The Ninth New Hampshire was assigned to Sturgis' division of the Ninth Corps—Burnside's—though at that time Burnside was in command of the First and Ninth Corps, which formed the right wing of the army. The regiment left Arlington Heights on the 6th of September, and, recrossing the Potomac, marched through Georgetown into Maryland. September 11, Lieutenant Brown writes: "We may be called into action soon. If so, I hope we shall do well. I am ready and willing to go where duty calls." Burnside was in the advance. On Sunday, September 14, he found the enemy in force at Turner's Gap, a pass in the South Mountain range. Cox's and Wilcox's divisions of the Ninth Corps were at once ordered into position, and the battle soon opened. Sturgis' division was brought into action still later in the day. The

Ninth New Hampshire then came under fire for the first time. "We went into the woods with a wild yell," writes Lieutenant Brown. "Fortunately we made the rebs think we were an entire fresh brigade. As we were going down a steep descent, we halted in order to straighten our line of battle. We happened to be in a little opening at the time, and in full view of a rebel battery. The sun shining upon our arms made us a good mark. We had five men wounded in our company in that one place." Among the wounded in that charge was Brown's Captain. Gradually the enemy was forced from his position, and darkness found Burnside's men far up the mountain's side. Under cover of that darkness the enemy withdrew from the points not already relinquished, and the pass was won. "We awoke the next morning feeling like veterans," writes Lieutenant Brown.

At Antietam, on the 17th, the Ninth New Hampshire was again in action. Here the regiment suffered still more than at South Mountain. "We went into action in good season," writes Lieutenant Brown; "were under fire now and then all day. Unfortunately we were brought into positions where we were shelled, but could do nothing in return. Lieutenant-Colonel Titus was wounded early in the day." At night, Company K was posted at the Stone Bridge, the capture of which that afternoon had cost Burnside so many men. Lieutenant Brown writes: "General Burnside came along, and told us to guard it well till morning, and he would send us reïnforcements. All the next day we were in line, just beneath the brow of a hill, expecting an attack. This part of the line it was very important to hold, and yet it was very weak. It was an anxious day for the Ninth." General McClellan's inactivity on the 18th, lost to our arms the fruits of the victory which had been won on the 17th. Lee unmolested retired across the Potomac, and the campaign was ended.

30

For a while after the battle, the Ninth Corps remained in camp near Antietam Iron Works. Early in October, crossing Elk Ridge, it encamped in Pleasant Valley. Nearly a month of rest followed. Up to that time Lieutenant Brown could say, "the heavens have been my only tent, and my only blanket."

On the 11th of October, he wrote, "I still hold that the enforcement of the Constitution is the direct object for which we contend; but I feel that peace would be premature if it should leave the slavery question as it now stands. Events marked by Providence are solving the accursed problem. While God is working, we should be willing to wait. I should regard it as a calamity if the armed violence that threatens the Constitution should be removed without removing the underlying cause. I hope we are now doing the fighting of centuries to come."

October 17th, he writes: "My testament is my nearest companion and dearest. I remember well that the next morning after the battle at South Mountain, as we lay along the slope of the mountain, I gained great consolation and peace from reading the fourteenth chapter of John. It was always a favorite chapter. 'Let not your heart be troubled,' seemed an antidote to the troubled scene. I felt that my heart should be easy, no matter what the outward danger."

Late in October, General McClellan resumed offensive operations. Burns' and Sturgis' divisions of the Ninth Corps were in the advance, and crossed the Potomac on the 26th at Berlin, a few miles below Harper's Ferry. On the 7th of November, General McClellan having been relieved of his command, General Burnside was placed at the head of the army of the Potomac. On the 19th of November, the Ninth Corps encamped on the heights opposite Fredericksburg. The battle of Fredericksburg was fought on the 13th of December. Sturgis' division of the Ninth Corps was hotly engaged. The failure of our arms that

day was an unlooked for disappointment; but Lieutenant Brown
had one pleasant remembrance of the fight in the good conduct
displayed by his men under circumstances most trying. "We
have passed through a fire of grape and canister as hot as the
hottest," he writes, "and then fired from sixty to one hundred
rounds of ammunition." The regiment went into the fight about
noon, and was engaged till night put an end to the conflict. That
night it remained on picket—also during the next day. On the
night of the 15th, it recrossed the river with the rest of the
army, and reöccupied its old camp.

Early in February, 1863, the Ninth Corps was detached from
the army of the Potomac, and ordered to Newport News, Virginia. Soon after, General Burnside, who, January 26th, at his
own request, had been relieved of the command of the army of
the Potomac, was assigned to the command of the Department of
the Ohio. Willcox's and Sturgis' (now Potter's) divisions of the
Ninth Corps accompanied him to his new field of duty. They
were at once sent into central Kentucky. The rebel forces which
had so long overrun the State, were speedily driven south of the
Cumberland river. While his regiment was engaged in these
movements, Lieutenant Brown received a First Lieutenant's commission, dated March 1, 1863, and was transferred to Company B.
The Captain of this company was at that time absent sick—a
Second Lieutenant had not yet been commissioned—so that the
command devolved wholly on him.

When General Burnside had nearly matured his plans for a
movement into East Tennessee, the Ninth Corps, under General
Parke, was detached from his command, and ordered to report to
General Grant, then in the rear of Vicksburg, Mississippi. The
Ninth New Hampshire left Crab Orchard, Kentucky, June 4, and
proceeded to Cairo, Illinois, by way of Cincinnati. Transports
were in waiting at this point, and the troops were soon moving

down the Mississippi. With other regiments of the Second Division, the Ninth New Hampshire disembarked at Sherman's Landing, on the west bank of the Mississippi, and a few miles above Vicksburg; but, after a short delay, the troops reëmbarked, and, moving up the Yazoo river, landed at Haines' Bluff June 17th, and proceeded to Milldale. The duty assigned to the corps was the defence of the rear of General Grant's army, then threatened by Johnston, who had assembled a considerable force on the east bank of the Big Black, and was only awaiting reïnforcements before commencing offensive operations. An unexpected obstacle now lay in his path, and Pemberton, failing to receive that coöperation which he had hitherto expected, surrendered on the 4th of July. That afternoon a large force, including the Ninth Corps, under the command of General Sherman, left Vicksburg in pursuit of Johnston, who now, with all possible haste, fell back on Jackson, the capital of the State. The pursuit was a most wearisome one on account of the extreme heat. On the 10th, Sherman was before Jackson. The next morning he drove the enemy into his works, and laid siege to the place. The Ninth New Hampshire held the extreme left of the line, its left resting on the Pearl river. "The land was low," writes Lieutenant Brown, "and covered with a small growth of trees and bushes. In the night there was the most entire absence of light. The enemy during the day kept at a distance, but in the night the rebel pickets would come up and throw a stick into some brush near, and so make a rustling. Our men would fire in the direction of the sound — the flash would reveal their position — and then, before the sentinel could load, the rebels would rush up to the post and knock him down with the butt of a gun. We had one in our company thus killed. * * * A deserter came in a few days ago, and told General Welch that the Texas Rangers who have been in our rear took one of our regiment prisoner and hung him. They shot another from our brigade. In Virginia we had a somewhat civilized warfare. Here it is brutal."

Johnston finding that Sherman was threatening his rear, hastily evacuated Jackson on the night of the 16th, and our forces entered the city in the morning. After destroying the railroads in the vicinity, Sherman returned with his army to Vicksburg. "We have had a long, hard march," writes Lieutenant Brown, July 25. "Many died by the wayside from exhaustion. Rations were short. Roast corn was our main dependence. Water was very bad and scarce. Many a time I have drank the water from the puddles." The Mississippi campaign was now ended, and the corps, with "Vicksburg and Jackson" on its colors, was returned to its old commander.

So severe, however, had been the campaign, that the corps returned to Kentucky a mere skeleton. It nevertheless, after a little rest, followed Burnside into East Tennessee, and aided in its deliverance from rebel rule. The Ninth New Hampshire did not participate in this campaign, but remained on provost duty at Paris, Kentucky. Here, on the 1st of November, Lieutenant Brown was promoted to the Adjutancy of his regiment. The regiment remained in Kentucky till late in February, 1864, when it was ordered to join the corps. It proceeded to Knoxville by way of Cumberland Gap. On reaching Knoxville, Adjutant Brown found that the Ninth Corps had been ordered to Annapolis, Maryland. After a rest of three days, in which he visited Fort Sanders, and other places made historical by the events of the late siege, his regiment falling into its old place in the corps, commenced, March 21, the return to Kentucky. The corps recrossed the mountains at Jacksboro', and reached Nicholasville, Kentucky, the terminus of the railroad from Covington, in ten days—a march of nearly two hundred miles. The Ninth New Hampshire arrived at Annapolis, April 7.

Here the corps was reörganized. The diminished ranks of the old regiments were not filled, but its numbers were greatly increased by the addition of new regiments, and a division of colored troops. In regard to the latter, there then existed in the army a prejudice which Adjutant Brown did not share. When in Mississippi, he wrote to a friend: "I have seen several colored regiments. Surely the black soldier shoulders his gun and walks his beat for all the world like a human being. If we had a race of orang outangs, who could imitate so well, we should have had them in the field long ago."

While at Annapolis, the corps was reviewed by General Grant and General Burnside. In a letter to a friend, speaking of this review, Adjutant Brown, while making honorable mention of the former, reveals in simple yet beautiful language his affection for the latter: "O, how I love that General. I would think myself happy, if I could be an orderly, and follow him from place to place. How I wish I knew him personally. How proud I was to have him speak to me the night of the battle at Antietam, while I happened to be on duty at the famous Antietam bridge. There may be greater generals than Burnside, but nowhere a more honest, noble, patriotic hero."

The destination of the Ninth Corps was a mystery so long as the corps remained at Annapolis. Nor was that mystery solved when, April 23d, the corps received marching orders, and set out for Washington. On the 25th, about noon, the corps entered the Capital. It was a proud day for the troops. President Lincoln stood on the balcony at Willard's Hotel, looking down on the men whose courage and endurance had been proved on so many fields, and receiving their heart-felt salutations. That night the corps encamped near Arlington Heights. It was now manifest that it was to coöperate with Grant in his spring campaign in Virginia.

That campaign opened early in May. Burnside, who was holding the Orange and Alexandria Railroad, hurried to the Wilderness battle ground at the summons of Grant. The Ninth New Hampshire was not present at that action. At Spottsylvania Court House, on the 12th of May, it was in position on the right of the corps, and lost heavily both in officers and men. The Lieutenant-Colonel and the Major were severely wounded. About two hundred of the men were killed, wounded or captured. The Colonel was absent sick, and of the captains only one was left present for duty. On the 18th, the regiment was again in action at Spottsylvania Court House. It participated also in the battles on the North Anna. Near Bethesda Church, May 31, it was once more brought face to face with the enemy. "We advanced alone and unsupported," writes Adjutant Brown, "and drove the enemy from a strong position. Our loss was one killed and twenty-five wounded." Again, on the same day, he writes: "Every one is cheerful and confident. * * * * O how I wish the people of the north could witness the earnestness and determination of the campaign, the endurance of the soldiers—marching all night, and fighting all day, sometimes with nothing to eat but the corn left by the mules."

Late at night on the 2d of June, Adjutant Brown made his way through the darkness and the rain in search of a college friend, whose regiment chanced to be in line near his own. The morrow was to bring with it battle, perhaps death; but Adjutant Brown was still "cheerful and confident." Sitting down under a tree, the two chatted till about day-break, and then, shaking hands, parted never to meet again. His friend was wounded in the early morning, but Adjutant Brown passed through the action "without a scratch."

On the morning of June 17th, Potter's division of the Ninth Corps made a gallant and successful attack on the enemy's lines before Petersburg. "At day-break," writes Adjutant Brown, "we made a charge, and drove the rebs from a strong position, capturing three pieces of artillery with their horses, and three hundred and seventy-five prisoners. Our loss was slight. * * * When the charge was made, our regiment and the Thirty-Second Maine were ordered to stay in the pits and hold them; but one regiment broke, and ran back. General Griffin came up, and cried out, 'Up, Ninth, and at them!' Up we got, and in a few rods we came upon the three pieces of artillery." The enemy's works at once were turned, new lines were established, and the siege of Petersburg commenced.

July 30, on the springing of Burnside's mine, the Ninth New Hampshire again went into action. The regiment lost five officers and ninety-two enlisted men. Captain Hough, commanding the regiment, was killed. "Our brigade," writes Adjutant Brown, several days after the battle, "was yesterday commanded by a Captain. Not a field officer survived the storm." Still later he writes: "You don't know what a feeling of gratitude there was in my heart for several days after the battle. Think how God has spared my life while so many have fallen all around me. I feel as though He must have some work for me to do."

But incessant marching, fighting, and watching, had well-nigh exhausted his physical energies. About the middle of August he writes: "If it were not that I am so much needed with the regiment, I hardly feel as though I could keep up a great while longer without rest." For a while, therefore, he remained at his post, but a change became necessary, and, early in September, he went home on sick leave.

On the 13th of October, and while at home, Adjutant Brown received a Major's commission in the Eighteenth New Hampshire —a new regiment. Well had he earned this promotion. "Since the regiment entered the service," writes a brother officer, urging the appointment, "Adjutant Brown has been with it in every battle, skirmish and march, and, by the fidelity with which he has performed every duty devolving upon him, has won the high esteem and admiration of every officer in the regiment. He is brave, cool, and judicious under fire. When it was proposed to confer the rank of Brevet Major upon the officer who had conducted himself with the most conspicuous gallantry during the campaign, Adjutant Brown's name was the one most prominently mentioned."

Major Brown joined his regiment about the middle of November. It was then stationed in the defences at City Point, and he remained on duty at that post till the opening of the spring campaign. Speaking of his reception, he writes : "I never received so hearty a welcome from any set of men before. They had been expecting me for several days." In the years which had passed since he entered the army, he had lost none of that spirit of true devotion to his country which marked his entrance into the military service. December 31, having reviewed the scenes of the past year, he turned towards the future. What would it bring? "If I should fall," he writes, "I should make no greater sacrifices than many have already made. They have left just as dear ones behind, and just as bright prospects. I would be a coward if I would not go, and stand with the rest. I often think of Shakspeare's words: 'I will do all that becomes a man.' That motto has had a great influence upon my life for many years." His cheerfulness amid the annoyances of a life which in itself became more and more distasteful to him, appears in a letter written January 5, 1865: "I am very happy, to-night," he says, "am thinking how blessed I am with friends, health, pleasure, honorable position, and all the comforts of life which can be expected in the army. Yet, most of all, I feel that God has blessed me in His love revealed to me through His Son. O

31

what more can I ask! * * * * Yet I long to be out of this turmoil, and unholy manner of life. * * * But the country is in peril—wants men who will serve her. I will be one to do my whole duty if there be many who 'sham' it." The slightest thought of any lack of real earnestness on the part of the people at the North troubled him. "When the flag,—O 'tis a dear old flag,"—he writes, February 26, "now baptized in the blood of thousands—when the flag was first fired upon at Fort Sumter, the President was not compelled to beg men to rally around it. To many the privilege was denied. But now, when the battles of 1861-2-3-4 and 5, have succeeded in bringing down from Fort Sumter the 'rebel rag,' and have run up the 'red, white and blue,' only see how the army goes a begging for men. People talk now of quotas, not men. If gold could fight they would give it—but not men, not life itself."

Shortly after the middle of the month of March, the Eighteenth New Hampshire was ordered to move up to Meade Station. It was evident that active operations were soon to be resumed. In the absence of the Colonel, Major Brown was now in command of the regiment. As the men had not yet been under fire, he felt not a little anxious with regard to the approaching campaign. "The tears stood in his eyes," writes a friend, who visited him about this time, "as he grasped me by the hand, and said, 'I am not afraid to face death, or even to meet it; but what if my regiment should disgrace itself.'" The hour of trial came sooner than he expected, but the young soldier's most ardent wish in regard to the conduct of his men was more than realized. March 27, the Eighteenth New Hampshire was assigned to the Third Brigade, First Division, Ninth Corps. The next day Major Brown writes from Fort Steadman: "We are now in the fort which was captured and recaptured on Saturday morning. It is the old life of last summer over again—only not so dangerous and disagreeable." On the 29th, writing to his father, he says: "Sheridan, I expect, started this morning at four o'clock, on another raid to the left. The whole army is under marching orders. I think the Ninth Corps will remain where it is till the enemy in front become weak or evacuate. We have our head-quarters in a bomb-proof in Fort Steadman, and hold quite a length of the line to the right of it. * * * * We feel that it is quite an honor to begin our life at the front in so famous a place." Still later in the day he writes to a friend: "Was up all night— feared an attack, and were under arms; but have got along finely thus far. I feared at first for the conduct of the men, but they do splendidly—I would not ask more of them." "9 P. M.—Want to see you, but can wait. * * * * Am tired and sleepy—think an important movement is on foot."

These few words, dated 9 P. M., were the last he wrote. Sensible of the responsibility of his position, he felt that his place that night was with his men. No one should know that he was "tired and sleepy." In order to be sure that every man was ready for instant service, he moved up and down the line regardless of the danger he thereby incurred. His men, who, in the short time he had been with them, had learned to love him because of what he was to them, kindly warned him against such an exposure of his life. But he thought only of his duty, and moved on. He had gone but a little way, when suddenly he fell. A Minié ball had entered his head just back of the right ear, and in a moment and without a struggle life was extinct. He wanted rest, and God gave "His beloved sleep."

A few days after, when the whole country was rejoicing over the fall of Petersburg and Richmond, and the prospect of the speedy overthrow of the Rebellion, a group of mourners gathered around the remains of the fallen soldier in the house of God which had echoed to his early vows. Friends and neighbors

were there; classmates were there; brothers and sisters and
parents were there; and with them one yet nearer and dearer
than they all. Lovingly the last offices of affection and friendship were performed. Then bearing him hence they laid him
away, far from the din and tumult of battle, and amid the scenes
which he loved so well. At the open grave of no one could it
be said more truly,

> " He lived as mothers wish their sons to live,
> He died as fathers wish their sons to die."

At the next Commencement at Brown, when the class of
1862 came together to celebrate their first Triennial, the Class
Poet, Mr. Henry F. Colby, in the lines which follow, gave expression to the one thought which filled all hearts, and hallowed the
hour :—

> " But while so many faces around the board appear,
> There is one face we looked for that will not meet us here :
> Hushed is the voice that cheered us, and still the heart so brave,—
> Our classmate, Brown, is sleeping within a soldier's grave.
>
> We knew his earnest purpose, his pure, unselfish aim,
> How much he gave his country, how little asked for fame ;
> Heaven's never-fading laurels now rest upon his brow,—
> We hoped to meet him here, boys, but angels meet him now.
>
> Our festal wreath of flowers is dewed with sorrow's tears,
> Among its smiling blossoms the amaranth appears ;
> But at each new Triennial, affection shall be true
> To the memory of the martyr of the Class of Sixty-Two."

HERVEY FITZ JACOBS.[*]

Class of 1863.

ERVEY FITZ JACOBS was born in Thompson, Connecticut, on the 3d day of August, 1838. His parents were Joseph D. and Sarah C. Jacobs. Hervey's boyhood is easily pictured by one familiar with New England life. The summer he gave to the labors of the farm; the winter found him at work in the school-room. Every seventh day came a respite from this simple round of duties, and the youth, accompanied by his brothers and sisters, and guided by his parents, went up to the house of God. Quiet and simple indeed was this life, but in his case, as in thousands of others, there came out from it a strong and noble character. At the age of eighteen the farmer's boy looked out upon the great world. The importance of attaining a better education than could be furnished by the district school, was impressed upon him, and he decided to prepare for college. Norwich presented the two-fold advantage of an excellent Academy and a home in the family of his maternal uncle; and thither he directed his steps. This was in the autumn of 1856, and on the 29th of September of that year, the name Hervey Fitz Jacobs was enrolled

---

For the materials of this sketch the writer is indebted to L. A. Gallup, Esq., of Norwich, Connecticut.

on the books of the Norwich Free Academy. It was not long after this time that the young student became a learner in the school of the Great Teacher, and began that new and better life which has no end.

Three years glided swiftly away, and the prescribed course of preparatory studies was finished with honor. Among the closing exercises of the Academy was the reading of an essay by Jacobs. His theme was, " National Progress dependent upon the Efforts of the Scholar." This was in July, 1859. He little thought then that to secure *our* nation's progress, he would soon be called to buckle on the warrior's sword,— that only four years hence, the anniversary of that festive day would find him in a southern city, dying from wounds received in battle for his country.

July 8, 1859, young Jacobs was admitted to the coming Freshman Class of Brown University. Those who knew him then will recall his mild blue eyes, his ruddy face, and his compact frame. As a scholar his rank was above the average. During his first term in college, he received the appointment of Class President. Frank and genial, he was a good companion, and deservedly popular among his classmates. Says one who knew him well in college: " He was one who entered at once into your confidence and love. He once remarked to me when speaking of a fellow-student who had complained of the coldness of the people of Providence: 'I believe the fault is his own. I always had all the friends I ever cared for.' Above all, I esteem him for his consistent Christian life. Though not a member of a Christian church, he cherished the hope that he had experienced a change of heart. Scarcely have I lost a friend whose memory is dearer to me than that of my classmate."

Early in 1861, Jacobs left college and entered the store in Norwich, of his uncle, L. W. Carroll, Esquire. Here the rebellion found him. At the very outset of the struggle the question of enlistment presented itself to his mind, but the oft-repeated predictions of many over-sanguine prophets that sixty or ninety days would see the end of the war, together with his newly formed business relations, sufficed to keep him at home. He was, however, no indifferent spectator of the unwonted scene which the country presented. Politically in favor of the abolition of slavery, he early foresaw that the rebellion would result in the destruction of this relic of barbarism, and in the complete triumph of the principles of the Declaration of Independence. The year 1861 wore away, and then the early months of 1862, and still the rebellion existed with scarcely diminished proportions. The question of duty became still more urgent.

The July call of the President for three hundred thousand men to serve nine months came. It was thought that during their term of service an overwhelming blow might be struck, and the war finished. Young Jacobs desired to have some part in the great work of saving his country. He also felt that of all his father's sons he was the one to enter the army, since he was unmarried and was in other respects more favorably situated for such action than his brothers. Thus the conviction of duty grew upon him.

When the papers for a company of infantry were received in Norwich, he was ready. His name was among the first upon the roll. This was August 28th, 1862, and, on September 5th, the company was organized, at which time Jacobs was chosen Second Lieutenant. At once the young officer commenced the work of preparing himself and his men for active service. It is, however, unnecessary for us to dwell upon the routine of camp life, and we turn to notice for a moment two or three scenes of a more private and personal nature.

The first of these occurred soon after his election to the position of Lieutenant. A large party of friends gathered at the residence of his uncle and presented the young officer with sword, sash and belt. His response to the presentation speech gave evidence that no romantic or ambitious views impelled him to the field, but simply a stern sense of duty. Again, a little later, we see him visiting for the last time the scenes of his childhood. His afflicted friends will never forget that visit. The daily gathering at the family altar will long recall the hour when their brave young soldier knelt with them and implored the blessing of God. We next see him parting from his friends in Norwich, where he had found a second home in the house of his uncle, Mr. L. W. Carroll. Here he had spent the three years of his preparatory course, and the year and a half of his business life. To take leave of these kind friends was a sad duty. As he bade his aunt adieu, both were deeply moved. If it had been the parting of mother and son, it could not have been more tender and affectionate.

The two months of preparation were now over, and, November 13, 1862, the Twenty-Sixth Connecticut broke camp and embarked for New York on the steamer Commodore. Arriving in that city the regiment went into camp at East New York, and remained there till December 4, when it again broke camp and embarked on the steamer Empire City. The destination of the regiment was then unknown. Two weeks later, after a somewhat rough passage, during which Lieutenant Jacobs suffered much from sea-sickness, the troops disembarked at Camp Parapet, Carrollton, Louisiana. Here they remained for five months. During this time the regiment was engaged in performing garrison duty and in receiving instruction in regimental and brigade movements. It was attached to the First Brigade, Second Division, Nineteenth Army Corps. General Neal Dow commanded

the brigade, and General T. W. Sherman, of Port Royal fame,
the division. We give the two following extracts from letters
of Lieutenant Jacobs, written during the period of delay. They
exhibit the character of the man :—

"CAMP PARAPET, January 28th, 1863.

"DEAR UNCLE :—

"Your letter dated December 31st, 1862, came to hand on
the 26th instant, having been a long time on its passage. However, it was received, and afforded me no less pleasure. Its contents were exactly what I wanted to hear. The new store, the
church, and many other things you were pleased to mention, are
subjects of interest to me. Please accept my thanks for taking
the trouble to write to me while you are so busy. You probably
have not thought that it is just two years ago to-day since I left
Brown University and came into your store. How quickly the
years fly away; yet I can but acknowledge they have passed
pleasantly as well as profitably. But I did not think at that time
that at the expiration of two short years, I should be found in
arms on rebel soil. How fortunate it is that the future is
unknown to us. * * * I still hold to the same principles as
regards the right and wrong of slavery, but I was deceived in
regard to the ability, intelligence and energy of the freedmen.
Many are indolent, and some are reported to have starved outside
our camp. Yet I have visited sugar plantations and seen the
carpenter, the cooper and the blacksmith using their tools with
the same ease and skill as our northern mechanics. Education is
the secret of our success, and the want of it is one of the most
important causes of their present degraded condition. The
majority of the people in this section of country are of French
descent, short, of rather dark complexion, and in general appearance rather slovenly. They are decidedly of the secesh order,
even in their outward appearance. * * * The soil is rich and

32

fertile, such as we are not accustomed to see in Connecticut and Rhode Island. A man of means and business tact, I think, might be very successful in agriculture here.

"Please let me hear from you again, soon.

"I am, yours,

"H. F. JACOBS."

A month later he wrote the following:—

"CAMP PARAPET, LOUISIANA, March 2, 1863.

"DEAR UNCLE:—

"Words fail to express how happy I am in reading your kind letter of the 16th of January, which I have just received. How can I reciprocate so kind a favor otherwise than by writing you a few lines in return, and this can be but a poor compensation, as no words or letter that I can write can produce half the pleasure that yours has afforded me.

"I am happy to learn that you are well and able to perform your daily duties, the amount of which I think I can well conceive, judging from what they were when I left; and at this time, complicated in the multitudinous affairs, both public and private, and by your ability and natural inclination to industry, I think they have not materially diminished. I should like to meet and spend an hour in social intercourse with you, but time is fast flying away, and three or four months will soon be gone, and if my work shall have been done in this capacity, and I— be it the will of our Common Protector—then survive, I shall probably avail myself of the first favorable opportunity of looking in upon you. But what is before me I know not. When I see the strong, able-bodied stricken down to-day, and to-morrow borne lifeless behind a corps of muffled drums, and when I turn my eyes westward and see the newly-turfed mounds that are rapidly coming to view, I see the future destiny of many, more plainly than words can tell. And it is only the finger on Time's dial-plate that can point out the man, the next, and his successor, that shall be relieved of his volunteer duties in his country's cause. We all hope with cheerful hearts, as we perform our daily duties, that at the expiration of our term of service, should it not occur before, peace will welcome us all triumphantly to our happy northern homes.

"I cannot say I do not enter with my whole heart into the work in which I have engaged, or that I am disheartened either by the prolongation of this unjust war, or through fear of the impending battle. The same part that I enlisted to play in this national drama I still stand ready to perform. Yet I look forward with pleasure to the time when I shall be relieved of my voluntary obligations, and shall be permitted to engage in peaceful pursuits, which are more congenial to my nature.

"In camp there is nothing new worthy of mention. We have company, regimental, and brigade drills daily. Our active little General manœuvres the brigade twice a week. We are constantly receiving reports that we are on the eve of our departure, but they come so often and our destinations are so numerous, that they create distrust and are believed unreliable.

"The country and climate are now delightful. The air is filled with the perfume of fragrant flowers. All kinds of vegetation grows rapidly and luxuriantly. * * * *

"With much love to all, I am, yours truly,

"H. F. JACOBS."

Notwithstanding the proclamations of dame rumor, over two months passed after the writing of the above letter before the Twenty-Sixth Connecticut left Camp Parapet, and moved up the river. During this period of preparation for active service, Lieutenant Jacobs was constantly at work, and, by his ability and cheerfulness in the performance of whatever duty devolved upon him he secured many friends, and came to be regarded as one of the best officers in the regiment. Owing to the large amount of sickness in the camp, he was detailed much of the time to command companies destitute of officers, and thus developed independence and self-reliance.

At length the monotony of camp life was interrupted by the reception of orders to embark at once on board the steamer Crescent City, then lying at the levee. This was on the 20th of May, 1863. The order was obeyed with alacrity. Every soldier felt that active service in the field was now at hand. Reports of movements up the river had been circulating for some time. General Banks had crossed the Mississippi, and was rapidly advancing to the rear of the rebel works at Port Hudson. Fighting had already commenced. The dread work of war for which the patriot sons of Connecticut had enlisted was just before them, and every pulse beat quicker at the thought. Lieutenant Jacobs was gratified at the prospect. He had often said that he would rather take the chances of battle than to return home without once having met the rebels face to face.

Four days after embarking, two of which had been spent in guarding artillery at Springfield Landing, the Twenty-Sixth arrived in the rear of the Port Hudson batteries, and assumed its place in the brigade to which it belonged. Introduction of these men to the real business of war came without delay. At five o'clock of the same day of their arrival upon the field, they were ordered to "fall in" and charge the enemy's rifle-pits. The charge disclosed the fact that the pits were deserted, and also exposed the regiment for the first time to artillery fire. The division of General Sherman, to which the Twenty-Sixth belonged, had moved up from the south of Port Hudson to meet General Banks' army which was descending from above. At the close of this day the two bodies of troops were not far apart, and Lieutenant Jacobs, with his company, was ordered to open communication with General Augur's pickets on the right. This movement was executed promptly in the face of the enemy. This first day's experience in the business of war, was only a foretaste to what occurred three days after. On the morning of the 27th of May, the troops were early in motion. The light artillery responded sharply to the rebel fire, and there was every indication that serious work was at hand. After marching and countermarching, and advancing through thick woods until about two and a half o'clock, P. M., the Twenty-sixth Connecticut, with the other regiments of its brigade, was ordered to charge the rebel works. The brigade was formed in column by regiments, and the Twenty-Sixth was the second in the column. General T. W. Sherman led the charge in person. In the advance, which was at double-quick time, the smouldering ruins of a large plantation house that had just been burned by the pickets, together with the passing of several fences, caused the brigade to become somewhat confused. On they went, however, till they reached the open field in front, and within easy range of the rebel works. Here they were met by a murderous fire. They did not cease the advance, however, till it became evident that to continue was certain death, and that nothing could be accomplished, as the enemy had every advantage. This fight lasted little more than half an hour. The number who were killed and wounded in this short time, will attest the bravery of the advance. Out of about two thousand men in the brigade, one-fifth or four hundred were killed or wounded. Among these were General Sherman, who lost a leg; General Neal Dow, wounded and afterwards taken prisoner; Colonel Kingsley, Twenty-Sixth Connecticut, dangerously wounded in the mouth; Colonel Cowles, One Hundred and Twenty-Eighth New York, killed; and Colonel Clark, Sixth Michigan, wounded and carried from the field. The Twenty-Sixth lost one hundred and seven killed and wounded. Of this number, nine were in Company F, (of which Lieutenant Jacobs was an officer.) After the repulse, Lieutenant Jacobs, regardless of the rain of rebel bullets, remained on the field, and rendered all the assistance in his power to his wounded comrades, till his company was ordered to reform with its regiment. It is the testimony of those who were with him in this his first engagement, that he showed coolness and bravery unsurpassed by any.

From the 27th of May till June 13th, the men of the division, in addition to their other duties, were busily engaged in building magazines and earth-works for artillery, and in digging rifle-pits. These labors, carried on as they were, night and day, were very exhausting to the soldiers, and, naturally enough, evoked some murmuring. Lieutenant Jacobs remained at the post of duty all the time, and by his example and words cheered his weary men.

Saturday, the 13th of June, was marked by skirmishing and heavy artillery firing all along the line. Every one was satisfied that this presaged a more general and determined strife on the morrow. The men of the Twenty-Sixth Connecticut were in fine spirits and confident of success in the coming charge. The expected orders came, and before day-break, Sunday morning, the 14th of June, the regiment was called out. After marching several miles to the extreme left of the line, it was massed with the division, preparatory to the advance. The day was bright and beautiful, but exceedingly warm. The young Lieutenant, reared in New England, amid Christian influences, himself in full sympathy with those influences, could not but feel deeply the painful contrast between these noisy preparations for war, and the peaceful observance of the Sabbath in his far-off home. Not the sweet peals of the church bells, but the angry roar of cannon now greeted his ear. Cheerful, because he felt himself in the path of duty, he nevertheless expressed his disapprobation of Sunday fighting when circumstances did not imperatively demand it.

The following extract from a letter written on the field by Captain L. A. Gallup, will give an idea of the charge, and the circumstances in which Lieutenant Jacobs received his wound:—

"HEAD-QUARTERS, TWENTY-SIXTH CONNECTICUT VOLUNTEERS,
BEFORE PORT HUDSON, LOUISIANA, June 14, 1863.

"MR. L. W. CARROLL, NORWICH, CONNECTICUT:—

"MY DEAR SIR:—Early this morning we were ordered to prepare for immediate action. Yesterday we had been skirmishing in front of our position, while our artillery was firing upon the enemy with good effect. We knew nothing of the plan of attack. Our entire division was massed on the extreme left, near the river, at daylight. Skirmishers had been deployed, and, at half-past five o'clock, General Dwight, commanding our division, ordered our brigade, commanded by Colonel T. S. Clark, to advance in column, and make a strong assault on the enemy's works where the road intersects the parapet. We supposed the ground had been reconnoitred, but it had not. Deep ravines and thick underbrush rendered an advance impossible except at a slow pace. It is said that our brigade advanced splendidly, ploying and deploying under a galling fire of shell and shrapnell. The rebels handled their artillery admirably. Lieutenant H. F. Jacobs had been detached from my company to command Company A, which is next on the right of Company F. As we were advancing up the main road in column by divisions, in easy range of the enemy, we were ordered to deploy the column. Soon after the line had been established and Lieutenant Jacobs had assumed command of his own company, (A,) a twelve-pound shell exploded between the two companies, killing four and wounding sixteen men. Lieutenant Jacobs was among the latter. He was wounded in the thigh by a ball from the shell. The bone is injured. I assisted him as well as I could to shelter, found that he was not bleeding, ordered two men to take him from the field, bade him good bye, and advanced up the road.

"I cannot describe my feelings when I was compelled to leave the Lieutenant. He was cheerful and hopeful. His bravery could not be exceeded as he led his men on, constantly cheering and encouraging them. All who saw him speak of him in the highest terms of praise. Since we left Connecticut he had been constantly on duty, and I had learned to regard him as a brother. Could I have shared his wound with him, I would willingly have done so. We hope to hear he is doing well.

"We were congratulated in general orders, number four, from General Dwight's head-quarters, for the bold advance we made. The loss in my company was nine wounded, two fatally. The loss in our regiment was between sixty and seventy. As soon as I can hear from Lieutenant Jacobs I will write you again. We have had a hard campaign, and are as well as we can expect.

"Yours truly,   "L. A. GALLUP."

The sad story of Lieutenant Jacobs' sufferings we may best gather from his own record. The following extracts are from his diary :—

"The morning I was shot, the regiment deployed from column by divisions into a line of battle. We were advancing steadily in front of the works, the rebels firing all the time. I called out to Company A, as I commanded it, 'Come on, boys, we are going over the parapet,' and I thought so, when a ball brought me to the ground. I was wounded about six o'clock, A. M., (14th June,) and was carried from the field. I had to ride to the old cotton press, where my wound was dressed at seven, P. M. I remained there till nine, A. M., 15th, when I was carried to Springfield Landing, then by steamer to Baton Rouge. Was carried to Church Hospital; wound very painful all night."

June 16th, he writes: "Out of my head half the time."

June 18: "Oh how I suffered last night. The pain from my head—my wound was almost more than I could bear."

June 19: "It seemed to me this morning as though I could not survive but a few days; strength all gone. Was fighting and building fortifications all night under heavy fire. Have suffered much to-day."

June 21: "In great pain all day."

June 22: "Woke up this morning feeling quite smart, but have since been quite sick."

June 24: "Kept quiet as possible all day. Pain unceasing. Cannot sleep. Head hot almost all the time."

June 25: "Moved this morning from Church Hospital to the officers' hospital. Was carried in my bunk. Got along well till I was taken out and put upon an iron bestead, when pain was excruciating."

June 26th: "Am fast losing strength. Am conscious I must die. I wanted to live to get home, but it is all right. I have tried to do my duty here. I shall make arrangements to have my body embalmed when I am dead, and sent home, as I think it will be a consolation to all my friends to have it there. I have suffered much since I was wounded, as I have lain on my back all the time. I had as great prospects to live for, and as bright, as almost any one. I should like to live, but if it is designed to be otherwise, I am reconciled."

June 27: "Feel quite smart this morning. Wound quite comfortable."

33

June 28: "Took some morphine last night, and slept till this morning. This is the best sleep I have had since I was wounded. Feel quite like myself."

June 29: "Slept till ten o'clock last night. Feel better now I can sleep. Head continues to feel heavy and dull. Think wound is doing well."

June 30. "Get along very well."

[It is evident from the hand-writing that he is fast declining, and *is not* getting along well.]

July 2: "Learned brother Wyman is sick with measles. Says will now go "—— (unintelligible.) "I expect to be on my way very soon."

This is the last date against which the dying soldier wrote. Poor fellow, he *was* on his way soon, yet not to the home, visions of which doubtless filled his troubled brain, but to another and better home where is neither sorrow nor crying, nor pain nor death. Three days and his spirit returned to God who gave it.

Wyman, to whom he refers above, was his brother, Wyman D. Jacobs, a private in Company F, Fiftieth Massachusetts Volunteers, and at that time in a hospital at Baton Rouge. Neither of the brothers knew that the other was in hospital till the day of the above entry in Hervey's diary. Only two days intervened between their deaths—the Lieutenant dying on the 5th of July, and his brother on the 7th.

The news of their comrade's death produced a sensation of profound regret in the Twenty-Sixth, then in the rifle-pits at Port Hudson. All felt that a true friend and valuable officer had been taken from them. On this point the words of a brother officer in arms, the Captain of our friend's company, may be taken as the best of evidence. The extract is from a letter written to Lieutenant Jacobs' sister :—

"I have just received the intelligence of the death of your brother, Lieutenant Jacobs. This is the saddest moment in my experience as a soldier. While your heart is bowed down under this great affliction, I feel that I can sympathize with you as but few others can. This occurrence has touched a tender place in my heart. As fellow-officers, we had associated together so much that I had come to regard him as a brother. These ties had been strengthened by mutual duties in the camp and on the battle-field, and amid the hardships of the campaign. He has died with a reputation that any soldier might envy. All who saw him on that fatal day, testify to his coolness and bravery. I can speak from personal observation. When that dreadful shell came that killed or disabled twenty men, including himself, he was cheering and encouraging his men, and pressing onward with the assurance of success. * * * * After he was wounded, the noble spirit that animated him was manifested by his refusing to be taken to the rear until all the wounded about him had been removed. Very few can appreciate my feelings when I was obliged to leave him without the power to administer to his necessities. I think he was conscious, from the beginning, of the seriousness of his wound. I am assured that his treatment was as good as could be expected. I would be resigned to the will of God, but it is difficult to see why one so noble and good should be cut down just as life was opening to him in all its most interesting features. Very few had more to live for than he. His prospects were flattering for a happy and useful life. Often has he told me of his purposes as he looked forward with happy anticipations to the time when he should return."

It was not till the middle of October that the remains of Lieutenant Jacobs arrived in Connecticut. Funeral services were held in the church near his father's residence, on the 20th of that month.   The following account appeared in the Norwich Bulletin, of October 27th.   After giving a rapid sketch of Lieutenant Jacobs' life, the report goes on to say that the funeral " was an occasion of unusual interest.   A large congregation evinced their deep sympathy with a most interesting family, in the great loss which they were called to deplore.   The coffin and hearse were draped with war-worn flags of the Forty-Seventh Massachusetts Volunteers, which were sent from Boston for the occasion, as a token of respect for a brave companion-in-arms. The pall was borne by the former commanders, teacher, and classmate of the deceased.   The services were conducted by the Reverend Messrs. Hawley and Dunning.   The feeling incident to the occasion was greatly deepened by the fact that the same mail which brought the intelligence of the death of Lieutenant Jacobs, also brought the tidings of the death of a younger brother in the same department.   Thus were the obsequies of two brothers of hope and promise observed upon the same day.   The readers of the Bulletin will call to mind many endearing recollections of the young man whose career we have so briefly sketched.   He left his home in the freshness and innocence of boyhood, and was carried back to it in early manhood, a voluntary offering to the welfare of his country."

At his grave, Mr. Elbridge Smith, his former teacher in the Norwich Free Academy, and Lieutenant Selden, of the Twenty-Sixth Connecticut, addressed the friends, both bearing testimony to the worth of the departed.   A hymn, composed for the occasion, was sung by a company of young friends.

Thus were laid to rest the ashes of the young soldier.   Noble, pure, heroic Christian in life, he sacrificed himself upon his country's altar.

A beautiful monument of Italian marble marks the spot where sleep the two patriot brothers.   Military emblems — shield, sword, and musket—adorn two of its sides, while the remaining two are occupied with tablets giving a short account of the departed. Beneath the record of the life of Lieutenant Jacobs are inscribed his last words:—

"I DIE AT THE POST OF DUTY."

CHARLES LOUIS HARRINGTON.

Class of 1864.

CHARLES Louis Harrington was born in Beverly, Massachusetts, July 12, 1843. His mother became a widow during his infancy, and he was the last survivor of her four sons, two of whom died just at the opening of a manhood of unusual promise. Charles' early years were passed in his native town, where he attended the Briscoe Hall Grammar School. He continued his studies at the High School in Salem, Massachusetts, giving attention especially to the classics. While at this school he expressed a desire to obtain a cadetship at West Point, and even went so far as to apply to Mr. Alley, then Representative in Congress from the district in which he resided. Unsuccessful, however, in his application, he diverted his thoughts for the time from a military life, and, with a classmate in the High School, entered Brown University in the fall of 1860.

During his Freshman year occurred those stirring scenes which characterized the outbreak of the rebellion. His desires for a military life were again awakened. Much of his time he spent in drilling with a volunteer company of which he had become a member. At the first call for troops he sought from his mother permission to enter the service. Twice before the year closed he repeated the request, but his mother's wishes held him back.   With regret he saw his comrades depart without him.

After the close of his first year in college he went to Wisconsin.   His desire to enter the military service followed him. He was restless and discontented, and, at length, on the advice of friends, his mother withdrew her objections, and he was left to enter the path which he had so long desired to tread.   A newly adopted resolution to live a thoroughly Christian life, only intensified his wish to serve his country, and seemed to kindle within him a warmer enthusiasm than ever in the national cause.

He writes to his mother under date of April 29, 1862:   "It seems to me as if I were made for a soldier.   I want to do my country some good if I can.   I don't fear to die.   Light is coming into my soul.   * * * Now you can have your boy's name in Beverly's Roll of Honor.   I hope he will honor God and his mother, wherever he may be. * * * When the war is over, I shall come home to see you, and I hope to show myself a true soldier of the Cross also."

His first intention was to join a Minnesota battery; but arriving in St. Louis a little too late for this, and accidentally hearing that recruits were wanted for Taylor's battery, then in active service at Corinth, he immediately went to Chicago, and enlisted in the First Regiment of Illinois Artillery, Sherman's division.

He writes of his enlistment, thus: "I start Thursday evening for the seat of war—shall arrive at my destination on Friday evening or before.   So I may be under fire next week.   I hope you will be satisfied with my course, as I did what I thought would be best for me.   Don't put too much faith in my coming back.   I've seen enough to convince me that there is a very small chance for that.   And the worst of it is, I may not fall in battle, but by disease.   There are a hundred chances to one, in favor of the latter. While I was in St. Louis, twelve hundred sick and wounded soldiers were brought up from Pittsburg Landing. Four hundred of them I saw myself, and, of these, not one was wounded—all were sick. I think nothing would sicken a young man of going to war 'for the fun of it,' more than a trip to St. Louis, and a view of the hospital boat when she is discharging her dreadful cargo. I'm not blue or discouraged—do n't think it. I would not have enlisted if I had been. I feel that I am doing right, and no man but a traitor can say nay. I only wish I had enlisted sooner."

His next letter is dated near Shiloh. He says: "We arrived at Pittsburg Landing Sunday morning, and found that our battery was stationed ten miles distant. We started afoot, but fortunately we got a ride on a baggage-wagon nearly the whole distance. We arrived at our camp this morning. We are in the advance, and shall see some rather hard fighting."

June 10, he wrote to his friends for the last time. He was evidently very ill, but he was in such good spirits, and his letter was so full of pleasantry, it was difficult to suppose his condition dangerous. He doubtless might have recovered but for a relapse consequent upon the exposures of the march, and he utterly refused to be left behind.

"So, at last," he writes, "Corinth has got to be an old story, and our cry is now to be, 'On to Memphis!' One week ago last Friday, we were startled, early in the morning, by several heavy explosions, which were very dull, giving no reverberations, like those of cannon. Various conjectures were made, and all came to the conclusion that Corinth was evacuated. Our battery was unhitched, and the men were scattered in all directions. I was at a spring, getting some water, at a little distance from camp. I happened to look up, and saw that the horses were

34

being hitched, and in five minutes from that time I was on my way to Corinth.

"We were the first battery in Corinth on the right wing. Such a ride I hope is my first and last. We tore over the ground as if we were mad.

"But taking Corinth came very near taking me also."

Then follows an account of a sudden and violent attack of fever, and of his feelings in the near prospect of death.

"I did want to see you all once more," he says, "but death would have had no pang, even if I was in a distant country, with friends far away, and strangers to close my eyes. I felt that God would receive me, sinner that I am; and it seems so bright a prospect even now, that I almost wish to go.

"I lay sick in camp two or three days, and then was sent to the Artillery Hospital, where I remained until Sunday afternoon, when I was about to be sent to the General Hospital, at Monterey. If I had gone there, I should probably have been discharged, without money and without friends. They have been doing so for the last week,—discharging every man that was not able to advance with his company. Feeling a little better, I requested that I should be sent to my company, and here I am. I can't make them think I am entirely well, and I am afraid that they will leave me behind, if they advance. But they will find me a thorn in their back if they do. For I shall pursue them, and perhaps I shall get well in the exercise. Please do n't worry about me, as I do n't feel worried at all.

"We are going to Memphis across the country, the length of our march to be determined by the condition of the railroad track, which we shall repair as we go along.

"By the way, at last I've been under fire. My duty is to take the shot, shell, or canister, as the case may be, cut the fuse of the shell, and pass it along. On the Wednesday previous to the evacuation, the enemy attacked both our right and left. We were attacked by cavalry; that was all we could see. I have n't any feelings to describe, as some have. At one minute I was kicking up my heels under a tree, thinking of you all at home, and two minutes after pulling ammunition from the limber-box about as fast as I wanted to. The air for about twenty minutes or half an hour, was full of bullets, with their 'zip! zip!' and 'w-h-e-w! w-h-e-w!' going by our ears. Once I looked up just in time to see the bark fly off from a tree about two feet from me, in a line with my head. But I didn't have time for thinking or wondering. All I had to do was to see that I cut the fuse right. N. B.—Secesh 'skedaddled.'

"Should I never write again, may our dear Father bless you all."

The next intelligence was received from the captain of his company, announcing his death, June 25, of typhoid fever. Everything that soldiers on a hurried march can do for a comrade was done for him, during his illness.

They laid him to rest in a grove by the roadside, at Lafayette, Tennessee, where he still sleeps. His mother survived him but one year,—as truly a victim of the war, as the son upon whom her hopes for life were centred.

His captain wrote: "He gave promise of making a fine soldier, and is a great loss to us." And messages from his companions came, which showed how much he had become endeared to them in sharing the enthusiasm and the sufferings of a noble cause. Dying before he had completed his nineteenth year, the red flood of war overflowing his grave by the roadside so early in the struggle, his life seems but a blighted promise. And yet, who will say that even one month of whole-souled service could have been given to the armies of the Union in vain?

MATTHEW McARTHUR MEGGETT.

Class of 1864.

ATTHEW McArthur Meggett, son of Alexander and
Sarah Meggett, was born in Chicopee Falls, Massachusetts, July 24, 1836. The story of his life is but a simple record
of the struggles of a poor boy, who desired the benefits of a liberal education, not so much for the sake of learning, as to make
it the means by which good could be accomplished. He early
evinced an interest in the subject of religion, and deep religious
feelings marked his whole life. It is natural that a young lad
thus constituted, should look to the ministry of the Gospel as the
proper sphere for his efforts in life, and that a Christian mother
should hope to see such a son consecrated to the duties of the
ministerial office.

His father's death occurred when Matthew was but eight
years old. This event left a deep impression on his mind, which
is frequently discovered in his letters and journal. The subject
of death often engaged his thoughts, while anxious fears of his
own unfitness for that last solemn change, often vexed his heart.
"I often think of death," he says, "and ask myself the question,
Should I be prepared, if Christ should call me now? I fear I
should not. Faith in Jesus Christ is the only thing that can
make the dying bed feel soft as downy pillows are. Possessing

this faith, the Christian need have no fears when entering the dark valley, for Christ is there to accompany him. His rod and His staff will comfort and sustain him." And again: "May we all," referring to his immediate family, "so live that we shall be prepared to die whenever God calls for us to leave the world. This is my heart's wish and prayer to God."

As his boyhood was necessarily devoted to manual toil, for the support of himself and of his aged mother, he could not avail himself of the advantage of a common school education. In after years, when he commenced his studies, this proved a very serious hindrance,—one, too, which he often deplored when he experienced the increased disadvantages under which he labored when he came to realize these deficiencies. "I feel the need," he writes to his mother, " of that early training which was lost to me, and which I ought to have had to make me a good scholar." He hoped, however, by diligence in his studies to make up much which he had' lost; and feeling that his circumstances were such as the Lord had willed, he determined to leave all with Him, trusting that He would in His own good time and way accomplish for him what his own strength could not secure.

In the year 1842, his family removed from Chicopee Falls to Slatersville, Rhode Island, where Matthew, though but a child, was employed in a mill. After some years he united with the Congregational Church in that place. His pastor, the Reverend S. A. Taylor, now dead, became deeply interested in the young disciple, and, with other friends, encouraged his desires of obtaining an education. At length, when the fitting time to commence the work seemed to have arrived, he was influenced by good and kind friends to enter Phillips Academy, at Andover, Massachusetts. This event, so important to him, as it was the first step in an enterprise which he had long anticipated with no little anxiety, occurred in the spring of 1854.

The undertaking did not prove at first an encouraging one. He realized now, in its fullest extent, the need of that solid foundation for an education which is best laid in the systematic drill of the common school. He had been so unused to study that, when he attempted it, he found his mind wholly undisciplined. It required time to learn how to study, and it is not surprising that when he sat down to his daily lessons he often seemed to be involved in an almost inexplicable maze. Continued exertion, however, did much to remove the difficulty which at first had appeared insurmountable, and he hoped by faithful attention to his duties to make amends, in the course of time, for all he had lost. His letters written from Andover always evinced persevering effort, filial affection and religious zeal. " I am often discouraged," he says, " when I see how much is to be done, and how difficult it is for me to do it. I try, however, to look on the bright side, and am determined to struggle on. I have advantages beyond many others, and my trust is in God."

" I have been thinking of mother to-night. I hope she is not lonely. It often makes me feel sad to think that I have to leave her alone while I am here endeavoring to get an education."

And again, as vacation draws near, and he begins to look forward to a short respite from study, he writes: " I have had thoughts of home to-day. In a few weeks I hope to be there, to see mother and to have a pleasant rest and a good time at home."

In all religious enterprises he took a deep interest. He was very active in the Sunday school, first as a pupil and later as a teacher. It was the custom of some of the pupils at the academy to meet together on some appointed evening during the week, for social conference and prayer. In these meetings Meggett felt the liveliest interest. He always considered that it was his duty to do what he could for Christ, while it was ever his pleasure to declare himself upon the Lord's side. " It was my privilege," we find written in his journal, "to lead the prayer meeting to-night. I felt that God was with us. Some of our classmates are becoming personally interested in the subject of religion."

His course was somewhat broken, as occasionally he left school for a while to replenish his funds. On returning to studies, it was all the more difficult for him to make up what his class had passed over during his absence, but he was becoming more used to study, and growing more confident of ultimate success. His persevering, conscientious spirit of industry gained for him the sympathy and esteem of his teachers, who gave him from time to time, such assistance in the preparation of his lessons as they could render. He speaks with feeling of their kindness and patience, thanking God that it had been his lot to have such instructors. There were also older students in the academy who often assisted him. He refers, not unfrequently, with gratitude to one who had first interested him in the school, had been of much service to him while there, and had promised him such aid as was in his power whenever he should enter college. In accordance with the advice of this friend, he relinquished the idea of entering Amherst College, in favor of Brown University, which he entered in the fall of 1858.

His limited means caused him almost unceasing anxiety, and now that he had entered college it became still more essential for him to increase them as much as he was able. To do this he gave instruction in the public evening schools of Providence during the winter of the year in which he entered Brown. He shrank from no honest employment in which he might gain even a little to assist him in his course. But these supplies were not adequate to his wants and necessities. He remained in college, therefore, hardly a year at this time. Two years were then passed in teaching. He was engaged most of the time in Woonsocket, Rhode Island, where he was successful as a teacher, esteemed as a gentleman and friend, and respected as a Christian.

In the autumn of 1861, he resumed his studies at Brown, entering now the class of 1864. He naturally experienced no little regret, when he thought of his former classmates, now Seniors, but he found many friends in the class with which he connected himself; and, though quiet and unassuming, gained their sympathy and affection. As at school, so in college, whatever he did was accomplished by perseverence and industry. His was not a mind to grasp a subject on the instant, but by work he laid hold of its principles and made them his own. His religious zeal did not abate, but his duties as a disciple of Christ were conscientiously performed. These were to him first in the order of importance, believing that "the highest intellectual attainments are of but minor importance when compared with even a slight degree of spiritual advancement."

From the first breaking out of the Rebellion, Meggett felt it his duty to enlist in the army. The thought of his aged mother, mourning over her separation from her "young Benjamin," as she often called him, was all that restrained him from entering the ranks at once. For some time he battled with his conviction of duty, but, at length, when near the close of his Sophomore year, there came from the President another call for men, he decided to go. Saturday, May 24, 1862, he wrote in his journal:

"I have been thinking a great deal to-day about entering the service with those who enlist for three months. Ex-Governor Dyer goes on with a fine company from Providence, and I should like to go with him. He will have none but moral men in his company, it is said. I look upon my going as a duty. I shall be ashamed to say that I contributed nothing by way of personal

35

sacrifice toward restoring my country. I will try, however, to settle the question of my going in the right manner."

He communicated his feelings to Doctor Sears, President of the University, and to Doctor Blodgett, of Pawtucket, his pastor. He also prayed that God would direct him aright. At length, having gained the consent of his mother, he enlisted, with several other students from Brown, in Company B, Tenth Regiment Rhode Island Volunteers. It pained him to leave his friends, and especially his mother; he was sad, too, at the thought that he had now broken in upon his studies once more, but in his country's call for armed men he heard the voice of God speaking to him, and he could not be true to his convictions of duty and remain quietly at home.

On the 27th of May, 1862, the regiment left Providence. Proceeding to Washington direct, and thence to Tenallytown, it was assigned to garrison duty in the defences of Washington. Some changes in the situation of the regiment were afterwards made, but it soon returned to its first position, where it was located during the remainder of its period of service. Meggett writes to his brother: "Our 'mess' is mostly made up of college boys. Almost all are pious, and not an oath is heard in our tent. We had a prayer meeting Sunday afternoon, at which Captain Dyer and Lieutenant-Colonel Shaw were present and made some remarks. It was an impressive meeting. We have prayers also in our tent every night."

In all his letters home, he spoke cheerfully of his condition as a soldier, expressing himself contented in camp, and by no means sorry for the step which he had taken. In his last letter to his mother, written a short time before he was taken sick, he speaks of his return home with pleasure, and lovingly plans what he will then do for her comfort and delight.

On Sunday, August 10th, Matthew went into the hospital, and was attended by Doctor Wilcox. He had not been well for some days before. It was thought at first, by himself and by his friends, that he was suffering from a slight attack of camp fever, which had been prevalent among his comrades. The disease assumed a graver form, however, in a few days, and was pronounced by the physician typhoid. Under date of August 17, a friend, at Meggett's request, wrote to his mother, informing her of his condition; saying that, as they expected to start for home in a few days, it might be necessary to leave him behind in the hospital, but that he would be well cared for by friends who were then with him. The next day, August 18, 1862, the Reverend Doctor Blodgett, of Pawtucket, received from the Chaplain of the Tenth, the Reverend A. H. Clapp, the following telegram: " Please inform Mrs. Sarah Meggett that her son Matthew died this morning. Remains will be embalmed and forwarded by express. Particulars by mail." It was not until a day or two after this telegram was received that the letter, which was kindly intended to prepare the mind of his loving mother for what might follow, arrived by mail.

His bereaved friends could hardly credit the startling intelligence that he who had left them strong and vigorous, and apparently for so short a time, had been cut down by death just on the eve of his return to the loved ones at home. The sad news was soon verified by the letter promised by the Chaplain. It came with the particulars of his death, bearing testimony to the confiding trust in his Savior's love with which he fell asleep.

Religious services were held in the hospital on Sunday, the day before he died, "and it was noticed that Matthew did not take that interest in those exercises which he ordinarily manifested, as he was too drowsy to realize what was going on." At about ten o'clock in the evening of that day, the physician informed the Chaplain that he considered his case very critical, and that he had doubts whether he could live. Hastening to his bedside, Mr. Clapp found that he had been suffering very much, though he seemed then somewhat relieved. He looked up, recognized his Chaplain, and expressed his pleasure in seeing him. "You feel discouraged about me, do n't you?" said Matthew. "No, not discouraged," was the reply. "We hope you may yet be well, and go home with us. You know that all is possible with God. He can raise us from the weakest state if He sees best." "Yes," he answered, "and He knows best." He then said that he knew that he was very sick, and when he caught the word "Savior" from the Chaplain's lips, he cried out, "He is *my* Savior. I can cheerfully leave all with Him." "Can you say, 'I know whom I have believed, and am persuaded that He is able to keep that which I have committed unto Him against that day?'" "These words express my feelings exactly," said he; "they are just what I was saying this morning to mother and sister, and they are of the same mind with me." After reciting some passages of Scripture, among them the twenty-third Psalm, the Chaplain rose to leave him, Matthew eagerly grasped his hand, and bade him "good night."

One of his comrades watched with him then until midnight had passed. After this hour he said little that was coherent. About two o'clock in the morning, he revived a little, and, seeming to think that he had been in a religious meeting, said: "What a beautiful meeting we have had. I have enjoyed it very much. And now, brethren, before we close, I want to tell you how much I have enjoyed it. My hope is bright, and I am determined to press toward the prize for the high calling of God." His mind then became confused, and these were the last words he uttered.

He lingered along, breathing very heavily at times, until about six o'clock of the morning of the 18th, when he began to respire more slowly, " and, at quarter past six," says one who stood by his bedside, " he quietly ceased to breathe; not the faintest struggle marking the moment of departure."

> " How blest the righteous when he dies !
> When sinks a weary soul to rest !
> How mildly beam the closing eyes !
> How gently heaves the expiring breast !
> So fades a summer cloud away ;
> So sinks the gale when storms are o'er ;
> So gently shuts the eye of day ;
> So dies a wave along the shore ''

The telegram previously mentioned, was at once sent to his home in Pawtucket, Rhode Island.   And, as it was expedient to the success of the embalmment that there should be as little delay as possible, funeral services were held that day in the afternoon. . Three companies were present. The body was then taken to Washington and embalmed, after which it was forwarded to his friends.

In accordance with the request of his company, the funeral services in Pawtucket were delayed until their return home. The regiment arrived in Providence on the morning of August 28, 1862, and, on the day following, his funeral was solemnized in the Congregational Church, Pawtucket. His comrades-in-arms were present to take part in those last sad offices of respect and affection.   His pastor, the Reverend Doctor Blodgett, together with the President of Brown University and the Chaplain of the Tenth regiment, bore cheerful testimony to his faithful, earnest, devoted Christian life.   And then we laid him away in the tomb, to sleep that sleep which shall know no waking, till the trump of the archangel shall summon him from the grave, to a glorious share in the resurrection to the life eternal.

EUGENE SANGER.

UGENE, the youngest son of Charles H. and Hannah J. Sanger, was born at Waltham, Massachusetts, November 5, 1842. In his early youth his parents removed to Concord, New Hampshire. Here he received the usual common school education. A bright, handsome boy, inclined to study, he was unfortunately kept out of school for a year or two, and deprived of his mother's care by her suffering from a distressing malady.

In 1859, Eugene entered the family of the Reverend S. Farrington, pastor of the Unitarian Church in Concord, who was attracted by the promise which Eugene's disposition gave of his profiting by a liberal education. Under Mr. Farrington's instruction and at his expense, Eugene was fitted for college, and entered Brown University in September, 1860.

His Freshman year passed without any unusual event. Eugene was quiet, studious, always attentive in recitation, maintaining a rank in his class fully up to the average. He was beloved and respected by his classmates, though his retiring disposition led him to form few if any intimate friendships.

At the close of his Freshman year, he returned to Mr. Farrington, who, in the meantime, had removed to East Bridgewater,

Massachusetts. Full of interest in what he had seen of military preparation in Providence, he was enthusiastic regarding the war. The disaster at Bull Run made it clear to his mind that his place was in the army. He obtained a reluctant consent to his enlistment from Mr. Farrington, and a conditional one from his father. At this time, July 27, 1861, he writes thus to his brother Austin, who was a private in the Second New Hampshire Volunteers.

"I want to enlist, and Mr. Farrington has given his consent, and I have written to father, and he says I may go, and join your company if you will say that I had better come. *Now, Austin, I want you to write and tell me to come.* I can stand it as well as you. I have never been sick as much as you, and honestly think I can stand the marching and other inconveniencies of a soldier's life as well as a great many others. * * * I know what I shall have to put up with if I enlist, and shall make up my mind to make the best of it, and to do my duty and not run."

Alluding to his disinclination to be a burden on Mr. Farrington, he gives the real reason of his desire to enlist: "I feel as though I could be of more use, and be better satisfied with myself, as a soldier than I can now." The desire to do his duty and to be of use to his country was always the controlling motive which regulated his conduct.

His letter, as might be expected, received a negative reply. Accordingly, Eugene, in deference to the wishes of Mr. Farrington, returned to college at the beginning of his Sophomore year. He devoted himself to his college duties with his usual assiduity. His thoughts, however, continued to run in the same channel, and his only wish was to enlist. October 15th, he writes to his brother: "Father is trying to obtain for me a situation in one of the New York regiments as one of the medical staff." If he does not obtain this, he threatens to enlist as a private. Every topic he writes about at this time, and everything he sees, leads him in one direction. " I can hear," he says, " the orders of an officer, drilling a squad of men, and I wish I were doing as they are, only in your camp. Things are going along about as usual in college; nothing of any importance happening, except studying and recitation, and they are too old to be new. 'Left! left! left!' I can hear the drill-master say, but still they will break step."   Again, he says: " You need not be surprised to see me walk into your camp sometime when you do not expect me, with my knapsack strapped upon my back and my rifle slung upon my shoulder, singing ' Glory Hallelujah,' or 'America.' "

He remained at Brown till November, when he wrote home so earnestly asking to leave college, that Mr. Farrington did not any longer feel at liberty to withhold his consent. His father's positive refusal to sign his enlistment papers was a fresh obstacle in the way of his plans. He passed the winter uneasily at Concord, still longing to be in the army. In the spring he returned to East Bridgewater, where he passed an equally uneasy summer, engaged in teaching a grammar school.

When the first call for three hundred thousand volunteers was made, the question of duty was solved so far as he was concerned.   He felt that he ought to devote himself to his country in its hour of peril.   How strong was this conviction of duty, may best be judged by the following extract from a letter to his father, dated August 3, 1862 :—

" You will no doubt be very much surprised to learn that I have enlisted, that is, have put my name down to go to the war, as one of the quota from East Bridgewater. The reason why I have done so, is that I think the time has come when everybody, who is able to bear arms, ought to go and do his part towards sustaining this government in the execution of the laws. As I

36

am willing and able to go, and am well and strong enough to handle a musket, I am sure that it is my duty to do my part in this work. I have not made up my mind *rashly*, but have thought it over, and have considered the hardships, the pleasures and the dangers of camp life. I am finally convinced of my *duty* to go, and have given up my school, and hope to go into camp in a week or ten days. Five of my friends in this town have enlisted —the High School teacher, a young lawyer, another High School teacher, two mechanics, besides several whom I do not know. The quota for the town is forty-three, and we hope to have it filled this week. We have the choice of our regiment and company, so that we can go *into a good regiment*. We talk of the Thirty-Fourth Massachusetts Regiment. I will let you know as soon as we are in camp, where we are. I have had the advice of Mr. and Mrs. Farrington in regard to this step, and have their entire approval, and I hope that I shall have yours also. I know that you have given one son to the cause, and feel unwilling to give another. But if the cause is not worth fighting for, why are we fighting? and if it is worth fighting for, then it is worth our lives, and I, for one, am *ready and willing* to give up my life to assist in putting down this accursed Rebellion. Do not try to discourage me, for I am perfectly satisfied that it is my duty, and I am going to try and do it. If I lose my life in the cause, I shall have given it for the best cause in the world, and one worth many such lives. Some lives must be sacrificed, and I am willing that mine should be one."

August 8, he writes to his brother Austin, informing him of the enlistment of a friend, and adds: "I am also to be in the same regiment, the Thirty-Eighth Massachusetts, for I have enlisted, been examined, and this evening shall take the oath. Father has given his consent, as have also Mr. and Mrs. Farring-

ton.   Quite a large number of young men here have enlisted,
who have given up a great deal at home and go with patriotic
feelings, and will make good soldiers.   * * * *   We shall go
with the Plymouth company, in the Thirty-Eighth Massachusetts, under Colonel Paul Revere; that is, he is spoken of as the
Colonel, and I hope that he will get the appointment.   He, as
you probably recollect, was Major of one of the Massachusetts
regiments, and was taken prisoner at Ball's Bluff, kept at Richmond six months, and finally exchanged.   We shall go into camp
at Camp Stanton, Lynnfield, Massachusetts, next week."

The regiment, when organized, was ordered to Baltimore.
Here it was stationed, doing guard duty with an Indiana battery.
Eugene was not satisfied with this probationary life, though he
admits its necessity in a letter to his brother Austin, of September 28th: "I hope that our regiment will move soon towards
Washington, or somewhere, for I am tired of staying here.   I do
not think the regiment is fit to go into the field yet.   Some of
the companies are backward in drill, ours among the number.
* * *   We use the Enfield rifle, and a most miserable arm it is,
too.   Mine is a pretty fair one, but the tube was broken off once,
and the screw which holds the hammer on is lost.   A great many
are in a worse predicament than mine.   I hope we shall never
go into action with them."

Eugene's health at this time was very good and had been
most of the time since his enlistment.   In November, his regiment was assigned to the Department of the Gulf, and ordered
to report to General Banks.   Embarking on board the steamer
Baltic, the Thirty-Eighth was detained for some time at Fortress
Monroe.   Life on shipboard was monotonous and dull.   Yet, in
a letter to Mrs. Farrington, dated November 30, he says: "The
time passes very quickly indeed.   I generally rise from my soft
bed—which is my blanket laid on the soft pine floor of our

bunk — about half-past seven, go on deck, and wash from my canteen of water — if I have any left from my allowance, which is a canteen full each day. By the way, there is something curious about the water. It is the color of pale brandy, and is brought from the Dismal Swamp by United States tugs for the troops on board the transports. Our Surgeon says it is the healthiest water that can be obtained here, and that it is colored by the roots of the juniper. It does not taste much different from other water, and I have got so used to it that I like it now. After washing I go to breakfast, which usually consists of fresh bread and a poor apology for coffee."

The steamer at length arrived at Ship Island, where the regiment disembarked. Eugene, whose health had not been good while on board the transport, now gained rapidly in health and spirits. He did not, however, fancy being cooped up on a sandbar "where nothing can grow." The change of climate, however, was agreeable to him, and especially did he relish the fruits with which the regiment was supplied from New Orleans. On Christmas day, the enlisted men of the regiment were allowed to overturn the established order of things, and had a guard-mounting and dress parade under officers chosen from their own number. "The peculiarities of some of the officers, especially the Adjutant, were well taken off by our officers *pro tem.* Several of the officers were sent to their tents to have their buttons brightened. We had as good a parade as we have ever had, and none of the officers had anything to do with it, except as orderlies or privates. One of our sergeants was Captain of Company D, and I was First Lieutenant. Everything went off in tip-top shape, and proved to the officers, who think they are a clan above us in the ranks, that there were men in the ranks who are as fit to command as they are, and that they are nothing but men with shoulder-straps and broadcloth coats on their backs. In the evening, most of the officers who did not appear on dress parade were put in the guard house, and with them the Colonel and Surgeon. They court-martialed the Colonel, and the excuse he made was that the man, who was President of the Court, stole his equipments."

The regiment did not remain long on Ship Island, but was soon ordered up the Mississippi river, and went into camp at Carrollton. It remained here, and in the vicinity of New Orleans, till March. The time was chiefly spent in drill. Occasionally Eugene was employed in the Quarter-Master's Department, though most of the time he did regular soldier's duty. The gift of "a beautiful verbena, one of the deep scarlet, almost purple, just like" some at home, leads him to write thus: "This is a fine country for flowers, and, in fact, for almost everything that grows; and what a pity it is that everything is going to ruin on account of the ambition and love of power of some of its inhabitants. You can have no idea how desolate are all the plantations and towns one sees in going up and down the river. When the boat stops, you see the inhabitants lounging around the buildings, looking lazy and surly." He speaks of flocks of negroes coming to the Union station, and approves of General Banks' plan of making them work on the plantations. But, at Plaquemine, he " saw a large number of slaves, who had left their masters, driven through the streets by the Provost Guard. Their masters had taken the oath of allegiance, and were going to take their slaves home with them." He adds: " I hope I shall never be ordered to drive slaves home to their masters."

The Thirty-Eighth Massachusetts was at length ordered to Baton Rouge. During its stay at that place the regiment changed camp occasionally, making what seemed to be fruitless excursions in the mud and rain. Eugene complains that " he has not yet seen an armed rebel." In his last letter to Mrs. Farrington, dated March 25, 1863, he details his experiences in a change of camp: "I was on picket when the regiment moved, and was not relieved till after dark, and had to march all alone from the picket station to our old camp, and then to the city, (Baton Rouge,) trying to find my regiment in the dark. The road was through a swamp, and the mud was more than ankle deep. No one knew where the Thirty-Eighth had encamped, and I was unable to find it. So, after wandering around an hour or two, I made up my mind that I might as well give up the search for the night, and, with two men from the One Hundred and Sixth New York, lay down in the wet grass by a fence, and went to sleep, with only two rubber blankets. About twelve, it commenced to rain, and I was soon in a puddle of water, two or three inches deep, and the rain pouring down upon me, But as I have got the habit, as all soldiers are obliged to, of making the best of things, I lay still till daylight, and got up with most of my clothes wet through, and started again to look up the Thirty-Eighth. I finally found a negro who told me where they were encamped, and started for the place about tired out and wet through."

Few of Eugene Sanger's letters have been preserved, and the above extracts are from the last that are accessible. The tone of his correspondence shows that his enlistment was freely an act of duty, of patriotism. He cheerfully welcomed the perils and exposures of a soldier, and never repined at the absence of home comforts. His sole regret seemed to be that the results achieved were so small, and his only fear was that his comrades might become exhausted and disheartened on account of the long delay.

In April, the regiment was ordered up the Bayou Têche, and the men of the Thirty-Eighth entered upon their first really important active service. On the 13th of that month they had their first engagement, at Fort Bisland. Eugene was mortally wounded early in the action. The particulars of his death are given in letters from Lieutenant Russell, and from his intimate friend and comrade, George L. Faxon.

Lieutenant Russell writes :ⁱ. "He was wounded on our first advance, while going forward towards the entrenchments of the enemy, and was the first man to fall from our company. He, with two others, was on the extreme right of the regiment, as it was deployed, and skirting the woods on our right. We were advancing steadily against the enemy, when we were startled by a sharp fire on our flanks. It was then your son fell, shot through the side. As soon as the fire abated, he was carried to the rear, to the hospital of the One Hundred and Fifty-Sixth New York, where his wound was dressed. His comrades then returned to their posts, Eugene was carried to the rear in an ambulance. Of course no one could accompany him, for every one has his part to perform."

Mr. Faxon says : "My acquaintance with Eugene commenced at East Bridgewater. I was at that time teaching the high school in the same house where he taught the intermediate. Our acquaintance ripened into intimate friendship, which continued till his death.

"On the 13th of April, 1863, the battle of Bisland, on the Bayou Têche, was fought. Bisland is the name of the fort. It is situated about five miles above Pattersonville. Our regiment was, on the morning of the 13th, on the right bank of the Bayou Têche, as you ascend, and was ordered to advance and relieve the Thirty-First, as skirmishers. During that advance, a ball struck Eugene, and, it is supposed, entered the kidney. He suffered some pain, groaning at times. He was carried from the field. I was not with the regiment at the time, being under orders on the other side of the Bayou. Hearing of his wound, in the morning of the 14th, I commenced a search for him, intending to give him any assistance he might need. Eugene had become one of my dearest and best friends, and my anxiety for him was great. I inquired of the surgeons of the Thirty-Eighth. They could give me no information. I applied to the Medical Director of the division. He knew nothing about him. Receiving permission to remain, while the army moved on to Franklin, I passed the morning going to all the hospitals, visiting each room, examining every face. I could not find him. Still I continued my inquiries. One day I dismounted and sat down with a group of strangers under a shady tree. A Hospital Steward asked me to describe Sanger, and upon my doing so, told me that he knew him, and was with him in the hospital of the One Hundred and Fifty-Sixth New York Volunteers. He said that he bore his wound heroically, but desired to sleep, and asked the Doctor to give him an opiate. This was done. The wound he told me was mortal. Since then Company D has received notice of his death. I cannot find that notice, but the entry on the company book is: 'Died at Bisland, April 13th, 1863.' I think that this is an error, and that he died on the morning of the 14th. A Lieutenant of Company D tells me that the Surgeon of the One Hundred and Fifty-Sixth says that he saw him buried.

"You ask me to tell you of the past life of your brother Eugene while in the army. I would that my pen could do justice to him, and render all that is due to his many virtues. He came to my room in East Bridgewater, and, in conversation, told me he felt it to be his duty to go forth to fight in the sacred cause of his country. In the army his conduct was always honorable. He was attentive to his duties as a soldier, and often received the commendation of his officers. None of his company surpassed him, and few equalled him in the details of a soldier's life. He was strictly temperate, and never guilty of the profanity and vulgarity of the army, so common among many who are esteemed worthy men. He was very high minded and pure,

one of the number whose patriotism is so exalted that it admits
no doubt of success, allows no carping at the government or its
resources, but, determined in the severest trials, looks hopefully
forward. He was greatly under the influence of Mrs. Farrington;
his respect and affection for her were singularly strong, and I
need say no more to assure you of the excellence of his principles and motives, than to tell you that that lady's advice was the
magnet of his life.

"You are a soldier, and as such will best appreciate the soldier's life. To be a good man in the army, has a stronger meaning than in civil life. The vices and allurements of military life
often infest the best minds. Amid them all, in thought, word and
action, Eugene was true to himself. While we mourn the loss of
so dear a friend and brother, while all feel sad that one so amiable,
talented and good should perish so early in life, still we find consolation in reflecting on his many virtues, and in the knowledge
that he lived nobly and died bravely, and that he has only been
advanced to a better life in another world."

To this we must add what Lieutenant Russell says: "Sanger
was a great favorite with all the company, always pleasant and
genial to all, always ready to do his share of work. The first
part of the time I was with the company, Eugene was detailed
in the quartermaster's department, and was with me only a short
time. I had just appointed him acting-corporal, designing him
for the first vacancy."

"Eugene lived well," writes his friend, Mr. Farrington, to his
father. He did more—he died well. He was of quiet, unobtru-
sive habits, but of noble and steadfast purpose. His retiring disposition led him to form but few friendships, but his few friends
were strongly attached to him for his genuine manliness and self-
sacrificing devotion. He died as he had lived, caring more for

his duty than for renown, and anxious only to contribute even with his life to the redemption of his country.   He left the noble example of a brave and spotless manhood.

LEVI CAREY WALKER.

Class of 1865.

EVI CAREY WALKER was born in Hartford, Connecticut, on
the 30th of October, 1840. His father was the Reverend
William Carey Walker, and his mother Almira L. (Palmer) Walker.
His boyhood, while wanting in all sickly precocity, gave promise
of a well-rounded life. His early love of the beautiful in art
and in literature, his rare keenness and studious inclinations, his
indomitable perseverance in the pursuit of knowledge, alike
heralded a future of distinction. At seventeen he entered the
Connecticut Literary Institution, at Suffield. Here his talents and
devotion to study soon attracted the attention of his instructors,
while his hearty frankness and genial good fellowship, placed
him in the high tide of academic popularity. Probably no period
of his life was better calculated to strengthen his powers and
develop his manhood, than the two years spent in Suffield. The
school was less provincial in its character than many academies,
and, with a thorough course of study, combined many advantages
of higher institutions of learning. These advantages Walker was
not slow to improve. Though standing first in his class in point
of scholarship, his rank was not attained through the midnight
vigil, or absence from the weekly debate. None spoke more
fluently than he, while in elegance of composition he had no

equal. The excitement, the thrill of those debates, will not be soon forgotten. To be sure, the speeches were adolescent in thought, and *sub fresh* in diction, but they kindled patriotic fires which only blood could quench, and set hearts beating that only death could still. The country was anxiously waiting the issue of the struggle at Washington, and the exciting discussions in Congress had their miniature counterpart in our weekly assemblies. Little the speakers knew how soon their patriotism was to be tested by the ordeal of battle or a southern stockade! When the summons came, class after class sent its quota to the field; and to-day the Institution can point to a roll of honor as long as that of many of her more pretentious sisters. Walker shared in the general enthusiasm, and entered a military company with the expectation of soon joining those already in the army. For good reasons, however, he delayed enlisting until the following year.

While he was at Suffield, an event took place in Walker's history which was to exert a powerful influence on all his future life. During a season of religious awakening he gave his heart to the Saviour. A high moral tone had always characterized his life, but henceforth a new, divine impulse was to possess and vivify his generous nature. "To do something for God and humanity," was the sublime desire that controlled all his future action. Two years of suffering and an early grave witness his devotion to this heaven-born aspiration.

Walker was graduated from the academy with the highest honors, and in the ensuing fall entered Brown University with the class of sixty-five. In college the same success attended him as in the preparatory school. He at once advanced to a high rank in scholarship, while his chivalric nature and sunny disposition gathered about him the choicest spirits of his class. He was no mere book-worm, but engaged as heartily in the sports of the

Campus as in the duties of the class-room. Although he identified himself with the religious interests of the college, his energy did not confine itself there, but sought other fields of usefulness beyond the college walls. The Sunday school and suburban prayer meetings were his weekly resort,—places where the memory of his pleasant face is as fresh to-day as ever.

Thus the months of the Freshman year rolled away, till May came, bringing with it the sickening news of disaster to the Union army. Stonewall Jackson had sent Banks whirling down the Shenandoah, and was driving the Union forces pell-mell into the Potomac. On the 25th, at midnight, the news reached Providence, with the pressing summons for troops; and before another sun had set the Tenth Rhode Island was under marching orders.

The college shared in the general enthusiasm, and contributed her full quota to the new regiment. Here was the long sought opportunity for Walker. With many a student, he had hesitated to leave his studies while men were plenty. But this was a louder call than had yet gone forth, and for him it had no uncertain sound. The difficulty of obtaining his parents' consent greatly troubled him. He was far from home, and, before he could hear from them, the company he had selected would be full. His diary thus briefly reveals his inward strife:—

"Monday, May 26: A great struggle in my mind this morning. The country has called for men. I want to go. Cannot consult my parents. * * * * Have at length enlisted, with a prayer that God will keep me.

"Tuesday, 27: Father has not come, and I am a soldier of the United States. I have taken an important step. * * * Whilst busy packing the knapsack, father came. He made no objection to my going, but felt rather bad. Wrote mother. Started for Washington."

How vividly do these brief pencilings call up the thrilling emotions of the young soldier, as he packs his knapsack for the first time, and ponders his unknown future. I cannot forbear quoting a part of the letter mentioned above. It speaks for the writer in better words than I can use:—

"My Dear Mother:—

"There is no thought connected with my enlistment that gives me so much pain, as that I shall by thus doing increase your burden of anxiety and solicitude on my account. * * * * I have studied to make myself worthy of your affection and your sacrifices. I know I have often erred, but as often have I repented. I do not wish to go to Washington without your full, free, hearty consent. It would shut up every avenue of pleasure, did I know that you regarded my enlistment as an act of disobedience. Never would I stir one foot against your wishes. But mother, many parents have given up their dear ones to bleed, yes, die in their country's cause. Many have gone forth from the paternal roof as dear and better fitted for life or death than I; and can you hesitate? I should think your bosom would swell with pride at the thought that you were represented in your country's struggle for liberty."

Of the departure of the regiment, and its journey to Washington, others have told. The same enthusiasm greeted the Tenth that greeted all the sons of gallant Rhode Island. The trip through Broadway, the bountiful table and hearty "God bless you" of Philadelphia, the march through Baltimore, and the repulsive fare and hard boards of the den, yclept "Soldiers' Retreat," at Washington,—what Yankee soldier can ever forget them! On the morning of the 30th, the regiment marched to Tenallytown, the sun pouring down its hottest rays. In his journal Walker writes next morning:—

" Arose somewhat lame after a long march. Spent the day hard at work pitching tents and throwing up embankments. Retired early and weary. Feel a little dispirited, but do not regret my enlistment. I am in the service of my country. God helping me, I will do my duty."

Again he writes, June 3d :—

" Have performed various camp duties. A soldier's life is rough and full of hardship, but I like it. I fear lest the wickedness abounding here, may have its influence on my character. My prayer is to God."

A classmate writes as follows :—

" He always made a point to see that the evening devotions in the tent where he messed were never omitted; and, while there were two others who shared the duty with him, when present he made it his especial charge to see that one of them at least was present between 'tatoo' and 'taps,' to conduct these devotional exercises. * * * His cheerfulnes and his wit were no less prominent than his piety, both being so well timed that all might laugh heartily at his *bon mot*, and join reverently in his evening prayer. These two elements of his character were so consistently united that irreverence on the one hand, and sanctimoniousness on the other, seemed in him impossible."

We now find the first record of illness in Walker's journal, though his comrades had long seen that he was failing under the effects of climate and the laborious work of the trenches. On Thursday, June 5th, his journal speaks of " raising blood in large quantities."

" Friday, 6th : Bleeding continues."

"Saturday, 7th: Arose very weak. Our company is on guard. Could not join them. No bleeding to-day, but do not feel much better, however."

After this he seems to have rallied sufficiently to perform the full routine of duty. Fearful of increasing the anxiety of friends at home, he writes guardedly of his illness: "I am sorry that my absence from you occasions so much solicitude, and if a candid statement of facts will relieve your anxiety, I hope this letter will accomplish the desired purpose. I was somewhat worn down and exhausted when I arrived in camp. My change of diet, united with my change of occupation, affected my system, and for a few days I was unfit for duty. The rest of the time I have been as well as usual. I perform my daily duties with the rest— even go further than some. My appetite is good. I sleep more than ever before, and am *in the best of spirits.*"

On the arrival of the regiment at Washington, the various companies had been distributed among the forts which commanded the approaches to the city. Company K, to which Walker had been transferred, was assigned to Fort Pennsylvania. On the 27th of June, the whole regiment marched to Cloud's Mills, eighteen miles distant. Twelve miles Walker marched with the rest, but was then compelled to seek the ambulance. Here the regiment remained but a day or two, when it returned to the neighborhood of the forts, marching nearly all night. The fatigue of this weary march broke Walker down completely. The dreaded bleeding again commenced, and he began to fear for his life. Sometimes he would improve rapidly for a day or two, but only to sink again under the disease. About this time we read in his journal:—

"Monday, July 28: Reported at the hospital. For the first time in a long while failed to go on guard when my turn came. Had much anxiety for friends at home."

Remaining in hospital about a week, he again reported for duty, "though weak and languid." He thus writes of the death of Meggett, one of the college boys in the regiment:—

"Many of our boys are prostrate in the hospital. One, alas! this morning, after a brief illness, passed away from earth. He was a fine fellow, full of generous impulses, a member of the Sophomore class of Brown, where he stood well as a scholar, I believe. Our camp is pervaded with sadness. The loud laugh, the shouts, are hushed while our friend sleeps. Thank God, he had the Christian's hope."

Concerning himself he again makes the following entries:—

"Thursday, August 21: I feel very sad. Life with its bright prospects to be given up! But God is good. I will try and trust.

"Saturday, 23: The doctor gives me no encouragement. I can hardly curb my feelings. * * * * To be cut down so young! *O God! I look to Thee.*"

In a few days the Tenth was on its way to Providence, bringing the sick, discouraged soldier to his yearning friends. The following are the last entries in his army journal:—

"Wednesday, August 27: Took the Bay State to-day for Providence. The sick occupy the ladies' cabin. My lung painful all day. I fear it is growing worse fast. *O God! must I die so young!*

"Thursday, August 28: Arrived this morning at Providence, both glad and sad. Sad that I was not able to march with my company,—a deep disappointment."

Such is the brief military career of Levi Carey Walker. He went to the field with as lofty a patriotism as ever inspired a Union soldier. After the Second Bull Run defeat, he resolved to reënlist, so deeply did he feel the wounds of the nation. Only the pleadings of anxious friends stayed the act which would have hastened the consummation of his great sacrifice. Walker returned a mere wreck of his former self. He had not been permitted to taste the *gaudium certaminis*, or go down in the bloody strife. But he gave to the country a life full of all noble promise, as truly as the slumbering hero of Stone River, or of the Wilderness.

For several weeks after Walker's return from the army, his friends despaired of his life. But, under their tender care, he rallied sufficiently to return to college the following February. Before the close of the year, however, it became evident that his days were numbered. And now ensued the long struggle for life. For more than eighteen months he fought his disease with all the energy of his nature. Hoping, fearing, sometimes despairing, he sought in vain for the elixir of life. The West seemed to promise lengthened days, if not recovery, and thither he turned his face. Provided with tent, gun and fishing-rod, and accompanied by a younger brother, he traversed the prairies, pierced dense forests, and camped on the banks of the Mississippi. But the vision of health dissolved into thin air before him. He tried the boasted climate of St. Paul, but returned to Wisconsin "more dead than alive." On his twenty-third birthday he writes in his journal:—

"My birthday finds me a confirmed invalid, struggling to resist the inroads of a fearful, well-nigh invincible disease. God only knows what the result may be. If I can have the supporting arm of my Saviour, I care not. Yet I am not wholly indifferent. Life is sweet. I would accomplish something for my fellow-men before I die. I hope to live, but thank God, I am not wholly unwilling to die if it be His will. Let this thought comfort the hearts of the loved ones at home, after I am gone."

On the 1st of January, 1864, we read :—

"Many have entered upon '64 who will not see its close. The sweeping scythe of Time is continually wet with the blood of his victims. I may be cut down. There is *more* than a *possibility* of this. The fangs of a fearful disease are fastened upon me, and it is struggling to make its fatal sting. I dare not promise myself one moment of futurity. Standing upon the threshold of another year, step by step I must traverse its halls, and, only as I thus progress, can I understand its mysteries. Father, I implore Thy blessing upon me. I would not take one solitary step alone. I only ask for grace that my life may be full of the fruits of Christianity, and my death be the triumphant transit of the righteous."

Again, we read :—

"April 13th: Five weeks ago to-day, I was unexpectedly made the victim of a copious hemorrhage. Raised nearly a quart of blood. For a few days was almost helpless. I shall never forget W.'s care and devotion. Friends and neighbors have been very attentive. Above all, I have had grace given me to trust my Heavenly Father and to leave myself in His hands. My experience has been so precious, so invaluable, that I do not really regret my illness. Very sick, far from home, I had much need of the consolations of religion, and they were vouchsafed to me. My soul is full of thanksgiving in view of God's mercy. If suffering can alone fit me for Heaven—if by passing through the crucible I can best glorify my Maker—then let me suffer. I ask only that my Saviour will place beneath me the Everlasting Arms. Then let the storms come, my soul shall abide beneath the shadow of His wing."

The last words written in his journal are these: "How have my hopes been blasted! Yet I thank God my trust is still firm in Him."

Fainting and weary, he now turned his longing footsteps homeward. For nearly six months he lingered, tenderly nursed by loving hands. But neither skill of man nor prayer of woman could prolong his stay. On the 21st of February, he was seized with paralysis of the right lung, and for two days his sufferings were intense. On the 23d, the pain was gone. The long struggle for life was ended. The prayer of faith was merging into the song of triumph. · Calling about him the stricken family, he breathed upon them his parting blessing, and left the last message of affection for the absent father and brother. Asking for the Sacred Word, he desired his sister to read the last prayer of Jesus, and that other passage, "To him that overcometh will I grant to sit with me in my throne." These words he repeated in a clear voice, saying: "This has always been my rallying cry when the enemy pressed close upon me, and, through Christ, I believe I have overcome." Then, at his request, some of the Sunday-school children were called in, who sung with him the last song of earth. Soon afterwards, in response to the inquiry, if all was well, he replied: "O, yes! yes! yes!" An hour of unconsciousness followed, and Walker was at rest.

The funeral services were held in the Huntington Street Baptist Church, New London, Connecticut. An address, portraying the life and character of the departed, was delivered by the Reverend Doctor Ives, of Suffield, his former pastor. The remains were then borne to the cemetery by his classmates, and tenderly committed to their last resting-place.

JAMES PECK BROWN.

AMES PECK BROWN, son of Eleazer Arnold and Charlotte Wright (Peck) Brown, was born in Rehoboth, Massachusetts, on the 4th day of November, 1844. At an early age he manifested a strong desire for a liberal education. To gratify this ambition, his parents spared no effort consistent with their means. At the age of fifteen he commenced the study of Latin, which he continued with some interruptions, until he arrived at the age of seventeen. He then began to attend the University Grammar School, at Providence, where he remained nearly two years.

He was at this school when the news of the fall of Fort Sumter came, followed by the call for seventy-five thousand men. He longed to enlist, but his parents would not consent. Deeply moved by the varying fortunes of the struggle, he repeatedly renewed his entreaties until the summer of 1862, when his parents gave their consent that he should enlist in a company with his oldest brother. He accordingly enlisted in the Tenth Rhode Island Volunteer Infantry, Company B. The regiment left Providence on the 26th of May, 1862.

No person could have been happier than this young man of seventeen as he marched through the streets with his musket

and knapsack, on the occasion of the departure of his regiment.
He felt that a new life was opening before him, and he was eager
to participate in all its experiences. Yet he felt keenly the sorrow of parting from those whom he loved.

The Tenth Rhode Island during a greater part of its period
of service was stationed at Fort Pennsylvania, near Washington.
But little duty was required of it, except that of guard and
picket. James was enthusiastic in the performance of these
duties. He seemed to enjoy the responsibility of the sentinel at
night. Yet at such times he says his thoughts were often turned
to his home and friends. His letters during this period contain
many evidences of his affectionate regard for his parents and
friends.

After his return in August, he continued his studies at the
University Grammar School, but his heart could not so readily
yield its strong desire. He longed for an opportunity to reënlist.
Meanwhile he gave much attention to military studies, drilling
with the home guards whenever he had an opportunity. In
September, 1863, having completed his preparatory studies, he
entered Brown University. His heart, however, was still with
our armies in the field, and late in the year his parents consented
to allow him to reënter the service. The Fourteenth Rhode Island
Heavy Artillery was organized at that time. He applied to Governor Smith for a commission on the recommendations of some
of his friends. He was referred to General Casey's board for the
examination of officers, then in session at Washington. He passed
a satisfactory examination, and was commissioned Second Lieutenant, January 13th, 1864. He joined his regiment at Dutch
Island, in Narragansett Bay, and started at once for the Department of the Gulf.

Strong and athletic, full of life and energy, nervous and
impulsive in his temperament, yet having so much of good feel-

ing in his heart as not to leave any room for incivility and petulance, he was well fitted for a soldier's life. One of his strongest traits was his conscientiousness. Although impulsive, he was yet to a remarkable degree moved by principle. The thought, "Is it right?" seemed almost to anticipate the consciousness of the motive for action. As a consequence he seldom erred when left to himself, in the exercise of his judgment as to the right or wrong of his proposed action. He was frank and generous in his address. He possessed a confiding disposition, and was disposed to rely, perhaps, too much upon others in matters which pertained to his outward life. The great worth of his nature he never entrusted to others. Over this reserve he always exercised a jealous control. It was easy to become acquainted with him, but relations of intimacy he sustained with but few. He commanded the respect and enjoyed the confidence of all. Those much older than himself confided in him to an unusual degree. He was dignified, yet not stiff. His dignity was that of an ambitious spirit that loved the right, and scorned to do that which was low; or it was rather a high toned self-respect which guided and controlled his whole life and nature.

On religious subjects he thought much and felt deeply. He was not a professor of religion after the established forms of any sect, but in his life he was an enthusiastic lover of truth and honor. Before leaving home the last time, he told his mother that he hoped he was a Christian.

His first leaving home opened before him a new life. It gave him a valuable experience with men, and an opportunity of seeing something of the world. His second experience was to have not less of novelty about it. He had formed the habit of making new resolutions whenever entering upon any new duty or into any new relation. The resolutions formed at this time had reference to a course of study in military science and tactics, and a close attention to all those studies and duties which would make an efficient and accomplished officer. With how much fidelity he kept these resolutions, extracts from his letters will best determine. They will also give us the best knowledge of his subsequent history. His first letter was written off Cape Florida, January 28, 1864. He says:

"DEAR MOTHER:—

"When I arrived in camp the troops were ready to go on board the transport. We sailed the next morning at seven o'clock. I was sick for the first two days, but am quite well now, and am enjoying the voyage very much. We were off Charleston about noon on Monday, and were boarded by the United States gun-boat Connecticut, of twelve guns. It has been as warm here to-day, as it is at home in July. The clouds broke over us as though we should have a thunder-storm.

    *   *   *   *   *   *   *   *

"As soon as you hear from me again I wish you to send me my geometry and French grammar."

"JANUARY 31, 1864.

"DEAR MOTHER:—

"We are now in the Gulf of Mexico, about two hundred miles from land. We shall reach the mouth of the Mississippi about Tuesday noon. I feel perfectly well. We expect to be stationed near Galveston, Texas, and it is possible that we shall be used in the attack on that place."

Under date of February 9th, he speaks of having been asked by his Captain to tent and mess with him, which invitation he accepted, as he thought it would give him a better opportunity of becoming acquainted with the duties of a soldier. February 14th, he sends directions to have one of Brewerton's automaton regiments of infantry sent to him. Under date of February 15th, writing to his youngest brother, after speaking of his situation, his camp and its surroundings, he says: "I wish to say a few words to you, suggested by my own experience. I want you to go into society more than I have done, and associate with those who are older than yourself. You will learn much in this way, which you cannot learn in any other manner. Enter into all the innocent sports of those about you. In your manner towards mother and father, you must be gentle and cheerful. Cultivate those virtues which you most admire in those about you. * * * * I am feeling very well. In a year or two I shall be at home and resume my studies with more vigor than ever."

The regiment did not go to Texas as he had expected. It became scattered throughout the country surrounding New Orleans, where the only duty it was required to perform was that of guard and picket. Company H, to which Lieutenant Brown belonged, was stationed at Plaquemine.

Writing from Plaquemine, April 13, 1864, he says:—

"I have been detached from my regiment and placed in command of the provost guard of this parish. I have thirty-six men, and they are furnished with horses. Yesterday I took twelve men, went outside of our lines about fifteen miles, and captured about ninety bales of cotton."

June 17, 1864, writing to his brother in the army of the Potomac, he says:—

"My love for the service increases daily in proportion as I become acquainted with its details of duty. I desire nothing more than a permanent position in the army. I am growing stronger and larger. I weigh one hundred and sixty pounds, and enjoy the best of health and spirits at all times. You ask me if I have discipline. I am not the best judge of that fact,

39

but I believe I have the reputation of being one of the most severe disciplinarians in the battalion."

June 27, writing to his youngest brother, he says:—

"Tell George that soldiering is to be my occupation through life. You would be surprised to see me, I have changed so much in appearance. I have grown much taller and stronger. I sometimes walk almost all night in visiting my outposts, and then read all the next day without sleep. I have kept myself free from all intemperate habits."

"JULY 9, 1864.

"DEAR MOTHER:—

"Since writing my last to you I have been quite sick with intermittent fever. I have fallen away from one hundred and sixty to one hundred and forty pounds. I am feeling better now. I have been under the care of Dr. H., a native of this State, who is practicing here."

"AUGUST 4th, 1864.

"DEAR MOTHER:—

"Our battalion has been doing picket and fatigue duty since coming to this post, but General Sherman has now ordered that we practice the manual of the piece in the heavy artillery drill. My company has target practice this afternoon. We use a thirty-two pounder, at the distance of fourteen hundred and thirty-three yards, firing solid shot, shell and canister. Each company is assigned a separate bastion. The one to which my company is assigned has three guns *en barbette.*

*   *   *   *   *   *   *   *

"You ask about my habits. I am very careful in selecting those with whom I associate. There are many temptations to do wrong, and one has to be constantly guarded. I can see in myself, and in those about me, a tendency to a certain coarse-

ness and freedom of manner which I did not notice when at
home. I suppose this is not to be wondered at, situated as we
are, with so little society. But the army is a good school. There
is none to fall back upon here. One stands by his own merit, if
he stands at all. I am studying artillery tactics with the greatest
earnestness. Tell G., that with a thirty-two pounder, at the distance of one and one-half miles, I can plump a target twelve feet
square the first time."

"OCTOBER 6th, 1864.

"DEAR MOTHER:—

"The weather is fast growing cooler. After this month there
will be but few cases of chills and fever. I have never given the
real cause of my long delay in writing. I have been very unwell
with chills and fever. I have done but little duty since September 3d. I am improving, though still off duty."

"OCTOBER 27th, 1864.

"DEAR MOTHER:—

"I am much more busy now than I have been at any time
since I entered the service. I go on picket nearly every other
day, and when off picket, I attend artillery drill in the morning
and battalion drill in the afternoon."

"NOVEMBER 4th, 1864.

"DEAR GEORGE:—

"We are still moving in the same beaten path. The weather
has grown cooler, but with our new houses and fire-places we are
comfortable enough. I have been reading Tom Brown at Oxford.
Hardy seems to have been just such an one as we could wish to
meet with in our college life. So far as love for muscular exercise and sports is concerned, I think Tom must have been a family-
connection of ours. However, as he was a pretty good fellow, I
think we will claim him. You will meet in your course just such

fellows as were associated with him, and his experience will be of value to you."

" NOVEMBER 12th, 1864.

"DEAR MOTHER:—

"I have spent most of my time lately in reading and in studying. I have not been well, and have been on duty as member of a court-martial for two weeks or more. I try to study four or five hours each day. I wish the service was more active. I feel the need of variety and of change. It is not to be wondered at that officers and soldiers become intemperate and reckless, as many do. There are no associations here to make them better. I would like to be in the army of the Potomac. It is very dull here, and I feel that I need more experience than I shall be likely to get in garrison. Write to Edward about getting me a position there if possible."

" MARCH 8th, 1865.

"DEAR MOTHER:—

"Since last writing we have had the glorious news of the capture of Charleston, Wilmington and Columbia. These successes are the results of Sherman's masterly movements. With such men as Grant and Sherman to plan and execute, the Rebellion cannot possibly last longer than the coming summer. I regret that I shall probably not have any part in the grand campaigns that are to be witnessed this summer. I am studying very hard preparing to be examined for West Point. In fact, I have made my application. Whether I shall succeed or not, I cannot tell, but I hope for the best. I have retained my habits of study perfectly, and have thought of little lately except the profession of arms."

" APRIL 17th, 1865.

"DEAR MOTHER:—

"We have had glorious news for a month past. Yesterday we fired two hundred guns in honor of Grant's victory over Lee. I should like to have been in the army of the Potomac. But a soldier cannot choose his own field of duty, and it becomes him to be contented wherever he is placed. If these successes continue, I see no reason why I may not come home on leave of absence in the course of three or four months. You will be surprised to see me. I have grown much stronger and taller, and besides, the profession has given me a steadiness and independence of character that I think is valuable. I have made it a principle never to ask a favor that is not for the good of the service, and I grant none to others. I never hesitate to say what I think to be right, (under the proper circumstances,) whether it pleases or displeases."

"MAY 8th, 1865.

"DEAR MOTHER:—

"I still continue to like the service as well as ever. I am enjoying better health than formerly. I feel happy and contented at all times. I read a great deal, and try to improve my mind by every possible means at my disposal."

"JUNE 13th, 1865.

"DEAR MOTHER:—

Am unusually busy with my lessons in tactics. There is to be an examination of the officers of the regiment in two or three weeks. I think there is reason for expecting that I shall soon be promoted. I prefer to remain in service for a long time yet. I was not successful in my effort to be admitted to West Point. You speak of my coming home this fall. I should like to do so if I am promoted, otherwise not. I am glad that the war is over, but I regret that I have never been engaged in battle. I shall never think of mentioning my military history at home. It has been so insignificant compared with that of the brave heroes of these last campaigns. I have, however, the consolation that I have worked hard and have cheerfully and faithfully performed every duty that a soldier could do in garrison."

"June 28th, 1865.

"Dear George:—

"I have just written to mother. She will tell you what news, and also what I have written about my future prospects. I have decided to remain in the army. I still keep up my habits of study. I have read within the past year at least twelve volumes, and this in addition to the study of tactics. I am in the best of spirits, and have not felt unwell in at least three months."

The last letter that he wrote was addressed to his mother, under date of August 11, 1865:—

"Dear Mother:—

"I have little news that would interest you. We have all the dullness of a soldier's life in time of peace, with very few comforts.

"Do you hear anything about our relations with Mexico? Troops are still on their way to the Rio Grande, and quarter-masters are increasing, instead of diminishing their supply of stores. Everything seems to indicate a movement into Mexico for some purpose. I would like to go too. Tell me, please, in your next, what you think about it."

Lieutenant Brown died August 23, 1865, at Donaldsonville. The letters written to his friends by the several officers of his battalion will give us the best account of his sickness, his last hours, and the estimate in which he was held by his comrades. Lieutenant Gaskill, his commanding officer, writes under date of August 23, 1865:—

"Mr. E. P. Brown:—

"Dear Sir:—It is with feelings of sadness that I communicate to you the death of your brother, James. He died about four, p. m., to-day, at the hospital, of congestive chills. He had not been well during the past two months, but was not considered dangerously ill until a few hours previous to his death. Nearly two weeks since he was sick in his quarters with the fever, but said very little to any one about it. The Doctor visited him but once. He was taken to the hospital across the bayou. In a few days he felt better and returned to his company, believing he had sufficiently recovered to do so. I think, perhaps, here he was imprudent, but his anxiety to be with his company was so great, that he left the hospital before he had recovered his strength. He did not gain at all, and a few days again found him quite unwell. I called on him from time to time, but he always appeared cheerful until yesterday. The Doctor assured me that he was much better, his fever having left him, and that weakness alone was the cause of his despondency. I remained with him that evening until ten, P. M., and then returned to camp. Lieutenant Coggeshall called on him to-day, but found him out of his head at times during the conversation. As he was about to come away, James remarked that he should never get off his bed again. The words were too true, for not an hour afterwards the Doctor rode into camp, bringing the sad intelligence of his death. It was not apparent to any one that he was so near his death until about fifteen minutes before he passed away, in a congestive chill.

"It is useless for me to speak to you of his merits, for who should know them better than a brother? It is sufficient for me to say that he was an excellent officer; for in such an officer is embodied every quality pertaining to manhood. He was a strict disciplinarian. He possessed that firmness and decision of purpose and that ability to command, that few of his age are endowed with. He strove to excel. One would always find him when off duty poring over some military work that he had recently added to his already extensive collection. If a person can ever be said to be generous to a fault, I surely think he could be said to be that person."

Captain Addeman, his former commanding officer, writes:—

"We have now for nearly two years been associated with each other. I had learned to love him as a brother. Our acquaintance began in our short term of service in the Tenth Rhode Island Volunteers, and it has been ripened and cherished by our friendly connection since. His high sense of honor, his conscientious attention to every duty required of him by his superiors, his temperate habits, his generous and kind heart, not only attached me to him as his Captain by the strongest ties, but also awakened the deepest love and respect of all his brother officers. There are none who are free from the weaknesses of frail humanity, but I have often thought, and as often remarked to others, that James was remarkably free from the common errors of young men. His character was pure and irreproachable. His life was unblemished.

"When I left the regiment a few weeks since he was unwell. I urged upon him the necessity of a change of climate, and of making some effort to reach his home. His sense of duty which impelled him to remain at his post stood in the way; but he promised me that as soon as his health improved he would make an application for a leave of absence.

*   *   *   *   *   *   *   *

"I do not know of any trait in his character more conspicuous than his earnestness, of the spirit of which he seemed to be the very impersonation. For one so young he was remarkably free from any disposition to trifle. Not that he was misanthropic or morose in the least, but, with his naturally taciturn disposition his thoughts turned within himself, and an earnest desire to fit himself for future usefulness seemed uppermost in his mind.

This disposition served to keep him free from the many vices of camp life.

"He was fond of military life, and always expressed a strong desire to enter the regular army.

"He possessed a high degree of physical and moral courage. In the moment of threatening danger his cheek would often blanch, but it was from no source of fear. He fully appreciated the extreme peril of the hour, and heroically nerved himself to meet it. I do not think the torture of the stake or of the rack would have extorted from him a murmur. His brave soul would have rendered him equal even to that emergency. He was often envied by his brother officers for the splendid physical development with which nature had endowed him. We had supposed that with his powers of endurance he would have survived those perils of climate to which weaker men would necessarily succumb. Almost any exposure at night to the malaria seemed to bring back fresh attacks of the dreaded ague, and at times his sickness was most alarming, but his unconquerable will carried him through many a trying ordeal, when medical aid and attention of friends seemed almost unavailing."

Captain Cragin thus speaks of him:—

"I was struck from the first with the remarkable interest James manifested in military duties. He seemed to be peculiarly fitted for the profession of arms. His manly air and bearing, erect figure, powerful muscular development, ability to endure protracted labor and fatigue, undoubtable courage, resolute spirit, and especially his love for the service, seemed to furnish an unusual number of qualifications for the trying exigencies of military life. I need not say that subsequent experience proved that he possessed all these soldierly qualities in a rare measure. He suffered very severely from the chills. He frequently went

40

on duty when he was not able to do so, but was never known to utter a word of complaint. He was selected for the dangerous post of Plaquemine on account of his habits of strict discipline, and for his successful command over his men. He was selected at two different times as a member of a board for directing the issue of rations to the needy people in and about Plaquemine; a duty requiring much discretion."

The officers of his regiment during his sickness cared for him with a tenderness more than filial, and, after his death, they entombed him with all the solemn and stately ceremonies of war. His remains now rest in his native village.

THE MEMORIAL TABLET

IN MANNING HALL.

THE MEMORIAL TABLET.

WHEN the war had come to an end, and college life once more began to go on undisturbed in its quiet paths, the thoughts of the students turned often in fond remembrance to their brothers, who never came back from the field, who perished there in defence of their country. Some of these, now so sadly missed, had been personally known and loved by many, who were still in college, and others, though graduates or students of earlier years, had yet come to be near and dear to all hearts, their names familiar and honored, and cherished with grateful affection ; and the career of each was talked over many a time in college-rooms and circles, and traced with an ever-fresh interest, from its beginnings of noble purpose and resolve, on through scenes of patient suffering or of heroic achievement, to its issue of swift death on the battle-field, or of wasting dissolution in hospital or in prison. Sad indeed were the regrets, and yet proud and grateful the memories awakened and uttered, as fellow-students thus conversed together of the noble lives and the martyr deaths of those who once had sat where now they were sitting, to whom college-halls and college-grounds were also once familiar places, whose had been a like companionship in the studies and the friendships of college life. Along with these regrets over their early loss, and these memories of the priceless blessings, which they had sacrificed everything to secure, came also the thought, how signal was the honor they had conferred upon the place of their education by their examples of devotion to patriotism, to freedom, and to duty, and how worthy that honor was of being kept in lasting remembrance. They had achieved a fame, more precious in the sight of their *Alma Mater* than the best academic honors she had ever held out to their ambition, higher than the loftiest professional distinction they could have reached in a long life through the nurture she had given them. And even because their best monument was their own remembered lives, it seemed most fitting and desirable, that within the walls of the college, some visible memorial should be set up, which, though it were slight and simple, might be a perpetual witness of the beauty and worth of those lives, and so keep them fresh in the memory of their fellow-students—their brothers all in letters, and many of them brothers in arms as well—and hand them down to the admiration and love of successive generations of students in after times.

It was thus that the movement arose, which ended in the erection of the Mural Tablet in Manning Hall. The idea once suggested by one student to another, and warmly adopted, spread through the college, and found such immediate and general favor, that measures were at once taken to carry it into execution. A general committee was appointed, representing the several classes, to which the whole subject was entrusted; and from them some were detailed to procure designs for a tablet, and others to make the pecuniary estimates, and obtain by subscription, the requisite funds. With the exception of a few subscriptions from citizens of Providence, well-known friends of the college, the amount found necessary was contributed by the undergraduates themselves. The design was furnished by Mr. Alpheus C. Morse, a distinguished Providence architect; and, after many consultations, and inspection of designs sent in by others, Mr. Morse's design was adopted by the Committee, and in the same form in which it was first presented. Mr. Morse has furnished the following description of the tablet: "The centre of the tablet bearing the inscription is decorated by angle-shafts with floriated capitals and moulded bases. The head of it is obtusely pointed with moulded angles, returned vertically, and stop-chamfered immediately above the abacus of the capitals; and is decorated in the centre by a gothic panel enclosing a flori-ated cross clasping a shield, and over this is carried an incised moulding, which forms an equilateral pointed arch, with the spandrel compartments filled by panels, charged with quatrefoil and leaf ornament. The whole is wrought in white Vermont marble, the extreme dimensions being as follows, viz.: the height, seven feet one inch, the width, three feet five inches, the projec-tion from the wall, eight inches."

The tablet bears the following inscription : —

IN · MEMORIAM · FRATRUM · SUORUM

QUI · PRO · LIBERTATE

ET · PRO · REIPUBLICAE · INTEGRITATE

IN · BELLO · CIVILI · CECIDERUNT

LITERARUM · STUDIOSI

IN · HAC · UNIVERSITATE · COMMORANTES

HANC · TABULAM · POSUERUNT.

MDCCCLXVI.

The tablet was executed by Messrs. Tingley, of Providence, and set in its place in the north wall of the Chapel, in the summer vacation, in 1866. It was at first intended that the names of those whom it commemorates, should be inscribed upon it, before it was erected ; and for that purpose, space was left under the inscription. But as a full list had not yet been obtained of the sons of the college, who had died in the service, this part of the work was postponed to some later period.

A service of dedication was held in the Chapel, on the afternoon of Tuesday, September 4, 1866, the day before Commencement. A large company was assembled, consisting of the Faculty and students, of graduates, and of ladies and gentlemen of the city. Mr. J. B. Mustin, of the class of 1866, Chairman of the Committee of Undergraduates, presided, and opened the service with an account of the movement, which had now reached its consummation. After prayer by the late Reverend Professor Dunn, Professor Diman addressed the company as follows:—

"If I speak, at this time, in behalf of the Faculty, it is for the purpose of making it distinctly understood that their part in the work now consummated has been merely formal. To the undergraduates all the praise belongs. From them the suggestion came, and save that to my colleague, the Professor of Latin, they owe the terse and admirable inscription, they have had the matter wholly in their own hands. I need hardly say that this gives a peculiar interest to our present services. So far as I am aware, no such tribute has been paid in any of our sister colleges. Some, with imposing ceremonies, have commemorated their unreturning dead. One has, with great propriety, decided to devote a chapel to the precious memory of sacrifices which in an earlier age would have swelled the list of saints and martyrs, while our most ancient University seeks expression for her proud sorrow in a Memorial Hall, whose stately front will bear the names of her heroes, while its inner walls will be eloquent with their pictured lips. But such costly offerings can come only from the whole body of Alumni, while the simple Tablet, which we set up to-day, derives its distinctive value from the fact that it is a students' tribute. And if, as the Roman historian holds, next to the doing of great deeds must be reckoned the right appreciation of them, this Tablet will serve in two ways as an enduring testimonial; for while, on the one hand, it will bear witness to the magnanimity and love of country of those, *qui pro libertate et pro reipublicae integritate* laid down their lives on the blood-stained field, or languished them away in the unwholesome prison, so, on the other, will it furnish equal evidence that one mind animated the mass, and that those who could not themselves share in the sacrifice, were prompt to testify their sense of its greatness.

"To the Faculty, and to the students, alike, it seemed eminently fit that such a memorial should be erected here; that here, as we gather to our daily devotions, we might be reminded of those who, only a short time since, sat with us on these benches, and joined with us in our accustomed hymns of praise; and that here those, who in years to come shall fill our places, may learn that study is not an end in itself; that liberal culture looks to larger results than are included in mere academic success; that the finest discipline becomes contemptible if not coupled with the manly virtues. Not what we learn, but the use we make of our learning is what tells the story. Surely if the instructors in this institution ever grow negligent in inculcating these high lessons, the very stone will cry out.

" And if any of you, who have been long out of college, are curious about the kind of training that has been furnished of late years, you may study the best proof of it in that inscription. *Abeunt studia in mores,*—let the lofty public spirit of these children of our common mother, their fidelity to duty, their valor,

41

their endurance, speak for the training that she gave them. She
carves their names in her holiest place, in recognition of the new
lustre they have added to her ancient fame. The evidence here
furnished of the intrinsic worth of our established method of
academic discipline is the more striking. because it is just here
that the common objections to it are urged with the greatest
force. That method, you are aware, has been severely criticised
as unsuited to the present age. Such exclusive devotion, it has
been claimed, to abstract studies, but poorly fits the understanding to deal with practical concerns; such prolonged contact with
the past is ill adapted to awaken sympathy with the living
present. Thus we purchase a puny intellectualism at the price
of those manly qualities which are the conditions of all real
success. How far these reproaches were well founded let the
experience of this, and of kindred institutions, show. When the
call of the President revealed the public peril, who sprang to
arms? Where all professions, all ranks, all conditions showed
such alacrity, it might seem invidious to claim special praise for
any single class, but let it never be forgotten that among those
who hurried earliest to the strife, in those shameful days when
one and another of the men who had been trained at West Point
was proving faithless to his trust, was a large proportion of the
students of our colleges; a proportion, in some instances, so large
as seriously to interfere with the routine of academic duties. It
is safe to affirm that no one-class of the American people was
represented in so liberal a ratio as the very class whose training
had been decried as tending to keep them at a distance from the
questions of the day. And in this respect our experience has
been the experience of those before us. In that matchless eulogy,
which Pericles pronounced at the beginning of the Peloponnes-
sian War, he proudly claimed that Athens had lost nothing in
the cultivation of those arts to which she owed her highest fame;

and we too, looking back on our record, remembering the readiness with which so many of our educated youth made sacrifice of the hopes of years, recognizing the conspicuous ability so often shown in the novel and arduous positions to which they were summoned, bewailing, alas, what may not even now be mentioned without renewing in the hearts of some here present, a grief too sacred and too recent to be disturbed, may repeat with added emphasis the words of the great Athenian orator, 'We have not been enfeebled by Philosophy.'

"And never again let it be said, as more than once it was said before the Rebellion, that our educated men, as a class, are the most disloyal to our institutions. There is no such antagonism between liberal culture and republican ideas. From a certain narrow national conceit, the offspring of ignorance and prejudice, culture, of course, emancipates the mind; it renders love of country a rational sentiment; it leads us to regard political forms as possessed not of absolute, but only of relative excellence; it warns us against supposing that any contrivances of man are perfect, or destined to endure forever; but that an enlargement of the understanding, in the study of philosophy and history, a thoughtful survey of the forces which have shaped society, a just appreciation of the controlling political ideas that underlie the mighty movements of modern times, have any tendency to shake our confidence in the great experiment for which the New World was reserved by Divine Providence for so many years, our recent experience has triumphantly disproved. It is the wiser judgment of one of the profoundest political thinkers of our day, whose views have had no little influence in moulding the present generation of American students, that a political system like ours is precisely the one which requires the 'greatest maturity of reason, of morality, of civilization, in the society to which it is applied,' and if, as Guizot affirms, modern society has penetrated the ways of God, it is because the scope and motive of modern politics are coming to be the more adequate expression of that Divine and Universal Justice, which men of genuine culture have been in all ages most swift to recognize, and in advancing which they have come nearest the prize of the mark of their high calling.

"But as I am speaking I see before me one who barely escaped having his name cut on this Memorial Tablet, and whose wounds make all words seem poor. I gladly give way to Major-General Underwood."

Remarks were then made by General A. B. Underwood, of the class of 1849, the Right Reverend Bishop Smith, of the class of 1816, Abraham Payne, Esq., of the class of 1840, and the Reverend James B. Simmons, of the class of 1851.

This sketch of the history of the Mural Tablet in the College Chapel it has been thought proper to append to the biographies contained in this volume. As the inscription upon it declares, it is a memorial offering of the undergraduates to their brothers, who fell in the late Civil War, in defence of the sacred cause of freedom, and of the Union. There it stands, imbedded in that sacred wall, as in the nation's history and fame are the names and lives of the brave souls it commemorates, pure in its marble whiteness as their loyalty to their imperilled country, firm and enduring as their faith in freedom, in truth, and in God, its clasped cross and shield fit emblem of their blended patriotism and piety. And, as in all the coming years, teachers and pupils daily go up together to that sacred place at the hour of prayer, may that memorial marble, as it catches the eye, and straight recalls the heroic dead, be to all a living source of noble inspiration, infusing a deeper sense of what is worthiest and best in human living, kindling a more generous ardor of patriotism, a purer devotion to duty, and a stronger faith in that life everlasting, which awaits him that endureth to the end.

ROLL OF STUDENTS,

GRADUATES AND NON-GRADUATES,

WHO SERVED IN THE ARMY OR NAVY OF THE UNITED STATES DURING THE REBELLION.

THE ROLL.

CLASS OF 1825.

GEORGE W. PATTEN. Brevet Second Lieutenant, Second Infantry, United States Army, July 1, 1830; First Lieutenant, February 13, 1837; Captain, June 18, 1846. Wounded —lost right hand—at the battle of Cerro Gordo, April 18, 1847; Brevet-Major, April 18, 1847; Major, Ninth Infantry, April 30, 1861; Lieutenant-Colonel, Second Infantry, June 7, 1862. Retired from active service, February 17, 1864.

CLASS OF 1829.

JOHN A. BOLLES. Captain, and additional Aide-de-Camp on the staff of Major-General John A. Dix, February, 1862; Major and Provost Judge at Fortress Monroe, June 20, 1862; Judge Advocate, Seventh Army Corps, September 3, 1862; Brevet Lieutenant-Colonel, March 13, 1865; Brevet Colonel, July, 1865; Brevet Brigadier-General, May, 1866. Resigned, July, 1865, and appointed Solicitor and Naval Judge Advocate.

BENONI CARPENTER. Surgeon, Twelfth Rhode Island Volunteers, October 5, 1862; Surgeon, Eleventh United States Heavy Artillery, (colored,) September 5, 1863; Medical Director and

Inspector of the District of Carrollton, Louisiana, June 18, 1864. Mustered out of service with regiment, October 2, 1865.

ELISHA DYER. Captain, Company B, Tenth Rhode Island Volunteers, May 26, 1862. Served in Virginia. Mustered out of service with regiment, September 1, 1862.

CLASS OF 1830.

FRANCIS J. LIPPITT. Colonel, Second California Volunteers, August 23, 1861. In command of the Northern District of California from January, 1862, till July, 1863. Mustered out of service, October 11, 1864. Brevet Brigadier-General United States Volunteers, March 13, 1865.

CLASS OF 1832.

JOHN B. WHITE. Chaplain, One Hundred and Seventeenth Illinois Volunteers, August 4, 1864. Mustered out of service, July, 1865.

CLASS OF 1834.

THOMAS POTTER. Assistant-Surgeon, United States Navy, October 17, 1839; Passed Assistant-Surgeon, January, 22, 1848; Surgeon, July 13, 1853. Served during the Rebellion on the Atlantic Blockading Squadron. Still in the service.

CLASS OF 1837.

CHARLES K. NEWCOMB. Private, Company D, Tenth Rhode Island Volunteers, May 26, 1862. Served in Virginia. Mustered out of service with regiment, September 1, 1862.

CLASS OF 1839.

JOSEPH S. PITMAN. Lieutenant-Colonel, First Rhode Island Volunteers, April 18, 1861. Served in Virginia. Mustered out of service with regiment, August 2, 1861.

James B. M. Potter. Additional Paymaster, United States Army, June 1, 1861; Major and Paymaster, United States Army, July 15, 1864; Brevet Lieutenant-Colonel, United States Army, March 13, 1865. Still in the service.

CLASS OF 1840.

George H. Browne. Colonel, Twelfth Rhode Island Volunteers, September 18, 1862. Served in Virginia and Kentucky. Mustered out of service with regiment, July 29, 1863.

Thorndike C. Jameson. Chaplain, Second Rhode Island Volunteers, June 11, 1861; Major, December 13, 1862. Resigned, January 8, 1863. Major, Fifth Rhode Island Heavy Artillery, March 2, 1863. Served in Virginia and North Carolina. Mustered out of service, February 2, 1865.

Henry S. Newcomb. Midshipman, United States Navy, July 21, 1838; Passed Midshipman; Lieutenant, June 28, 1853; Lieutenant-Commander; Commander, September, 1862. On duty in the South Atlantic and East Gulf Blockading Squadron. Died, October 24, 1863.

CLASS OF 1841.

John M. Thayer. Colonel, First Nebraska Volunteers, June 13, 1861; Brigadier-General, United States Volunteers, October 4, 1862. Served in Missouri, and under General Grant in Kentucky, Tennessee and Mississippi. In the fall of 1863 was transferred to the Department of Arkansas, and assigned to the command of the Army of the Frontier. Brevet Major-General, United States Volunteers. Resigned, July 19, 1865.

CLASS OF 1842.

Edwin Metcalf. Major, Third Rhode Island Heavy Artillery, August 27, 1861. Resigned, August 4, 1862. Colonel, Eleventh Rhode Island Volunteers, September 15, 1862; Colonel, Third

42

Heavy Artillery, November 11, 1862.   Resigned, February 5, 1864.

CLASS OF 1843.

TRACY P. CHEEVER.   Captain, Thirty-Fifth Massachusetts Volunteers, August 13, 1862.   Served in Maryland and Virginia. Discharged, June 23, 1863, on account of wounds received at the battle of Antietam, September 17, 1862.

LEWIS RICHMOND.   Private, Company C, First Rhode Island Volunteers, May 2, 1861.   Served in Virginia.   Mustered out of service with regiment, August 2, 1861.   Captain and Assistant Adjutant-General, United States Volunteers, on staff of Major-General Burnside, September 13, 1861; Major, April 28, 1862; Lieutenant-Colonel, July 22, 1862; Brevet Colonel, August 1, 1864; Brevet Brigadier-General, March 13, 1865.

ABRAM VAN BUREN.   First Lieutenant and Adjutant, Twenty-Sixth Missouri Volunteers, January 17, 1862.   Served in Missouri. Resigned, April 26, 1862.

CLASS OF 1844.

LEWIS H. BOUTELL.   Major, Forty-Fifth Missouri Volunteers. Mustered out of service, March 7, 1865.

WILLARD SAYLES.   Major, First Rhode Island Cavalry, September 27, 1861; Lieutenant-Colonel, February 21, 1862; resigned, July 7, 1862.   Colonel, Third Cavalry, July 1, 1863.   Served in Virginia, and in the Department of the Gulf.   Mustered out of service with regiment, November 29, 1865.

CLASS OF 1846.

S. R. GIFFORD.   Private, Seventh New York Volunteers, April, 1861.   Served in Maryland and Virginia.   Mustered out of service with his regiment.   Twice again during the war, Mr. Gifford went to the field with his regiment.

WILLIAM GODDARD. Major, First Rhode Island Volunteers, June 27, 1861. Served in Virginia. Mustered out of service with regiment, August 2, 1861. Major by special order, and Volunteer Aide on staff of Major-General Burnside at the battle of Fredericksburg, Virginia, December 11, 1862. Brevet Lieutenant-Colonel; Brevet Colonel United States Volunteers, March 13, 1865.

WILLIAM W. PEARCE. Corporal, First Light Battery, Rhode Island Volunteers, May 2, 1861; Sergeant. Served in Virginia. Mustered out of service with battery, August 6, 1861.

CLASS OF 1847.

THOMAS S. ANTHONY. First Lieutenant, First Rhode Island Light Artillery, March 17, 1862. Served in Virginia. Mustered out of service, October 15, 1862.

FREDERIC DENISON. Chaplain First Rhode Island Cavalry, November 7, 1861; resigned, January 19, 1863. Chaplain, Third Rhode Island Heavy Artillery, January 20, 1863; mustered out, October 5, 1864 — term of service having expired.

JOSHUA J. ELLIS. Assistant Surgeon, Thirty-Seventh Massachusetts Volunteers, August 18, 1862. Served in Virginia. Resigned, March 10, 1863. Died, March 17, 1863.

WALTER H. JUDSON. Second Lieutenant, Thirteenth Massachusetts Volunteers, July 16, 1861. Served in Virginia. A prisoner at Richmond, Virginia, November, 1862. Died at New Haven, Connecticut, March 10, 1863.

CLASS OF 1848.

FAYETTE CLAPP. Surgeon, on General Fremont's staff, November, 1861. Regimental Surgeon, December, 1861, and ordered to Jefferson City, on hospital duty. Resigned, 1862. Surgeon,

United States steamer Marmora, December, 1862.   Transferred to the Benton, and then to the Louisville.   Died, September, 1864.

JOSEPH B. CLARK.   Captain, Eleventh New Hampshire Volunteers, August 21, 1862.   Wounded at the battle of the Wilderness, May 6, 1864.   Served in Virginia, Kentucky, Mississippi and Tennessee.   Mustered out of service with regiment, June 4, 1865.

AUSTIN S. CUSHMAN.   Second Lieutenant, Company L, Third Massachusetts Volunteers, April 23, 1861; Adjutant, April 29, 1861.   Served in Virginia.   Mustered out of service with regiment, July 21, 1861.   Major, Forty-Seventh Massachusetts Volunteers, November, 7, 1862.   Served in the Department of the Gulf.   Mustered out of service with regiment, September 1, 1863.

WILLIAM B. WEEDEN.   Lieutenant, First Rhode Island Light Artillery, June 6, 1861; Captain, August 8, 1861.   Served in Virginia.   Resigned, July 21, 1862.

CLASS OF 1849.

WILLIAM R. BROWNELL.   Surgeon, Twelfth Connecticut Volunteers, October 7, 1861.   May, 1862, on staff of Major-General Butler; July, 1862, on duty at St. James' General Hospital, New Orleans, Louisiana; August, 1863, Medical Director, La Fourche District, Louisiana; December, 1863, Division Surgeon, First Division, Nineteenth Army Corps; August, 1864, Medical Director, Nineteenth Army Corps.   December, 1864, appointed Staff Surgeon, United States Army.   Served in Louisiana and Virginia.   Resigned, April, 1865.

LLOYD MORTON.   Surgeon, Ninth Rhode Island Volunteers, May 26, 1862.   Served in Virginia.   Mustered out of service with regiment, September, 1862.

ISAAC N. TOURTELLOTTE.   Private, New York Volunteers.

ADIN B. UNDERWOOD. Captain, Second Massachusetts Volunteers, May 24, 1861; Major, Thirty-Third Massachusetts Volunteers, July 11, 1862; Lieutenant-Colonel, July 24, 1862; Colonel, April 3, 1863. Wounded at Lookout Mountain, Tennessee, October 29, 1863. Brigadier-General, United States Volunteers, January 22, 1864; Brevet Major-General. Served in Virginia, Maryland and Tennessee. Mustered out of service, September 1, 1865.

H. LINCOLN WAYLAND. Chaplain, Seventh Connecticut Volunteers, September 18, 1861. Served in the Department of the South. Mustered out of service, January 7, 1864.

CLASS OF 1850.

JAMES BROWN. Captain, Thirty-Third Massachusetts Volunteers, July 31, 1862; Major, November 29, 1862. Served in Virginia. Mustered out of service, May 11, 1863.

HENRY F. LANE. Chaplain, Forty-First Massachusetts Volunteers, November 4, 1862. Served in the Department of the Gulf. Mustered out of service, August 25, 1863.

EDWARD L. PIERCE. Private, Company L, Third Massachusetts Volunteers. Served in Virginia. Mustered out of service with regiment, July 20, 1861.

CLASS OF 1851.

EMMONS P. BOND. Private, Fourteenth Connecticut Volunteers, September, 1864; Chaplain, October 12, 1864. Served in Virginia. Resigned, May 5, 1865.

FRANK WHEATON. First Lieutenant, Fourth Cavalry, United States Army, March 3, 1855; Captain, March 1, 1861; Lieutenant-Colonel, Second Rhode Island Volunteers, July, 1861; Colonel, July 22, 1861; Brigadier-General, United States Volunteers, November 29, 1862; Major, Second Cavalry, United States Army,

November 5, 1863; Brevet Lieutenant-Colonel, United States Army, May 5, 1864; Brevet Major-General, United States Volunteers, October, 19, 1864; Brevet Colonel, United States Army, October 19, 1864; Brevet Brigadier-General, United States Army, March 13, 1865; Brevet Major-General, United States Army, March 13, 1865; Lieutenant-Colonel, Thirty-Ninth Infantry, United States Army, July 28, 1866. Served in Maryland and Virginia. Still in the service.

CLASS OF 1852.

SULLIVAN BALLOU. Major, Second Rhode Island Volunteers, June 11, 1861. Served in Virginia. Died near Sudley Church, Virginia, July 26, 1861, of wounds received at the battle of Bull Run, July 21, 1861.

MILES J. FLETCHER. Aide-de-Camp to Governor Morton, of Illinois. Killed, May 10, 1862.

CHARLES H. PARKHURST. Captain, Eleventh Rhode Island Volunteers, September 19, 1862; Lieutenant-Colonel, Third Rhode Island Cavalry, August 31, 1863. Served in the Department of the Gulf. Resigned, May 26, 1865.

CHARLES B. RANDALL. Second Lieutenant, Company A, Twelfth New York Volunteers, May 13, 1861; Captain, September 25, 1861. Mustered out of service with regiment, May 17, 1863. Major, One Hundred and Forty-Ninth York Volunteers, March 17, 1863; Lieutenant-Colonel, June 5, 1863. Wounded at Gettysburg, Pennsylvania, July, 1863. Killed before Atlanta, Georgia, July 20, 1864.

CLARENDON WAITE. Private, February 18, 1864. Served in North Carolina. Mustered out of service, May 20, 1864.

Lucius A. Wheelock. Second Lieutenant, Company A, Forty-Third Massachusetts Volunteers, November 10, 1862. Served in North Carolina. Mustered out of service with regiment, July 30, 1863.

CLASS OF 1853.

Osborn E. Bright. Sergeant-Major, Twenty-Second New York Volunteers, June 28, 1862. Served in Virginia. Mustered out of service with regiment, September 15, 1862.

Henry W. Diman. Acting Assistant-Paymaster, United States Navy, January 14, 1862. Served in West Gulf Blockading Squadron. Resigned, August 13, 1862.

George D. Henderson. Chaplain, United States Navy, July 2, 1864. Served in North Atlantic Blockading Squadron. Ordered to the Naval Academy, September 12, 1864. Detached, December 20, 1865. June 23, 1866, ordered to take passage from New York for Brazil, and report for duty on board steamer Brooklyn. Detached from the Brooklyn and ordered to the Guerriere. Still in the service.

Charles H. Henshaw. Captain, Company K, One Hundredth New York Volunteers, October, 1861. Served in Virginia. Resigned, August, 1862.

Leonard B. Pratt. Second Lieutenant, First Rhode Island Cavalry, December, 1861; Quartermaster, First Battalion; First Lieutenant and Regimental Commissary, November 1, 1863. Served in Maryland and Virginia. Mustered out of service December 14, 1864.

George H. Woods. First Lieutenant, First Minnesota Volunteers, April 29, 1861; Acting Regimental Quartermaster, July 3, 1861; Chief Quartermaster, Corps of Observation, Brigadier-General Charles P. Stone, commanding; Captain and Commissary of Subsistence, November 16, 1861; Commissary, Richardson's Division, Second Corps, April, 1862; Chief Commissary of Subsistence, Second Corps; Lieutenant-Colonel and Chief Commissary of Subsistence, Third Corps, January 1, 1863; Chief Commissary of Subsistence, Cavalry Corps, (General Sheridan,) March 28, 1864; President Board of Examination for Officers of the Subsistence Department, December, 1864. Mustered out of the service, June 11, 1865.

CLASS OF 1854.

FRANK W. CHENEY. Lieutenant-Colonel, Sixteenth Connecticut Volunteers, August 15, 1862. Wounded at the battle of Antietam, September 17, 1862. Served in Virginia and Maryland. Discharged on account of wounds, December 24, 1862.

ARTHUR F. DEXTER. Captain, First Rhode Island Volunteers, May 2, 1861, (date of muster.) Served in Virginia. Mustered out of service with regiment, August 2, 1861. On staff of Brigadier-General Tyler, April, 1862. Resigned.

WILLIAM G. ELY. Lieutenant-Colonel, Sixth Connecticut Volunteers, September 4, 1861; Colonel, Eighteenth Connecticut Volunteers, July 24, 1862. Served in South Carolina and Virginia. Captured at Winchester, Virginia, in June, 1863. Wounded at Lynchburg, Virginia, June 18, 1864. Discharged on account of wounds, September, 18, 1864. Brevet Brigadier-General, United States Volunteers, March 13, 1865.

FRANCIS W. GODDARD. Private, Company C, First Rhode Island Volunteers, May 2, 1861, (date of muster,); Captain, (carbineers,) June 27, 1861. Served in Virginia. Mustered out of service with regiment, August 2, 1861.

THOMAS P. IVES. Lieutenant, United States Revenue Service, May 15, 1861. Resigned, November 6, 1861. In command of steamer Picket, Burnside's flag-ship, December 2, 1861. Resigned, May 12, 1862; Acting Master, United States Navy, September 3, 1862; Acting Volunteer Lieutenant, May 26, 1863. Assigned to duty in the Ordnance Bureau, December 3, 1863. Acting Volunteer Commander, November 7, 1864. January 26, 1865, relieved from duty on account of ill-health with permission to travel abroad. Died at Havre, France, November 17, 1865.

HENRY C. PARSONS. Sergeant, Eleventh Pennsylvania Volunteers, April 25, 1861. Served in Virginia. Mustered out of service with regiment, July 25, 1861. Captain, Pennsylvania Volunteers, 1863.

AMOS D. SMITH, JR. Second Lieutenant, Tenth Light Battery, Rhode Island Volunteers, May 26, 1862. Served in Virginia. Mustered out of service with battery, August 30, 1862.

WILLIAM TILLMAN. Major and Paymaster, United States Volunteers, September 9, 1861. Served in Virginia and in the Department of the Cumberland. Brevet Lieutenant-Colonel, March 13, 1865. Mustered out of service, January 15, 1866.

THOMAS VERNON. Corporal, Seventy-First New York Volunteers, April 19, 1861. Mustered out, July 30, 1861. Reëntered the service, May 28, 1862. Mustered out, September 2, 1862. Entered the service again, June 17, 1863. Mustered out, July 22, 1863. Served in Virginia, Maryland and Pennsylvania.

CLASS OF 1855.

LOUIS BELL. Captain, Company A, First New Hampshire Volunteers, May, 1861. Served in Maryland. Mustered out of service with regiment, August, 1861. Lieutenant-Colonel, New Hampshire Volunteers, September 3, 1861; Colonel, May 16, 1862. Commanded Third Brigade, Second Division, Tenth Army Corps. Served in South Carolina, in Virginia, and in North Carolina.   Killed at Fort Fisher, North Carolina, January 15, 1865. Brevet Brigadier-General, January 15, 1865.

WILLIAM P. GRIER.   Assistant Surgeon, Third Cavalry, United States Army, 1861.   On duty at the hospital, Chester, Pennsylvania, and at the Medical Inspector's office, Philadelphia.   While sailing up Arkansas river, on his way to join his regiment, January 22, 1866, killed by bursting of the boiler on steamer Miami.

MOSES B. JENKINS.   Private, Company C, First Rhode Island Volunteers, May 2, 1861, (date of muster.)   Served in Virginia. Mustered out of service with regiment, August 2, 1861.

HORATIO ROGERS, JR.   First Lieutenant, Third Rhode Island Heavy Artillery, August 27, 1861; Captain, October 9, 1861; Major, August 18, 1862; Colonel, Eleventh Rhode Island Volunteers, December 27, 1862; Colonel, Second Rhode Island Volunteers, January 29, 1863.   Served in South Carolina and in Virginia.   Resigned and honorably mustered out of the service, January 14, 1864.   Brevet Brigadier-General United States Volunteers, March 13, 1865.

CHARLES A. SNOW.   Chaplain, Third Massachusetts Volunteers, October 10, 1862.   Served in North Carolina.   Mustered out of service with regiment, June 26, 1863.

JOHN F. TOBEY.   First Lieutenant and Adjutant, Tenth Rhode Island Volunteers, May 26, 1862.   Served in Virginia.   Mustered out of service with regiment, September 1, 1862.

WILLIAM M. TURNER.

CLASS OF 1856.

GEORGE W. ADAMS.   Private, First Light Battery, Rhode Island Volunteers, May 2, 1861, (date of muster.)   First Lieutenant,

First Rhode Island Light Artillery, August 12, 1861; Captain, January 30, 1863; Brevet Major, October 19, 1864. Served in Maryland and in Virginia. Mustered out of service with battery, June 24, 1865.

CHARLES H. ALDEN. Assistant Surgeon, United States Army, June 23, 1860; Surgeon, July 28, 1866; Brevet Major, March 13, 1865. Still in the service.

NICHOLAS B. BOLLES. First Lieutenant, Tenth Rhode Island Volunteers, May 26, 1862. Served in Virginia. Mustered out of service with regiment, September 1, 1862.

JAMES M. CUTTS. Private, Company C, First Rhode Island Volunteers, May 9, 1861. Served in Virginia. Discharged to accept promotion, June 23, 1861. Captain, Eleventh Infantry, United States Army, May 14, 1861. Judge Advocate on staff of Major-General Burnside. Detached from staff, September 28, 1863. Brevet Major, United States Army, August 1, 1864; Brevet Lieutenant-Colonel, August 1, 1864. Captain, Twentieth Infantry, United States Army. Still in the service.

J. HALSEY DEWOLF. Private, Company D, Tenth Rhode Island Volunteers, May 26, 1862. Served in Virginia. Mustered out of service with regiment, September 1, 1862.

THOMAS EWING, JR. Colonel, Eleventh Kansas Volunteers, September 15, 1862. Brigadier-General, United States Volunteers, March 13, 1863; Brevet Major-General, United States Volunteers, March 13, 1865. Served in Missouri, Arkansas, and the Indian Territory. Wounded at Pilot Knob, Missouri. Resigned, March 13, 1865.

CHARLES H. HOWE. Assistant Surgeon, United States Army.

FRANK A. RHODES. First Lieutenant, Tenth Light Battery, Rhode Island Volunteers, May 26, 1862. Served in Virginia. Mustered out of service with battery, August 30, 1862.

SAMUEL STARKWEATHER. Private, Company D, Eighty-Fourth Ohio Volunteers, May 26, 1862. Served in Virginia. Mustered out of the service, September 20, 1862.

JOHN E. TOURTELLOTTE. Captain, Company H, Fourth Minnesota Volunteers, October 5, 1861; Lieutenant-Colonel, August 24, 1862; Colonel, November 24, 1862. Wounded at Alatoona, 1864. Brevet Brigadier-General. Served in Mississippi, Tennessee, Georgia, South Carolina, North Carolina, and Virginia. Captain, United States Army, and still in the service.

CLASS OF 1857.

GEORGE W. CARR. Assistant Surgeon, First Rhode Island Volunteers, April 18, 1861; Assistant Surgeon, Second Rhode Island Volunteers, August 27, 1861; Surgeon, September 12, 1862. Served in Virginia. Mustered out of service, June 17, 1864, term of service having expired.

ROBERT H. IVES. August 19, 1862, Lieutenant and Volunteer Aide-de-Camp to Brigadier-General I. P. Rodman, commanding Third Division, Ninth Army Corps. Mortally wounded at the battle of Antietam, September 17, 1862. Died at Hagerstown, Maryland, September 27, 1862.

CHARLES H. POPE. Sergeant-Major, First Light Battery, Rhode Island Volunteers, May 2, 1861, (date of muster.) Served in Virginia. Mustered out of service with battery, August 6, 1861. First Lieutenant, First Rhode Island Light Artillery, October 17, 1861. Served in Virginia and in North Carolina. Resigned, October 6, 1862. Captain and Commissary of Subsistence, United States Volunteers, February 21, 1863.

Josiah G. Woodbury. Acting Assistant Paymaster, United States Navy, December, 1862. Served in South Atlantic Squadron. Killed on board the iron-clad Catskill, in the attack on Forts Wagner and Sumter, August 17, 1863.

CLASS OF 1858.

Samuel W. Abbott. Assistant Surgeon, United States Navy, November 11, 1861. Served in North and South Blockading Squadrons. Resigned, May 27, 1864. Surgeon, First Massachusetts Cavalry, November 2, 1864. Served in Virginia. Mustered out of service with regiment, June 26, 1865.

Edward L. Clark. Chaplain, Twelfth Massachusetts Volunteers, June 26, 1861. Served in Virginia. Resigned, June 16, 1862.

Stephen A. Cobb. Captain, Fourth Kansas Volunteers, 1862. Provost Marshal of the Eighth and Ninth Districts of the Department of the Missouri. Mustered out of the service in 1863. Appointed Captain and Commissary of Subsistence in the spring of 1864, and assigned to duty on the staff of Major-General Gordon Granger. Chief Commissary, Thirteenth Army Corps; Brevet Major; Brevet Lieutenant-Colonel. Served in the Departments of the Missouri, and of the Gulf. Mustered out of the service, September 23, 1865.

Elisha Dyer, Jr. Sergeant, First Light Battery, Rhode Island Volunteers, April 18, 1861.

Robert H. I. Goddard. Private, Company C, First Rhode Island Volunteers, May 2, 1861, (date of muster.) Mustered out of service with regiment, August 2, 1861. Lieutenant and Volunteer Aide-de-Camp, on staff of Major-General Burnside, September 20, 1862. Captain, March 11, 1863; Brevet Major,

August 4, 1864; Brevet Lieutenant-Colonel, April 2, 1865; Assistant Inspector-General, Ninth Army Corps. Served in Maryland, Virginia, Kentucky, and Tennessee. Mustered out of service at the close of the war.

ARNOLD GREEN. Private, Company C, First Rhode Island Volunteers, May 29, 1861. Served in Virginia. Mustered out of service with regiment, August 2, 1861.

EDWARD M. GUSHEE. Chaplain, Ninth New Hampshire Volunteers, July 10, 1862. Served in Maryland, Virginia and Kentucky. Resigned, October 20, 1863.

JOHN HAY. Secretary to President Lincoln, 1861. Volunteer Aide-de-Camp to Major-General Hunter, in 1863; Major and Assistant Adjutant-General, January 12, 1864. Ordered to Major-General Gilmore, commanding Department of the South, April, 1864. Ordered back to Washington as Aide-de-Camp to the President, May 31, 1864. Brevet Lieutenant-Colonel; Brevet Colonel.

CHARLES L. KNEASS. First Lieutenant, Eighteenth Infantry, United States Army, May 14, 1861; Adjutant, July 2, 1861; Captain. Served in Tennessee. Killed at the battle of Murfreesboro, December 31, 1862.

ROBERT MILLAR. Assistant Surgeon, Fourth Rhode Island Volunteers, August 27, 1861; Brevet Major, United States Volunteers, March 13, 1865. Served in Virginia. Mustered out of service, August 26, 1864, term of service having expired.

WILLIAM A. MOWRY. Captain, Company K, Eleventh Rhode Island Volunteers, October 1, 1862. Served in Virginia. Mustered out of service with regiment, July 13, 1863.

AARON H. NELSON. Acting Assistant Paymaster, United States Navy, July 7, 1863. Served in North and South Blockading

Squadrons. Resigned, March 28, 1865. Assistant Paymaster, United States Navy, February 24, 1867. Still in the service.

WALTER B. NOYES. Chaplain, Fifth Rhode Island Volunteers, November 7, 1861. Served in North Carolina. Resigned, August 15, 1862.

SAMUEL THURBER. Private, Company K, Eleventh Rhode Island Volunteers, October 1, 1862; Second Lieutenant, November 3, 1862; First Lieutenant, March 26, 1863. Served in Virginia. Mustered out of service with regiment, July 13, 1863.

CLASS OF 1859.

THEODORE ANDREWS. Private, Company D, First Rhode Island Volunteers, May 2, 1861, (date of muster.) Served in Virginia. Mustered out of service with regiment, August 2, 1861.

LUCIUS S. BOLLES. Assistant Surgeon, Second Rhode Island Volunteers, March 9, 1863. Served in Maryland and Virginia. Resigned, September 10, 1863.

WILLIAM E. BOWEN. First Sergeant, Battery E, First Rhode Island Light Artillery, September 30, 1861. Served in Virginia. Discharged on surgeon's certificate, March 14, 1862.

ADONIRAM B. JUDSON. Assistant-Surgeon United States Navy, July 30, 1861; Passed Assistant Surgeon, June 22, 1864; Surgeon, December 26, 1866. Served in South Atlantic and Gulf Squadrons. Still in the service.

WILLIAM W. KEEN. Assistant Surgeon, Fifth Massachusetts Volunteers, July 1, 1861. Mustered out of service with regiment, July 31, 1861. Acting Assistant Surgeon, United States Army, May 8, 1862; Assistant and Executive Officer, Eckington Hospital, Washington, D. C.; Surgeon in charge of Ascension

Hospital, Washington, D. C. On field duty, Second Bull Run battle, August, 1862, and for a while a prisoner. Afterwards on hospital duty at Philadelphia. Mustered out of service, July 2, 1864.

CHARLES H. PERRY. Assistant Surgeon, United States Navy, September 2, 1861. Served in the West Gulf and North Atlantic Blockading Squadrons. Resigned, May 9, 1865.

SAMUEL T. POINIER. Chaplain, Fifteenth Kentucky Volunteers, June 3, 1863. Served in Tennessee and Georgia. Mustered out of service, February, 1865.

GEORGE L. PORTER. Assistant Surgeon, United States Army, July 17, 1862. Served with Best's Battery, United States Artillery, and with Fifth United States Cavalry. Captured during Banks' campaign in the Shenandoah Valley. Wounded at Boonsboro', Maryland, July 9, 1863. Assigned to duty as Post Surgeon, at Washington Arsenal, Washington, D. C., May 12, 1864. Brevet Captain ; Brevet Major, United States Army, March 13, 1865. Still in the service.

CHARLES M. SMITH. Private, Company C, First Rhode Island Volunteers, May 2, 1861, (date of muster.) Served in Virginia. Mustered out of service with regiment, August 2, 1861. Second Lieutenant, Eleventh United States Colored Heavy Artillery, January 14, 1864. Served in Department of the Gulf. Mustered out of service October 2, 1865.

ROBERT H. THURSTON. Third Assistant Engineer, United States Navy, July 29, 1861 ; Second Assistant Engineer, (Ensign,) December 18, 1862 ; First Assistant Engineer, (Master,) January 30, 1865. Served in North and South Atlantic, and Gulf Blockading Squadrons. Still in the service, and on duty at the Naval Academy, Annapolis, Maryland.

THOMAS F. TOBEY. Sergeant, Company D, Tenth Rhode Island Volunteers, May 29, 1862; Captain, Seventh Rhode Island Volunteers, September 4, 1862; Major, January 7, 1863. Served in Virginia, Kentucky and Mississippi. Resigned, February 9, 1864. Second Lieutenant, Fourteenth Infantry, United States Army, May 3, 1865; First Lieutenant, May 6, 1865. Still in the service.

RICHARD WATERMAN. Private, First Light Battery, Rhode Island Volunteers, May 2, 1861, (date of muster.) Served in Virginia. Mustered out of service with battery, August 6, 1861; First Lieutenant, First Rhode Island Light Artillery, Battery C, August 8, 1861; Captain, July 25, 1862. Served in Virginia and Maryland. Mustered out of service, September 2, 1864.

CLASS OF 1860.

HENRY S. ADAMS. First Lieutenant and Adjutant, Forty-First Massachusetts Volunteers, September, 1862. Served in the Department of the Gulf. Mustered out of service, November 10, 1863.

CRAWFORD ALLEN. Second Lieutenant, First Rhode Island Light Artillery, November 7, 1861; First Lieutenant, November 18, 1862; Adjutant, First Regiment Rhode Island Artillery; Captain, Battery H, First Rhode Island Light Artillery, September 30, 1863; Brevet Major, April 2, 1865; Brevet Lieutenant-Colonel. Served in Virginia. Wounded at the battle of Fredericksburg, Virginia, May 3, 1863. Mustered out of service, June 28, 1865.

GEORGE N. BLISS. Private, Company B, First Rhode Island Cavalry, September 28, 1861; Quartermaster-Sergeant, October 4, 1861; First Lieutenant and Regimental Quartermaster, October 12, 1861; assigned to duty in Company G, December 21, 1861; Captain, July 15, 1862; Judge Advocate General, Court-

Martial at New Haven, Connecticut, from August, 1863, till May, 1864; Assistant Provost Marshal, General Sheridan's Cavalry. Wounded at Waynesborough, Virginia, September 28, 1864, and taken prisoner. In hospital at Charlottesville, Virginia, and, at the Libby Prison, Richmond, Virginia, December 9; selected as a hostage and placed in close confinement. Exchanged, February 8, 1865. Mustered out of service, May 15, 1865.

HORACE S. BRADFORD. Acting Assistant Paymaster, United States Navy, February 24, 1862. Served in West Gulf and Atlantic Blockading Squadrons. Resigned, December 1, 1863.

DAVID P. CORBIN. First Lieutenant, Company G, Twenty-Second Connecticut Volunteers, August 25, 1862; Captain, February 19, 1863. Served in Virginia. Mustered out of service with regiment, July 7, 1863.

SAMUEL W. DUNCAN. Captain, Company F, Fiftieth Massachusetts Volunteers, November 10, 1862. Served in the Department of the Gulf. Mustered out of service with regiment, August 24, 1863.

HARRIS HOWARD. Chaplain, Seventh Rhode Island Volunteers, September 6, 1862. Served in Maryland, Virginia and Kentucky. Resigned, June 3, 1863.

PARDON S. JASTRAM. Private, Company C, First Rhode Island Volunteers, May 2, 1861, (date of muster.) Served in Virginia. Mustered out of service with regiment, August 2, 1861; Second Lieutenant, First Rhode Island Light Artillery, October 16, 1861; First Lieutenant, December 6, 1862; Assistant Adjutant-General, Artillery Brigade, Third Army Corps. Served in Maryland and Virginia. Resigned, March 29, 1864.

FREDERIC A. MITCHEL. Captain and Aide-de-Camp on staff of Major-General O. M. Mitchel, September 3, 1862. Mustered out of service, November 7, 1862. Second Lieutenant, Sixteenth Infantry, United States Army, March 25, 1863. Served in the Department of the Cumberland. Resigned, August 7, 1863.

BENJAMIN F. PABODIE. Corporal, Company H, Tenth Rhode Island Volunteers, May 26, 1862. Served in Virginia. Mustered out of service with regiment, September 1, 1862.

ANDREW C. POLLARD. Paymaster's Clerk, United States Navy, April 17, 1865. Served in the West Gulf Blockading Squadron. Discharged, December 20, 1865.

HENRY K. PORTER. Private, Company A, Forty-Fifth Massachusetts Volunteers, October, 1862. Served in North Carolina. Mustered out of service with regiment, July 8, 1863.

LIVINGSTON SATERLEE. On staff of Colonel (afterwards Major-General) Butterfield, April 19, 1861; Captain, Company K, Twelfth New York Volunteers, (National Guards;) Lieutenant-Colonel, 1862. Taken prisoner at Harper's Ferry, Virginia, September, 1862. Brevet Brigadier-General, United States Volunteers.

WILLIAM S. SMITH. Private, Company C, First Rhode Island Volunteers, May 2, 1861, (date of muster.) Served in Virginia. Mustered out of service with regiment, August 2, 1861. Captain, Tenth Rhode Island Volunteers, May 26, 1862. Served in Virginia. Mustered out of service with regiment, September 1, 1862.

HENRY J. SPOONER. Second Lieutenant, Fourth Rhode Island Volunteers, August 27, 1862; First Lieutenant and Adjutant, October 1, 1862. ·

ALBERT G. WASHBURN. Private, One Hundred and Thirty-Fourth New York Volunteers, July, 1862; Sergeant; First Lieutenant, Company I, September 12, 1862; Captain, Company E,

October 24, 1862. Served in Virginia. Died at Falmouth, Virginia, January 26, 1863.

JOHN WHIPPLE. First Lieutenant and Adjutant, First Rhode Island Cavalry, October 4, 1861; Captain, February 21, 1862; Major, June 27, 1862. Served in Maryland and Virginia. Resigned, February 17, 1863.

ALFRED M. WILLIAMS. Private, Company K, Fourth Massachusetts Volunteers, August 12, 1862. Served in the Department of the Gulf. Mustered out of service with regiment, August 28, 1863.

CLASS OF 1861.

ORVILLE A. BARKER. Private, Thirty-Ninth Massachusetts Volunteers, August 5, 1862; Corporal, January 1, 1863; Hospital Steward, October 13, 1863; Second Lieutenant, November 8, 1863; First Lieutenant, September 13, 1864; Adjutant; Captain, April 3, 1865. Served in Maryland and Virginia. Mustered out of service with regiment, June 2, 1865.

JOHN K. BUCKLYN. Private, First Rhode Island Light Artillery, 1861; Quartermaster-Sergeant, September, 1861; Second Lieutenant, March 1, 1862; First Lieutenant, December 31, 1862. Wounded at Gettysburg, Pennsylvania, July 2, 1863. Brevet Captain, United States Volunteers, October 19, 1864; Captain. Served in Maryland and Virginia. Mustered out of service with regiment, February 2, 1865.

HENRY S. BURRAGE. Private, Company A, Thirty-Sixth Massachusetts Volunteers, August 1, 1862; Sergeant, August 5, 1862; Sergeant-Major, August 27, 1862; Second Lieutenant, Company D, May 16, 1863; First Lieutenant, November 17, 1863. Wounded at Cold Harbor, Virginia, June 3, 1864. Captain, June 19, 1864. A prisoner at Richmond and Danville, Virginia, from November

1864 till February 22, 1865. Brevet Major, United States Volunteers, March 13, 1865. Acting Assistant Adjutant-General, First Brigade, Second Division, Ninth Army Corps. Served in Maryland, Kentucky, Mississippi, Tennessee and Virginia. Mustered out of service, June 8, 1865.

CHRISTOPHER C. BURROWS. Quartermaster-Sergeant, Company C, First Rhode Island Cavalry, December 14, 1861. Served in Maryland and Virginia. Discharged, April 20, 1864, to accept the Chaplaincy of the Twenty-Second Regiment, United States Colored Troops. Served in the Department of the Gulf. Resigned, June 17, 1865.

FRANK H. CARPENTER. Hospital Steward, Twelfth Rhode Island Volunteers, October 13, 1862. Served in Virginia and Kentucky. Mustered out of service with regiment, July 29, 1863.

THOMAS T. CASWELL. Assistant Paymaster, United States Navy, (Master,) September 9, 1861; Paymaster, (Lieutenant-Commander,) September 17, 1863. Served in West Gulf and North and South Blockading Squadrons. Still in the service.

CHARLES H. CHAPMAN. First Lieutenant and Adjutant, Fifth Rhode Island Volunteers, November 30, 1861. Served in North Carolina. Resigned, May 14, 1862. Sergeant-Major, Thirty-Ninth Massachusetts Volunteers, September 1, 1862; Second Lieutenant, August 30, 1863; First Lieutenant, September 6, 1864. A prisoner at Richmond and Danville, Virginia, from August 19, 1864, till February 22, 1865. Served in Maryland and Virginia. Resigned, April 29, 1865. Captain, Forty-First Regiment, United States Colored Troops, April 30, 1865. Served in Department of the Gulf. Mustered out of service, December 10, 1865.

JAMES A. DEWOLF. Private, Company C, First Rhode Island Volunteers, April 17, 1861. Served in Virginia. Mustered out of service with regiment, August 2, 1861. Acting Medical Cadet at McDougall General Hospital, New York Harbor, March 10, 1863. Acting Assistant Surgeon, United States Army, at Hampton General Hospital, Fortress Monroe, Virginia, June 1, 1863.

WILLIAM W. DOUGLAS. Second Lieutenant, Fifth Rhode Island Heavy Artillery, November 30, 1861; First Lieutenant, June 7, 1862; Captain, February 14, 1863. Served in North Carolina. Mustered out December 20, 1864, term of service having expired.

T. HENRY EDSALL. First Lieutenant and Adjutant, One Hundred Seventy-Sixth New York Volunteers, (Ironsides,) December 31, 1862. Served in the Department of the Gulf. Mustered out of service with regiment, November 16, 1863.

CHARLES H. HIDDEN. Private, Company D, Tenth Rhode Island Volunteers, May 26, 1862. Served in Virginia. Mustered out of service with regiment, September 1, 1862.

WILLIAM W. HOPPIN. Private, Company D, First Rhode Island Volunteers, April 17, 1861. Served in Virginia. Mustered out of service with regiment, August 2, 1861.

CHARLES E. HOSMER. Private, Company B, Tenth Rhode Island Volunteers, May 26, 1862. Served in Virginia. Mustered out of service with regiment, September 1, 1862. Assistant Surgeon, United States Navy. Discharged at the close of the war.

LELAND D. JENCKES. Private, Company D, First Rhode Island Volunteers, April 17, 1861. Wounded, July 21, 1861, (battle of Bull Run,) and fell into the hands of the enemy. A prisoner at Richmond, Virginia, and Tuscaloosa, Alabama. Paroled, March 1,

1862, but retained a prisoner at Salisbury, North Carolina, till May 23, 1862; then exchanged. Mustered out of service, June 1, 1862.

CHARLES F. MASON. Second Lieutenant, First Rhode Island Light Artillery, December 24, 1861; First Lieutenant, October 1, 1862. On staff of Colonel Tompkins, Chief of Artillery Brigade, Sixth Army Corps, November, 1863. Served in Maryland and Virginia. Resigned, April 21, 1864.

ELISHA C. MOWRY. Private, Company D, Tenth Rhode Island Volunteers, May 26, 1862. Served in Virginia. Mustered out of service with regiment, September 1, 1862.

STEPHEN F. PECKHAM. Hospital Steward, Seventh Rhode Island Volunteers, September 6, 1862. With Medical Director, Ninth Army Corps, May 21, 1864. In charge of Chemical Department, United States Laboratory, Philadelphia, January, 1865. Served in Maryland, Virginia, Kentucky and Mississippi. Mustered out of service, May 26, 1865.

DUNCAN C. PHILLIPS. First Lieutenant, Company M, Fourth Pennsylvania Cavalry, September 9, 1862; Captain, Company F, November 21, 1863; Major, January 1, 1865. Inspector of Cavalry at Elmira, New York, from July, 1864. Mustered out of service, February 16, 1865.

JOHN W. ROGERS. First Lieutenant, Seventh Massachusetts Volunteers, June 15, 1861; Captain, Thirty-Eighth Massachusetts Volunteers, August 12, 1862; Captain, Fortieth Massachusetts Volunteers, August 18, 1862. Declined commission. Served in Virginia.

FREDERIC M. SACKETT. Private, Company D, First Rhode Island Volunteers, April 17, 1861. Mustered out of service with regiment, August 2, 1861. First Lieutenant, Battery C, First

Rhode Island Light Artillery, October 5, 1861. Wounded at the battle of Chancellorsville, Virginia, May 3, 1863. Served in Maryland and Virginia. Mustered out of service, October 3, 1863.

SUMNER U. SHEARMAN. Second Lieutenant, Fourth Rhode Island Volunteers, August 27, 1862; First Lieutenant, November 25, 1862; Captain, March 7, 1863. Captured before Petersburg, July 30, 1864. A prisoner at Columbia, South Carolina. Exchanged, December 7, 1864. Served in Virginia and Maryland. Mustered out of service, December 17, 1864.

HENRY K. SOUTHWICK. Second Lieutenant, Second Rhode Island Volunteers, August 29, 1862; First Lieutenant, August 9, 1863; Captain, Eleventh Regiment, United States Colored Heavy Artillery, February 1, 1864. Acting Inspector-General on staff of General T. W. Sherman. Served in Virginia and in the Department of the Gulf. Mustered out of service with regiment, October 2, 1865.

JOHN H. STINESS. Second Lieutenant, Second New York Artillery, December 13, 1861. Served in Virginia. Mustered out of service, November 1, 1862.

LUCIEN B. STONE. Second Lieutenant, Company E, First Rhode Volunteers, April 18, 1861. Served in Virginia. Resigned, June 5, 1861.

WASHINGTON B. TRULL. Assistant Surgeon, United States Volunteers, July 6, 1863; Brevet Captain, November 30, 1865. Served in Tennessee. Mustered out of service, December 8, 1865.

JAMES C. WILLIAMS. Second Lieutenant, Forty-Fifth Ohio Volunteers, September, 1861. Acting Aide-de-Camp on staff of General O. M. Mitchel, September 29, 1861. Second Lieutenant, Twenty-Fourth Ohio Volunteers, December 20, 1861. Appointed

Aide-de-Camp, (rank Second Lieutenant,) July 1, 1862, to date from April 11, 1862. Captain and Aide-de-Camp, September 15, 1862, to date from September 3, 1862. Died at Beaufort, South Carolina, October 29, 1862.

CLASS OF 1862.

JOSHUA M. ADDEMAN. Private, Company B, Tenth Rhode Island Volunteers, May 26, 1862. Mustered out of service with regiment, September 1, 1862. Captain, Company H, Eleventh Regiment, United States Colored Heavy Artillery, November 23, 1863. Acting Assistant Adjutant-General on staff of General Cameron, commanding District of La Fourche, Louisiana, 1864. Served in Virginia and Louisiana. Mustered out of service with regiment, October 2, 1865.

GEORGE H. BABBITT. Private, Company F, Thirty-Ninth Massachusetts Volunteers, August 5, 1862; Sergeant, September 1, 1862. Served in Ambulance Corps, Fifth Army Corps. Mustered out of service with regiment, June 2, 1865.

JOHN T. BLAKE. Sergeant, Battery B, First Rhode Island Light Artillery, August 13, 1861. Wounded at the battle of Gettysburg, Pennsylvania, July 2, 1863. Second Lieutenant, Battery A, October 28, 1863. Served in Virginia. Mustered out of service, August 12, 1864.

T. FREDERIC BROWN. Corporal, Battery A, First Rhode Island Light Artillery, June 6, 1861; Second Lieutenant, Battery C, August 13, 1862; First Lieutenant, Battery B, December 29, 1862; Captain, April 7, 1864; Brevet Major, December 3, 1864; Brevet Lieutenant-Colonel, April 9, 1865. Inspector-General, Artillery Brigade, Second Army Corps. Wounded at Gettysburg, Pennsylvania. Served in Maryland and Virginia. Mustered out of service, June 12, 1865.

WILLIAM I. BROWN. Second Lieutenant, Ninth New Hampshire Volunteers, August 10, 1862; First Lieutenant, March 1, 1863; First Lieutenant and Adjutant, November 1, 1863; Major, Eighteenth New Hampshire Volunteers, October 13, 1864. Served in Maryland, Kentucky, Mississippi, Tennessee and Virginia. Killed before Petersburg, Virginia, March 29, 1865.

FRANK W. DRAPER. Private, Thirty-Fifth Massachusetts Volunteers, August 10, 1862. Captain, Thirty-Ninth Regiment, United States Colored Troops, April 14, 1864. Acting Aide-de-Camp, July 12, 1864; Acting Assistant Adjutant-General, First Brigade, Third Division, Twenty-Fifth Army Corps, October 20, 1864. Served in Maryland, Virginia, Kentucky, Mississippi, Tennessee and North Carolina. Mustered out of service, June 23, 1865.

JOSIAH R. GODDARD. Sergeant, Company K, Eleventh Rhode Island Volunteers, October 1, 1862. Served in Virginia. Mustered out of service with regiment, July 6, 1863.

JAMES B. M. GROSVENOR. Private, First Light Battery, Rhode Island Volunteers, May 2, 1861, (date of muster.) Served in Virginia. Mustered out of service with battery, August 6, 1861.

RHODOLPHUS H. JOHNSON. Private, Company I, Ninth Rhode Island Volunteers, May 26, 1862. Served in Virginia. Mustered out of service with regiment, September 2, 1862.

JASON B. KELLY. Corporal, Tenth Rhode Island Volunteers, May 26, 1862. Served in Virginia. Mustered out of service with regiment, September 1, 1862.

GEORGE E. MASON. Assistant Surgeon, First Massachusetts Heavy Artillery, April 7, 1865. Served in Virginia. Mustered out of service with regiment, August 25, 1865.

JOSHUA MELLEN. Private, Company D, Tenth Rhode Island Volunteers, May 26, 1862. Served in Virginia. Mustered out of service with regiment, September 1, 1862.

ADDISON PARKER. Private, Company B, Tenth Rhode Island Volunteers, May 26, 1862. Mustered out of service with regiment, September 1, 1862. Sergeant, Company I, Forty-Sixth Massachusetts Volunteers. Mustered out of service, July 28, 1863. Served in Virginia and North Carolina.

JAMES H. REMINGTON. Captain, Seventh Rhode Island Volunteers, September 4, 1862. Wounded at Fredericksburg, Virginia, December 13, 1862. Served in Maryland and Virginia. May 2, 1863, honorably discharged on account of wounds received in action. Captain, Veteran Reserve Corps. Brevet Major.

CHRISTOPHER RHODES. Private, Company D, Tenth Rhode Island Volunteers, May 26, 1862. Served in Virginia. Mustered out of service with regiment, September 1, 1862.

ISAAC H. SAUNDERS. Private, Company D, First Rhode Island Volunteers, May 30, 1861. Served in Virginia. Mustered out of service with regiment, August 2, 1861.

EDWARD H. SEARS. First Lieutenant, Second Rhode Island Volunteers, June 6, 1861; Captain, July 22, 1861. Resigned, October 18, 1861. First Lieutenant, First Rhode Island Light Artillery, October 19, 1861. Served in Virginia and Maryland. Resigned, November 14, 1862. Acting Assistant Paymaster, United States Navy, August 27, 1863. Served in North and South Atlantic Blockading Squadron. Still in the service.

RICHARD WATERMAN. Private, Company C, First Rhode Island Volunteers, May 2, 1861, (date of muster.) Mustered out of service with regiment, August 2, 1861. First Lieutenant, Company

F, First Rhode Island Cavalry, October 4, 1861. Resigned, December 5, 1862. Served in Maryland and Virginia.

EDWARD N. WHITTIER. Private, Company C, First Rhode Island Volunteers, May 2, 1861, (date of muster.) Mustered out of service with regiment, August 2, 1861. First Sergeant, Fifth Maine Battery, November 29, 1861; Second Lieutenant, September 1, 1862; First Lieutenant, May 5, 1863; Brevet Captain, United States Volunteers, October 19, 1864. Acting Assistant Adjutant-General, Artillery Brigade, Sixth Army Corps, June, 1864. Served in Maryland and Virginia. Mustered out of service with battery, July 25, 1865.

GEORGE T. WOODWARD. Private, Company F, Thirty-Ninth Massachusetts Volunteers, August 25, 1862. Sergeant, Signal Corps, United States Army. Served in Virginia and Louisiana. Mustered out of service, June 2, 1865.

CLASS OF 1863.

WILLIAM AMES. Second Lieutenant, Second Rhode Island Volunteers, June 6, 1861; First Lieutenant, October 25, 1861; Captain, July 24, 1862; Major, Third Rhode Island Heavy Artillery, January 28, 1863; Lieutenant-Colonel, March 22, 1864; Colonel, October 10, 1864. Chief of Artillery, Department of South Carolina. Served in Maryland, Virginia and South Carolina. Mustered out of service, August 27, 1865.

WILLIAM B. AVERY. Private, Company A, First Rhode Island Volunteers, May 2, 1861, (date of muster.) Served in Virginia. Mustered out of service with regiment, August 2, 1861. Master's Mate, United States Navy, December 25, 1861. Second Lieutenant, New York Marine Artillery, February 15, 1862; First Lieutenant, July 1, 1862; Captain, August 1, 1862. Chief of Artillery, on General Ledlie's staff, January 17, 1863. Acting Ensign,

United States Navy, June 15, 1863. Served in North and South Atlantic Blockading Squadrons. Passed an examination as Acting Master, and honorably discharged, August 10, 1865.

CHARLES E. BAILEY. Private, Company D, First Rhode Island Volunteers, May 30, 1861. Served in Virginia. Mustered out of service with regiment, August 2, 1861.

DANIEL R. BALLOU. Sergeant-Major, Twelfth Rhode Island Volunteers, October 13, 1862; Second Lieutenant, Company G, November 20, 1862. Served in Virginia. Resigned, April 25, 1863.

WILLIAM W. BLISS. Private, Company K, Tenth Rhode Island Volunteers, May 26, 1862. Mustered out of service with regiment, September 1, 1862. Private, Company B, One Hundred Seventy-Sixth New York Volunteers, September 11, 1862; First Sergeant, December 18, 1862; Sergeant-Major, March 1, 1863; Second Lieutenant, August 20, 1863; Captain, First Corps d' Afrique, Engineers, September 2, 1863; Lieutenant-Colonel, Eighty-Seventh Regiment, United States Colored Troops, September 28, 1864. Served in Virginia, Mississippi, Louisiana, and Texas. Resigned, September 7, 1865.

AMOS M. BOWEN. Private, Company A, First Rhode Island Volunteers, May 2, 1861, (date of muster.) Captured at the battle of Bull Run, July 21, 1861. A prisoner at Richmond, Virginia, and Salisbury, North Carolina. Exchanged, May 22, 1862. First Lieutenant, Second Rhode Island Volunteers, January 22, 1863. Aide-de-Camp, on staff of General Eustis. Served in Virginia. Mustered out, June 17, 1864, term of service having expired.

JOSEPH M. BRADLEY. Private, First Light Battery, Rhode Island Volunteers, May 2, 1861, (date of muster.) Served in Virginia. Mustered out of service with battery, August 6, 1861.

CHARLES R. BRAYTON. First Lieutenant, Third Rhode Island Heavy Artillery, August 27, 1861; Captain, November 28, 1862; Lieutenant-Colonel, October 22, 1863; Colonel, March 22, 1864. Served in the Department of the South. Mustered out, October 5, 1864 term of service having expired.

EDWARD P. BROWN. Second Lieutenant, Fourth Rhode Island Volunteers, August 27, 1862; First Lieutenant, January 4, 1863; Captain, March 2, 1863. Acting Assistant Commissary of Subsistence, First Brigade, Second Division, Seventh Army Corps, July 28, 1863. Acting Inspector-General, Post of Williamsburg, Virginia, May 15, 1864. Aide-de-Camp on staff of First Brigade, Second Division, Ninth Army Corps, July 4, 1864. Acting Assistant Inspector-General of same brigade, August 19, 1864. Acting Assistant Inspector-General, Third Division, Ninth Army Corps, March 26, 1865. Brevet Major, April 2, 1865. Served in Virginia. Mustered out of service, June 5, 1865.

CHARLES C. CRAGIN. Private, Company B, Tenth Rhode Island Volunteers, May 26, 1862. Mustered out of service with regiment, September 1, 1862. Captain, Eleventh Regiment, United States Colored Heavy Artillery, December 5, 1863. Served in Virginia and Louisiana. Mustered out of service with regiment, October 2, 1865.

AGUSTUS N. CUNNINGHAM. Sergeant, Company D, Second Rhode Island Volunteers, June 5, 1861; (First Lieutenant, Company H, Seventy-Eighth New York Volunteers, December 23, 1861; Captain, February 30, 1862, but not mustered.) Mustered out of service, July 13, 1865.

JOSEPH H. CURTIS. Private, Company F, Forty-Fourth Massaachusetts Volunteers, August, 1862. Served in North Carolina. Mustered out of service with regiment, June 18, 1863.

EDWARD P. DEACON. Aide-de-Camp, on staff of Major-General
Heintzleman, commanding Third Army Corps, May, 1862; Captain, Second United States Cavalry, February, 1864; June, 1864,
ordered to duty with Eighteenth Army Corps; Acting Aide-de-
Camp to Brevet Major-General Devens, commanding Third Division, Twenty-Fourth Army Corps; Twice Officer at Aiken's Landing, Virginia; Brevet Major, United States Volunteers; Brevet
Lieutenant-Colonel. Served in Virginia and Maryland. Mustered out of service, June 25, 1865.

SAMUEL R. DORRANCE. Sergeant, Company D, Tenth Rhode
Island Volunteers, May 26, 1862. Served in Virginia. Mustered
out of service, July 15, 1862.

FOREST F. EMERSON. Private, Company B, Tenth Rhode Isl-
and Volunteers, May 26, 1862. Served in Virginia. Mustered
out of service with regiment, September 1, 1862.

HENRY G. GAY. Private, Tenth Rhode Island Volunteers,
May 26, 1862. Mustered out of service with regiment, Septem-
ber 1, 1862. Private, Company F, Twenty-Sixth Connecticut
Volunteers, September 3, 1862. First Sergeant, September 19,
1862. Wounded at Port Hudson, June 13, 1863. Served in
Virginia and Louisiana. Mustered out of service with regiment,
August 17, 1863. Second Lieutenant, August 17, 1863, but not
mustered on account of expiration of service.

CHARLES W. GREENE. Private, Thirty-Fifth Massachusetts Volunteers, July 25, 1862; Captain, Company F, One Hundred and
Sixteenth Regiment, United States Colored Troops, July 21, 1864;
Served in Maryland, Virginia, Kentucky, Mississippi, Tennessee
and Texas. Mustered out of service, July 8, 1865.

JOHN J. HOLMES. Private, Company K, Tenth Rhode Island
Volunteers, May 26, 1862. Served in Virginia. Mustered out
of service with regiment, September 1, 1862.

HERVEY F. JACOBS. Second Lieutenant, Company F, Twenty-Sixth Connecticut Volunteers, August 29, 1862. Wounded before Port Hudson, Louisiana, June 14, 1863, and died July 5, 1863. Served in the Department of the Gulf.

J. ALBERT MONROE. First Lieutenant, First Rhode Island Light Artillery, June 6, 1861; Captain, September 7, 1861; Major, October 21, 1862; Lieutenant-Colonel, December 4, 1862; Chief of Artillery, Ninth Army Corps. Served in Virginia. Mustered out, October 5, 1864, term of service having expired.

ALEXANDER PECKHAM. Private, Company L, Ninth Rhode Island Volunteers, May 26, 1862. Served in Virginia. Mustered out of service with regiment, September 2, 1862.

DUNCAN A. PELL. Private, Company A, First Rhode Island Volunteers, May 2, 1861, (date of muster.) Mustered out of service with regiment, August 2, 1861. Lieutenant and Volunteer Aide-de-Camp, on staff of Major-General Burnside, December 1, 1861; Captain, April 4, 1862; Brevet Major, December 2, 1864; Brevet Lieutenant-Colonel, March 13, 1865; Brevet Colonel, April 2, 1865. Served in North Carolina, Maryland, Virginia, Kentucky, Mississippi, and Tennessee. Mustered out of service at the close of the war.

S. HARTWELL PRATT. Private, Company B, Tenth Rhode Island Volunteers, May 26, 1862. Served in Virginia. Mustered out of service with regiment, September 1, 1862.

LIVINGSTON SCOTT. Private, Company B, Tenth Rhode Island Volunteers, May 26, 1862. Mustered out of service with regiment, September 1, 1862. First Lieutenant and Adjutant, Third Rhode Island Cavalry, July 1, 1863; Captain, January 2, 1864. Served in Virginia and Louisiana. Mustered out of service with regiment, November 29, 1865.

ORVILLE B. SEAGRAVE. Private, Company B, Tenth Rhode Island Volunteers, May 26, 1862. Served in Virginia. Mustered out of service with regiment, September 1, 1862. Acting Assistant Paymaster, United States Navy, October 19, 1863. Served in West Gulf and South Atlantic Blockading Squadrons. Honorably discharged, October 18, 1865.

ORSMUS A. TAFT. Corporal, Company E, Tenth Rhode Island Volunteers, May 26, 1862. Served in Virginia. Mustered out of service with regiment, September 1, 1862.

ANDREW F. WARREN. Private, Company K, Tenth Rhode Island Volunteers, May 26, 1862. Served in Virginia. Mustered out of service with regiment, September 1, 1862.

CLASS OF 1864.

SETH J. AXTELL. Corporal, Fifty-First Massachusetts Volunteers, August 25, 1862. Served in North Carolina. Mustered out of service with regiment, July 21, 1863.

W. WHITMAN BAILEY. Private, Company D, Tenth Rhode Island Volunteers, May 26, 1862. Served in Virginia. Mustered out of service on account of sickness, July 15, 1862.

GEORGE B. BARROWS. Private, Company D, Tenth Rhode Island Volunteers, May 26, 1862. Served in Virginia. Mustered out of service with regiment, September 1, 1862.

EDSON C. CHICK. Private, Company K, Tenth Rhode Island Volunteers, May 26, 1862. Served in Virginia. Mustered out of service with regiment, September 1, 1862.

JOHN S. CHICK. Private, Company K, Tenth Rhode Island Volunteers, May 26, 1862. Served in Virginia. Mustered out of service with regiment, September 1, 1862.

HARRY C. CUSHING. Corporal, Battery A, First Rhode Island Light Artillery, June 6, 1861; Second Lieutenant, Battery F, Fourth United States Artillery, November 1, 1861; First Lieutenant, Battery H, Fourth United States Artillery; Brevet First Lieutenant, United States Army; Brevet Captain; Brevet Major. Served in Virginia, Maryland and Tennessee. Still in the service.

EDGAR J. DOE. Private, Company K, Tenth Rhode Island Volunteers, May 26, 1862. Served in Virginia. Mustered out of service, September 1, 1862.

JOHN K. DORRANCE. Private, Company D, Tenth Rhode Island Volunteers, May 26, 1862. Mustered out of service with regiment, September 1, 1862. Second Lieutenant, Second Rhode Island Volunteers, September 15, 1864; First Lieutenant, December 5, 1864. Wounded before Petersburg, Virginia, April 2, 1865. Brevet First Lieutenant, April 2, 1865; Brevet Captain, March 13, 1865. Served in Virginia. Mustered out of service, June 20, 1865.

G. LYMAN DWIGHT. Corporal, Battery A, First Rhode Island Light Artillery, June 6, 1861; Second Lieutenant, Battery B, November 29, 1861; First Lieutenant, Battery A, November 4, 1862. Acting Assistant Adjutant-General, Artillery Brigade, Second Army Corps. Served in Maryland and Virginia. Mustered out of service, September 30, 1864.

JOHN D. EDGELL. Corporal, Company K, Tenth Rhode Island Volunteers, May 26, 1862. Mustered out of service with regiment, September 1, 1862. Second Lieutenant, Company F, Fifty-Third Massachusetts Volunteers, September 12, 1862. Served in Virginia and Louisiana. Mustered out of service with regiment, September 2, 1863.

DAVID FALES. Corporal, Company I, Forty-Fifth Massachusetts Volunteers, September 17, 1862. Served in North Carolina. Mustered out of service with regiment, July 8, 1863.

SIMEON GALLUP. Corporal, Battery F, First Rhode Island Light Artillery, October 29, 1861; Sergeant. Served in Maryland and Virginia. Mustered out of service, October 28, 1864.

CLARENCE T. GARDNER. Private, Company E, First Rhode Island Volunteers, May 2, 1861, (date of muster.) Mustered out of service with regiment, August 2, 1861. First Sergeant, Company H, Third Rhode Island Heavy Artillery, October 5, 1861; Second Lieutenant, July 8, 1862; First Lieutenant, January 21, 1863. Detached for service with Battery B, First United States Light Artillery, March 24, 1863. Served in Virginia and in South Carolina. Resigned, October 24, 1863. United States Contract Surgeon, Army of the Potomac, from March 4, 1865, till June 4, 1865.

ALBERT E. HAM. Private, Company D, Tenth Rhode Island Volunteers, May 26, 1862. Served in Virginia. Mustered out of service with regiment, September 1, 1862.

CHARLES L. HARRINGTON. Private, Taylor's Battery, First Regiment, Illinois Artillery, May, 1862. Served in Tennessee. Died near Lafayette, Tennessee, June 25, 1862.

FRANK T. HAZLEWOOD. Private, Company A, Tenth Rhode Island Volunteers, May 26, 1862. Served in Virginia. Mustered out of service, September 1, 1862.

DAVID A. HOLMES. Corporal, Company A, Third Rhode Island Heavy Artillery, August 20, 1861. First Lieutenant, Second Rhode Island Volunteers, March 3, 1863. Served in South Carolina, Georgia and Virginia. Resigned, August 18, 1863.

JOHN S. HOLMES. Private, Company B, Tenth Rhode Island Volunteers, May 26, 1862. Served in Virginia. Mustered out of service with regiment, September 1, 1862.

WENDELL P. HOOD. Private, Company A, Tenth Rhode Island Volunteers. Mustered out of service with regiment, September 1, 1862. Hospital Steward, —— Massachusetts Volunteers.

BENJAMIN D. JONES. Corporal, Fourth Rhode Island Volunteers, October 30, 1861. Wounded at Antietam, September 17, 1862. Second Lieutenant, Eleventh Regiment, United States Colored Heavy Artillery, December 5, 1863. Served in North Carolina, Virginia, Maryland and Louisiana. Mustered out of service, October, 1865.

HENRY H. JUDSON. Private, Company M, Fifteenth New York Heavy Artillery, January 28, 1864. Served in Virginia. Mustered out of service, December 12, 1864.

GEORGE H. KENYON. Private, Company B, Tenth Rhode Island Volunteers, May 26, 1862. Served in Virginia. Mustered out of service with regiment, September 1, 1862.

OSCAR LAPHAM. Private, Twelfth Rhode Island Volunteers, August 23, 1862; First Lieutenant, October 13, 1862. Aide-de-Camp to Colonel D. R. Wright, commanding First Brigade, Casey's Division, November 7, 1862. Regimental Adjutant, December 27, 1862; Captain, March 29, 1863. Served in Virginia and Kentucky. Mustered out of service with regiment, July 29, 1863.

HENRY S. LATHAM. Private, Company B, Tenth Rhode Island Volunteers, May 26, 1862. Served in Virginia. Mustered out of service with regiment, September 1, 1862.

FRANK W. LOVE. Private, Company K, Tenth Rhode Island Volunteers, May 26, 1862. Served in Virginia. Mustered out of service with regiment, September 1, 1862.

HORACE W. LOVE. Second Lieutenant, Third Rhode Island Heavy Artillery, July 8, 1862. Served in the Department of the South. Resigned, June 12, 1863.

ROGER W. LOVE. Private, Third Rhode Island Heavy Artillery, April 3, 1862. Sergeant-Major, July 1, 1864. Served in the Department of the South. Mustered out of service, April 12, 1865.

MATTHEW M. MEGGETT. Private, Company B, Tenth Rhode Island Volunteers, May 26, 1862. Served in Virginia. Died at Fort Pennsylvania, near Washington, August 18, 1862.

GEORGE B. PECK. Second Lieutenant, Second Rhode Island Volunteers, December 13, 1864. Wounded at the battle of Sailors' Creek, Virginia, April 6, 1865. Served in Virginia. Resigned, June 30, 1865.

MATTSON C. SANBORN. First Lieutenant, Twentieth Maine Volunteers, August 29, 1862. Served in Maryland and Virginia. Mustered out of service, June 4, 1865.

NATHANIEL T. SANDERS. Private, Tenth Rhode Island Volunteers, May 26, 1862. Served in Virginia. Mustered out of service with regiment, September 1, 1862.

EUGENE SANGER. Private, Thirty-Eighth Massachusetts Volunteers, August, 1862. Served in the Department of the Gulf. Died of wounds received in action at Fort Bisland, Louisiana, April 12, 1863.

A. JUDSON SHURTLEFF. Private, Company I, Ninth Rhode Island Volunteers, May 26, 1862. Served in Virginia. Mustered out of service with regiment, September 2, 1862.

T. Delap Smith. Private, Company A, First Rhode Island Volunteers, May 29, 1861. Taken prisoner at the battle of Bull Run, July 21, 1861. Hospital Steward, United States Army. In the service till the close of the war.

John Tetlow. Corporal, Company B, Tenth Rhode Island Volunteers, May 26, 1862. Served in Virginia. Mustered out of service with regiment, September 1, 1862.

Francis M. Tyler. Private, Company H, Ninth Rhode Island Volunteers, May· 26, 1862. Served in Virginia. Mustered out of service with regiment, September 2, 1862. Sergeant, Nineteenth Unattached Company, Massachusetts Volunteer Militia, August 8, 1864. Mustered out of service with company, November 16, 1864.

William H. Underhill. Private, Company K, Tenth Rhode Island Volunteers, May 26, 1862. Served in Virginia. Mustered out of service with regiment, September 1, 1862.

Louis O. Walker. Private, Company G, Tenth Rhode Island Volunteers, May 26, 1862. Served in Virginia. Mustered out of service with regiment, September 1, 1862.

Rufus Waterman. Midshipman, United States Navy, September 25, 1861. Still in the service.

CLASS OF 1865.

Zephaniah Brown. Corporal, Company K, Tenth Rhode Island Volunteers, May 26, 1862. Mustered out of service with regiment, September 1, 1862. First Lieutenant, Eleventh Regiment, United States Colored Heavy Artillery, October 24, 1863. Acting Adjutant, First Battalion. Served in Virginia and Louisiana. Resigned, June 1, 1865.

Israel M. Bullock. Private, Company K, Tenth Rhode Island Volunteers, May 26, 1862. Served in Virginia. Mustered out of service with regiment, September 1, 1862.

Charles M. Corbin. Private, Company B, Tenth Rhode Island Volunteers, May 26, 1862. Served in Virginia. Mustered out of service with regiment, September 1, 1862.

William P. Davis. Corporal, Company G, Ninth Rhode Island Volunteers, May 26, 1862. Served in Virginia. Mustered out of service with regiment, September 1, 1862.

Frederic A. Dockray. Second Lieutenant, Company L, Third Heavy Artillery, February 11, 1862. Served in the Department of the South. Resigned, June 12, 1862.

James G. Dougherty. Private, Company D, Tenth Rhode Island Volunteers, May 26, 1862. Served in Virginia. Mustered out of service with regiment, September 1, 1862.

George B. Hanna. Private, Company K, Tenth Rhode Island Volunteers, May 26, 1862. Served in Virginia. Mustered out of service with regiment, September 1, 1862.

William C. Ives. Private, Company K, Tenth Rhode Island Volunteers, May 26, 1862. Served in Virginia. Mustered out of service with regiment, September 1, 1862.

George H. Messer. Private, Company K, Tenth Rhode Island Volunteers, May 26, 1862. Served in Virginia. Mustered out of service with regiment, September 1, 1862.

Frank J. Leonard.

Robert H. Paine. Private, Company D, Tenth Rhode Island Volunteers, May 26, 1862. Served in Virginia. Mustered out of service with regiment, September 1, 1862.

J. AMMON PRICE. Private, Company D, Tenth Rhode Island Volunteers, May 26, 1862. Served in Virginia. Mustered out of service with regiment, September 1, 1862.

HOSEA M. QUIMBY. Sergeant, Twenty-Seventh Maine Volunteers, September 14, 1862. Served in Virginia. Mustered out of service with regiment, July 17, 1863.

GEORGE W. SHAW. Private, Company K, Tenth Rhode Island Volunteers, May 26, 1862. Served in Virginia. Mustered out of service with regiment, September 1, 1862.

WELCOME A. SMITH. Private, Company F, Twenty-Sixth Connecticut Volunteers, September 20, 1862. Served in the Department of the Gulf. Mustered out of service with regiment, August 17, 1863.

HEBRON H. STEERE. Second Lieutenant, First Rhode Island Cavalry, June 14, 1863; First Lieutenant, May 19, 1865. Served in Maryland and Virginia. Mustered out of service with regiment, August 3, 1865.

CALEB E. THAYER. Corporal, Company C, Tenth Rhode Island Volunteers, May 26, 1862. Served in Virginia. Mustered out of service with regiment, September 1, 1862.

LEVI C. WALKER. Private, Company K, Tenth Rhode Island Volunteers, May 26, 1862. Served in Virginia. Mustered out of service with regiment, September 1, 1862.

JOSEPH WARD. Private, Company D, Tenth Rhode Island Volunteers, May 26, 1862. Served in Virginia. Mustered out of service with regiment, September 1, 1862.

WILLIAM C. WITTER. Private, Company K, Tenth Rhode Island Volunteers, May 26, 1862. Served in Virginia. Mustered out of service with regiment, September 1, 1862.

CLASS OF 1866.

BENEZET A. HOUGH. Private, Company B, Twenty-Fourth Connecticut Volunteers, August 25, 1862; Sergeant, October 25, 1862. Served in the Department of the Gulf. Mustered out of service with regiment, September 30, 1863.

CLASS OF 1867.

PHANUEL BISHOP. First Lieutenant, Company B, Eleventh Regiment, United States Colored Heavy Artillery, September 14, 1863; Captain, November 9, 1864. Served in the Department of the Gulf. Mustered out of service with regiment, October 2, 1865.

JAMES P. BROWN. Private, Company K, Tenth Rhode Island Volunteers, May 26, 1862. Mustered out of service with regiment, September 1, 1862. Second Lieutenant, Company H, Eleventh Regiment, United States Colored Heavy Artillery, December 31, 1863. Served in Virginia and Louisiana. Died at Donaldson, Louisiana, August 23, 1865.

ELMER L. CORTHELL. Private, First Rhode Island Light Artillery, May 15, 1861; Corporal, August, 1861; Sergeant, Battery F, September, 1861; Second Lieutenant, Battery H, October 11, 1862; First Lieutenant, Battery G, November 11, 1863; Captain, Battery D, November 2, 1864. Served in North Carolina, Maryland and Virginia. Mustered out of service with battery, July 17, 1865.

JOSEPH F. FIELDEN. Private, Sixtieth Massachusetts Volunteers, July 15, 1864. Served in the Department of the Ohio. Mustered out of service, December 4, 1864.

JAMES N. GRANGER. First Lieutenant, Company H, Second Rhode Island Volunteers, 1864. Served in Virginia. Mustered out of service with regiment, July 13, 1865.

47

WILLIAM R. HARMOUNT.   First Lieutenant, Twenty-Seventh Connecticut Volunteers, October 4, 1862.   Served in Pennsylvania, Maryland and Virginia.   Mustered out of service with regiment, July 27, 1863.

MARTIN S. SMITH.   Second Lieutenant, Company K, Eleventh Regiment, United States Colored Heavy Artillery, January 8, 1864.   Served in the Department of the Gulf.   Mustered out of service with regiment, October 2, 1865.

HENRY A. WINN.   Private, Sixth Massachusetts Volunteers, July 15, 1864.   Served in Virginia.   Mustered out of service with regiment, October 25, 1865.

ROLL OF STUDENTS

CLASS OF 1866.

JAMES W. BLACKWOOD. Private, Company B, Tenth Rhode Island Volunteers, May 26, 1862. Served in Virginia. Mustered out of service with regiment, September 1, 1862.

EDWIN B. FISKE. Private, Company B, Tenth Rhode Island Volunteers, May 26, 1862. Served in Virginia. Mustered out of service with regiment, September 1, 1862.

HERVEY A. FOSTER. Corporal, Company D, Tenth Rhode Island Volunteers, May 26, 1862. Served in Virginia. Mustered out of service with regiment, September 1, 1862.

N. NEWTON GLAZIER. Private, Company G, Eleventh Vermont Volunteers, afterwards First Vermont Heavy Artillery; Corporal, November 23, 1862; Acting Ordnance Sergeant; Second Lieutenant, Company A, November 2, 1863; First Lieutenant, January 21, 1864. Wounded at Spottsylvania Court House, Virginia, May 18, 1864, (lost left arm.) Served in Virginia. Discharged on account of wounds, September 3, 1864.

Edward K. Glezen. Sergeant-Major, Tenth Rhode Island Vol
unteers, June 9, 1862. Served in Virginia. Mustered out of
service with regiment, September 1, 1862.

William H. Spencer. First Sergeant, Sixty-First New York
Volunteers, September 6, 1861; Second Lieutenant, January 8,
1862; First Lieutenant, January 24, 1862; Captain, June 14,
1862. Wounded at Charles City Cross Roads, Virginia, (lost
right leg,) June 30, 1862. Commissioned Major, but not mustered. Discharged on account of wounds, December 29, 1862.

CLASS OF 1867.

Frederic B. Hall. Private, Seventeenth Connecticut Volunteers, August 10, 1862. Served in Virginia. Mustered out of
service, August 8, 1863.

Joseph D. Kirby. Corporal, Third Massachusetts Volunteers,
May 4, 1864. Mustered out of service, August 2, 1864.

James McWhinnie, Jr. Sergeant, Twentieth Connecticut Volunteers, August 6, 1862. Wounded at Chancellorsville, Virginia,
(lost left leg,) May 2, 1863. Served in Virginia. Discharged on
account of wounds, May 4, 1864.

John C. Sullivan. Sergeant, Fourth Massachusetts Volunteers, September 9, 1862. Served in Louisiana. Mustered out of
service with regiment, August 29, 1863.

CLASS OF 1868.

Sabin T. Goodell. Private, One Hundred and Fifty-Seventh
Pennsylvania Volunteers, August 18, 1863; Second Lieutenant,
Twenty-First Regiment, United States Colored Troops, October
17, 1864; First Lieutenant, August 17, 1865. Served in the
Department of the South. Mustered out of service, April 25,
1866.

GEORGE R. READ. Private, Forty-Seventh Massachusetts Volunteers, August 30, 1862. Served in the Department of the Gulf. Mustered out of service, August 30, 1863.

XENOPHON D. TINGLEY. Private, Company I, Eleventh Rhode Island Volunteers, September 15, 1862. Served in Virginia. Mustered out of service, July 13, 1863.

CLASS OF 1869.

JAMES C. BUTTERWORTH. Private, —— Rhode Island Artillery.

JOSEPH H. COWELL. Private, One Hundred and Thirty-Ninth Illinois Volunteers, May 1, 1864. Served in the Middle Department. Mustered out of service, December 1, 1864.

ALVIN M. CRANE. Second Lieutenant, Twenty-First Connecticut Volunteers, September 5, 1862; Captain, October 12, 1864. Served in Virginia and North Carolina. Mustered out of service, June 20, 1865.

ALBERT R. GREENE. Private, Company K, Eleventh Rhode Island Volunteers, September 25, 1862. Mustered out of service with regiment, July 13, 1863. First Lieutenant, Seventy-Eighth New York Volunteers. Aide-de-Camp on staff, Third Brigade, Second Division, Twentieth Army Corps. Served in Virginia and in the Department of the Cumberland. Mustered out of service, July 11, 1864.,

DURA P. MORGAN. Private, Eleventh New Hampshire Volunteers, August 26, 1862. Hospital Steward, United States Army, June 21, 1864. Served in the Army of the Potomac. Mustered out of service, June 30, 1866.

WILLIAM T. RICHMOND. Private, Fifteenth Independent Company, Massachusetts Volunteers, July 25, 1864. Mustered out of service, November 11, 1864.

CLASS OF 1870.

ELISHA B. ANDREWS.   Private, First Connecticut Heavy Artillery, April 30, 1861; Second Lieutenant, August 27, 1863. Wounded before Petersburg, Virginia, August 24, 1864. Mustered of service, October 29, 1864.

JAMES H. ARTHUR.   Private, Seventh Connecticut Volunteers, August 19, 1862. Wounded at Fort Wagner, June 11, 1863. Served in the Department of the South. Mustered out of service, September 20, 1864.

IRVING W. COOMBS.   Private, Fifteenth New Hampshire Volunteers, October 21, 1862. Served in Louisiana. Mustered out of service, August 12, 1863.

NEWELL T. DUTTON.   Private, Ninth New Hampshire Volunteers, August 6, 1862; Sergeant-Major, February 1, 1865. Served in Maryland, Virginia, Kentucky, Mississippi, and Tennessee. Mustered out of service with regiment, June 15, 1865.

THOMAS G. FIELD.   Corporal, Eighty-Fifth Ohio Volunteers, May 15, 1862. Served in the Department of the Ohio. Mustered out of service, September 28, 1862.

WILLIAM H. FISH.   Corporal, One Hundred and Forty-Fourth New York Volunteers, September 6, 1862. First Lieutenant, Twenty-First Regiment, United States Colored Troops, February 9, 1865. Served in the Department of the South. Mustered out of service, April 25, 1866.

LEWIS MUNGER.   Private, Second Connecticut Heavy Artillery, July 22, 1862; Second Lieutenant, March 15, 1864; First Lieutenant, February 4, 1865; Brevet Captain, April 2, 1865. Served in Virginia. Mustered out of service, August 18, 1865.

TOTAL, GRADUATES AND NON-GRADUATES, - - - - 294.

INDEX.

CORRIGENDA.

Page 31, line 2, for "John R." read "John K."
Page 31, line 5, for "Jelley" read "Jelly."
Page 55, line 31, for "Seagraves" read "Seagrave."
Page 56, line 5, for "Keene" read "Keen."
Page 92, line 22, for "watch" read "watchful."
Page 235, line 16, for "Willcox" read "Wilcox."
Page 359, line 6, for "Twice" read "Truce."